Penguin Books

NADINE

Matt Cohen was born in Kingston, Ontario in 1942 and educated at the University of Toronto. He taught religious studies at McMaster University before becoming a full-time writer.

His first novel was published in 1969. Since then, he has received critical acclaim for many books, notably ''The Salem Novels'' — *The Disinherited, The Colours of War, The Sweet Second Summer of Kitty Malone* and *Flowers of Darkness*. *Café le Dog*, his most recent collection of stories, was published in the Penguin Short Fiction series, and *The Spanish Doctor*, a novel, is also available in a Penguin edition. *Intimate Strangers*, a collection of new stories from Quebec which Cohen co-edited with Wayne Grady is also available in the Penguin Short Fiction series. Cohen has contributed articles and stories to a wide variety of magazines including *The Malahat Review, The Sewanee Review* and *Saturday Night*.

Matt Cohen now lives in Toronto, Ontario.

NADINE

MATT COHEN

Penguin Books

Penguin Books Canada Ltd., 2801 John Street, Markham,
Ontario, Canada L3R 1B4
Penguin Books Ltd., 27 Wrights Lane, London W8 5TZ (Publishing &
Editorial) and Harmondsworth, Middlesex, England (Distribution &
Warehouse)
Penguin Books, 40 West 23rd Street, New York, New York 10010,
U.S.A.
Penguin Books Australia Ltd., Ringwood, Victoria, Australia
Penguin Books (N.Z.) Ltd., 182-190 Wairau Road, Auckland 10,
New Zealand

First published by Penguin Books Canada Limited, 1986
Published in this edition, 1987

Copyright © Matt Cohen, 1986

All rights reserved.
Manufactured in Canada.

Canadian Cataloguing in Publication Data
Cohen, Matt, 1942-
   Nadine

ISBN 0-14-008870-9

I. Title.

PS8555.038N32 1987   C813'.54   C85-099862-X
PR9199.3.C64N32 1987

For P. A.

Suppose the universe has a code. Suppose the maps we make of the sky are the maps of our own psyches, and the constellations in fact the countries of the heart.
from *Shooting Stars* by D.B. Miller

PROLOGUE
Paris 1982

I am at a table in the living room of Léonie's apartment. The sun, warm and friendly, shines through the window just as it must have forty years ago. I see the soft spring sky, I smell the soft spring smells, I smile at the soft clouds that drift by.

This morning I went to the doctor's. "Madame will remove her blouse, please." At one time I would have been embarrassed to stand naked in front of a doctor, even a woman doctor, but now I am a patient, an object. When I take off my upper garments, the doctor can inspect the miraculous results of the latest surgery—the place where they reconstructed the nipple and its supporting tissue. "Excuse me Madame," says the doctor, touching the newly grafted flesh. "Does Madame have sensation?"

The tip of her finger is cold and sandpapery, like her voice. "Yes."

We pass on to other, less sensational injuries. It is amazing to think what a mess an explosion can make.

Of course it is exciting to be back in Paris. As I walk through the streets I find myself reconstructing my favourite movie—the one about me. Scenes of an infant being wheeled past soldiers. Scenes of an infant surrounded by death and the fear of death. Scenes of an infant being moved from one apartment to another in the middle of the night. Then time passes, the movie speeds up and crucial developments are skipped over as the infant becomes a young girl and the cradle is exchanged for the comfortable web of lies necessary for survival. Because how do you teach a two-year-old child to conceal the truth—when truth is life and death? Better to teach the child the lies and tell the truth later, when it is safe. Better to build the lies into every word the child knows than to let a mere baby betray herself.

So now I am hungry for the scenes I was too young to remember, the truths that were covered up by lies, the past I was too young to live. For example, the other day I was standing on the Quai d'Orsay soaking up the sun while waiting for a break in the traffic. The light changed, I didn't notice, a thickset grey-haired man bumped me into action as he hurried confidently across the street. I followed him, taking note of the pure wool blue suit, the expensive black shoes, the supple leather briefcase, the military cut of his hair. Without having to try I imagined him as a collaborator during the war, betraying and torturing innocent Jews.

"Look at him," I thought to myself. "He is the prosperous one now. No doubt he too paid a price. Lost a few teeth to the Nazis, got kicked in the groin by some resistance hero after Paris was liberated, endured a silence or two from his wife."

I was inventing the history of this Fascist who had committed unknown horrors when a little mental arithmetic started up in my brain. The man I had been condemning with such certainty, this fifty-year-old businessman with his clipped hair and his confident stride, would hardly have been old enough to lift a rifle during the war.

Léonie watches over me. It is now two months since I was flown here from Jerusalem. Warm weather has arrived for good, which means that the windows are always open to the noise and heat of the city.

Most of the operations are over. The skin along my hips and thighs has been rearranged because of the grafts, and there are angry ladders of stitches running across my belly. I go a week between visits to the doctor now. In the mornings I wake up starving and gulp down my breakfast with the enthusiasm of the newly reborn. Then I set out to explore the city; with the aid of an elegant and ladylike cane—a gift from Léonie—I can walk for miles.

The afternoons I spend at the table by the window, looking at my mementoes and writing stories to myself. Therapy, yes, because the mind must be healed as well as the body. Especially that is true in my case—I who had been blown apart in order to come together. On the other hand, the libraries are surely overflowing with the memoirs of one war orphan or another. Was it not Albert Camus who repeated the old adage that while everyone's happiness is the same, suffering is individual and unique?

Insane! Only a man could pretend to believe such garbage. In truth, happiness is what is precious. Happiness is what requires courage.

Here in Paris, I have become a heroine of sorts. Nadine Santangel—the amazing Jewish Joan of Arc who has had her week in the magazines—the exiled French orphan of the Holocaust come back to the homeland.

"You brought good weather," one of Léonie's neighbours remarks every day. The whole building knows me, is friendly to me. Of course everyone saw me arrive: a van drove me direct from Charles de Gaulle airport and then I emerged, blanketed like a sausage from neck to feet, pale face bathing in the popping of flashbulbs. Miller was carrying the suitcases, but it was Yaakov who was pushing the wheelchair. As you might expect he was the one to attract the cameras: a burly black-bearded soldier, nice white teeth that look good in the photographs; but he could use a haircut, it's been twenty years since he was the *wunderkind* of the Israeli infantry.

After a few days, Yaakov went back to Israel. Then Miller returned to his classes in California. But there is still Léonie to take care of me. She watches over me. She holds my hand when I have nightmares. Bit by bit we exhume the past.

The stories of my parents, their friends—I can't get enough of them.

Finally Léonie takes me to meet Robert Lemieux.

We don't eat at his usual hangout. That is a café Léonie pointed out to me on one of our walks, a rundown bar with the electrified picture of a dog in the window. As though we were strangers, Léonie introduces me to Lemieux. He looks older than I expected, but he isn't surprised to see me. "I've read about you in the papers," he says. Then he kisses me on both cheeks and presents me to some of his journalist friends. "Nadine Santangel," he calls me, no mention of the fact that I had briefly carried his name.

During the meal, very nice, we drink a lot of wine and Lemieux talks about the war. Afterwards we walk back with him to his hotel.

By the time we arrive, Robert Lemieux's hands are quivering with the effort of the walk, and his face is dangerously flushed. He says goodbye to me, then embraces Léonie, holds her to him and hugs her fiercely. When he pulls away his eyes are wet and the three of us stand in a tight little circle, dizzily looking from one face to the other.

On the way home Léonie and I stop to sit in a park. We are at the Luxembourg Gardens, on a little bench near the pond where children are taken by their nannies to lose their sailboats and throw breadcrumbs on the water. The sun bobs up and down on the tiny waves. I close my eyes. Points of light ricochet through my brain; I am lying on the street again, the noise of the explosion has blocked out my whole life, my soul has torn free and is flying through the universe like a runaway star.

But I am feeling better, I want to walk. Exercise can't hurt me, the doctor has said. When Léonie has to go back to work, I decide to stroll down to the river and back.

On the Boulevard St Michel the traffic—the human traffic— is so heavy that I can't find a place. I turn off at random and soon I am wandering along streets I haven't been on since I was a child. I find myself stopping before each corner, closing my eyes and trying to predict what I will see next.

When I get back to the apartment I lie down on my bed. I can't sleep, but I try to imagine how it must have been for Léonie and Lemieux. First in Paris, during the war, and finally now, seeing each other when their lives—lived and unlived— are almost over. Which were their real lives? I wonder. The ones in which Léonie lived out her spinster years while Lemieux put himself through the paces of his marriage? Or their phantom lives, the forbidden underground ghosts that spent useless decades yearning for each other?

Meanwhile, back to myself: my name is Nadine Santangel. I am neither young nor old. I am a woman, a scientist, a Jew. I was born in France and am now a citizen of Canada. There was a time when I fancied the idea of being a citizen of the world—and when I was a child I believed in another world altogether, the lost planet of our hopes where the tortured and cremated have escaped to a happy existence.

At this moment I am back where I began—in the Paris apartment where I was born.

But even here, as I busily recreate myself amidst the letters, the documents, the photographs—silence strikes. The fabric of new lives and old tear apart.

I splash cold water on my face, I look for reassurance in the mirror. I see green-black eyes, skin pale from illness, black hair just shampooed and trimmed by Léonie's favourite hairdresser. The bangs hide the scar at my hairline, sleep and a little make-up have almost erased the dark shadows beneath my eyes.

I am trying to seize the moment—but sometimes the moment seizes me. I come to consciousness to find myself crouched on the carpet, or twisted awkwardly in my chair. For a few seconds my body has been inhabited by another self—a little explosion of memory has laid me out again.

Then I pick up my pen and continue where I left off, writing this memoir. Léonie, Gabrielle, Piakowski, Yaakov,

Lemieux—each of them will find their place. But most of all this will be my story—and that of the man who is my soul mate. For most of our lives we were like twin stars, revolving around each other, sometimes finding ourselves dimmed and obscured by our closeness, but at our best and most rare moments, casting our light in harmony.

BOOK ONE
Paris 1940

August 12, 1940 is the date—two months after the German soldiers swept through France like a fist poking through thin silk. The place is Paris: to be exact, the house of a well-to-do American called Henry Brimmer. It was early evening and at this normally sentimental time Robert Lemieux was on his knees behind a thick oak door. By peering through the mail slot he could watch the German soldiers who had been standing, apparently without purpose, in front of the house for the past hour.

"You'll be careful?" With that Lemieux felt the American's heavy hand descend onto his shoulder. "You don't want to get caught with those pictures."

"I won't get caught," said Lemieux.

"It was very heroic of you to come," Brimmer now murmured.

"I'm no hero, believe me." The soldiers had concluded their discussion and were now marching down the street. A few seconds later they turned the corner and the sound of their steel-toed boots against the pavement could be heard receding into the distance. Lemieux stood up. He was tall and slender, with fine narrow features stranded between youth and manhood. He had a habit of stooping as he talked, to avoid towering over his listeners. Now he shook hands with Henry Brimmer.

"I don't want to bring you trouble," the American said.

"Don't think of it." Lemieux wanted a cigarette, but when he reached inside his coat pocket, he felt only the thick wad of pictures that Brimmer had given him.

"Good-night," Lemieux said. He stepped into the street, and immediately the August heat pressed against his skin. Starting and stopping, using short streets and back alleys that could be easily surveyed, Lemieux crossed through the luxurious quarter where the American lived to his own shabbier district.

Once he thought he heard a voice speaking to him—a man's voice soft and direct. He froze, hidden in a doorway's shadow, and waited. Since his last visit to Lyon, in the Free Zone, it seemed he was hearing these voices all the time: in the streets, in his dreams, even whispering to him in the cafés where he took his coffee. "Be careful," they would say, like the voice of Henry Brimmer. Or, as his wife wrote: "Robert, please come home, we miss you—" But most of all they were voices without words, just the low imploring voices of the foreigners and refugees who had crowded the streets of Paris in increasing numbers for five years now.

"*Bonsoir*, Lemieux."

This time the voice was a mocking whisper, one which came to him from the adjacent doorway.

"Piakowski," Lemieux said.

"*L'état, c'est moi.*"

Lemieux stifled a laugh. One of these days, Piakowski's Polish officer's French was going to get him into trouble. "I thought the soldiers had frightened you away."

"But Robert, I thought you *trusted* me . . . "

Lemieux again was starting to laugh when suddenly the door against which he had been bracing himself gave way. Before he could turn around a fist like a rock had pumped into his ribs and sent him sprawling into the street.

"Go home, you idiot, before I call the police." Then the door slammed shut and Lemieux and Piakowski raced away into the darkness, making for the safety of their hotel. But when they had arrived, and were ensconced in Lemieux's room, Piakowski wanted not to see the pictures Lemieux had obtained, but to tell him of his own triumph of the day—his meeting with the fabulously beautiful Santangel sisters.

"I insist," said Piakowski, "these women are absolutely splendid, beautiful, irresistible. They are like melted wax waiting to be shaped in the hands of real men."

"You always say that."

"But this time it is true. One of them works in the laboratory where my half-brother is employed. The other—the more beautiful—is a student at the Sorbonne. Tragically, both their parents have recently died—and the two sisters are without protection against the brutalities of the world. I met them absolutely by chance. Sir, if you were a true Frenchman, a gentleman, you would help me to rescue them."

"Alas, my friend, I am a married Frenchman with a wife I adore and a child who depends on the fidelity of his father. Whereas you—" Lemieux looked at Piakowski, remembering that Piakowski would soon be going back to Poland where he would undoubtedly be killed.

"I am also married, with a wife and *two* children." Piakowski laughed, the crazy broken laugh that had first attracted Lemieux to him—a laugh that made his white teeth flash, his dark eyes narrow, his mock-sinister V-shaped scarred eyebrow shoot up into his forehead at a crazy angle, as though it might leave his face altogether and shoot off into space.

The name of Piakowski's half-brother was Jakob Bronski. Over the six months he had worked in the same laboratory with Gabrielle Santangel, he had never dared speak to her, except to ask, "Would you mind if I borrowed your—" or "Do you have a copy of the latest—" Then, shopping one day in the market with Piakowski, he had found himself beside Gabrielle and her sister, Léonie. Gabrielle was the one who had spoken first. Then there had been introductions all around, smiles, a few more awkward lines of conversation followed by a hasty retreat.

Unlike Piakowski, Bronski did not have the heroic look. His was a narrow ghetto face with a slightly bulging forehead and weak eyes masked by wire-rimmed glasses with thin and delicately curving lenses. His skin was a stranger to the sun, so transparent that the shadow of his beard glowed luminously from his jaw and upper lip. But behind the glasses his eyes were a bright and piercing blue, a colour so fierce and energetic that Gabrielle had been watching him since the day he entered the laboratory. Also, she had noticed his hands—slender and artistic—and the way his wrists protruded awkwardly from the threadbare cuffs of his blue serge suit. On his wrists, too, the skin was transparent: there she could see the rivers of his blood flowing close to the surface, a suicide's dream.

"He moves like a dancer," Gabrielle Santangel said to her sister after their encounter in the market. "Did you notice the way he holds himself, the way he walks? I think he must be at least a prince-in-exile."

Of course, Jakob Bronski had no means of knowing about this conversation. Nonetheless, he had decided to act. But preparing to speak to her in the laboratory, he found himself blushing repeatedly with nervousness. Finally, the sentence he had planned—a fine ironic statement to get their relationship off to a glowing start—was uttered.

"Mademoiselle Santangel, to spend an evening with you would be to share an excellent bottle of wine. Would you like to take a drink with me after work?" He had gone to stand beside Gabrielle at her bench, but after he spoke, there was only total silence. The words, meanwhile, hung in the air—totally ludicrous.

Gabrielle turned to Bronski and smiled.

"Did I say something wrong? You must excuse my French. It is always worse every day."

"No, you spoke perfectly. And now it is time for me to go home." Gabrielle stood up. She had a heart-shaped face with a quick smile. Like her sister, Léonie, she had dark eyes, but her hair was all her own—a glossy chestnut colour that shone even in the dingy light of the laboratory.

"I'm sorry if I have disturbed you."

"Not at all." She looked at him. He was handsome, yes, but was also one of the thousands of foreigners who were clutter-

ing up Paris in the wake of the German advance through
Europe. "Jews without a home but too stupid to hide their
foreign ways." That was Léonie's verdict. Of course the San-
tangels were also Jews: Jews second, French citizens first. Now
that the Germans had reached Paris, Bronski was no doubt
hoping to escape to Unoccupied France. At least that was
what Léonie, who read the newspapers, said that the foreign
Jews were going to do. "But we should help them. Otherwise
we will all finish in the same place."

"Good-night." Bronski turned away. Gabrielle remembered
the first day he had come to the laboratory. There was a
rumour that he was a relation of the famous Madame Curie,
that in Poland he had been an important scientist.

"Monsieur Bronski. Don't hurry away without me."

When she got home, Gabrielle would also tell her sister
about the peculiar conversation that had taken place in the
café. Bronski had spoken not at all about himself, but about
his half-brother Stefann Piakowski. According to Bronski this
half-brother was indeed a formidable man: a physicist who
already published important articles in journals, as well as a
man of action—a soldier who had escaped Poland in the midst
of the German invasion.

"But you, also, escaped," said Gabrielle.

"Oh yes, but for me there were no difficulties. I left earlier,
doing nothing more dangerous than to take a train with false
papers."

"I would find that very frightening," Gabrielle said.

After their glass of wine, Bronski stood up and offered to
see her home.

"It isn't necessary."

"I insist."

It was the dinner hour, the streets were full of people returning home from work and shoppers with their bags full of
groceries for the evening meal. Hundreds of times Gabrielle
had made her way home at this hour; but now, with Bronski
by her side, the streets had been transformed into a dangerous and frightening maze. She told herself to be calm, to

breathe deeply, to concentrate on putting one foot in front of the other. She couldn't help wishing she were invisible: even her eyes were an embarrassment—for the first time in her life she noticed herself avoiding the glances of passers-by.

And then, suddenly, they were in front of a group of German soldiers. But Jakob didn't walk around them, only whispered something to her and kept walking, slowly. Now the fear swept through her, gusts of terror coming right from the soles of her feet all the way through her body to her scalp, where they tingled so strongly it felt as though her actual hairs wanted to leap and run.

"Good-evening," she heard Jakob say. For once his accent was plausible. For a moment the soldiers stared at them, and she could see their eyes passing quickly from her to Jakob, taking in his hooked nose, his narrow face, his wire-rimmed glasses.

Finally a man of Jakob's age smiled at her and said, in return, "Good-evening," and stepped aside so they could pass through. When they stopped at Gabrielle's door she realized her hand linked to his arm had tightened into a claw which now had to be unfolded, a finger at a time.

"Thank you for seeing me home."

"It was my pleasure."

They were standing outside the apartment building where Gabrielle Santangel had lived her whole life. She was twenty-one years old. If not for the war and the shadows its coming had cast on her, she might already have been married. As it was, there had been other nights she had stood outside this door, other boys and men to whom she had bid farewell.

"Until tomorrow, then," said Gabrielle. She offered her hand, cool and formal: the self-possessed Gabrielle Santangel—an orphan girl who had preserved her reputation. Then she unlocked the door and went into her building. Only as she climbed the stairs did she say the words she had been suppressing: "If you're going to be a Jew in France, learn how to disappear."

Two weeks later, Lemieux had his chance to meet the famous Santangel beauties. It was the last Sunday in August, in the

Bois de Boulogne. The worst of the summer's heat had passed: now, through the green leaves of the chestnut and plane trees, a pale blue sky filtered its late summer gifts. It was a sky so perfect it should have been sold to a museum, a dusty blue sky that rose from the paths of the Bois and hung like a marriage canopy over the delighted ladies with their fancy hats and dresses, the gentlemen wearing suits and walking stiffly in their best patent leather shoes. Indeed, the entire bourgeoisie of Paris—aspiring and arrived—seemed to be parading their happiness and splendour. Had it not been for the German soldiers, had it not been for the lack of tourists, had it not been for the fact that *le tout Paris* was here rather than fleeing the city as was its August habit—well then, it might have been easy to believe that the war had never happened.

Even Lemieux, loosening his tie to let the cool breeze search out the skin of his neck and chest, found himself hoping that the scattered knots of soldiers were nothing more than a bad dream, a temporary inconvenience that a few more weeks of summer would sweep away.

"People don't want to think about the war," Lemieux's editor had told him.

Lemieux, silent, had reached for a cigarette. The photographs were spread out on the desk between the two men.

"Where did you get these?"

Lemieux shrugged. "A man gave them to me."

"And I suppose you exposed yourself to much danger in order to show them to me."

"Yes," Lemieux said. His father had told him that Theodore Caron was a man of integrity. Why he had said this, he had never explained, but perhaps it was only because Caron had honoured their old friendship by giving his friend's son a job at one of Paris's most influential newspapers.

"And now," said Caron, "I am going to save the life you so bravely risked." From his drawer he took a pair of large scissors and very rapidly began to cut the images into tiny pieces. These were the pictures Henry Brimmer had given to Lemieux, photographs showing how the Germans were setting up a network of death camps across Europe. "You must be crazy, walking around the streets with these. Did I hire you to get yourself killed? What's wrong with you? Do you want me to have to write your obituary and send it to your father? Do you even know where these pictures were taken? Germany? Poland? Russia? Certainly not here. Look at these faces. These are not French faces."

"And if they were?" Lemieux was astonished to hear himself saying.

Caron swept the remains of the pictures into his wastebasket. "Monsieur Lemieux, in the 1914 war, two million Frenchmen died in the trenches. Frenchmen who would have been my age had they lived, who were your age when they died. Frenchmen who were young and had wives and children and lives to live. And after that war, Monsieur Lemieux, the world had not changed for the better, the angels of heaven had not descended to earth, but the earth of France was pocked with the graves of the Frenchmen who had died for it. Some of us, Monsieur Lemieux, are sufficiently old to have learned the lesson of history. We will survive this war with dignity, with sorrow, with patience, with whatever is required to get through."

"No French faces," said Lemieux.

"That is correct."

"Not even the faces of French Jews."

"Monsieur Lemieux, let me commend you on your concern for your fellow man. But I promise you—when the war ends, even French Jews will be alive to drink themselves sick, with the rest of us."

Lemieux had stood up. There were times in his life when he had been this angry, only a few, and on those occasions, too, he had felt the blood draining away from his face, his fingers, his toes—draining away so completely and severely that his toes and fingers began to chatter as though they were already bones stripped of flesh.

"Monsieur Lemieux, let me also remind you that you are a journalist, with a responsibility to the truth. Next time you bring me pictures make sure that they are pictures you have taken yourself. That way you can be certain they are not forgeries. You must realize, at a time like this it is easy to be taken in."

Lemieux stubbed out his cigarette and walked towards the door.

"Lemieux, there is a military parade on the Champs Elysées this afternoon. I want you to go and photograph it. Just so we both know that your attraction to interesting pictures is not wasted."

Black photographer's hood over head, one knee on the ground, Lemieux looked through the reflex lens at the sisters. They were as beautiful as Piakowski had promised. They spoke the faultless French of well-born Parisian daughters, but seen through the camera the impression of their name, Santangel, was reinforced: with their olive skin and flashing white teeth they had the perfect look not of camellia-white Frenchwomen but of something more exotic, perhaps Italian. And how deliciously their lips curled when they smiled—dark, well-defined lips with mischievous messages painted into their every expression. High cheekbones, like gypsies, dark round eyes that looked into the camera without blinking or blushing.

Except for their hair—Gabrielle's a saucy reddish hue, whereas Léonie's was glossy and dark—they might have been twins. How extraordinary to think of them living alone.

Behind the sisters stood Piakowski and his half-brother, Jakob Bronski. Piakowski, as was to be expected, was clowning it up, his face radiating happiness to find himself in such proximity to beautiful women. But Bronski, though his fingers seemed to be groping for Gabrielle's shoulders, looked utterly serious, his skin so white and pasty he must have spent the whole glorious summer in his laboratory.

"What are you waiting for?" shouted Piakowski. "Everyone is already getting hungry."

"Oh, I'm sorry, I was just admiring you all. Now, don't move ..." He held up his hand to signal them—three fingers, two fingers, one. Then the lens of the camera opened—so

confident and mechanical it might have been thinking that it
was, incarnate in glass and metal, the lens of history—it opened
like a monster's mouth, whirred for the requisite seconds,
then closed again. In the meantime, through the sensual and
dusty blue of the sky, the sun's ray had found the eager young
faces of the brothers and the sisters, magical arrows of light
sent across the solar system to bounce from their young and
hopeful skin to the waiting silver oxide plate of the camera.
Lemieux withdrew his head from the cape. The couples
applauded gaily. As he put away his equipment Lemieux
noted, walking only a few metres away from them, two men
who were clearly veterans of the shattering German attack.
One of the men was on crutches, the other sported an empty
sleeve.

"*There* are some French faces for you to photograph," Caron
had told him, speaking of the victims of the two-week war,
"Had it lasted longer, one of them might have been your
own." But Lemieux, seeing the looks on the faces of these two
men—envy and contempt as they took in the well-dressed
and healthy party of picnickers—found himself not thankful,
but ashamed. And after a few minutes, he made his excuses
and began walking home.

The afternoon which had been so perfect in the park had
spread its charms to the city as well. The streets were almost
empty: the occasional family out for a stroll on its way to or
from relatives, a few single men like himself, the odd policeman making sure that France stayed under wraps.

It was a week, now, since he had written to his wife. Despite
the war, letters flowed easily between Lyon and Paris. Of
course, letters were no substitute for being together, and twice
he had made the trip into the Unoccupied Zone to visit her.
The visits had been a relief from loneliness—but also unsatis-
factory. His wife had returned to her parents' house in Lyon
because they had envisioned a Paris demolished, a Paris unsafe
for their unborn child. To save money, Lemieux himself had
moved from their former apartment back to the hotel where
he had stayed as a student, the Left Bank hotel managed by
his older sister.

"You see," Marguerite had said bitterly, during his last visit, "this wonderful job, this wonderful opportunity, has brought us nothing but problems. Now we have not even a place to live together."

These unwelcome words had been whispered, because their baby son was in the room with them and they didn't want to wake him—and because in the room adjacent to theirs Marguerite's parents were sleeping.

"It's the war," Lemieux had replied, "you know I don't want to be apart from you." And, it was true—he had no desire to be separated from his wife and child. Without them he felt isolated and adrift, cast back into a student life he was too old to live.

"Why don't you let us move back to Paris with you?" Marguerite had pleaded. "Even in your hotel room, at least we would be together."

"But here you are free, out of danger," Lemieux had pointed out, not for the first time. And by then it had been almost dawn, only hours until his train, so to give themselves a memory they could live with they had made love. Lemieux remembered noticing how different his wife's body had become in the three years of their marriage, how she had changed from an untamed, frightened girl into a woman who knew how to want and how to take.

Thinking about this, Lemieux arrived back at the hotel. His sister was waiting for him. As always, they would eat their Sunday supper together, talking about the old times with the family, the memories of their parents; and then Lemieux would go to his room to spend the rest of the evening writing to Marguerite. After that, he knew, he would feel close to her—as though they had made up after a quarrel. Even now, opening the door, he felt a hint of the satisfaction he would have sitting down at his table, forming her name with his pen, writing to her about how much he missed her, what he did during his days, the books he was reading and planning to read. And then, at the very end of the letter, Lemieux would allow himself to begin writing the name of their son—Christophe—a saint's name chosen by Marguerite in the hope that God would protect a child so respectfully named.

"How long do you think the war will last?" Piakowski's voice, in the darkness.

Jakob lifted his wrist from beneath the bedclothes and looked at his watch. Three A.M. "It will definitely last until morning."

"Lemieux has information that the Americans are going to join the war any day. When they do I predict it will be over. Right away. Pppht."

Jakob took the slowest of breaths, trying to control the cough which threatened to explode out of his lungs every time the cold air tickled its way down his throat. "I want the war to be over," Jakob said. "I hope Lemieux is right."

"Of course you want the war to be over." Piakowski's laugh. "Then you can marry your beautiful Gabrielle. Why do we never see them any more? Have you got another girlfriend?"

"I see her at work all the time," Jakob said. "Do you expect us to have picnics in December?" In his sudden irritation with Piakowski he breathed too quickly, a cough tore its way free from his chest, and then, when Jakob sat up to clear his lungs, he banged his head into the eaves. Whether he had been asleep when his half-brother had first spoken he could no longer remember. He lit a cigarette. In the match's flare he could see the walls that surrounded himself and Piakowski so closely. The room they occupied was on the top floor of the hotel managed by Robert Lemieux's sister. It was a corner room and there were places where it was impossible to stand up, or, in any case, where it would have been impossible to stand up had not most of the room been filled with the beds which contained Jakob Bronski and Stefann Piakowski when they slept at night.

"And when you see her, what do you think?"

In spite of the teasing tone of Stefann's voice, Jakob could not help remembering that he had promised himself to stop—a hundred times a day—glancing over from his work to feast his eyes on the lovely face of Gabrielle bent over her papers. Sometimes he caught himself staring, hypnotized, at the soft skin of her cheeks, the long shy curve of her eyelashes, the way her lips parted—as if for a kiss—whenever she was writing something down. When his infatuation completely devoured him he would find an excuse to walk by her. Then he would imagine that, instead of merely admiring her in passing, instead of merely drowning his fantasies in the soft scent of her perfume, he was about to declare his love. But before he could speak she would smile at him and ask him how he was, how was his brother. And Jakob, face impassive, would give her the desired information while resting his eyes on the fine gold necklace that curled into the warm hollow of her collarbone.

Now Piakowski spoke again: "Today Lemieux told me he could provide papers for us to leave France. You could go to America. There's nothing to keep you here."

"What are you going to do?"

"I'm going to be a good soldier," Piakowski said. "Lemieux has connections with the Free French Army. I will have the privilege of liberating Warsaw."

Jakob lit a second cigarette from the butt of his first. It was almost a year now since Stefann had appeared in Paris and come to stay with him. In that year he had spoken of his wife and daughters only once, to say that he had left them behind in Warsaw. But then, what else was he to say? That he missed them? That he hoped theirs were not among the subhuman faces in the concentration camp pictures Lemieux kept showing to them?

"And you?" Piakowski asked. "What is your destination of choice?"

"I want to stay for a while. I am in the middle of my research." Jakob listened to the words as they filled the room. He was amazed to hear himself saying that he wanted to be in Paris, even more amazed to hear the lie about the research.

When he next looked at his watch it was after four A.M. As he settled back under the covers he heard a slow and

careful step on the stairs. That, he knew, would be Lemieux—
it seemed that every night Jakob heard Lemieux creeping
in just before dawn. Piakowski, breathing deeply, seemed
to be asleep. Jakob rolled over carefully in his bed, trying
to move without the springs squeaking. Then, lying frozen
into position, his ears quivering with concentration, he heard
Lemieux draw his chair up to his desk, the scratching of
his pen.

In December 1940, on an afternoon when the sky had already
turned from slate grey to black, the director of the laboratory
asked Jakob to prepare certain statistics that he would need
for a meeting in the morning. Jakob, of course, agreed.

And so it was his turn to be bent over, absorbed in his work,
when Gabrielle approached him at the end of the day.

"Monsieur Bronski."

Jakob looked up. Gabrielle was standing over him, so close
that for a moment he thought she had put her hand on his
shoulder. Then he saw that she was hesitating.

"Monsieur Bronski, my sister and I would like to invite
you and your brother to dine with us some evening."

"That would be very nice," Jakob Bronski said.

"And I am also wondering, if you will excuse me, why the
long silence from the man who once said that to spend an
evening with me would be to drink an excellent bottle of
wine."

"I am a Jew," Jakob said.

"Is that all?"

"It is enough."

"I see." She stepped away from him. Jakob swung around
on his stool and stared fixedly down at his desk. As he heard
her steps recede he kept his eyes resolutely on his work.
He didn't look up. Not then, not until he had finished his
calculations an hour later and was putting his slide rule back
in his case. That was when he saw she was still there, standing
by the door, waiting.

"Are you finished?"

"Yes."

"Good." Gabrielle reached for the lightswitch and turned it off. Jakob sat for a moment without moving. He was aware of the sound of his breathing, of Gabrielle's. He wondered how she could have been there the whole time without his hearing them both breathing, without his knowing he was alone in a room with this woman he loved so intensely.

"I am a Jew," Jakob said, again.

"You keep telling me."

Gabrielle came to him. He took her in his arms, he was surprised to realize she was almost as tall as he was, surprised at how easily his lips melted into hers, surprised at the soft connivance of their bodies as they pressed together. After a certain length of time, not too long, Gabrielle separated herself from Jakob. Breathless, he found himself sitting down on his stool, still holding her hands in his. For a few moments, they looked at each other in the shadows. Then Gabrielle pressed the head of Jakob Bronski between her breasts. Gradually his hands found the courage to caress her. Eventually he undid the top button of her blouse, then the next. By the time they were lying on the floor, making love, he was ready to die for her, ready to follow her every movement, ready to explode when she whispered his name into his ear.

But at the doorway of her apartment building, there were no farewell kisses—just a clasping of hands, like the first time, a promise to keep their secret to themselves. Even in their wedding picture, taken by Robert Lemieux, they are shaking hands the same way. After the kiss, of course: it is their permanent private joke, the monument to their first night together. In the picture Jakob is wearing a black suit and a borrowed shirt with a high stiff collar. As Gabrielle had predicted to her sister, he is photogenic: under the scrutiny of the camera it is impossible not to marvel at the way his high Slavic cheekbones give way to the cavernous shadows of his undernourished cheeks. Gabrielle is a radiant angel.

The marriage was inspired by the fact that on a certain day Gabrielle discovered she was pregnant. On September 15, 1941,

Nadine Bronski duly and legitimately appeared. Along with
the photographs of the infant have been kept only three letters of felicitation; the first from the rabbi who performed the
ceremony, the second from Robert Lemieux, the third from
Stefann Piakowski.

It has already been noted that the sisters resembled each
other. But beyond the cosmetic details, looking at their lives
from this distance, who can doubt that they shared the
virtues—if they are virtues—of passion and courage. In any
case, what Léonie did was brave enough: instead of allowing
Gabrielle to register herself after her marriage, she went in
Gabrielle's place—in the company of Jakob Bronski. Her purpose? To sign Gabrielle's name but without the quickly swelling belly that might have been noted by some sharp-eyed
official. In November of 1941, after the round-up of the lawyers, another census was taken and this time Léonie went
again for Gabrielle—her excuse being that since the fraud
had been begun, it had better be perpetuated.

*And so my birth went unrecorded. No one knew I existed, therefore
no one ever searched for me. It was Léonie who protected me. I owe
her everything—despite everything.*

June 1942:
   Lemieux had been playing with Christophe when the argu-
ment between Marguerite and her parents began. At first it
was angry whispers, quickly built up to words and sentences
he couldn't help hearing, which finally became guilty accusations shouted directly at the wall. Then Marguerite came into
their bedroom and proposed that they walk together down to
the train station, without Christophe.

   "You can say goodbye to him here," Marguerite proposed
brightly, as though the idea was a happy inspiration that had
just flown into her head like a pretty-coloured bird.

   But it was only when they were nearly at the station that
she had found the courage to begin. "I don't understand you."

   "What don't you understand?"

"Don't you care about us?"

Lemieux stopped. He led Marguerite to a bench and sat down beside her. "You want a cigarette?"

"You never used to smoke so much." But she accepted, just the same, and when he lit the match she cupped his hand in hers. "Robert, I want you to move back to Lyon."

"I can't. My job is in Paris. You know that."

"He's going to get killed," Marguerite's mother had bellowed at the wall: *"Tell him he's going to get killed and then ask him who's going to send you money every week. What does he think we're made of?"*

"And besides your job? Papa says you are doing other things."

Lemieux shook his head.

"He went to Paris to find out. Caron told him."

"Your father came to Paris to spy on me?"

"Not to spy on you, Robert. My father is worried about you, that's all. He's worried about me and Christophe."

"Why doesn't he speak to me?"

"He went to your hotel and asked for you. Your sister said you were out. He waited until midnight and then he left. Robert, what were you doing out after midnight? Have you found—"

Lemieux took his wife's hands, folded them into his own. Every month of the war seemed to be adding a year to her life. When they had married her face had been slender and girlish. Now her eyes had dark hollows beneath them, and there was a determined set to her mouth and jaw.

"What do you do after midnight?"

Lemieux didn't answer.

"Then it's like Caron says. Do you know what my father told me? That for every German the Resistance kills, two hundred Frenchmen are killed. And they aren't all Jews, either. Haven't you seen their names in the papers? There are even camps where they keep the hostages, ready for the next time a German is killed. And you know what else my father says? If the Resistance becomes too strong, then the Germans will occupy Vichy."

Lemieux let go of his wife's hands. "What do you want me to do?"

"Stay out of trouble. Or, if you must fight for France, why don't you join de Gaulle in England? Then when the war is over you can come back to France, and our Christophe will have a father."

"A wonderful idea. Go to sleep until the war is over. Then everything will be perfect again. You and General Pétain would make a wonderful team. *Vive La France! In Sleep We Find Our Freedom!*" Lemieux stood up. "I had better catch my train now." In one hand he grasped his suitcase. The other he extended to Marguerite. "Goodbye until next time."

"No," Marguerite said. She stood up and was facing him. "Robert, my father says you are spending your time in Paris helping Jews. Is this true?"

Lemieux felt his fingers tighten around the handle of his suitcase. "If I am, what is wrong with that?"

"Robert, would you really trade the happiness of your family in order to lend yourself to such a hopeless cause? Robert, to fight for France is one thing. But this—you must know how much you are hurting me."

The trip to Paris was even slower than usual. There had been a series of unexpected stops, each one bringing the gendarmes through the train to check the papers of the passengers. Lemieux, of course, was in no danger. His papers were in perfect order. He had even the required certificate from his Lyon prefect swearing that he was not a Jew.

"You must know how much you are hurting me." Why had Marguerite said this? Did she have anything against Jews? Before the war, the subject had never been mentioned. Why would it be? Even he had never thought about such questions. He had no distant Jewish relatives that he knew of, no Jewish friends from his childhood, knew no Jews whatsoever save for the half-brothers above him in the hotel.

And yet, and yet—every time there was a new ordinance against them he found himself shaking, as though he was feeling an earthquake no one else seemed to notice.

The first had been the compulsory marking of Jewish stores, right at the beginning of the Occupation. Lemieux remembered walking along streets made unfamiliar by the war, seeing stores he had walked into without a thought now given special placards in the window. A few times, to test his own courage, he had gone inside to buy cigarettes or a newspaper. And then he had stopped using them—in any case, it soon seemed that their doors were always locked.

Later, Jews were forbidden to use public parks, public museums, even public toilets. Now Jews were permitted to shop only at the end of the afternoons, when other Parisians had had their opportunity to use their ration cards to buy whatever was available. And since the lawyers had been rounded up, Jewish doctors, dentists, bankers, stockbrokers—even journalists—were being forced to leave their jobs.

The latest regulation was that Jews were going to have to wear a yellow star, the size of a hand, on the left side of their coats.

"Like the Middle Ages," Caron had said. "If I had the courage, I myself would wear a star."

The train pulled into Gare St Lazare. Leaving the station, for Vichy France, it had been packed but, as always, there were only a few passengers coming back. Lemieux stepped down from the car and walked along the platform. Soon he was in the central station, making his way through the crowd. One hand was tightly wrapped around the handle of his suitcase. He was walking very rapidly, through the station towards the toilet. When he got inside the cubicle he opened up the suitcase. What he was looking for was in the bottom of his shaving kit, wrapped in cellophane. He pulled it out, pinned it onto his coat. Then he picked up his suitcase and walked out of the toilet into the main station.

Sweat masked his face and covered his eyes so that he could hardly see. But he forced himself to take his usual path. Though he didn't look down, he could feel the yellow star burning, as though his chest was on fire. Soon he was, as planned, in the line-up to buy cigarettes. For a few moments the press of people made him anonymous again. And then, finally, he was standing in front of the vendor, asking for his usual package of Gitanes.

The face he had seen and talked to on every trip to and from Lyon now looked not at Lemieux's face, but at the badge on his coat.

"Monsieur?"

"Please, a package of Gitanes."

"I am sorry, monsieur, it is not permitted to sell cigarettes to Jews."

And then, before Lemieux could protest, the man behind him had shoved him out of the way and was placing his own order.

Lemieux walked out of the station and began making his way towards the hotel. It took him an hour and half to cross Paris. When he arrived at the hotel, his sister opened the door. He was still wearing the star.

"Robert!"

"I had to."

The next day, at the newspaper, Caron told him that all of Paris had revolted against the new outrageous edict against the Jews. "You should have seen the Champs Elysées," laughed Caron. "There must have been a thousand Frenchmen wearing stars beside their decorations. It was a real party, let me tell you; the Germans have learned just how far they can push us."

The identity card: *carte d'identité*: a yellow cardboard folder. On top is printed the number of issue.

NAME: Stefann Piakowski

DATE OF BIRTH: 22 October 1905

NATIONALITY: Polish

PROFESSION: Astronomer

And then, aside from his fingerprint, there are the details of height, eye colour, colour of hair. All leading to the one organ about which everything must be known—the nose.

First a photograph—nose straight on. Next, a series of questions designed to specify the semitic grade of the object in question. Its length, the width of the base, the overall dimension. Imagine the inspector inspecting the nose. The height of a man can be described in centimetres, the colours of hair and eyes can be found in the rainbow—but to describe a nose? This is a task for a poet, not an official. And yet, for the hundreds of thousands of Parisian Jews who were issued identity cards, the poor underling at the local police station rose to the occasion. No doubt there were internal memoranda circulated about the problem. Perhaps there was clandestine consultation with the Académie française. We can easily imagine the conscientious clerks—most of whom, let's face it, would never have aspired to such a job—tossing in their sleep as their imaginations struggled to find the right vocabulary, the perfect rhythms, the syntactical solutions, to the vexing problem of describing the noses of Jews.

Piakowski plunges into the life of the city. Yes, he thinks about his wife and children, but in the abstract because for some reason he is unable to remember their faces. From Robert he gets whatever news there is about the round-ups in Poland, the placing of the Polish Jews into ghettos, the growing tensions in Warsaw. Meanwhile there is Léonie. She is shy, a beautiful twenty-three-year-old girl who has never permitted a suitor. At first Piakowski draws her out because it is a challenge, because he is so happy to be alive. And then he becomes infatuated with her. Why not? He feels guilty but, as always, desire is greater than guilt. And, anyway, Piakowski admires Léonie. Behind the shyness, he decides, is a woman of infinite strength, a woman so sure of herself that Piakowski finds himself leaning on her, needing her.

One night he kisses her in the hall. It is a surprise manoeuvre. He grabs her by the shoulder and lifts her to him as though he were forcing her. He expects her to resist, but she does not. Not at all. When she leans against him he feels she is holding nothing back. That night, in his hotel room, he remembers the soft press of her breasts and belly. She is eager, the kind of eagerness he used to dream about.

Meanwhile there is more news from Poland. All the remaining Jews have been placed in a ghetto in Warsaw. Robert Lemieux relates this one night when they are alone.

"I must go back," Piakowski says. "Can you still arrange it?"

Lemieux nods. "But why be killed for nothing? Here you are doing valuable work—saving lives instead of throwing them away."

The next day Lemieux tells Piakowski that one of his colleagues at the paper, a Jew, has been arrested and deported from Paris to a holding camp. The camp is called Drancy: it is on the edge of Paris. Piakowski ponders this bit of information. Of course he does not yet know of the Drancy Express, because it is not yet in existence. But he does know, for example, that almost a hundred thousand Jews have immigrated to Paris within the past few years—most of them, like himself, escaping harsh fates in Eastern Europe. These new would-be French Jews are no secret: how could they be? Their foreign clothes, their poverty, their insistence on speaking their own language in the street set them apart as surely as if they were lepers. Nor does Robert Lemieux have to show Piakowski the newspaper articles about his compatriots: everywhere there are columns saying that the rights of these new immigrants must be restricted, that France must be kept for the French, that massive deportations are the only solution.

One night Piakowski and Lemieux stay out late at a café, drinking an extra bottle of wine with their supper. It is a careless thing to do. On their way home they are stopped by the police and their identification is demanded. As Piakowski withdraws his wallet, Lemieux lurches drunkenly into him, then begins a long and slurred tirade about the rights of French citizens in *La Belle France*, rights for which his father had died during the First World War. During this verbal onslaught he praises the French Army, the French state, the French police, the bravery of a certain group of Frenchmen from the west who singlehandedly held off the Germans for two months in 1916. He is making jokes, singing snatches of songs, pushing Piakowski ever deeper into the shadows while he puts on his performance. Finally the policeman laughs and tells them to hurry home. At the hotel Lemieux explains that he recognized the Breton accent.

"Thank you," Piakowski says.

"Show me your papers."

Piakowski produces his Polish passport, his immigrant's visa, the yellow identity card.

After that events begin to move more quickly. The deportations increase—soon everyone knows a family, a friend, a co-worker who has been taken away in the night. Sometimes even by day a Jew is stopped in the street and hustled off to the nearest police station—never to reappear. The danger has grown, but with it Piakowski's vision. He has learned to see both the foreign Jews and the French Jews, those in the resistance and those who are collaborating.

Meanwhile Piakowski continues with his "valuable work." He is a courier for Lemieux's network. He delivers false papers and instructions for Jews whose escape has been arranged.

Piakowski also carries packages to Henry Brimmer. Like Lemieux, the American offers him papers, advises him to leave. One night, Brimmer invites Piakowski to take a glass of wine. The glass becomes a bottle. And Piakowski, after declaring that his deepest wish is to join the Free French Army, finds himself talking of the last time he was in Paris, his student days, his crazy ambition to study with Marie Curie and turn the world of physics upside down.

Once he goes to the Gare St Lazare with Lemieux and sits in a corner while Lemieux stands talking with a man in a kiosk. Lemieux hands Piakowski the letter that was given to him by the man: it describes the deportations from Warsaw, then explains that those left in the city are barricading themselves to fight to the death against the Nazis.

"What do you think about that?" Lemieux asks.

"Suicide?"

"Will the Poles not help the Polish Jews?"

"In another year there will be no Polish Jews." Piakowski has spoken only once to Lemieux about his wife and children.

Now that he knows their fate he cannot speak again. The next
night he goes to the apartment of the sisters. Piakowski stays
up late with Léonie. They talk in whispers, moving closer
and closer to each other in the night. It is too late to go home,
Léonie says. She looks at him sadly as she says this and Piakowski has the sudden intuition that she knows the Warsaw
Jews have been killed. Then Léonie says that Stefann can
sleep in the parlour. He lies down on the sofa and she returns
from her bedroom, carrying a blanket for him. His eyes are
closed. He does not know whether to imagine his wife dead
or living in terror. He pretends he is asleep. Léonie slips the
blanket over him. She is leaning down, tucking it around his
shoulders. He can feel her breath on his face. When she bends,
just a little further, to plant a sisterly kiss on his brow, Piakowski draws her down. "Please," she whispers. Piakowski holds
her in place. For a long time—minutes—she lies unresisting
on top of the blanket, while Piakowski moves his hands over
her. When his hands stop she gets up, whispers something to
him that he cannot hear, then pads down the hall to her
bedroom. A few minutes later, Piakowski follows her. He turns
the doorknob slowly—it isn't locked—then opens the door.
Until a match flares, the room is completely black. Then he
sees a man's face: Lemieux.

The train moves faster yet. Piakowski gets more deeply
involved with Lemieux, going to meetings, now daily delivering exit visas to certain Jews and resistance workers as the net
tightens in Paris. One afternoon, Piakowski is arrested. He is
taken to the station and thrown in a cell with a man who has
been horribly beaten. All night Piakowski waits, sweating, for
his turn. Like the nights he waited with his regiment for the
fall of Poland. He wishes he had fought his way back to Warsaw and died with his wife. He wishes he had committed
suicide. He wishes a bomb had fallen on him and wiped out
his future. He wishes he had been born in a different country.
He is afraid he will be tortured, that in being tortured he will
betray Lemieux. He is afraid that if he does betray Lemieux
in order to save himself, then Lemieux's friends will kill him.

He grows angry at Lemieux and feels used by him. Now that Lemieux has compromised him, has provided him with false papers whose falseness will be discovered, where is he? In a restaurant somewhere, no doubt, eating and drinking wine while Piakowski prepares to die. For the first time in months Piakowski finds himself able to remember his daughters, the sweet smell of their baby skin, the warm kissable bundles they made in his arms. He tries to remember every time he ever saw them, ever cooed to them, ever felt their lips on his. In the morning the cell is opened and Piakowski is led to the desk. A man he has never seen before greets him by the false name on his papers. Piakowski nods in recognition. The stranger offers him a cigarette and smiles. "Don't worry," he says, "with me you are perfectly safe."

A week later, June 12, 1942, the ordinance concerning yellow stars was made public: as of that date all Jews over the age of six would be required to wear a yellow star of David on which the word Jew was written in black letters. *Juif* or *juive* in fact, the dignity of sexual distinctions being maintained. These stars were to be the size of the palm of an adult's hand, and were to be sewn on the left side of the garment, preferably over the heart. Each Jew was to be assigned three stars, and the amount of cloth used was to be deducted from the textile ration. These regulations were printed, among other places, in Robert Lemieux's newspaper.

In July of 1942 the Prince of Darkness himself, Adolf Eichmann, came to Paris. The purpose of his visit? To confirm, in person, the date on which *La Belle France* would join in the Final Solution. In brief, the plan was that the Jews of France would leave for Eastern Europe where their souls and bodies would part company at various sites already built for that purpose. Plans had been long in the making. Already there existed on the outskirts of Paris two of the main holding camps—waiting rooms, you might call them.

The first of these was the Vélodrome d'Hiver, an indoor sports arena in the fifteenth district. The arena was to serve as the assembly point for the 28,000 Jews to be rounded up in the first wave—The Spring Wind, it was to be called. From there they would move on to the second waiting-room—Drancy: an enormous half-finished apartment complex in a suburb northeast of Paris. Eventually, seventy thousand Jews passed through Drancy on their way to points east—the most popular being Auschwitz. Two thousand returned.

There are pictures of the Bronskis during those weeks in limbo. One of them, taken by Robert Lemieux, shows Jakob, Gabrielle, and their baby daughter in front of the apartment building. Both of the adults are wearing their yellow stars. Baby Nadine is trying to stand, her arms wrapped round one of her father's legs. In the same album are pictures of Piakowski, also smiling. He is shown alone, with his half-brother and sister-in-law, with his arm around Léonie, and even holding Nadine. Now, forty years later, I look at my baby self, at the good-natured joker Piakowski, at my parents and Léonie and Lemieux. Amazingly, they are all smiling, all alive and burning with excitement.

One night the five of them—Lemieux, Jakob, Gabrielle, Léonie and Piakowski met in the apartment.

"If you don't leave now," Lemieux said, "you won't have a chance."

"We're in no danger," Jakob insisted. "I am virtually running the laboratory. Without me—"

"Without you, your child will be an orphan."

Jakob sputtered. "This is crazy. Why are we panicking?"

"No," Lemieux said, "*you* are crazy. Where have you been the last three years? Have you not heard of the Third Reich? Have you not heard what has happened to the Jews of Germany? What sort of dream are you living in? Where are your friends of six months ago? Do you think they went to Drancy for a holiday? Let me tell you something: if Hitler has his way, every Jew in France will be dead within one year."

"Of course," Jakob said, "you don't have to tell me that it is dangerous to be a Jew. Do you think I am blind?"

"Sometimes, yes. If you want your child to live, do something about it."

"So you say. Do something about it! At least here, we are still alive. If we take Nadine on some wild journey and we are caught, then what—"

"Then nothing," said Léonie. "Do you really want to save Nadine? I have a different plan, a better one." She turned to Lemieux. "You have said you would help us—"

At this point the story I like to tell myself, the story of how I survived the war, becomes fragmented and disconnected. Some of the scenes have been twisted out of shape by memory, some covered over by lies, some never known except by those who lived them. On that last night in the Santangel apartment, everyone was together. For three years their fates had been intertwined and they had kept each other safe. Now it was time to move on. Piakowski had brought the false papers and forged exit visas. For Jakob, with his heavily accented French, escape was the only option. He and Gabrielle were going to try to reach Spain. But thanks to Léonie, my existence had never been officially registered, and so it was decided that I was to be hidden with her until the war was over. What must it have cost Gabrielle to leave me in order to accompany Jakob? Dare I even imagine what went on in my mother's heart? Did she really have a choice? But this was a night for brave talk. They toasted the reunion to come at the end of the war. Piakowski swore he would find his own family in Warsaw. Then eventually the bottle was empty and it was time to go to sleep.

"First class, believe me you're going to love it." Sweet smelling fresh straw. Through the gapped planks stripes of bright white sunlight stretched like frozen glass. "Do you want a cigarette?"

"Thank-you."

The guard, standing at the open door, tossed a blue package across the floor. Gabrielle Santangel was sitting on her suitcase, the only furniture in the car—unless you counted the four shining new galvanized iron buckets, one in each corner. Gabrielle bent over, picked up the package, then took

out a cigarette. While she was still smoking she heard the
footsteps of the other women being marched along the cin-
ders, towards her.

"I told you to eat," the guard said. "Now the others will be
hungry."

"Good. It is good to be hungry. When I am released from
this illegal detainment, I also will be hungry."

The guard slapped the shoulders of his uniform into place,
tugged at his collar. "If you're not going to eat you might as
well keep the cigarettes." Then he added: "Here come your
friends. Not too many of them. There were supposed to be a
hundred. This is only twenty, if you ask me. I told you the
trip would be first class." On the straw at the door was a kettle
of the broth the guard had offered to Gabrielle. Now he
pushed it aside.

Gabrielle stood up. Her face moved into the light and suddenly she looked like a woman peering out a very narrow
barred window. "Don't you understand? I am a French citizen, like yourself."

"Keep the matches, too," said the guard. "Who knows when
you'll get more? And don't forget to be careful of fire. In a
few days that straw will be as dry as a—anyway, you know
what I mean."

The column was now so close that mingled in with the
footsteps could be heard the laboured breathing of the marching women.

The guard turned towards Gabrielle. For the first time she
looked at his face: brown eyes, dark sunken cheeks, a large
nose with a bridge knobbed in the middle, as though it had
been broken.

"Before the war I was training to be a priest, in Alsace."

"I'm glad to know that," said Gabrielle. She was still standing, the full force of the white light illuminating her violet
eyes, the coffee-tinted skin of her face and neck, the sugges-
tive perfection of her long dark hair.

"God save you," said the guard. Then he leapt from the car
and barked out a salute.

In an hour the train was moving north. Twice, during the night, it stopped to pick up additional passengers. At the first there were women only, another two dozen. As though they were on their way to a party they introduced themselves. Addresses were exchanged, along with the occupations of husbands and the names and ages of children. At the second stop over a hundred new passengers were taken on. These were women, and children too. Suddenly the car was crowded, and through the cracks between the whispered conversations fear and panic began to bloom. Some of the children were crying. In the dark Gabrielle moved over to make room for two girls who lay down with their arms wrapped round each other for comfort.

At dawn the train stopped again. Gabrielle found herself looking up at the steep hills of Burgundy. In the half light they were creased by rivers of darkness, long deep moving shadows into which Gabrielle wished she could slip unnoticed and sleep until the nightmare was over. Above the hills: neon blue sky, pulsing with the arrival of the sun. Below: mist, shadows, grey stone station. Gabrielle closed her eyes, but she could still see the rivers of darkness flowing down the hills, across the floor of the valley into her own veins and arteries. They were driving out the blood and replacing it with fear. Until finally Gabrielle, trembling, turned for comfort to her husband, as though he were still sitting beside her, as though, forged papers in hand, foolish hearts filled with hope, they were still travelling through Free France towards their imaginary haven in Spain.

For three days Gabrielle watched the sun as it played hide-and-seek with the hills. During those days the door of their car remained sealed. Nothing in. Nothing out. It was no longer a first-class or even a third-class car. The furniture in the corners overflowed. Shouts of outrage. Screams of pain. Cries of children beginning to die of thirst. On the third day Gabrielle distributed the guard's cigarettes. It was surprising to see how quickly they were taken. The air was still filled with paralysed clouds of smoke when the door opened and bottles of water and buckets of broth were passed in. While mothers shouted insults, a guard threw them armloads of stale bread, scattering it as though he were feeding starving animals who might trample each other to death.

Gabrielle rejected the soup as too salty, took some sips of water—not too much at first—and then slowly chewed her way through half a stick of the dry bread. When she was done, she found the butt of her cigarette and re-lit it, smoking it this time until her fingers were burned.

The door closed, the train began to move. Gabrielle let her eyes shut, she began to sleep. In her sleep she dreamed the rest of her life. The train picked up speed, passing out of the town and into the countryside. Gabrielle opened her suitcase, took out a piece of paper, wrote an address on it. She took the ring off her finger, a dark ruby set in gold, wrapped it in the paper. With a length of thread she bound and tied the tiny package. And then, as soon as it became dark, Gabrielle pushed the package through the gapped planks and into the night.

> *Dear Robert,*
>
> *I do not understand what you are doing or pretend to read your heart. But after our last visit I can have no doubt that you are no longer the man I married. I feel as though the Demarcation Line between Occupied France and Free France has become a battle line between husband and wife. For the sake of our marriage vows and for the sake of our child, I hope you will continue to come to Lyon. Other than that I scarcely know whether we can still think ourselves husband and wife.*
>
> *Your faithful Marguerite.*

In accordance with Léonie's plan Robert Lemieux rented an apartment on the outskirts of Paris for himself, his "wife," Léonie, and his ten-month-old "daughter," Nadine. As was required, he was able to show papers which had been stamped by the police, and in any case the building was owned by a friend of Lemieux's employer, Theodore Caron.

April 1943

Piakowski's last night has finally arrived. Since Jakob's marriage he has had the hotel room to himself. This has given him not the feeling of luxury, but insomnia. Jakob's former bed is now the resting place for innumerable newspapers, magazines, novels. Also, in one corner, scientific journals and sheets of paper covered with calculations.

These papers, along with most of his clothes and books, would be left behind. Eventually the police or the Gestapo would probably find the room—it would appear he had vanished into thin air. Along with Jakob and Gabrielle who were now surely in Spain, and Léonie and Nadine who were living with Lemieux.

Piakowski thinks about Lemieux: everything always revolves around him. Even at this moment it is Lemieux he awaits. When he arrives, it will be with his final package. Included among the false papers and exit visas will be his own. These will take him to North Africa, and from there to Poland.

Piakowski tries not to think about Poland: according to Lemieux the Russians and the Free French will join to overthrow the Nazis, but Piakowski finds this impossible to imagine. All he can see is the battlefield he escaped, a night-covered countryside lit only by exploding shells, one of which will eventually find him.

June 1943

Léonie was in the stuffed armchair, trying to sleep. That was where she spent her nights now, ever since Lemieux had stopped coming home. As always, through her dreams she heard the footsteps in the street, the sound of the front door opening to a key. The sounds mixed with her dreams. Soon Lemieux would be in the door, soon Lemieux would be kneeling on the floor in front of her. Soon the hands of Lemieux would surround her now, his face would be in her lap, his lips kissing her, his lips whispering words he was ashamed to speak except in darkness.

"When I hear you coming, I want you," Léonie told him once. "I spend the day caring for Nadine, but as soon as night falls, I start hoping you will arrive. Even in my sleep I dream of having you. You know what our sex is like in my dreams? A knife stabbing into my blood. And then I wake up wanting you, and at the same time feeling so strange because Marguerite must be wanting you, too."

"When I am with you," Lemieux said, "I feel as if I am the only man in the world and you are the only woman." That had been at dawn one morning. Léonie had been lying in bed—cold and needing Lemieux's body beside her—while Lemieux insisted on dressing in his pants and undershirt so that he could look out the window while he smoked a cigarette.

Lemieux had laughed. "*You* are the faithless one." That was all he had ever said with reference to Piakowski. As for his wife—he only spoke of her as though she were already dead.

Now Léonie was totally awake, her heart hammering in her chest. She heard the man pause outside, breathing heavily with the effort of his climb. For a certain number of months, on a certain number of occasions, she had been woken by Lemieux's step, in the same way, had sat up in bed, breathless, while Lemieux fished for his key and caught his own breath.

But the man now outside the door was a stranger. He gave a hoarse, rasping cough. "Here it is," Léonie heard him mutter, and then he grunted as he bent over and an envelope was shoved under the door. Following this, the scraping of a match, the first inhalation of a cigarette whose smell immediately penetrated the room, then the gradually retreating sound of the stranger's descent.

When she had heard the front door close again, Léonie stood up from her chair. As she had slept through the comings and goings of Lemieux, Nadine had remained undisturbed by this new intrusion. Léonie felt her way to the crib in the darkness, then bent over it and let her hand rest on Nadine. As always, Nadine's arm was around her favourite stuffed doll, her fingers dug into the cloth so that nothing—at least nothing a two-year-old baby could foresee—would wrench it away from her.

"Thank God it is not *her* mother I am betraying," Lemieux had once said when they were standing together in the dawn light, admiring the fiercely determined sleep of Nadine.

Léonie moved to the door and felt for the envelope she had heard. When she had it in her hand, she walked into the bedroom, closed the door so as not to wake up Nadine, then lit a candle. Sitting on the bed—fresh sheets, cleanly starched— she tore the envelope open. Inside was no letter. Only a photograph of Lemieux. On the back of the photograph was written, *for Léonie, with love from Robert*. On the front of the photograph a big charcoal *X* had been scrawled across Lemieux's face.

A few nights later there was, once again, the noise of heavy breathing in the stairwell. This time it sounded like more than one man, and it climaxed in the sound of a body being dumped outside the door. When the feet had run down the stairs Léonie undid the locks to see who had been left. It was Lemieux, half-dead, soaked in his own blood.

Dear Robert,

Thank you for your quick reply to my last letter. It is, of course, months since I received it, months during which I have been too busy to write. Here at Drancy it always seems that there is much going on, and my services are always useful since so many people arrive needing medical attention. How absurd that I would end up playing the doctor! I always wanted to be one as a child, so I suppose I must be happy that my opportunity has finally arrived.

Today is September 15th, 1943, the birthday of my dearest one. Now I have been here almost a year and a half and that makes me one of the senior citizens here. Nonetheless, I still have not had word from, or seen, Gabrielle.

I don't think I ever told you exactly how we were caught. It happened when we were on the train to Marseille. We had long passed the inspection at the Demarcation Line but we were stopped just south of Lyon for a final check. I presented our papers, as I had several times, and as always I answered Monsieur Sevigny when asked my name. This time, however, as I gave my name a little girl was standing beside me in the coach. She was Lucille Lavoie, you will remember that the Lavoies owned the bakery where we often shopped. When I said my name I winked at her, but she just looked up at the policemen as if it were all a big joke and, giggling, said, "that isn't Monsieur Sevigny, that is Monsieur Bronski."

We were taken off the train and to a police station for questioning. Then we were separated, without even a chance to say goodbye.

Meanwhile life here is not so bad. As you know, it is a fine autumn, and of course the food is as might be expected. I only ask you, if you can spare the time, to send some toilet paper, the more the better. Also, if you can lay your hands on some sweaters, as I have given most of my winter clothes away.

Thank you for your troubles.

Jakob.

When the war ended, it was time for Léonie and Nadine to go home. They simply took a taxi from the building where they had been hiding to the downtown apartment where Léonie and Gabrielle had always lived. Léonie had explained to Nadine—a dozen, a hundred, a thousand times—that they had the miraculous good fortune to be returning to the apartment where she had lived as a child, an apartment now to be shared with some distant cousins from the South of France. And although Léonie had also told Nadine, since the day of Lemieux's second disappearance—that her father had gone away during the war and would not be found for a long time, the child Nadine was absolutely sure he would be there, waiting in the apartment at the end of the rainbow. Yes, I am certain Nadine was expecting Lemieux. At least Léonie has told me that I was.

And then, according to Léonie, I ran up the last flight of stairs and beat my fist against the wooden door.

There were voices. Footsteps. The door opened a crack.

"I'm home. Let me in."

And here is my first memory: I look up to where my father's face should be, but see nothing through the narrow opening. I shove the door impatiently and it opens wider. Still, I can see nothing.

"Here," a small voice says.

In front of me is standing a boy. He is wearing black pants and a white shirt. He is as skinny as a grasshopper and his neck and his wrists protrude like narrow stems from his shirt.

"My name is Yaakov. And I know who *you* are."

"My name is Nadine Lemieux. And this is my mother, Léonie Lemieux. We live at—" That night Léonie told me the truth about my mother. I was three years old.

Like me, Yaakov was unable to remember his parents because they too had been deported. So together we invented a lost planet with an imaginary country where our parents still lived. On this planet, which was always the first star in the sky, and in this imaginary country, I was the Queen and Yaakov the King.

The imaginary time zone it inhabited was the present. In the imaginary country our parents were trapped in an imaginary countryside. People said that the war was over, but Yaakov and I knew that it was still going on, that the missing Jews were located in faraway caves where they were being held hostage by German soldiers who would never release them until we and the other parentless children became old and strong enough to come to the rescue.

It was a favourite fantasy, the lost planet. We would probably have gone so far as to make wooden swords except that something happened. One day Yaakov came and knocked at the door of the bedroom I shared with Léonie. I was reading aloud to my aunt from a newspaper. When I opened the door, Yaakov put one hand in front of his stomach, the other behind his back, and bowed deeply. That was what he always did, because I was the Queen and Yaakov was my most loyal subject. When he was finished bowing I curtsied, which was what I always did because Yaakov was the King and I was his most loyal subject.

"I found them," Yaakov said.

"Who?"

"Our parents."

I looked at Léonie for confirmation. Léonie smiled at Yaakov—a flashbulb smile hedged with a tremor of hesitation—the way her sister had once smiled. "Don't be silly," she said.

"I found them," Yaakov insisted.

"Where are they?" I asked.

"Come with me."

I followed Yaakov to his room. He opened the door. "Look," Yaakov said. He threw back the blanket of his cot as if it had been hiding a body. In fact, it was hiding thousands of bodies. Yaakov had discovered pictures of the concentration camps and brought them for me to see. In the pictures no one was fat or thin because they were only bones.

"Here they are," Yaakov said.

After a certain number of days the train arrived at its destination. By this time the butts of the guard's cigarettes had long been smoked into nothingness, and whatever life Gabrielle had lived before the train had become a memory blurred by fear and hunger.

How perfect it would be to describe the doors opening and Gabrielle stumbling into the daylight. The way her strength and purity shone through even this squalid situation. Perhaps they did. Perhaps in the end she was a true angel, a sainted luminous extra-mortal who eased the souls of the suffering as they fled from the emaciated bodies out through the chimneys of the crematoria. Unfortunately the fate of Gabrielle Santangel is entirely unknown. No one has ever stepped forward to say anything about what happened. It is up to the rest of us, should we so desire, to invent the details of her death. As for myself, I prefer to dwell on the moments of her happiness. Her love for my father, for myself, the strange seasons of excitement and danger that marked Paris during the war. What she felt leaving

*me behind I can only guess. Fear. Relief. Guilt. Perhaps even hope.
I know she was capable of hope because of the gesture of the ring.
Which found its way to me: a message, I like to think, carried on
the waves of chance from one soul to another.*

BOOK TWO
Toronto 1948

In the olden days, whole and golden decades ago, before the city of Miller's childhood and youth became a star-studded international metropolis complete with dazzling art galleries, world-class hotels, movie production companies, the world's tallest free-standing needle, major league baseball, Japanese and Vietnamese restaurants; in those ancient times when his city was only one of those dozens of post-war mid-sized faubourgs where a million or so decent people lived out their lives far from the bright winking lights; in that long forgotten era when outer space was still far away, when no human foot had marked the surface of the moon, when it was still possible to believe there might be life on Mars; in brief, when I was just off the boat, a young war orphan straight from Paris, a living reminder of the millions whose lives had been flattened by bombs, buried in the trenches, baked away to ashes and smoke—that was when I first met Miller.

Now, as everyone knows, Miller has made it into the public eye as one of the international *cognoscenti*, an expert on everything from terrifying black holes that can swallow a million solar systems in a single gulp to the domed sports stadium which is to be our city's crowning glory. As the Prime Minister said when Miller was presented with his prize by the Secretary-General of the United Nations: "In D.B. Miller is personified that quiet voice of reason and humanity which is ours alone in the family of nations. His achievement should make all of us proud, not only of him but of ourselves." That was Miller in his finest hour: a quiet ambassador for the best

in his modest country's tradition. And—give him credit—
Miller in his triumph was equal to fame. Modest, charming,
comfortable in the public eye. Fame had chosen him and
fame had prepared him.

Miller's first and greatest discovery was a comet. The newspapers dubbed it Miller's comet, especially when it became so
bright that for three nights running you could sit on the roof
of your house or apartment building and see not only the
magnificent explosively white head—brighter than the brightest star—but also the majestic sweep of its tail that lay like a
great glowing veil across the southern half of the sky. Miller's
comet: what a startling brightness. And after it came Miller,
shining in its wake, his name a password for the genius of
science, the mystery of space.

When I have told myself the story of my beginnings, I always
return to Miller. Miller my soul-twin. Between Miller and
myself, I often believed there could be one whole person. For
example: I am always the one to dive into inner space, the
land of memories and speculation. Miller was the opposite.
One day, he would say, outer space will be our home. Looking
back we will see ourselves swarming and struggling on the
surface of this aging planet, poor little things full of hopes
and superstitions. Just the way, for example, I can see my
mother huddled in her railway car, smoking her last cigarette, taking off her ring—the ring I'm now wearing.

When Miller was a boy he lived in a narrow house on a quiet
downtown street. The house was built of bricks, a hundred
years old, roof steeply peaked in the Victorian style shared by
all of its neighbours. Miller's room was on the third floor,
facing the street. From there he could observe certain comings and goings, and in the summer listen through his screened
window to certain conversations which might not have been
meant for him.

Across the street was another narrow house with three floors and a steeply peaked roof. Emma and Earl Borstein were the people who lived there. Like Miller and his family, they were Jews. But Miller's father was a doctor whereas Earl Borstein was in charge of major appliances in a downtown department store. This despite the fact that on the grounds of religion he refused to work Friday nights or Saturdays.

For hours before the boat pulled into Montreal harbour, I was on deck, in the very front row against the rail, as the others pressed against me, eager to see the details of our new country. And as the boat drifted into the cement wharf I was anxiously searching the faces in the crowd, looking for the attractive soldier of the photograph.

What did I expect of Stefann Piakowski? Everything, let's say. He was the half-brother of my father, he was the person who had arranged for me to leave Paris, he was the mysterious warrior-survivor of the storm which had obliterated my parents.

I was waiting in the giant clearing room before Immigration when I saw NADINE SANTANGEL printed in large black letters on a ragged cardboard sign. Carrying the sign was a woman, tall and thin; she would have towered over Léonie. When she caught sight of me she began quickly walking forward, still holding the sign out like a shield.

"Nadine Santangel?"

"Yes."

"You are Nadine?" She said this uncertainly. Her face, very thin and papery, wrinkled up in distaste. I felt suddenly conscious of how clean she was, how her clothes were pressed and fresh-smelling whereas my own black dress, the one Léonie had packed so carefully at the bottom of my suitcase, had even in the few hours of that day become tainted by the food I had eaten and the black and sooty smoke that belched from the ship's smokestack. I pressed my fingers to my cheek, took them away to inspect. They were shiny with grease.

"Yes."

"My poor girl." And as she said this she waved to a man across the room, then dropped to her knees and embraced me.

And so I met the Borsteins: the frosty awkward Emma, and her garlicky husband, Earl, with unshaven cheeks featuring half-grown golden whiskers and surprising little dimples.

We drove from the Montreal harbour where the boat had docked to Toronto, which was to be my new home. The journey took two days and by the time we arrived in Toronto I realized I had been sent to a country entirely beyond my imagination. Here, everything was raw, everything was without limit—the ground, the colours, the sky, the trees. Earl drove silently, occasionally smoking on a cigar. It was left to Emma to provide the entertainment.

"Nadine, look at that group of animals, those are Holstein cows." Or, "Nadine, in one hour we will be stopping for gas. Please be sure to go to the bathroom. But don't sit on the seat. In Canada you can catch very serious diseases from toilet seats, I hope your Aunty also warned you."

I was their duty, their own special orphan, the tragic little piece of garbage spewed out by the war in which they had lost so many relatives. "Every night we thank the Lord for you," Emma Borstein told me. Then she proceeded to recite the names of the lost loved ones. I had never before had a room to myself—now I was put in the large and lonely attic of the Borstein house. Lying in bed I would imagine that I was being kept company by the six million dead souls I had to replace in the Borstein hearts. Sometimes I would stay up half the night, listening to the streetcars going by, pretending they were cattle cars carrying people like myself to oblivion. In the morning the sun would pour its fierce yellow light through the east-facing window, blasting my dreams into space dust.

"She's wonderful," Emma kept saying of me as her various woman friends came round to admire and weep. "She's got perfect manners. She never reaches for food and her English is so good, too. Next week she's going to start school. Isn't it marvellous? We feel so privileged."

Piakowski, it turned out, had been at a conference in Philadelphia at the time of my arrival in Montreal. By the time he appeared to pay his compliments, the tone of my relationship with the Borsteins had already been set. I was the one who answered the door. As always, for these visits from the Borstein circle of friends, I was costumed in the black dress Léonie had given to me, white stockings supplied by Emma, very shiny black shoes with a brass buckle, also courtesy of Emma. My hair at that time was long—in pictures of myself from those first few months in Canada I look entirely the sad little orphan: long dark hair, a smile that hesitates for fear of being beaten, mournful eyes.

Yet I had no reason to be afraid: even had I burned down their house I'm sure the Borsteins would only have cooed and clucked over the ashes and then gathered me into their arms so that my new shoes needn't be dirtied by this regrettable accident. "After all," Emma once said to me when I had dropped a serving platter of roast beef and potatoes, "we must forgive you because you are a victim of history." She said this as though I had dropped the platter because my mind was full of the horrors of the crematoria.

"Look at you," Piakowski said, as soon as I opened the door; and before I could decide that he, too, was going to fail to live up to my expectations he had bent down, wrapped his arms around me, and lifted me into the air.

"Exactly like your Aunt Léonie, I can't believe it. Look at you. I'm *never* going to let you go."

Of course Piakowski was not the suave and slender soldier he had been. Even his hair had increased: instead of the slicked down dark hair of the photographs this live Piakowski had bushy black hair that the wind pushed out in every direction; and in place of the soldier's pencil moustache my uncle now sported a thick brush that straggled generously over his top lip so that when he talked his teeth were only half-visible through a veil of tobacco-stained hairs.

But I wasn't going to quibble over such details. That night, in my attic, I managed to make myself sleep by closing my eyes and dreaming of the time when my Uncle Stefann would realize how easy it was to take care of me, how perfectly mannered I was, how delightful I would be if only he would pluck me from the frozen hearts of the Borsteins and let me live with him until Léonie arrived.

Then I received the letter from Léonie and found out that my stay with the Borsteins would not be temporary.

Dear Nadine,

Your uncle Stefann will show you this letter and help explain to you why I am sending it.

You see, Nadine, life is not always predictable. I have decided I am too old to change my ways and marry. Meanwhile you are in Canada, in the care of your uncle, living with a family who loves you. Here in Paris I would be unable to provide you with even the basic essentials of food and clothing. I live from hand to mouth, only the generosity of others keeps me alive. But, nonetheless, Paris is my home—I cannot leave. For the moment, at least, we shall have to continue as we are. Be well, Nadine, take advantage of your good fortune at growing up in a country which is wealthy and free. All my love, your old unmarried aunt,

Léonie.

As one of the Santangel sisters, Léonie had been beautiful, desired, sought after. But after the war, despite her beauty, Léonie seemed uninterested in attracting a suitable man. The way she presented herself was totally severe. Her hair was pinned during the day into a spinster's bun, with only a few stray tendrils floating about her unkissed neck. Thin and long, supported by twin cords at the back, this neck, I always thought, told everything bad about Léonie.

At night, out came the pins and in an instant the whole effect was wiped away. Then, dark glowing hair falling richly past her shoulders, she exuded a faint perfumed smell from the folds of the housecoat she always wore through the evening. I would think that if only she could go out on the street

like this—her face free of make-up, her lips unexaggerated by
carelessly smeared lipstick, her hair disguising everything that
was cramped about her, the smooth white skin of her throat
and chest shining like a pale, triangular moon—a thousand
men would be sure to want her. Men with money and cars
and mansions with walls thick enough to keep out any disaster.

In fact, Léonie did have her suitors, but they were more the
stuff of nightmares than dreams. For example, there was Yasha
Rabinowitz, a never-married fifty-year-old who claimed he
had escaped death in his concentration camp only by playing
the flute while the commandant had intercourse with various ladies. This Yaakov and I discovered by listening through
his bedroom wall—with the aid of a cup—to the adults talking in the kitchen. Rabinowitz not only suggested the general
trend of what had happened, he insisted on describing the
events in great detail. Often he would weep over the soft
white bellies of the defiled, the long artist's fingers that trembled with each new brutality: but he didn't approach these
subjects crassly—in fact he preferred to use the most biblical
of language. "He put his mouth to the white mountains of
Babylon" or "the inside of her thighs gave off such heat they
would have kept King David warm for a year"—this of a
Dutch lady who was also described as "the Red Sea of love,
whole armies had made their way through her great divide"—
or even, "I could smell the land of milk and honey, believe
me, even my flute began to leap up."

So far as I know, he never followed his biblical descriptions
with biblical actions, but Léonie always smiled when he arrived
and made him a pot of ersatz tea flavoured with a bit of
honey. I was Jewish, yes, I *understood*, but I was also seven
years old and unprepared to take the whole burden of the
Holocaust on my shoulders. I didn't want to hear the details
of the camps, the numbers of dead and missing. I wanted to
sing and to dance and to know that I would never have to
walk to school with a yellow star saying "juive" on my dress. I
wanted Léonie to show off her breasts, to swing her behind, to
let down her hair during the day and to find us a husband

who would install us in a wonderfully large house with ten-course meals and servants. I wanted skirts made of wool as fine and tender as the wool of which the other girls' skirts were—the girls whose parents had not disappeared, the girls who were brought up in daylight—and I wanted stockings that didn't need to be mended with lumps of off-colour thread that stuck out like warts. I even wanted a coat that hadn't worn away so many of its threads that it was turning into the bone white of canvas—a bone white like the bones of skeletons, a bone white that nevertheless showed, on its left arm, the clear outline of where a yellow star had been sewn for a previous unlucky owner.

But, alas, Paris was not filled with rich Jews looking for a plain and spinsterish bride. Also, alas, most of the suitors I would have wished for Léonie had been machine-gunned or cremated, made into lampshades or glue.

Aside from Yasha, there were other charity cases—but it was only near the end that I realized that of the men I had been watching traipse upstairs, the only one who was serious was the very one I had ignored.

The settlement man—we called him that because he worked for the Jewish resettlement agency. Of course he had a real name, it was Henry Brimmer. The war had not been kind to him. He had stayed too long in Paris and ended up in an internment camp where he had almost starved to death. Now his big frame was still almost fleshless, and his hollow cheeks were like moon-craters on his wide-boned face. When he first started coming to the apartment I had thought that he was just another government official.

He always wore a grey suit, a white shirt, a tie. Even in summer he would appear in full costume, though if he was sitting in the kitchen and Léonie insisted he would strip off his jacket, then undo the thick jewel-studded gold cufflinks of which he seemed to have dozens of pairs, and roll up the sleeves of his white shirt. His face was cavernous, but his thick hairy arms seemed to belong to another person. That was the resettlement man aspect of him—with his powerful arms he plucked children up and then jammed them into the soil of another country, planted them with such force that they grew roots and never moved again.

Months before I started at the *Ecole Primaire*, Yaakov was sent to the Hebrew Day School that had been organized by the resettlement agency after the models of Hebrew Day Schools in the United States. The year was 1948, the year the state of Israel obtained its independence. Even while Yaakov was beginning his formal studies in Paris, the War of Independence was being fought a few thousand miles south. Despite the distance, the war seemed to us to be very close: a continuation of our childhood war—of the years in hiding, the carefully learned lies, the eventual triumph.

According to Henry Brimmer, the war in Israel was the final stage of the Liberation. When Israel was established, the Jews would finally have their legitimate place in the sun, never again to be threatened.

Yaakov, at his school, heard news of the war all the time. He would come home every night with authoritative tales of new triumphs, new massacres. His teacher, a Mr Esher, had been active in the Massad for years. According to Yaakov, the only reason he was now teaching children like himself in Paris was that his war injuries—tortures received in the British prisons—made him a burden to the state. In prison he had started to educate himself; now he was passing his knowledge on to boys like Yaakov so that when they grew up they—like good Jews—could go help to build the Kingdom of Israel.

Yaakov was so magnetized by this teacher that even the Hebrew alphabet became endlessly fascinating. He somehow obtained a large poster of it which he pinned above his bed so that entering his room you would see the thick black letters glaring accusingly from the wall. Accusingly, I say, because while Yaakov was turning himself into a patriot and resistance fighter, with the encouragement of his aunt, I was, along with Léonie, continuing to forget the war and sink into the simplicities of life. I loved the easy routine of my school. Henry Brimmer had used his connections to register me officially under my mother's maiden name of Santangel, a nice anonymous shelter which I have kept all my life; so when the others in my class prayed to their Christian Gods and saints, I could pretend to pray with them—eager to be assimilated, eager to be one of them, eager to believe the star's shadow on my coat had not already given me away.

Nonetheless, Yaakov and I remained each other's only real friends, and every night after school we would share the details of the new worlds we were entering. But we already seemed to know our time together was about to end. Yaakov's aunt was planning to take him to Israel as soon as the war was over. And Léonie, on the other hand, was weekly receiving letters from Stefann Piakowski—who, unlike my parents, had made it out of France and, ensconced as a professor of astronomy at the University of Toronto, was eagerly awaiting our arrival in the New World.

One sunny October day I came out of school and saw Henry Brimmer at the school gate.

I had never encountered him outside of our apartment. Standing on the sidewalk he looked towering, ghostly and—I feared—Jewish. He was wearing a trenchcoat with epaulettes and a matching grey hat, which he took off as he saw me approaching.

"Mr Brimmer," was all I could say. I had no idea what he might be doing at the gate of my school.

"Nadine, I was waiting for you. May I see you home?"

I began to walk down the sidewalk with him, a bit embarrassed that my classmates might have noticed me with this stranger. Would they have seen beyond his Jewish face to notice his American clothes, the fact that he talked to me in English? Perhaps they would even ask if he was my father.

As it turned out, the same question was on Henry Brimmer's mind. By the time we had turned the first corner he had informed me that he wanted to marry Léonie—if I would give my permission.

"I love her very much, Nadine. If you will let me take this momentous decision, I would make Léonie a very loving husband, and I would be honoured, also, to try to be a father to you."

With this he took my hand in his. His palm was as thick and as dry as the sole of a shoe.

The details of the "momentous decision" became clear more quickly than expected. As it turned out, despite Brimmer's eagerness to be a "father" to me, the plan was that I would precede them to America. I discovered this when I was shown a new letter from Piakowski saying that he had found a family to take care of me for as long as should be necessary. While I absorbed this news, Léonie and Henry Brimmer watched me across the kitchen table. I felt a sudden emptiness beginning to grow in my stomach, an emptiness that quickly turned into panic.

"What do you think?" Léonie asked.

My panic increased. Nothing had been said about Léonie in the letter: there was only the line, "they are very eager and willing to add a little girl to their family and to do their best to be her parents."

"I don't know," I said. I couldn't look at her face, only at the table where I saw Henry Brimmer's broad muscular hand sliding towards Léonie's arm, then possessively circling around it. "When are you getting married?"

"A month after you sail," Henry Brimmer said. "We want you to leave now, while the weather is still good. When you arrive in Toronto you can begin going to school right away." This is the same reassuring voice he had used to talk to me that day after school.

There was a nervous clatter—Léonie's cup rattling against the saucer as she tried to pick it up. I finally lifted my eyes. She was crying. Once Yaakov and I had talked about how families must have felt when the time came for some of them to be deported from Paris. "I suppose they must have kissed each other goodbye," Yaakov had said, making his wide lips grimace into the caricature of a last slobbering goodbye. I wondered how it had happened with Léonie and my parents— had there been tears and secret kisses with my father? Had she trembled nervously at the thought that their destination might be not a village outside of the Occupied Zone but quick death? And how had she said goodbye to Gabrielle? A kiss, a wink, a nudge? A turning away of the living from the dead? A begging to be forgiven for surviving?

And then, too, how had my parents felt? Most likely the same way I did now. A curtain coming down between those going and those staying—a curtain of indifference towards those who would be left behind, so that all my energy could be turned towards surviving the future.

"I want you to write every week," Léonie said. "And when Henry's work is finished here in the spring, we will come to join you."

That night she kissed me tenderly as I lay in my cot, waiting for sleep. I felt her lips on my forehead, but even as she kissed me I imagined how eagerly she must be awaiting my departure so that her kisses could land on Henry Brimmer's lips, so that her soft cheeks could be enclosed in Henry Brimmer's wide enclosing hands. "You know," Léonie said, "I always hoped your parents might be found alive. There was always one more place to look." She drew the ring off her finger, a dark ruby set in gold, the ring I have always worn since. "Do you see this? It came to me in a most peculiar way. Someone brought it to the door just after the war, when we had been back in the apartment only a week."

One last time Yaakov and I walked down from the apartment to the Seine. It was a November Sunday. The wind was cold and raw, and Yaakov kept shivering, his thin wrists and neck turning red in the cold. We sat on one of the benches. I could feel the cold iron bars pressing through my clothes and against my skin. By now I had seen the articles in magazines—pictures of Jews crowded into cattle cars, standing on the platforms of train stations, lining up for bars of stone soap at the actual camps. By now, too, the trials had begun, war criminals being "brought to justice." When we were at home alone after school Yaakov and I sometimes read these articles together, concentrating on the atrocities: while reading we would be pressed together—knee to knee, shoulder to shoulder—and between us an almost sexual current would pass. Not the sexual current of attraction—we were too young for that—but of being in a forbidden place, thinking forbidden thoughts. Even now, travelling through the sealed borders of my past, I feel uneasy. What special right do Jews have to mourn their own dead, when so many others have died? What right do Jews have to mourn their own dead at all, when they are killing others? We start by complaining about our individual fates, but surely our true oppressor is the one we all have in common, the unstoppable machine of human history.

Yaakov was wearing a hand-me-down leather bomber jacket with a fur collar that they had given him at the Hebrew School. From one of his pockets he pulled an American candy bar. Then he broke it in half and we ate it.

I was still chewing on my last bite when Yaakov stood up to throw his wrapper into the water.

"Goodbye," he said. Then I saw he was crying. His mouth was twisted and red, and his bright blue eyes were swollen with tears. I stood up and stepped towards him. "*Jew*," Yaakov hissed. He swung his fist and drove it into my stomach with such force that I fell to the ground. Along with my own gasping for breath I could hear Yaakov's footsteps as he sprinted away from me.

When I got home Yaakov was in his room. At suppertime he came out and sat, as always, across from me at the table. But his eyes avoided mine and as soon as the meal was finished he went back to his room. Even the next morning, as I was preparing to leave, Yaakov kept out of sight. And then, at the last moment, he appeared. Gravely, as though he were forty-five instead of five, he kissed me on both cheeks. Then he handed me a sealed envelope with NADINE printed carefully on the front.

I didn't open the envelope for a week. Then, I was on the boat, in the middle of the North Atlantic Ocean, clinging to my bunk as the grey seas battered the liner during one of the endless series of storms that carried us from Paris to Montreal.

The concentration camp pictures spilled out on my pillow as I tore the envelope open—Yaakov's last laugh. Also a piece of paper on which Yaakov had printed one word only, LIVE.

In fact I both lived and died. That is to say, a certain thin and shabbily dressed girl had boarded the boat at Calais. And when that same boat docked in Montreal, the passengers and crew could have sworn that the young girl was among those who disembarked. But when you leave, you leave something behind—a place, a time, a person. And when you arrive, you invent someone new. In Paris I had been a war orphan, yes—but so were tens of thousands of others. Now I was someone new, a Displaced Person landing on the shores of the continent of riches.

A few days after I moved to the Borsteins', before I had the chance to meet Miller on the street, tragedy struck the Miller family. Miller's mother was killed in an automobile accident. It happened at the bottom of our street—while the children were at school—and all of the neighbours, ourselves included, went to the funeral. Miller stood at the graveside, in the lee of his father's arm. I was near the back of the crowd, barely able to see him, but once he caught my eye and I tried to smile at him.

Later that month we met on the street, and after that we sometimes walked to or from school together. But we weren't in the same class; I was two years ahead of him. There was a sister, too; she was younger than Miller and when they were together she always held tightly to his hand. The route from house to schoolyard included the corner where the fatal collision had taken place: when we passed that Miller and his sister, Margaret, would stiffen.

Sometimes we played together. One winter day we built a snowman in Miller's front yard. Sticking our arms out and roaring like comic book bombers we ran through the falling snow, then plunged headfirst into the snowman to make our landing, screaming wildly as our heads pillowed into the soft melting snow of its paunch. Then the snow was falling more thickly, it was evening and the lights from the front windows illuminated the flakes into perfect crystals. We started making snowballs and throwing them at each other. Miller hit me on the ear. I jumped on top of him and brought him crashing down to the ground. But then he began to cry and, crying, he looked so much like Yaakov that I bent down and kissed Miller on the lips, sugary snow joining us mouth to mouth until Margaret began to call out, "Look, they're kissing! They're kissing!"

When I was twelve years old and my education had proceeded to that point of sophistication where the school system offered us a course in modern history, this is the line I found in my history book. *On August 25, 1944, the Americans liberated Paris.* Everyone has seen the pictures in the history books: Paris, black and white, in chains. American tanks rolling in from the outskirts, brightly coloured soldiers wrapped in flags and chewing gum. Guilty French men and women crawling up from the mud of collaboration and begging like dogs for cigarettes. Dancers dancing in the streets and bars. Drinkers swilling back everything they could find. Writers looking into the sky and writing immortal sentences about the eternal stars mixing with bullets.

"Nadine," my teacher said, "you were in Paris during the war. Is there anything you can tell the class about how you felt when the war ended?"

A silence while faces turned towards mine. On August 25, 1944, I had been three weeks short of my third birthday.

"Nothing?" asked the teacher. "Wasn't there a big celebration?"

And so, in order that no one be disappointed, I recited an episode from a movie I had seen: "For a week there had been fighting all around us. The electricity and the water were shut off and we had no food, except for some bread which the woman downstairs had given to us. My aunt made me hide under the bed the whole time. Then, one night, there was a long silence. Suddenly the whole room was flooded with light.

I came crawling out from under the bed and my aunt turned on the radio. The Marseillaise was playing, it was wonderful, and then the voice of a very nice man came on the radio and said how happy America was that France could be *La Belle France* one more."

"You see," said the teacher, "you did remember. You only had to try. Notice, you others, the way Nadine pronounces France. F-rrrr-ahnts. Now, everyone say after me, *La Belle F-rrrrahnts.*"

I had come a long way since I stepped off the boat. On the outside I was a quiet hard-working teenage girl, modestly dressed, speaking perfect Canadian English, almost a candidate for model citizen of the year. It was true that I had no close friends. But aside from the Borstein household I also spent time at the Millers' house, where Miller's father employed me as a babysitter and mathematics tutor for his daughter, Margaret.

Meanwhile, *chez Borstein*, life was less than ideal. The basic situation was that I spent my time in the attic, doing schoolwork or looking out the window, while downstairs the Borsteins put themselves through various kinds of hell. Why did they do this? I don't know, though I suppose the answer must be contained somewhere in the combination of Earl's half-shaven uncertain smile and Emma's thin stick-like arms. By the time I entered secondary school Earl had taken on a second woman: I wasn't told this officially but one day, home sick from school, I discovered in Emma's room a folder containing a report by a private detective. It was complete with photographs of the guilty party—a widow with two children who lived in a trailer park outside the city—and a list of times and places where the two had been seen together. To me the woman looked plain and unappealing, definitely not the scarlet siren type, but apparently most of the nights Earl "worked late" he was actually sitting in the widow's mobile home drinking beer and doing whatever lovers do in mobile homes that aren't going anywhere.

Emma, on the other hand, had consoled herself by taking a job as a cosmetologist. The dressing-table in her bedroom became the repository of so many brands and styles of make-up that it resembled the underground laboratory of an alchemist. Unfortunately, her efforts only went to prove the old adage that you can't turn lead into gold. Nonetheless, Emma seemed well amused spending her lonely evenings drinking wine and trying out different masks on herself. I didn't mind: the alternative was her coming to my bedroom for an excruciating heart-to-heart talk during which she never failed to remind me that, "Believe me, Nadine, I feel in every way as though I am your own mother, and no one could be prouder than me of the wonderful girl you have become."

Wonderful, yes. I was perfectly behaved. I had to be perfectly behaved because my categorical imperative was to be good—to strive, to succeed, to camouflage the alien DP as an acceptable person who would be allowed to live. Every night after dinner I did the dishes. My gigantic attic cavern was always spic and span. Not having the courage to invite anyone home, I had nothing else to do at night than to carefully go through my assignments so that, the next day, the teachers could find no fault with me. It was a ridiculous existence, yes, but in those days I was always afraid. Afraid of what? Of angry voices. Of reproach. Of the Borsteins sending me away. And if they did, where would I go? Léonie seldom wrote to me and Piakowski scarcely visited. I had to survive where I was. But despite the fear, I was bored. Boredom, yes, I used that as my excuse for what happened.

My geometry teacher was the one who started it. I suppose he was an expert in quiet girls like myself, but at the time I thought he was actually interested in me. As I left the room he would often stop me to congratulate me on the elegant solution I had made to a problem, to ask me if I was doing well in my other subjects. This progressed to his suggesting that since I was so adept at mathematics, perhaps I would be interested in reading various magazines he could supply me with. These he brought to school at first. Then, one day, he said he had forgotten at home a book he wanted to show me, but if I would drop over he would give it to me.

Nothing could have been more natural. I went to his place on a Saturday morning. He answered the door looking perfectly respectable, offered me a cup of coffee, gave me the book. The next visit was late in the afternoon. Coffee was augmented by brandy, the atmosphere enriched by music. At the door I suddenly found myself kissing him. He turned me away but by the time I got home I thought I was in love.

Now I had something to think about in my attic bedroom. Looking out the window I could imagine he was walking along the street, about to come into view. Lying down, eyes closed, I could wish the bed I was lying upon was his and that, music playing, he was leaning over me with his tobacco-laden breath. When I came down to dinner I looked at Earl through new eyes. He had his woman in a mobile home, I had my geometry teacher in his apartment. Sometimes I even convinced myself that one night I would wait up for Earl, long after Emma had gone to bed, to tell him that I had seen the private detective's file, but that he shouldn't worry because I was in the same situation myself.

Eventually fantasy became reality and I traded my infatuation for a few afternoons of hesitant but exciting sex. Now I was truly, totally, fatally, hooked. I had to see him every afternoon. He became withdrawn at first, then frightened by my persistence. I fell upon an old ruse and claimed that I was pregnant. In fact I even managed to convince myself. He panicked and offered to take me to an abortionist. I ran away in tears, schoolbooks clutched to what I was convinced were my maternally swelling breasts. I couldn't face going home. The next possibility was Piakowski. But the Piakowski I had hoped for on the boat, even the friendly uncle whose lap I could climb on, no longer existed. Now Piakowski was a middle-aged professor, growing fatter every year, who seemed to be sinking ever more deeply into an eccentric bachelorhood. I couldn't help suspecting—correctly, as it later turned out—that my once charming and gallant uncle had developed some very strange habits.

So finally I went to the only place left: the hospital office of Miller's father. There I explained that my life was destroyed and I was about to become a mother.

It was late afternoon. Walter Miller had been about to go home. Instead, we sat in his office with the lights off and he asked me various questions. At first the questions were about my relations with my geometry teacher. It became clear, as he explained, that if I were pregnant I couldn't be certain for several weeks. Then he asked me more questions—things I had never talked about since the day I got off the boat. What had been my life in Paris? Did I miss Léonie? What kind of food did she cook? Did I ever dream in French? Was I going back to Paris when I graduated from high school?

For a month, every afternoon, I went to see Miller's father. Same time each day, deepening darkness as fall gave way to winter, a torrent of words as I recreated the life I had forgotten and the shell of the life I was living broke apart. Finally, after three tests, I believed that I wasn't pregnant, my life wasn't ruined, I could go back to being a model student and channelling my energies into trying to win a university scholarship. Was I cured? No, in fact the episode with the geometry teacher turned out to be only the preview of a similar, but much grander, drama.

Piakowski once said to me that the imagination of every human being travelled compulsively around two points—birth and death.

I was born, as it were, into almost immediate orphanhood, and yet although for a long time I knew almost nothing about my parents, I spent thousand of hours imagining what they must have been. A lot of the details took shape for me after Léonie began showing me their pictures; others fell into place by necessity: for example, my father became tall after a very short bus conductor harangued me over a forgotten ticket.

The thinning brown hair of a hated teacher reminded me to emphasize the thick black hair—this was actually justified by the photographs—of my father. The bulbous nose of Earl Borstein confirmed the fine aristocratic organ of my own sire. Et cetera. A picture of my parents—the very one taken by Léonie from the steps of the building where she now works—was mounted in an old-fashioned frame that I placed on the dresser. But although I have devoted such intense efforts to inventing the parents I can't remember, imagining the voices I must have heard but can't hear now, my decade with the Borsteins has been almost erased from the official record.

Of course, in a certain way those years are always present: every time I go into a supermarket or take the subway I can see aged variations of Emma Borstein, who, after all, did her best with her sad little escapee from the Holocaust. Or certain actions—making tea, double-knotting the laces of Leandra's shoes—can suddenly remind me of moments from my childhood. But although a multitude of these little fears and recollections are always buzzing about like so many fireflies, I have learned to ignore them: they are there, yes, but when you look at them directly they vanish. And anyway, to tell the truth, even while I was living out my childhood, I willed it to pass as quickly as possible. Nights when I couldn't sleep I would comfort myself by wrapping the pillow around my ears and imagining myself a train, caroming at top speed through the tunnels of time—an ugly earthbound caterpillar, yes, but one destined to be reborn a butterfly the moment freedom was achieved.

Not only did I wish my childhood to be over—no Yeatsian angel I—but sometimes I refused to admit it had existed. My parents, whoever they were—had somehow left me behind while leaping on their own train to oblivion. And then Léonie had gotten rid of me for reasons I could never quite understand. If those who took care of me found me a burden, my only protection was to need no caretaker. The day I was waiting for was not the day I would finally be promised love and security; I knew that day could never come. The day I prayed for was the day I would finally be financially independent instead of an unwanted child shipped from one country to another.

To my amazement, that day actually arrived: it came wrapped up in a thick manila envelope—containing an austerely worded letter to the effect that the university had the pleasure of informing Nadine Santangel that she was to be the privileged recipient of an Open University Fellowship *and* the Ella Louise Mathers Bursary for Deserving Girls. *Deserving Girls*, that made me blush. I imagined writing back to ask if I would have to wear a yellow star for the duration of the scholarship. But my anger dissipated quickly enough as I kept reading and discovered not only the large amount of money being deserving had brought me—but an absolutely incredible offer: if I showed up at a certain place, on a certain date, during business hours, one half of the large amount of money would be paid to me by cheque.

Of course that date was far away, not until the following September when the academic year officially began. The place was a building I knew—an ivy-covered Victorian structure only a few hundred years away from Piakowski's office.

It was summer. In front of the Office of the Registrar was a gigantic chestnut tree, and under its shadow I stood reading and re-reading my letter. I wanted to rush inside so they could congratulate me—the deserving scholarship girl who had survived the Holocaust in order to become a spectacularly successful entrant into the Honours Science program of the University of Toronto. Instead, I just examined every detail of the thick paper, the embossed university crest, the impressive watermark. When I finally began to feel silly for showing off, I put the letter back in its envelope and walked over to my uncle's office.

By chance he was there, interviewing a student. As soon as I came in he stood up to welcome me—then introduced me as his niece. The student fled instantly. I, meanwhile, was waving my letter about in the air like a captured flag. When I showed it to Piakowski he took it in in a glance. I could hardly believe that his eyes had swallowed in one second what had taken me hours to digest—then he came around from behind the desk and kissed me on the cheek.

"Nadine," he said solemnly, "I am very proud of you." It was incredibly awkward. Even at the conclusion of our monthly meetings he had never kissed me—only clasped hands at the door. For a moment he held me by the shoulders, the way an uncle holds a niece, and for a moment I actually believed that the man who had kept me at such a distance the last decade—my only blood relation in the New World—might finally let down the barriers. "Your parents would be proud of you," Piakowski said. This, too, was incredible—never had he spoken such words. Of course I had looked into his eyes before—they were, after all, eyes that had known my parents, Léonie, even me as an infant: everything I tried in vain to remember or invent, Piakowski's eyes had seen. But now, finally, I found sympathy. *I know what you have been through*, he seemed to be saying, *I was the witness of your childhood and now I am the witness of its completion*. If Yaakov had been spying on us he would have died laughing. Instead, sentimentality won the day and I kissed Piakowski on the lips.

Then Piakowski congratulated me once more and after making a date to meet for lunch so we could look over the calendar and select my courses, I started back home. Except, of course, that it was home no longer.

I should say in favour of the Borsteins that their home had been my own: they even offered to adopt me well before I got the magic letter—and to house and to support me while I was a student at the university. It was in the kitchen that the offer was made. For the occasion Earl came home for dinner and sat sheepishly at the kitchen table while Emma explained how they would love me forever. I refused. I can't say why—only that accepting would have meant giving up my hold on my past. Borstein!!! Borstein!!! Borstein!!! How could I become Borstein—or anyone—when for over a decade I had been waiting to become myself, waiting for the moment when my real parents finally re-appeared, miraculously rescued from some faraway secret concentration camp, ready to take me back if only I had been faithful to them. It is pitiful, but true: even when I was old enough to go to university I still—not when fully awake—but in my heart—nurtured this ridiculous fantasy. Of course I also still had the pictures of skeletons that Yaakov had given me; of course I had seen the movie of allied soldiers coming in and cleaning up the camps with bulldozers. But my own parents had never been officially located, and there were occasionally preposterous stories of people who struggled back from the past... Did I really believe they might be alive or was I just haunted by them? In nightmares is there a difference?

For years I lived across from Miller—my third floor attic bedroom facing his; and, if during those years I can say I began to know Miller, well, I must admit my knowledge was far from complete. For example: if you had asked me whether I was betting on the future of Miller, if you had asked me whether I foresaw in Miller the fame he eventually achieved, if you had asked me whether Miller would grow into a man of passion and courage, I would have had to answer that such great expectations never crossed my mind.

Perhaps, aside from my own blindness, that is because Miller's first decisive moment did not even occur when he was living at home; it came when he was eighteen years old—to be exact, when he entered the residence of his university for the first time.

When was that? On a certain day, during a certain hour—but let us be scientific and admit that the moment of Miller's rebirth was a time interval too small to be located on a watch. In fact it was a micro-second so tiny only a heart could have room for it; it was the careless and unpremeditated moment when, with the afternoon sun streaming in the west-facing window so that his eyes were half-averted and the details of the room swum in a vague and coloured haze, the door which he had pushed shut, locked.

The sound was a well-oiled, mechanical click. It was only as Miller turned towards it, as the full brass and iron details of the sound registered and translated themselves into meaning, that the *true* moment of his arrival at the university began and ended. That is to say, the once and future D.B. Miller realized that

without making any conscious effort,

without having to ask permission,

without anything at all except a careless bump of his shoulder administered to the solid-core door,

he was for the first time in his life alone in a locked room.

The details of how that even came to pass—of how Miller left home for university because his doctor father decided to end his long widowerhood by marrying a woman of great physical charms—belong elsewhere. Enough to say that no sane man would want his eighteen-year-old son as witness to such nuptial raptures.

But what Miller felt upon his arrival had nothing to do with his father's plans. Instead, an entirely different phenomenon was taking place. Miller, *Miller*, was being born.

Putting down his suitcase, Miller stepped towards the window. His eyes had now adjusted and through the glare of the setting sun he could see that across the street from the university residence was a row of three-storey brick houses. Some of these houses were terminally ill, with plywood-covered doors and torn-away porches. Others, with their windows ajar to the warm fall air, and tattered sofas on their front lawns, were clearly still in use. Later Miller would learn that students expelled from the residences used these houses as an affordable and convenient alternative, but for Miller—intoxicated by the unexpected gift of privacy—the houses across the street had a rich and sinful look, the look of older women who planned their wardrobe and wore make-up for reasons he had only begun to imagine.

He closed the curtains, and instantly the room was filled with a pale shimmering light. Then, as Miller turned back to his suitcases, his eye was caught by the broad and freshly waxed surface of his new desk. In its centre, an echo of the locked door, was a glass ashtray. Unbelieving, reaching towards it to confirm this ashtray was real, Miller suddenly caught sight of himself in the mirror above his desk. He saw a wiry and athletic young man, dark hair cut too short, glasses perched askew upon a nose slightly bent due to a stray elbow caught during a scrimmage. He wore a button-down white shirt with the tie slightly loosened, but the effect was ruined because on the left-hand pocket, like the sign of a stained heart, was a large beige splotch of coffee that Miller realized he had been wearing since the uncomfortable breakfast he had shared only a few hours before with his father and his new mother.

Miller, at that instant, made his first decision about his new home. He took a dime from his pocket and unscrewed the mirror from its mooring above the desk. Next, he opened the closet door and placed the mirror at the very back. Psychologists might find great meaning in the gesture, and I would agree that if there was anyone Miller *didn't* want to know it was himself; but instead of self-evasion I prefer to see in Miller's gesture the reflex of an innocent. Give Miller credit, he didn't want to spend his whole first year away from home staring at his own face.

When he had disposed of the mirror Miller unpacked his suitcases where he found, in addition to what was expected, an envelope containing a fifty-dollar bill and a note from his father: *buy yourself a milkshake.* The sight of his father's handwriting, narrow-lined and almost indecipherable in a manner which Miller always assumed must have been cultivated to reflect the fast-moving mind of a man who communicated in prescriptions, gave Miller the sudden feeling he was being spied upon. He looked towards the door as if it had betrayed him. *I locked you.* Then he crumpled up the paper, squeezing it with such violence that the veins in his arms popped up. Again he looked towards the door—friend, betrayer—until he heard again in his mind the reassuring and final click of the lock.

*Miller was my twin, my complementary opposite. Locked doors
imprisoned me but—and not only on this occasion—they inspired
him. But just as I had looked forward to every aspect of university
life, Miller was overwhelmed by it.*

On the first day of classes, all Honours Science students were
summoned to a large room in the chemistry building. At the
front was a grey-haired woman sitting behind a desk. For a
moment she studied some papers in front of her, then she
lifted her head and smiled at them all benevolently.

"I am afraid we need to get some information from you.
Please form a line in the order of your final marks last year.
Thank-you." Having delivered this request in a high soprano
voice, the grey-haired woman—her name was Maria Ellsbach
and she was another of the many faculty members who had
escaped the theatre of disappearance in Europe—turned back
to her papers. Soon the room was filled with the buzz of
embarrassed students comparing grade averages. Miller, who
in his own high school had always effortlessly been one of the
best, found himself, in this rarefied crowd, more than halfway
down the line of two hundred.

That afternoon, in their first mathematics lecture, the
professor—who was Hans Ellsbach, the husband of Maria and
the possessor of a reputation for having helped invent guided
missiles, first on behalf of the Germans, then the Americans—
said, "I want everyone to look at their neighbours."

This was requested in a heavy accent. He had to repeat it
twice before heads began twisting curiously from side to side.

On Miller's left was a boy he had already noticed, the tall
red-headed scarecrow in a too-short grey tweed suit who
had stood conspicuously at the very front of the line and
was rumoured to be receiving a professor's salary in scholarships. On Miller's right was another person he had noticed in
the line, a girl who had stood quite near him—but ahead of
him—and who had been wearing a strangely attractive perfume smelling of peaches so that as Miller moved forward
towards the desk, he had been continually aware of being in

the wake of this out-of-place adornment. (Later, when everything fell apart for Miller and he found himself obsessively recounting all of this to me, in order to discover the key events in his march to oblivion, he would often pause at the episode of the perfume and speculate that there had been no perfume at all, that his over-excited nostrils, already aware that fate was about to demolish him, had simply invented it in a romantic gesture). The girl's name was Amanda Nelson. Miller learned this because turning to look at her he saw her name written out in rounded childish letters at the top of the notepad. "At the end of the year," said Professor Ellsbach, "one of your neighbours will have dropped out or failed. In this course, only one out of two candidates proceeds into second year."

There was a brief pause, then Ellsbach began his lecture. He spoke in a rapid and incomprehensible mumble heavily spattered with German words. From time to time he stopped to illustrate his point with indecipherable squiggles that quickly covered the blackboard.

Later Miller discovered that these tactics, and others like them, were simply standard warfare against students foolish enough to offer themselves up to the altar of science. By that time Miller had almost entirely stopped going to lectures. His room, which only a few weeks ago had been an emblem of freedom, became a cell in which he compulsively slept, later and later every day, until finally he had mastered the art of staying unconscious until twilight.

At that magical hour, rubbing his eyes with the strain of doing nothing, Miller would rejoin the normal stream of life in the university residence. Freshly shaven and showered, drops of water still clinging to his face, Miller would stand outside and suck in great gulps of cold autumn air before crossing the leaf-strewn commons on his way to supper in the dining hall. From there he made his way to the library where he guiltily stared at the various texts assigned for his courses. But these were so boring, so difficult, so reminiscent of the lectures he was missing and yet couldn't force himself to attend, that Miller found himself pushed into a reverie even deeper than sleep. Lying back in the library chair he looked about the room and at the students and asked himself which were the ones who looked interesting, who looked happy, who were enjoying their lives.

Having made this judgment, Miller then inspected their books. Were they reading about quantum mechanics? Multidimensional geometry? Mass spectroscopy? No, they were not. They were reading well-thumbed texts on the Punic Wars, clever little dissertations on word origins in Chaucer, French novels, biographies of lesbian poetesses. In brief, they were reading books that were easy to read, books in which one word followed the next and you knew exactly what was happening, books made up not of concepts that turned your brain into spaghetti, but books that could be started at the beginning and finished at the end without too much effort. They were reading books that you read with the same avid delight with which you plunged into a meal you were eager to eat.

Miller began sneaking a few of these very preferable books from the shelves. Soon, at his library table, they replaced his hated texts; and then he began taking them back to his room. There he would collapse in his armchair and, fresh from his long day of sleeping, he would read until dawn. While he read, he would smoke cigarettes and stub them out in the ashtray the university had provided, and with the fifty-dollar gift from his father he kept himself supplied with cheap red wine to lubricate his throat.

In the middle of November, exactly two months after the beginning of Miller's first term of university, Walter Miller, unannounced, came to the door of his son's room. He was dressed in the expensive wool suit he wore for hospital board meetings, or visits from adolescent girls who thought they were pregnant, but instead of a doctor's bag or briefcase he was carrying a cane. Miller immediately concluded that his father had been lamed by excessive sexual indulgence. Miller himself, already under that lucky star that protected him most of his life, had that very day tidied his room and, not drinking because he had decided to go into training for the university soccer team, was sitting at his desk working on a letter to the Dean of Men, announcing his resignation from the false calling of Science, so he could devote his academic career to "the study of man's mind, and to sounding the hidden depths that make us what we are."

"You're a fool," his father announced as he walked into the room. He brushed by Miller to stand in front of the desk where he bent over and read his son's letter. Then he turned to the bookcase and began pulling out the paperback volumes Miller had been collecting and throwing them on the floor: "Look at these—Dostoevsky, Nietzsche, Freud, Jung—do you think I sent you to a finishing school for young ladies? Where are your textbooks?"

Before Miller could answer, his father had raised his cane and poked him in the chest, sending him tumbling back into his armchair.

"It's three o'clock in the afternoon. You're supposed to be at your chemistry lab. What are you doing here? You really are an idiot. When I was your age I *begged* to go to university."

"I like it here."

"I'm sure you do." From the top of Miller's desk, his father picked up an empty wine bottle, adorned with the drippings of the candles Miller found it inspirational to burn while reading nineteenth-century philosophy. "What a stupid joke this is. You left home so you could spend your time watching candles burn? Why don't you come to visit us? We have a whole drawerful of candles."

At this moment Miller, even had he not previously unscrewed the mirror from the wall, would have been entirely unable to see himself because Miller, when he loses his temper, becomes deranged to the point of blindness. But we can imagine how Miller must have been. Broad-shouldered and thick-armed from the fifty push-ups he had practised nightly since going out for the soccer team in grade eleven, red-faced, glasses threatening to slide down his nose, voice beginning to break because it had not yet mellowed into that smooth baritone that later became a frequent visitor to the nation's parlours, we can see Miller stumbling and sputtering forward, eager to defend this new life in the face of any opposition, especially his father's.

And in Miller's mind, we can be sure, must have been fixed another scene, one which had taken place on the well-mowed grass of the back lawn of the primordial Miller residence, the version of a ritual that had been repeated every summer for more years than Miller could remember: the annual arm-wrestling match between Miller *père* and Miller *fils*. Even the previous year, the year before his high-school graduation, Miller's push-ups had made it possible for him to withstand his father's superior strength and weight for a few minutes. But this summer, as Miller had eased himself onto his stomach and reached out his hand to grasp his father's, he had seen something completely unexpected on the old man's face—doubt.

Miller, wearing a T-shirt that was shrunk into a narrow tube that showed all his ribs, looked across at his father and saw a man who was almost old, a man who was wearing a short-sleeved white shirt with a deck of Export "A" in the breast pocket, a man with a receding hairline, a nose surrounded by veins popped by several decades of beer and Scotch consumed at a steady pace, a man who grunted slightly as he adjusted his body to the contours of the ground.

Miller had grasped his father's hand and squeezed.

Ten minutes later the hands were still locked together in the midnight position. Father and son sweating. The lovely lacquered Bernadette hovering over them. "Careful, Walter. Now, why don't you two children just congratulate each other and call it a draw. You've both tried so hard. You should be proud. *Listen* to me. You're going to give each other heart attacks. Now, sweetheart why don't you set an example and just give up. After all, Dennis is your son. You must be proud. Please—"

Miller, looking at his father, seeing the sweat running through the little valleys of his wrinkles, almost ready to give up when his father, with a mighty groan, twisted his entire body, forcing Miller's hand towards—but not to—the lawn he himself had cut only a few hours before with the family's newest acquisition, an electric lawnmower with a red saw-toothed toe-guard. "Now," Miller's father grunted, once more pushing down on the hand of Miller, pushing with such force that the blades of grass, uncut, would surely have brushed against his flesh.

"Not this time," Miller said. Two years of fifty push-ups per night came surging through his teenaged veins and wrenched his hand back to the midnight position.

"Now you're even. Both of you. Listen."

But Miller heard another voice. It said to him: *You can do it.* He looked at his father. He was breathing deeply, the skin of his face and neck had turned a bright scarlet.

For an instant Miller loosened his grip. As his father, falling for the old trick, jerked forward, Miller reversed his direction and slammed his father's hand into the earth.

"I see you're smoking now."

"Sometimes."

"Then offer an old man a cigarette. But don't tell Bernadette. She made me promise to quit smoking and start taking care of myself." Bernadette was, of course, the new wife. The New Wife in the way that previous generations had had The New Car. The New Wife was still factory fresh, just at the nether edge of maturity, in her mid-twenties, and still reeking, from her lacquered shoes to her oddly modulated voice, of an intercontinental private-school education designed to equip young ladies to accompany wealthy young doctors on expensive vacations. Or so Miller liked to think, before his own compass led him in a similar direction.

"I hear you're not going to your courses."

"I'm sorry," Miller said. "I just don't have what it takes."

"Anyone can attend a few lectures. Are you some kind of moron who can't find your way to the right buildings?"

"I don't understand the work."

"You're not supposed to understand. They're trying to scare you. Did they tell you that old one about the people beside you failing? They used to tell that one to soldiers in the trenches in the First World War. 'Hey, Buddy, the next one's going to drop on you.' I can't believe you fell for it. For a person reading masterpieces on the nature of man, you have the insight of a toad."

"Other people understand."

"Some of them understand," Miller's father said. "The rest are faking it."

"Out of the two hundred that started, fifty-five have already dropped out."

"I don't care about them. I care about you. You're my son."

"Even if I don't become a scientist, I'll still be your son."

Miller's father stood up. "It's your life. Make your own decision. In the meantime, let me take you out to dinner, and if you don't mind, we will meet an old friend of mine."

Miller, who had scarcely breathed in the whole time since his father had barged into his room, was still standing half-paralysed, the shape of the word *no* still twisting his mouth, when he saw his father bend down and begin picking up his books, handling each one very carefully, and putting them back in the bookcase. The overhead light was on and it shone through the last wisps of Miller's father's thinning hair to the white scalp beneath. Miller, choking now with frustration and remorse, could see the scar where his father's head had been gashed by a hockey stick, another scar where the mole they had feared was brain cancer had been removed.

When the books were picked up they walked out of the residence and through the campus, past the building where his father had studied medicine, past the newer buildings where the lecture theatres Miller never attended were located, downtown to a steakhouse Miller had read about in the newspapers.

"After all," his father said, as they stood in the entranceway and inspected the menu, "you might as well get a decent meal out of this."

They went into the restaurant and worked their way to the very back. There, sitting at a table, was a man reading a newspaper.

Miller's father stopped. The man put down the newspaper and stood up. He had black hair, one of his eyebrows was misshapen, and his large dark eyes fixed on Miller intently. He was enormously fat. "Walter Miller," he said. His voice was a soft reverent whisper. "What a pleasure to see you. And this must be the boy you have sent us for his education. Let us hope, my dear Walter, that we will not fail him."

Miller always said that his meeting with Piakowski was his own crossroads, the instant in which his abandoned resolve to become a scientist was found again. But the truth, obvious to anyone who knew him, was different: Miller didn't find himself again—he had never had himself to begin with—what happened to Miller was that he fell in love with Amanda Nelson.

When Piakowski spoke of love it was a different matter. Oh yes, he knew how to use the word. But what love meant to him, like to his beloved Proust, was a comedy of manners, a multi-layered mirage so cunningly constructed that even its creator can finally become its victim.

But for Miller, love was no comedy. Miller did not fall in love: love struck Miller a near fatal blow. Love ran Miller over. Love grabbed Miller by the throat and rattled his bones until love betrayed Miller, which is what love always does.

For the Christmas vacation of his son's second year at university, Miller's father arranged something very special: a trip to England for the whole Miller clan—father Miller, the stepmother Bernadette Miller, Miller-the-son and Margaret-the-daughter. When Miller returned from this exotic treat he was still outwardly the Miller of old, that is the Miller whose chief thrill in life had been the sound of a door locking behind him.

But the shock of London had set something off in Miller. For example, he allowed his new mum to buy him clothes that made him look at least vaguely attractive. And from his cupboard he had resurrected the mirror that he had unscrewed so definitively little more than a year before.

Does this mean that love's first stirrings had already made their little waves in Miller's pink and unpractised heart? Biologists who believe in gradual change might say so, but my own theory is that love happens all at once, a traffic accident of the soul.

For the first few weeks of the second term, Miller faithfully went to lectures, did the assignments that were assigned, spent his designated hours in the laboratory. In sum—the Miller reformed by his encounter with Piakowski continued on his studious way.

However, the dutiful Miller had changed his plumage: chief among his vacation purchases was a Harris tweed jacket, and to go with it Bernadette had given her stepson a suitable array of button-down shirts and subtly patterned ties. It was thus in a mid-Atlantic college-boy outfit that Miller now presented himself in public—lectures, labs, even the library where he continued to waste his time on novels, philosophy, anything that struck his fancy as he browsed in the open stacks. These prizes he would, two or three nights a week, gather under his arms and take upstairs to read at one of the dozens of blond oak reading tables that were scattered through the building.

At one of these desks Miller's calamity occurred. He had taken off his jacket and rolled up his sleeves, carefully pushing back his cuffs so that they might survive another day without washing, and was fifty pages into *Appointment in Samarra* when a voice from across the desk said his name.

Miller looked up.

"Do you have change for a dollar?" Amanda Nelson asked. "I want to get some coffee."

Miller, who had often sat near or beside her since their first meeting, nodded and reached into the pocket of his new flan-

nel trousers. The top button of his oxford cloth shirt was
undone, his matching tie was loosened casually—in a manner
he had been practising by the hour in front of his resurrected
mirror—and as he stood up with a handful of change he had
a sudden last-minute consciousness of himself as a boy turning into an independent young man, a young man who,
despite pressure from his father and Stefann Piakowski, was
still riding that first sweet post-adolescent surge of infinite
possibility, a young man who might still emerge from his
chrysalis as anything from a lawyer to a wino to a businessman with a fleet of taxis.

Then he looked across at Amanda, still so far as Miller was
concerned one of that vague mass of vaguely friendly girls
who had populated his high-school and university life—that
is to say, one of those girls who lived out their passions and
tortures with other boys, boys who knew how to unlock their
secret doors.

"May I come with you?"

"I wish you would."

Amanda Nelson had just turned nineteen. Like Miller. Later
they discovered—oh, coincidence of coincidences—that they
had been born during the same hour of the same day. The
year she met Miller, Amanda's hair was short, a bleached
white blonde. She had a fine expressive mouth, white even
teeth. Her best feature was her eyes: coal black, long-lashed.
When she cried her long lashes would soak up the tears from
her cheeks and Miller would hold her in his arms to kiss
them, sucking the salt from her lashes, a sharp sparkling
taste that made his tongue jump with tiny electric shocks of
pleasure.

Miller picked up his coat but left *Appointment in Samarra*
lying face down on the desk. Amanda put the books and notes
she had been working on in her shoulder bag. Then she led
the way out of the reading room and down to the cafeteria.
For a few moments they sat in silence, drinking machine coffee. Amanda offered Miller a cigarette, which he accepted,
and then as they smoked he noticed that Amanda's cigarette

filter was gradually being painted by small flecks of red, from her lipstick.

"Well," Amanda finally said.

"Yes," Miller replied. At that moment, he later claimed, he already knew everything that would happen, it had all been rushing by him like ten movies playing at super-speed, all at once, from the very moment she had said, "I wish you would."

"Let's go for a drive." Again Amanda led and Miller followed. They climbed the steps from the basement cafeteria and got into Amanda's car. It was an MG with a canvas convertible roof, freezing in the winter. Amanda wore a fur coat. She could afford the coat, the car, anything she wanted, because her father had parlayed a small inheritance into a hundred thousand shares in a very successful brewery. Some of those shares had sent Amanda to Switzerland. A few others had been used to send her twin sister on a skiing holiday; on the way back the sister's plane had crashed in the Colorado mountains. Miller, whose residence was only a few hundred yards from the library, wore nothing but his genuine Harris tweed jacket, guaranteed hand-woven by sincere ladies from the Hebrides.

To keep warm, Miller smoked cigarettes. Amanda drove at top speed out of the city and to the airport where she parked in the metered parking for the handicapped. Then she led Miller to the bar where she ordered two Manhattans.

"I like to watch the planes take off," Amanda said.

Miller, who knew about her sister, nodded sympathetically. He couldn't take his eyes off Amanda's face. He was drinking it in, every pore. When Amanda spoke, when she breathed, when her coat made its half-silent furry rustle, these sounds tore through Miller's brain like a freight train roaring through a fog.

After two drinks Amanda stood up. "I have to go home." And then: "I like you."

"I like you."

"Remember the first day, last year, when the professor said that one of our neighbours—"

"I remember."

"I hoped it wouldn't be you."

"I hoped it wouldn't be you," Miller lied. In fact, it hadn't occurred to him that his neighbours would fail—he had been positive that the one to go would be himself. He looked into Amanda's eyes because they were looking into his. The first instant of surprise was over and the full extent of the calamity was beginning to sink in. Amanda Nelson, rich Amanda Nelson who lived with her rich daddy and her eccentric mama and who had a string of boyfriends who waited for her after class.

"It's all right," said Amanda. "Don't be afraid. I wasn't asking you to marry me or anything."

They laughed. "I'm not afraid," Miller said.

"I'm afraid. Inside of me is a big fear."

They got back into the car and Amanda drove Miller back to his residence. Nothing had happened. Everything had happened. She stopped the car but kept the motor running. Miller wondered if he was supposed to kiss her.

"I'll see you tomorrow," Miller said. He was looking into her coal black eyes again. His bare hands reached up to bury themselves in the warm fur of Amanda's coat, he pulled her towards him because he needed to feel all of her against all of him.

The first kiss wasn't a kiss at all, only his face against hers, breathing in her taste, her smell. They stayed locked, hardly touching, until Miller began to shiver.

"You're freezing." Amanda spoke her words directly into his mouth and Miller heard her voice as if it were his own.

"I know." Now their mouths had collided and Miller shivered again, this time with panic. He leapt out of the car, waved to Amanda, ran across the street, so dizzy with love that he was walking up the stairs of one of the disreputable non-residence houses before he realized where he was, dashed back across the street, skidding on ice, waved awkwardly to Amanda and ran inside the residence to his own room.

The next day he sat beside her in classes. When they took notes their elbows touched, and sometimes Miller forgot to copy anything down, so entranced was he by the soft girlish curves of Amanda's writing. When they walked from one building to the next Amanda pressed her fur coat into him; at lunch they sat together and Miller told her about the years he had spent doing push-ups so he could make the soccer team.

"You must be very strong," Amanda said.

"No," Miller giggled, suddenly embarrassed at his foolish story, "I'm actually very weak. I'm the weakest person I know."

"I am", Amanda said. "I'm *really* weak." She began to laugh, it was the sound of something very expensive breaking, Miller wanted to tear off his clothes and dive into it. Amanda kept laughing. She was laughing so hard she couldn't stop. Miller was aware that other people were looking at them. "I'm *really* weak," Amanda gasped, "we must have been born on a very *weak* day."

At this titanic pun Miller began to laugh uncontrollably, until finally, speaking directly to the audience, he spluttered out: "Don't you get it? We were born on a *weak day*." Then he got up and helped Amanda to her feet, and they were both still spluttering and gasping as they staggered out of the cafeteria and into the freezing air.

"Let's go to a hotel," Amanda said when she had recovered her breath. "I can't stand the suspense."

They went to the Park Plaza Hotel because that was the place where you went. Even Miller knew that. Amanda registered them under her name. "Not to worry, I've never been here before, if that's what you're thinking. Except with my mother this fall, when the house was being painted. My father went to tennis camp. My mother and I stayed here because paint fumes make my mother sick. That's why they know me. My mother is a big tipper."

They took off their coats and sat down on the bed, one on each side.

"I've never done it before," Amanda said, "not all the way."

"I've never done it at all."

"Let's lie on our backs with our eyes closed, looking at the ceiling."

Miller stretched out and cupped his hands behind his head. His body wasn't touching Amanda's but he could feel the mattress sagging with her weight beside him, hear the slow rhythms of her breathing.

"Now," Amanda said, "let's pretend we're lying on the bottom of a boat, drifting down a river, and that above us we can see a million stars. Do you see them?"

"I see them," Miller said.

"Is there a moon?"

"There's no moon," Miller said. "But the water makes a weird hollow sound because we're lying on the bottom of the boat. And at the edges of the stars are the trees along the shore. Poplar trees. The leaves are all silver from the starlight. Every leaf has its own private star. So does every drop of water. So does the boat. So do we."

"We have our own stars?"

"That's right." Miller said.

"I'm cold." The bed shook and then Amanda was lying against him, cuddled into his chest and legs. Miller put his arm around her to draw her closer; when his hand encountered hers their fingers laced together. "That's better." When she spoke her breath went into his chest, through the cloth of his button-down shirt and onto his skin.

And with his eyes closed and the press of her body against his, Miller *could* see the sky; inside the private dome of his eyelids rivers of stars were arcing across the darkness.

"Let's get under the blankets, Miller. Let's take off our clothes with our eyes closed and then hide under the blanket. Like our boat has come to shore now, we're going into our tent because the wolves are beginning to howl."

Miller sat up on the bed and began stripping off his clothes. He could hear Amanda's silk shirt reluctantly separating from her skin, the elastic snap of her brassière, the metallic murmur that betrayed the zipper of her skirt. But he didn't look, not out of modesty, but because he wasn't ready to see her yet;

for the moment he wanted to see nothing but shooting stars, and then he wanted to crawl into the tent.

Sliding beneath the sheets he had the sudden sensation of deep and textured linen against his skin. As he stretched out his arms and legs tangled with Amanda's, and without asking permission, his hands circled her waist. A child's waist enclosed by two curved ladders of ribs.

"Now, Miller, lie on top of me and open your eyes."

What he saw first was her face. It was strange to see a face so close up, a face that filled the whole screen so that at first his eyes couldn't focus but kept looking for the edges of the picture. Diamond studs in her ears. Hair making a perfect halo on the pillow. A nice chin, a chin that he had never noticed, and then her throat making its elegant triangle into her collarbone; and that was where he kissed her first, the vulnerable hollow of her throat where her skin was a sweet moist meadow and his tongue could feel the startled leaping of her pulse.

"Miller, promise me you don't know what happens next. Promise to love me forever. Promise me never to die."

Miller promised. He promised it all. His eyes were wide open, he said later, meaning that he understood what was going to happen—but the truth was that his wide open eyes were too busy feasting on the splendid vision of the naked Amanda Nelson to worry about life—past, present or future—on the other side of their locked hotel room door.

Had Miller by his second year transformed himself completely into a dutifully studying son of his father, then love might have derailed his newly won good habits. As it was, love saved Miller from slipping back into disaster.

In order to sit beside Amanda, Miller attended all his lectures, spent his afternoons in the laboratory, his evenings at the library. You might guess from this that it was Amanda who was dedicated to her work: you would be correct. Hidden inside the fur-coated, boy-crazy Amanda was a very boring teenager who used to set her alarm for five o'clock in the morning so that she could recopy her notes. It wasn't long before Miller, too, was taking notes at his lectures—notes less organized than Amanda's but notes nonetheless, using three colours of pencils to make graphs for his lab reports, and even reviewing previous work.

In addition to the courses begun in the first term, there was a new optional half-course in the second, an Introduction to Astronomy which was taught by Stefann Piakowski. It was a lecture course relying heavily on slides of the cosmos projected onto a screen at the front of the room. Piakowski, seated in the darkness, would expound on the mysteries of the universe while his assistant changed slides according to instructions previously given.

In this bizarre setting, lectures delivered in darkness while the constellations flashed by, Piakowski was at his best. Eloquent, mellifluous, always lucid, his lectures had a certain small fame among the science students. But even had Miller not been curious about this well-known course given by his father's friend, even had he not remained loyal to his boyhood belief in life on other planets, Piakowski's course would still have been his favourite because there, in the anonymity of darkness, the two lovebirds had the amazing opportunity to kiss and fondle during an official university lecture.

The lovebirds, in fact, was the name by which they rapidly became known. Mutually adoring, always deferring to each other, directing little bird-like whispers into each other's ears, holding hands during and between classes, constantly fetching each other coffee and cigarettes, they made their busy little nest wherever they went.

When the lights went out and Piakowski began to speak, I was the assistant who changed the slides. From my station at the back of the room I could observe, whether I wanted to or not—Miller's arm creeping around Amanda's back, his hand massaging her shoulders, his fingers sliding beneath the hair at the back of her neck to stroke the base of her skull, caress her earlobes, *anything* to maintain the constant stream of sub-erotic attentions by which they were joined.

Love saved Miller academically, but though it may have
made him feel a real Casanova, he was still more a boy than a
man of the world. Amanda, on the contrary, immediately blossomed from a rich spoiled teenager into a ravishing woman.
When she turned to Miller as the lights came up after the
slides, her black eyes shone with the passion of a movie star;
when her lips parted for a kiss, her mouth took on the perfect
proportions of desire caught in flight; and when she stood up
and brushed imaginary dust from her skirt, preparing to move
on to the next nesting place, each of the thousands of tiny
movements of her muscles and bones was like a separate and
delicate voice of the self-conscious chorus of her love—as if
she knew that her strange and seemingly inexplicable passion
for Miller had fixed her in the spotlight, transformed her
into the object of all our unfulfilled adolescent dreams and
fantasies—and as she left the theatre she would sometimes
glance back coyly as if to acknowledge our applause for her
startling performance.

Piakowski couldn't stop talking about her.

"That woman our friend Miller has found is absolutely
amazing. Do you see the way she *insinuates* herself next to
him? I swear that even from the front of the room I can
smell her musk. Miller has turned that bitchy little girl into
a ravishing cat in heat. Today I really and truly thought
they were going to fall out of their chairs and begin making
love right in the middle of my lecture on variable stars. Do
you know that the man who discovered variable stars was deaf
and dumb? That he devoted his whole life to astronomy?
What would he think if he knew his life's work was being used
to supply the musical background for a supernova of hor-
mones? You must find out that girl's name for me, everything. She is extraordinarily beautiful, don't you think? Or
are you jealous?"

In summer Piakowski wore beige suits, in winter grey. On the
rare occasions when he could be seen standing, these suits
made him look almost normal, as though they themselves fit

into the normal scheme of things. What a tribute this was to Piakowski's tailor. Closely examined—at least in retrospect—his trouser legs were vast cylinders through which baby elephants could have been born. And, when it was draped over the back of his chair, his jacket, too, could be seen for what it was, a gigantic sack made from a whole roll of cloth, so much material that folds and puddles of it gathered round each other, covered up the floor, often became entangled in any nearby furniture.

Piakowski's chair—and in a chair he was usually to be found—was generally located in the cafeteria of the physics building. Like all the chairs in the cafeteria it had a wooden seat and back supported by hooped iron legs. In fact, "it," the chair, was not a constant; that is Piakowski's chairs collapsed on an average of one every ten days. In any case, sitting in the chair of the moment, Piakowski would conduct his office hours, hold his seminars, answer correspondence, and even deliver lectures to his senior classes.

What, you might ask, had happened to the starving young soldier who grovelled in the trenches while the Nazi machine thundered across Poland? Where was the darkly handsome Piakowski who had graced photographs, who had skipped through the streets of Paris, who had courted and almost stolen the heart of Léonie Santangel? Where was the avenging warrior who had vowed death to the Nazis who had killed his family? Where, even, was the only mildly fat uncle who had sat me on his lap that first night at the Borstein house?

The only certainty is that by the time I became a student at the University of Toronto, the fleshly volume of Piakowski was fully matched by the legends that surrounded him. Except that whereas the actual body of the great scientist was virtually immobile—pinned to the earth by the almost incalculable gravitational attraction between our own modest planet and his own inestimable mass—the true identity of Piakowski was an ever-shifting concept shrouded by nebulous clouds of rumours and half-truths.

In brief: my uncle had turned out to be a complicated man.

The St James version, as it was known, actually contained elements of the truth. In it, his parents were Polish, second cousins of Marie Curie, who had brought the infant Piakowski to France so that he might receive his education at the feet of the eminent genius. A picture on Piakowski's office wall shows a skinny Piakowski, probably ten years old, posed beside the diminutive and aged — but still fierce-faced — Marie Curie. By the time the war came Piakowski had already delivered his little jolt to quantum theory, but the borders closed down when he was back in Poland, newly married. Forced to enlist, the story continues, Piakowski fought with great bravery until the collapse of the Polish army, when he courageously crossed the German lines and took his brilliant scientific mind to Paris. When he arrived he continued to starve, this time because of rationing, and when the Germans began to clean France of its Jews, Piakowski fled Paris — this time to return to Warsaw and attempt to rescue his wife and children. Alas, tragedy: despite the help of the resistance, Piakowski was unable to reach his destination. Stranded in North Africa, Piakowski had to listen to short-wave reports of the uprising in the Warsaw Ghetto. After that he managed to smuggle himself to Canada where the University of Toronto welcomed him with open arms. Overcome by years of suppressed grief and starvation, Piakowski commenced eating.

Other versions branch off in different directions: just one example — he *did* study with Marie Curie, but became a Nazi sympathizer after the fall of Paris and escaped the resistance by fleeing to Argentina where he sold war secrets until forged documents got him a job at the University of Toronto, a post he used to glean information in his avocation as a paid Soviet informer.

The young and skinny Piakowski, even the one in Léonie's photographs, like the mature Fat Man, had one eyebrow shaped like an inverted V, permanently raised. His eyes, too, were wideset; and if you looked at him through a rolled-up piece of paper, regarding only his mouth, the same innocent boyish smile often reappeared, complete with slightly gapped front teeth—top and bottom. (Although, it must be added, another rumour was that Piakowski had had his eyebrow surgically altered, and false teeth made to resemble the photograph; this fantasy was complete with the sworn testimony of a graduate student who claimed to have found two sets of similarly gapped dentures in the bottom drawer of Piakowski's desk.)

My own preference among the stories of Piakowski's origin—called the Big Bang theory—was that Piakowski was neither ex-Jew nor ex-Nazi, and had never even been to Paris. In this account Piakowski is merely a corpulent refugee from the slums of Brooklyn with an overactive thyroid gland.

When Piakowski laughed, which was often, his scarred eyebrow would shoot up, and one eye would be left entirely eyebrowless, rolled back and exposed like the eye of a wolf howling insanely at the moon. As his laugh diminished and the eye sank back into position, fixing one in its stare with a certain amount of fidgeting, like the nervous clothes-brushing of a drunk who has taken an embarrassing stumble, the eyebrow would twitch several more times, threatening to begin the whole chain of events once again.

"So," Piakowski would say at such moments, "where were we?"

On the arborite table in front of him were invariably to be found Piakowski's tools of the trade: a couple of lined pads of foolscap, a slide-rule, a few pencils, a can of Export "A" tobacco, a green package of cigarette papers, a Swiss army knife which he used to sharpen pencils, or, more often, to open the steady stream of confections which made their way from the take-out counter of the cafeteria to his belly.

"Pardon me," he would say, as a chocolate bar or doughnut would disappear with great haste behind his gapped teeth—the final bite was always followed by a flick of his surprisingly narrow tongue: a lizard's tongue, a slender devil's tongue which undoubtedly was another feature unchanged from the European version—"mind and body must be fed."

From ten o'clock in the morning, when he was delivered by taxi, until five o'clock in the evening, Piakowski—unless there was a department meeting or a lecture for his introductory course in astronomy—was to be found at his post in the cafeteria. From there, with the aid of a few of his most favoured students, he would make his way to a Chinese restaurant only a few hundred steps to the south of the physics building. These steps were accomplished with great ceremony and difficulty as Piakowski, breathing hard, stopped at every excuse in order to expound on some or other nicety, to point towards a window and deliver gratuitous insults to its owner, or just to turn and look down from his considerable height at we Lilliputians who were as discreetly as possible linked to his arms in order to help him support the accumulated bulk of his confections. What a man of substance my uncle Stefann had become! Since he had left Paris he seemed to have put on not years, not decades, but whole generations. Yet, I once calculated, the year I entered university Piakowski was in fact forty-four years old—still young enough to get into trouble, I realize in retrospect. And despite his bulk, Piakowski hadn't lost his looks; in fact during that era he had a very sweet and frequent smile, and fine handsome features derived, he claimed, from "my grandfather, the Count,"—a short narrow nose, wideset pale blue eyes, a forehead across which played a constantly changing symphony of interrogatory wrinkles. As we got to the restaurant, finally, he would always give us one of these special smiles and say, "Without you, I swear I would not be able to survive from one day to the next."

Once installed, Piakowski would get down to serious scientific discussions. At the time his interest had been shifting from pure physics—which he said had been morally destroyed by the invention of the atomic bomb, just as its twin, philosophy, had been destroyed by its use as the building blocks of totalitarianism—towards the ancient and speculative science of astronomy.

In this, he had begun by having various of his graduate students measure the bending of light as it passed by heavy stars. This was a repetition of Einstein's experiment, and in forcing its repetition Piakowski was reminding us of the lineage he liked to claim for himself. For just as Piakowski would speak of his genetic grandfather, the Count, he also made it clear that he occupied the same Olympian intellectual peak as Einstein, Plato and, very oddly, Marcel Proust. Proust was his eccentricity. Piakowski was always quoting him in a weird Polish-tinged French that made us think not of literature, but of the Curies and their colleagues, sitting about in Paris cafés glowing with their own excitement and the radioactive samples they carried about in their pockets until their clothes and fingers began to disintegrate.

Without having to be ordered, great steaming platters of food were placed in front of Piakowski. While he demolished the lion's share, we hangers-on would nibble away at the edges of his appetite, stuffing ourselves with his scraps.

When the history of modern science is written, Piakowski will not be in its galaxy of stars, but for us he was Olympus itself—not only because of his tremendous girth and his equally large interest in his students—but because his mind, like an ocean of which the ever-varying wrinkles on his forehead were only a hint of the enormous depths beneath, was always more than equal to anything we could set before it. In brief, Piakowski was one of those few professors you remember. Some will say that such professors, clever and charismatic men and women with a need to impress their students, are psychological cripples, using students to supply the support they can't get elsewhere. If Socrates had had a better marriage perhaps he would have spent more time by the hearth, instead of staying up all night asking his students questions. In any case, those whom Piakowski allowed near him seldom refused his invitation. His reputation as the campus genius was supreme, the spell he held us in complete. An invitation to join the inner circle who dined at the Chinese restaurant—usually delivered in an offhand manner such as "Why don't you come to watch me eat, I'm told it is quite a spectacle"—was practically the local equivalent to the Nobel Prize. And Piakowski's delight in giving was fully equalled by his delight in taking away. Even now I can see his sallow Slavic skin, his eyebrow shooting up with laughter, his tongue darting out to lick some stray morsel or just to make a sly circuit of his lips after he had, with a few devastating words, cleverly undermined some theory that a student had spent weeks constructing.

But his interest in us was not confined to the working hours of the university, during which he treated each and every one of his students with equal solicitude, or to his social hours at the restaurant. There were also those of us to whom he turned at the end of the meal, which was about nine o'clock, and asked, "If you don't mind, could you help me back to my apartment?"

Piakowski's apartment was only a few minutes, even at his pace, from the Chinese restaurant. It was located above a tailor's shop so ill-favoured that the bolts of cloth displayed in the iron-grilled windows had yellowed with sun and age, and it could be reached only by climbing two sets of twisting stairs. Perhaps buoyed by his evening meal, Piakowski always climbed these stairs with amazing speed, almost scampering, but then he would finish up puffing in front of his door, key weakly extended.

The role I played with Piakowski at this juncture is not something I have excuses for. Not that he was physically repulsive, objectively speaking. Despite his size he was, naked, more like a gigantic porpoise than a disturbingly fat person—in fact, ensconced in his over-large bathtub, drinking brandy and rubbing himself down with a genuine South Seas sponge, Piakowski revealed the true Count Stefann, an exotic shining marine creature mistakenly endowed with human limbs.

Long before psychedelic drugs became fashionable, Piakowski was well supplied with opium. This he smoked in pipes that I shared with him. With the first puff I was plunged into a weird aqueous world of dreams and the gloomy Germanic music that Piakowski played on his sound system. With the curtains drawn and a solitary candle flickering, Piakowski's

world became a planet of its own. Stranger even than Mars
could have been, it made of my consciousness an adolescent
limbo of half-formed dreams; and inching my way through
the night I was drawn into Piakowski's nightmare, the destruc-
tion of the old world, the music of the Holocaust, until finally
at dawn, when I stumbled out onto the street, I felt as though
I myself had survived a trip into the antechambers of Hell.

At the time I wrote it all off to experience, to love, to
whatever obscure debt I owed my dead parents. Then I began
to wonder if the love was less than love, if the experience was
more than an experience—a book read or a strange country
visited. First I progressed to the idea that it was something
that was making me; and then eventually I understood that it
wasn't something "outside" of me that was happening to me,
like a meteorite falling on a soft field—it was my life itself,
the absolute innermost part of me that had been in hiding
every since Léonie whisked me away to the outskirts of Paris
and started teaching me lies. Piakowski's planet wasn't his at
all—it was mine. But that was something I only discovered
much later, when Piakowski had transformed himself yet again
and I had meanwhile found my own ways of digging into the
centre of the night.

But right here I want to insist on what is already so obvious
to everyone else, that the secrets of science *are* the secrets of
the night, and that when we use our shiny twentieth-century
machines to gaze into the fabled dark mysteries of the universe we are fleeing from *human* truth to search out a truth
entirely different, a truth so harsh that there is no room in it
for the soft frailties of childlike souls, for the easy vulnerabil-
ity of human skin that is so easily crisped by radiation, for the
delicate balance of bodies that are so eager to dive into pleasure that they are poisoned and corrupted by almost everything they invent.

Drugged, lost in old childhood nightmares, touching Piakowski, kissing the smooth marbled expanses of his flesh, I
felt as though I was the anvil and Piakowski the hammer of
history collapsing impotently on top of me.

We who surrounded Piakowski seemed to make a constella-
tion of our own. Sitting in the restaurant with him and putting his leftovers in our hungry mouths, glancing at each
other in a conspiracy of amazement and awe as Piakowski
speculated on some new and transcendental set of equations,
some of us taking our turn at caring for the very flesh of the
master, we seemed to be joined in an intimate dance, a communal unlocking of the soul, the mind and the body.

For most, in retrospect, that dance was a moment of illu-
sion: an instant of transparent geographic proximity destined
to be sucked away by other lives, other events.

But for three of us—myself, Miller, Amanda Nelson—the
collision with Piakowski was the beginning of an intricate and
compelling dance. Not that we did not often live our separate
lives, go our own ways into love and ambition—but in the
end we have been locked together the whole time, like three
children holding hands and skipping around one centre—that
centre being of course Stefann Piakowski.

"Tell me which one of you has the greatest mind," Piakowski
asked me one night after his bath. He was wrapped in his gigantic maroon dressing gown, the air of the room was thick with
opium smoke. It was four A.M. I know this because Piakowski's
question was followed by the chiming of an absurd cuckoo clock
which he had beside his chair. As it counted out the hours I
could feel my numbed body trying to pull itself through its
mesh of half-dreams and into some sort of consciousness. There
was music playing, too, an Albinoni adagio which is often on
the radio, unidentified, and can bring me to tears.

"Spitzer," I mumbled, thinking of the tall red-haired boy
who had captured so many scholarships and was to go on to a
brilliant career in astrophysics.

"Not Spitzer," Piakowski said. Normally his voice was surprisingly high and clear, a classic fat man's voice, but with
opium its timbre lowered and become melancholy. "Spitzer,"
Piakowski went on, "has the *best* mind I have seen in years,
the *cleverest* mind in the whole university, a mind that is like a
splendid white wine—light and silvery and capable of awing

you on the first impression. But his is not a *great* mind. A hundred years from now we will hardly remember Spitzer except for the curiosities that he invents or discovers." Piakowski loved to speak of the distant future as if we would all be in heaven together, reading the roll-call of our accomplishments and taking the true measure of our lives and mistakes— "but he won't have changed the way we see things, the way we *understand* the world. The world may be a different place because of Spitzer, but it won't be better or worse."

Piakowski reached for a glass of the brandy he sipped at through the night and brought it to his lips, sniffing carefully as if to inspect the bouquet of the various minds he was considering.

"I like Spitzer," Piakowski said. "But his is a second-class mind, finally, though a second-class mind of the very highest type. If I were to choose one of you as my assistant, there would be no one I would rather have than Spitzer."

Despite Piakowski's shortcomings as a man, I still had respect for his judgment. In fact, my presence often seemed to be mostly meant as a mental rather than a physical stimulant. Not only would he interrupt my opium-soaked journeys to ask some unexpected question, but he often insisted on my reading aloud to him from various of the scientific journals he subscribed to, arguing the pros and cons of different theories while he was in the bathtub, even interrupting the act of love to dredge up some new detail from his encyclopaedic memory to demolish or augment whatever speculation he was engaged in.

Thus when Piakowski said this about Spitzer—who was a regular at the restaurant and had earned all of our envy by being hired as the personal assistant of Piakowski for two summers running—I was totally shocked. At the same time, I must confess, even as his statement woke me up, I wondered if Spitzer had earned Piakowski's dislike by refusing some final measure of his favours. Because, after all, despite Piakowski's relegation, it was Spitzer we all sought out for help with assignments that seemed impossible, for explanations of mathematics that seemed to have flown off the edge of the logical. And Spitzer, always, with absolute clarity and ease, was able to make simple what had been complex, unravel the knots and the short cuts to lay out in a language a virtual baby could understand the puzzle that had caused so many hours of frustration.

"We are only students," I said defensively.

"You are not *only students*. If you were *only students* I would find all of you too boring. Now, think again, be daring."

At this moment the candle was burning, the violins were descending through their minor-key waterfall, my brain pulsed with the energy of opium. "Me?"

"You!" he exclaimed, as if I had just tried to enrol a dog in his graduate course in particle physics. "You think that you have a great mind?" At that moment my skin suddenly declared its own consciousness: every place he had touched me burned in revolt, my lips quivered with the shame of kissing him, my eyes squeezed shut to block out the memory of his naked whale's corpse. One more derisory sentence and I wanted to believe I would leap to my feet and hack away at the gigantic mounds of blubber until only the skeleton that had escaped the camps remained. "You have a great soul," Piakowski said gently. "You are both blessed and cursed because you believe in the difference between good and evil. But you are not clever, not a juggler."

As the burning of my skin subsided, the truth of what Piakowski had said worked its way in. I was a scholarship student, true, but more and more I had begun to flounder in our restaurant discussions, writing off to fatigue my need to sit back and let others solve the conundrums Piakowski presented.

"Your danger," said Piakowski, still speaking in this new gentle voice of a doctor delivering the bad news, "is that you will underestimate yourself. You are a mixture of impossibly high hopes and the fear that you are worthless. Get rid of your fear. You don't need it. One day you will write a wonderful thesis and will be a full professor at a university. You will be a great teacher, I know. I myself am like Spitzer, the highest of the second class. If I had your gifts, too, I would be truly someone. As it is, I envy you."

These last words, *I envy you*, had been delivered in the tone Piakowski always used for ending a discussion. While I was thinking about what he had said I heard the cuckoo clock again. Five o'clock. Somewhere, in between two words perhaps, a pause scarcely noticed, the hour had fled by. I was aware that it was a long time since I'd heard the record. Outside, now, the sky would be growing light. It was time for me to go home, time for Piakowski to get his few hours of sleep before the taxi arrived to take him to the university.

"Miller is the one," Piakowski said suddenly. "He is not so human as you, not so brilliant as Spitzer. But he has the spark. Miller will come to something, wait and see."

"Miller! He was lucky to pass last year."

"I know," Piakowski said. "I made an intercession on his behalf. This summer he is to be my assistant. Next year he will be a first-class student, wait and see."

This *wait and see*, delivered twice, like two blows of the hammer, sent me spinning. Miller? Never in a dozen guesses would I have come up with his name. When he came to the university and I, then in my third year, discovered myself a lab instructor in his first-year course, I had rushed to greet him. For a few moments we stood opposite each other in the laboratory, our faces burning with embarrassment and delight. Then, after we found a few words to say to each other, Miller turned back to his desk. Soon he had begun to skip classes and I lost track of him until the next year. Only recently had he been invited to join the group at the restaurant, and as if by some pact made during that first encounter, we hardly spoke to each other.

Miller? Until Piakowski delivered his verdict I had regarded Miller as he seemed to be—an intelligent neurotic student who would be fortunate to get a degree. I still *liked* Miller, for old times' sake and also because—let me admit it—I liked all those rivals who obviously presented no danger—but the idea that Miller's shoulders were to bear some

mantle of destiny had never crossed my mind. And, to tell
the truth, despite all his successes I don't think my essential
judgment of Miller ever would have changed had Piakowski
not introduced the idea that behind the skinny awkward
Miller who was too lazy and mentally confused even to take
care of his university work was another Miller, a "great mind"
with a "spark." And then Piakowski, as if he knew my thoughts
about Miller, completed his pronouncement. "Miller's gift is
nothing super-human, only ambition and vanity. There is
nothing in that man to be envied, you can believe me. I know
his father, a real nobody."

But even as I walked out onto the street, as always amazed
that beyond the drawn drapes of Piakowski's planet the ordinary world had survived untouched, I couldn't forget that
Piakowski had called Miller a man whereas he always referred
to the rest of us as boys and girls, overly bright acolytes it
amused him to amuse himself with.

The first night Miller brought Amanda to the Chinese restaurant was in early spring. Piakowski put me up to it; and I was
so used to bending to his will that I met them in the library to
make sure that Miller did not back out.

It was a raw March night. The snow that had begun to melt
during the day was already frozen over, and an uncomfortable wind whistled through the pink and yellow twilight.

By the time we reached the restaurant Piakowski was already
eating, and when we sat down at the end of the table he
barely glanced up at us. This behaviour continued throughout the meal: his desperate desire to meet the fabled Amanda
seemed to have been replaced by utter indifference. Over tea,
Piakowski began discussing that hoary old conundrum of the
twins: one of whom stays home while the other goes out into
space for several years and then returns—having all the while
been travelling at close to the speed of light. According to the
theory, the twin on earth would have aged while the travelling one—since speed compresses time—would be just a little
older than when he left.

"What do you think of this theory, Miss Nelson," Piakowski suddenly demanded.

Amanda, who was holding hands under the table with Miller, blushed a bright scarlet. "What I've always wondered," she said, "is why the story is about twins. The one who stays home is bound to be jealous of the one who travels. The story should be about a husband and wife. Then, while the husband is at home becoming a wise old man with grey hair, the wife could be having adventures in space while keeping her looks. At the end of the story they would both be a perfect match."

Piakowski burst into laughter. "Have you ever heard anything so charming? Miss Nelson has actually succeeded in making me wish my own hair was grey, so that I could be a wise old man awaiting the return of my beautiful wife."

"First," Amanda said, "you would have to be married." Her face was still flushed, the blood rushing through her creamy transparent skin like a spectacular sunset invading a perfect desert sky.

Again Piakowski burst into laughter. The rest of us nervously followed suit. Then Piakowski stood up, laid the money for the meal on the arborite table, and very slowly walked to the doorway of the restaurant. There he stopped and turned towards us. "Come again, all of you. It does my heart good."

His eyes narrowed and drilled into mine. A plea for help? A call from the charred flesh of the Warsaw Ghetto? A cry from the heart of a helpless uncle to his niece? I wanted to rush to his side, everything forgiven, but was afraid I might ruin whatever exit he had planned. But I was half out of my chair, still struggling to decide, when Piakowski slid dramatically to the floor, his great bulk settling into the hardwood with a long deflating sigh.

Sometimes, as I drift into sleep, memory tricks me and I am plunged again into the fog of the opium dreams I dreamed with Piakowski, long semi-conscious tunnels with a warm wind whistling by my ears and half-seen doors whizzing by.

When I asked Piakowski what he thought at such moments he would answer that he went "travelling"; but whether these trips were returns to his past or deep forays into outer space I never had the courage to ask. Once, while he was "travelling" I found in a bookcase a leatherbound edition of a speech he had given. By this time I had almost stopped thinking of Piakowski as a practising scientist: it was a shock to see he had been given a prestigious award which required him to deliver a speech in Chicago.

At the front of this special edition was a photograph of Piakowski just after the war. He was already fat but the bones of his face were clearer, and an eager-to-flatter photographer had airbrushed away the errant eyebrow and replaced it with a cleverly pencilled-in substitute.

Piakowski's speech began with Einstein's statement that mathematical constructs arise independent of observed reality—which is a fancy way of saying scientists, like everyone else, just make things up. But scientists like to say things elaborately, with big words no one can understand. And there is nothing scientists like better than to plonk themselves down in their easy chairs and turn themselves into great philosophers: Piakowski's speech read like a primer on the history of human thought—complete with quotes from the Persian and the Chinese.

And yet—imagine—the heart-tugging sight of Piakowski earnestly bent over a table, trying with all sincerity to find the right high-sounding words. Piakowski on the train to Chicago, the flat fields of the mid-west rolling by like a sky without stars. Piakowski arrived at his hotel, dressing for the photographer, smoothing out the creases in his dark suit and trying to adjust his starched collar so that it wouldn't dig into his neck. Piakowski actually speaking, actually facing the audience, actually standing at the lectern with the lights in his eyes, bent over a bit to read the page, pausing for effect between sentences, speaking slowly and trying to erase, with every word, the French and Polish inflections. Piakowski back in his room, Piakowski giving himself a final drink before sleep, Piakowski allowing himself to think that the frightened Jewish boy who had started running in Poland, who had run so fast he could hardly remember the names of his own children, had finally found a safe place to hide.

When he had the leatherbound edition made, Piakowski must have been filled with pride, because he put it, not with the messy and unsorted pile of his magazine publications, but in a special place amongst his most treasured books.

When Piakowski swooned, someone had the wit to call an ambulance. Even by the time I was kneeling beside him I could hear the sirens in the distance. I loosened his tie, unbuttoned his shirt. His heart was beating strongly, pounding like a fist into the palm of my hand. But his face was deathly white. When he opened his eyes they were glassy and fogged over.

In the hospital Piakowski overflowed the narrow bed and they had to strap him into place for fear that he would slide off. Three intravenous tubes were required to feed him, and a patch of hair was shaved from his skull so they could attach wires to his brain.

The waves given off, the specialists explained to me, were entirely abnormal. For hours they would be absolutely flat, vegetable talk. Then there would be a burst of activity, dense conglomerates of peaks and valleys as though Piakowski was bounding through the alps.

Amanda came to visit him every day. "I hope you don't mind," she said to him the first afternoon. "I feel I was just getting to know you when you were struck down. Anyway, it must have been fate that the accident happened on that very night—so here I am." She smiled at him, and when Piakowski's lips moved in response, she bent down and kissed him. "Let me be your Florence Nightingale."

That night Amanda telephoned to ask what else she could do for Professor Piakowski. "I have a book," I said, "that you could read aloud to him."

The next afternoon Amanda began reading *Swann in Love* to Piakowski. "I hope you don't mind my accent. I went to school in Switzerland for a year, but my sister was killed and I had to come home in the middle of our course on pronouncing vowels."

Faced daily with Amanda's irresistible eagerness to please, Piakowski began to respond. At times he was even cheerful, laughing with all his old zest. But those explosions of laughter were the only time we heard his voice. He never spoke, nor did his right arm or leg function properly. The specialists conferred endlessly, but were unable to locate brain damage. Meanwhile Piakowski could use his left hand to write notes on a pad fixed conveniently in front of him; soon we learned to decipher his awkward printing and carry on conversations with him.

After a while they took out the tubes and fed him normal food. A special bed, too, was arranged so that he didn't have to be strapped in. Four times a day several nurses clustered around him and supported his bulk while he struggled up and down the halls. Soon fewer nurses were necessary because hospital food was melting Piakowski away.

But the Piakowski who emerged was not the handsome soldier of the Paris photographs. The first place he lost weight was his face, and the effect was to give his eyes the appearance of staring out intensely from large bony caves. This insane apeman look was emphasized by his hair, which grew long and stringy, and the dry cracked voice which escaped every time he laughed. No one knew why he wasn't talking, but using his pad he responded to all questions with his usual sarcastic diligence.

While Piakowski stayed in the hospital, I became the guardian of his apartment, feeding the fish, taking in the mail, saving the refrigerator from turning into a seminar for bacteriologists. On Piakowski's instructions I brought him various scientific journals, his slide-rule, several pads of graph paper. These were all stored in a briefcase which he kept locked—the key looped into a string tied around his neck. During the mornings and the early afternoons Piakowski—when the doctors weren't testing him—worked on his projects. At four, various students and colleagues would begin their visits. After those first few heady days, Amanda saved herself until after seven, when the others had drifted away. She would come in, talk with me or whoever else had stayed so long, then read Piakowski his few pages of Proust. During these readings, which Amanda would render in the clear soprano voice of a schoolgirl, Piakowski would lay his head carefully on the pillow—as if it were Amanda's lap—and close his eyes. Perhaps he even listened to the words—Amanda's accent was not so atrocious as she imagined. But, watching him, I couldn't help thinking Piakowski had transported himself back to the hotel room in Paris. There, too, he had spent long days and nights waiting for his fate to be decided. Or, perhaps, in those strange silent intervals which all of our lives have, it is we who decide our own fate, we who finally fill the emptiness with a newly minted version of ourselves.

Around nine, Miller would come to collect Amanda. Sometimes he would arrive earlier and they would work together on their various assignments, Piakowski helping with the mathematics, of course, sketching out the solutions on his pad. All this while other students were sweating over impending exams, getting drunk, playing tricks on one another—no wonder Miller began to attract attention as an exceptional student. He even began to believe in himself, until he fell into the elephant pit of vanity.

It happened one otherwise brilliant afternoon, one of the weekly afternoons he and Amanda consecrated to reinventing the world in Room 736 of the Park Plaza Hotel. Lying on his back enjoying the cool sizzle created by the evaporation from his skin of various sweet fluids, Miller was feeling so absolutely thoughtless that with one long arm he reached down into Amanda's open carry-all bag and plucked out, at random, one of his textbooks.

With better luck the book would have been a dictionary, a chemistry text, even Proust. Instead it was the large and unwieldy volume containing the second-year course in statistics and numerical analysis. Statistics and numerical analysis!

It was a course that Miller totally hated, a skullcrunching dinosaur of boredom. Even opening the book sent a chemical tide of dread and anxiety through Miller's love-soaked organs. Miller, his eyes unable to focus on the page, looked over at Amanda. She was lying on her side, asleep, and as Miller reached over her to get a cigarette he stopped to admire the perfect lines of Amanda's sleeping calf.

Unable to resist he ran his hand along the narrow curved sole of her foot, up the bristly runway of her shin, along her slender haunches. At his touch her breathing quickened, then she stirred in her sleep and her legs quivered, like an animal in mid-dream.

But when his cigarette was retrieved and lit, and anxiety had driven him off the bed and away from the temptations of Amanda to the desk, Miller found his stomach beginning to churn in a way it had entirely forgotten since the day he went for coffee with Amanda. Even *looking* at a problem, he felt a bilious mixture narrowing his throat, bubbling in his chest, putting an unhealthy haze between his eyes and the page. When his fingers gripped the hotel pen, the haze got worse, and when he actually wrote down the first equation, the haze thickened and he felt as though an invisible hand was clutching at his guts.

"What are you doing?"

Miller jumped at the sound of Amanda's voice.

"Come back to bed."

Miller stood up, carrying the book back to Amanda. "Do you get this stuff?" he asked, pointing to the problems he couldn't even see, let alone solve.

Amanda pulled him down beside her. Miller sank to the sheets. She took the book from him, inspected the page he had been looking at. "No one gets this. I just memorize it so I can pass the test."

"You *memorize* it?"

"Of course, stupid. I just *memorize* it. It only takes a minute. What do you do?"

"I try to understand it," Miller said. "Isn't that what you're supposed to do?"

"I guess so. But if I always did what I was supposed to do, how could I be here?" She pulled him closer and Miller's mind, as always, followed Miller's body.

That night when Miller came to the hospital to pick up Amanda, he arrived carrying the offending text, his face white and drawn as if he had received some terrible news.

I can remember exactly my reaction to Miller as he came in the door and hurried to Amanda's side. I thought it was too bad Miller had come so soon. I wondered how someone so apparently undeserving had managed to catch the fancy of the luscious and admired Amanda Nelson. And I also felt sorry for Miller—thinking along with everyone else that soon enough Amanda would tire of such easy pickings and move onto a more glamorous mate while Miller was left in a daze.

What's wrong with your friend? Piakowski wrote on his pad. Amanda handed the note to Miller.

"Nothing," Miller said.

"Tell him," said Amanda.

Miller explained how merely opening the mathematics textbook made him sick to his stomach because he couldn't understand the problems.

What are you going to do about it? Piakowski wrote.

"I don't know."

Don't be so worried. Your father was the same way. Let me see your book. When Miller handed the book to him, Piakowski leafed through it, found one of the most wickedly confusing chapters, then turned to the back page and circled several of the problems. *Bring me the answers tomorrow afternoon. And now, everyone, good-night.*

At that time I lived across the street from the men's and women's residences. I was, in fact, one of those who had been exiled; and I had sole possession of the third floor of one of the dilapidated houses due to be torn down for the new

lecture hall. My nights with Piakowski had gotten me into the
habit of staying up until dawn, even when I was alone. So,
still feeling sorry for Miller, I invited him to come up to my
attic after he had finished saying good-night to Amanda, and
to bring his textbook with him.

It took Miller an hour to make the climb from Amanda's
sports car to my room. His hair and clothes were dishevelled
and his eyes squinted in the light.

"True love," I couldn't help saying as Miller sank into
my armchair—a tattered Salvation Army relic that gasped
out dusty puffs of history every time someone sat in it—and
lit a cigarette. But Miller was too morose to rise to the
bait. I gave him a cup of coffee and while he drank it I looked
at the problems circled by Piakowski. For Miller, in second year and still frightened by the idea that other minds
were more capable than his own, they were indecipherable
scribblings.

But for me—two years older and having seen the same
thing in a hundred different formats—they were simple
enough. Of course, I can't claim that I really *understood* them,
the way Miller wanted to. But habit makes understanding
unnecessary; you don't have to take a course in meteorology
to know that rain comes from clouds.

I showed Miller how to solve the problem. At first Miller
didn't want to copy the method I used. I had learned enough
from Piakowski to know that what Miller was going through
was not only his own barrier of block-headedness—though it
was that, too, but also a little opening of scientific possibility
repeated hundreds of thousands of times each day in labora-
tories and classrooms around the world. Occasionally, the
refusal to understand the old way leads to a new perception,
and what was once complicated becomes suddenly simple and
new. However, that is a one-in-a-million chance and Miller's
ticket was not about to come up. Not yet. Instead he drank
another cup of coffee, smoked another cigarette, and finally
allowed himself to mimic what I was doing.

Watching Miller work I remembered another passage Pia-kowski had lifted out of Einstein's writings, a statement that systematic education probably destroys more minds than it creates. Of course Einstein liked to believe that scientific enquiry was as free as swimming in the ocean and that scientists were a select group of very intelligent men and women about to understand the secret of the universe. A wonderful idea—science as a nursery school of superbrains juggling their play-blocks until they lined up in the patterns of the cosmos—but you had to be born a long time ago to believe it. The generation that Miller and I belonged to had grown up with a different image of science: television specials on exploding atomic bombs, documentaries showing the melted faces of Hiroshima, university research projects fuelled by the money of defence departments.

Through television—itself a gift of science—we learned what science was. Science was the mysterious and marvellous wizard who brought everything from instant pain relief to watches that glowed in the dark to the ageless beauty of movie stars; but science, also, with its flying machines that dropped ever-more-efficient bombs, its chemical rain, its pollution of air and water, was the Death card in the tarot pack. Science the wizard, science the Black Angel. Science was the sponsor behind the sponsors, the great schizophrenic sponsor in the sky. Science put the fizz in Coca-Cola, invented runless nylons and miracle lift brassières, contributed secret ingredients to everything from car tires to cookies. Science was in the air, as necessary as air; anyone who didn't want to grow up to be a scientist was either blind or stupid. Science had invented rock and roll. Science had reached for the stars and brought them close with telescopes. Science had conquered superstition with two aspirins and a glass of chlorinated water. Science was sending bits of metal into the sky to circle like moons around our brainy little planet. Soon, any day, real live people would be whizzing deep into space, seeing the Milky Way in their Chevrolet. Somewhere out there—but not too far—was the secret of the universe. We scientists were going to find it and when we did everything was going to be different.

That was how I had seen science when Piakowski was no more than the friendly uncle who had let a little girl sit on his lap—and that was Miller's view when he came to university. He knew he was riding a wave subsidized for the most dubious of reasons, but he still believed in the Big Flash—not the atomic bomb, not Zen Buddhism, not even drugs—but the blinding intellectual insight that would demolish centuries of mistaken thinking, tear the blinders from mankind's jealous eyes and make him the envy of his relatives and friends.

Given all of this promise and romance, how could Miller ever have considered quitting science? Because Miller, the awkward inner Miller who had seen his own reflection the day he finally found himself in a locked room, the little inner Miller who was gradually sneaking into his owner's skin, had inexplicably become totally *bored* with science and everything about it. Amanda saved Miller for the pursuit of rational knowledge; it was Amanda who pulled Miller back into the play-pen of ideas, because when Amanda came along the little inner Miller who had been flexing his muscles by reading Kafka found something much more compelling than a battle of the minds—in brief, the feel, taste and smell of the beautiful Amanda in the flesh.

It was three in the morning when Miller had finally finished the problems Piakowski had set. I checked over his work, not forgetting as I scanned the pages the extravagant claims Piakowski had made on Miller's behalf. Let me say this about my reaction, because that occasion was the only opportunity I ever had to see Miller at work before the fabulous discovery which set him apart from the rest of us mere drones: what I saw of Miller that night included things to be admired. His handwriting was neat. He had persevered at a difficult task. He learned quickly and gained with each repetition. It was a solid B-plus performance from a student who had been failing. I was proud of Miller for spending his time on mathematics when he could have been screwing Amanda.

Or perhaps time has poisoned my memory. Because it is also true that when I was finished reading Miller's work I whooped with happiness and offered him a drink. Then we began to talk again, but this time, finally, our defences dropped away and we talked about the years we had lived across the street from each other.

"You should have been there when my father got married again. We wanted to invite you but no one knew your address. Do you remember the time we made a snowman?"

"Of course."

"After that, I was in love with you for years." And then he smiled, the unusual little boy, the Miller of old, the Miller I had kissed in the snow.

Up until dawn, as always, I felt as though a piece of the universe had fallen back into place. When the sun made its appearance in my tiny attic window I hurried downstairs and began the walk towards the hospital. The night nurses were still on duty—and they knew me well enough from the times when Piakowski had been in danger. But today they had a surprise for me: the universe had shifted indeed. At six o'clock in the morning, a steaming cup of coffee on his tray, Piakowski was sitting bolt upright, chattering away as though his stroke had never happened.

"Miller."

"Tell me."

"Miller, I'm bringing you home to my parents tonight."

"I know."

"Miller, I'm afraid you're going to hate me for them."

They were in their hotel room, door locked, chained and bolted. Miller was standing in front of the mirror. On his left foot was an argyle sock purchased during the watershed trip to London.

"Miller, you have to make me a promise."

"Tell me."

"*Listen* to me."

In Miller's hands, draped around his knuckles like boxer's tape, was his tie. Silk the colour of a night blue sky, narrow diagonal red stripes.

"For God's sake, Miller, do you need me to tie it for you?"

Miller's unsocked foot scratched its sole on the clean tufted wool of the Park Plaza broadloom.

"Where's your other sock?"

Miller's eyes slid along the surface of the mirror until they met Amanda's. Amanda could be seen, sitting in the stuffed velvet armchair, totally dressed, foot impatiently jiggling, smoking a cigarette and drinking the last of the wine they had ordered from room service.

"I don't know."

"For *Christ's* sake, Miller, we're going to be late. Do you want me to go downstairs and buy you another pair of socks?"

"I like these socks." Miller, speaking of them in the plural, had found the missing item. He had spotted it in the mirror, peeking out from under the pillow. It had come off during their second love-making, an impromptu dash into the sheets brought on by Miller's desire to fondle Amanda's right breast. He preferred it to the left because he was convinced that Amanda, in the passenger seat of her high-school boyfriend's car, had offered the left as a matter of convenience during a drive-in double bill. In fact he had wrung out of her a complete confession concerning the event, right down to the fact the she was so engrossed in the movie she would have offered him the right as well—but if Miller had used his reasoning powers to ask himself why he was so jealous instead of interrogating Amanda, he might have saved himself a decade of unhappiness. Instead, he had settled on Amanda as an Amazon, good and evil incarnate, a luscious geography with still enough virgin territory to keep him going for a lifetime of obsession. In any case, the point is that they had previously been completely dressed and composed, ready to face *mère* and *père* Nelson, when this need to touch and kiss had arrived in Miller, had been welcomed by Amanda, had led to its predictable conclusion.

Miller let go of his tie. He was currently wearing one sock, one shirt, one tie—unknotted. He put on his second sock.

"You really are an asshole, Miller. What are you doing?"

"Getting dressed," Miller said, thinking not for the first time that Amanda satisfied was Amanda ready to wipe her hands and throw away the bones. Miller's back was sore, his knees weak, his genital area a blissful throbbing vacuum. Meeting Amanda's parents was not his greatest desire, but he was getting dressed as quickly as possible, all things considered.

"Miller, in one minute I am leaving."

Miller pulled on his trousers. Then his face felt itchy and he walked into the bathroom to wash it. While he was bent over the sink Amanda went by him and out the door. "Take a taxi." The door slammed shut and Amanda proceeded soundlessly down the hall.

Miller dried his face and opened the door. He realized he had forgotten to put on his underwear. "You bitch," he shouted, as Amanda stepped into the elevator.

Miller retreated into the hotel room and picked up his suit jacket from where it had fallen on the floor. Across the back, at approximately the same angle as the stripes on his unknotted tie, was a deep crease created during the recent acrobatics. Miller pulled his cigarettes out of the pocket, lit one. He smoked it while he finished getting dressed, calming down, convincing himself that Amanda would be waiting for him in the lobby.

Curiosity leads us into strange compulsions. Miller and Amanda: I have heard it all, extracted it from both of them, elicited thousands of hours of confidences. They needed to talk, I to listen.

"You must be Miller."

As the taxi pulled away Miller silently extended his hands. They were filled with red roses, two bunches of six, bought from the hotel florist.

"How sweet of you." Cynthia Nelson, Amanda's mother, had a booming mannish voice, and long, long-fingered hands which enclosed Miller's own in a warm and welcoming squeeze.

"You *are* Miller, aren't you?"

Like Amanda, Cynthia Nelson had ash-blonde hair, and after that the resemblance ended. Amanda was petite, pretty, high-voiced. Cynthia was broad-shouldered, and almost as tall as Miller in her high-heeled leather boots that resounded against the marble hallway.

As Miller entered the living room, in which Harold Nelson, *père*, was waiting, he remembered Amanda saying that her twin sister had taken after her mother while she herself seemed to have descended from her father. On the mantel was a large picture of the twins as girls, in party dresses, but before Miller could inspect it Harold Nelson was standing in front of him: blue blazer, grey flannels, Amanda's fine features seen through a drinker's veil of surface veins.

"You must be Amanda's young man."

"For God's sake, Harold, offer the boy a drink. *Miller*—is that what I should call you? Amanda tells me that absolutely no one calls you Dennis. *Miller*, as you can see we're in the midst of having the house redone, but I felt we absolutely had to have you here before things got out of hand and Amanda eloped with a stranger."

"Yes, Miller, name your poison. I'm on the wagon myself, so I've forgotten what comes first."

Miller's excruciating discomfort, Amanda's casual happiness in this unusual nest, Harold Nelson's cleverness in pouring vodka straight from the bottle every time he went into the kitchen for a new glass of water—the gradual dissembling and dissolution of the dinner party could be explained in any of a dozen ways.

But let us move to the heart of the matter: after the first drink came a second, after the second, a third, and after the third, a fourth.

Why did Miller drink like this? Firstly because Harold Nelson encouraged him, so he himself could go to the kitchen for more vodka; but secondly, of course, because Amanda was giving Miller the old cold shoulder, the frost *extraordinaire*, in fact was behaving in the worst possible manner.

By the time they sat down to dinner, Miller's speech centres had entered the first stages of paralysis. To sober up he decided to counter the influence of alcohol by smoothing out his system with a quick shot of nicotine.

He inserted a cigarette between his lips. There was such an alarming lack of sensation that Miller squeezed it tightly. Then he struck a match. As he drew the flame towards the tip of his cigarette, the match broke in half and the burning portion exploded upwards. Briefly, the fireball hung suspended until, before Miller's astounded eyes, it began its dive homeward, down towards the thick linen tablecloth. Miller jerked forward, the second-string soccer player in full emergency alert, and in a miraculous demonstration of reflex got the palm of his right hand between the match and tablecloth. The first sound Miller heard was a gasp from Amanda, that sudden intake of breath he had previously associated with her orgasms; but then he became aware of another simultaneous sound, a low-level hissing as the fine layer of sweat and oil on the palm of his hand boiled away and his skin began to blister.

"*Miller.*"

"Sorry," Miller said.

"What are you doing?"

"Being a gentleman," interjected Cynthia. "Thank-you, Miller."

"Thank-you," Miller said, and then, to his great relief, he felt as a kind of peace offering, Amanda's stockinged foot inching its way up his shins until it settled complacently between his knees.

"Amanda tells me you are quite an athlete."

Miller blushed.

"I did the high jump in school," Cynthia said. She had a handsome smile, and when she leaned forward in the candlelight it was almost possible to imagine her sailing happily through the air, bloomers billowing in the breeze. "I beat all the boys. If I hadn't promised to stop, I swear my sex life would have been ruined."

"She always boasts about her sex life," Harold said. He held up his vodka, then tipped it towards his mouth, swallowing greedily.

"Harold!"

"You do. And there's nothing wrong with my saying so, Miller was bound to find out."

"I am a very sensual woman. But what Miller finds out is up to Miller. At least it was, until you opened your mouth." Then she leaned closer to Miller, put her hands over his. "Don't let us frighten you. We both love Amanda so much."

"Now she's trying to change the subject," Harold said. "Let me tell you, she's like one of those streakers who gives you the moon and then disappears into an elevator. Honestly."

Cynthia squeezed Miller's hands.

"She's got a heart of gold," Harold now said. "Why don't we drink to that?"

"You too, Miller." Cynthia released Miller's hands. "You'll have to learn to keep up with us if you're going to become a member of the family."

"To hearts of gold," Miller declared, trying not to slur, and raised his glass. He looked at Amanda across the table—he couldn't remember if Harold Nelson had been talking about mother or daughter—and saw that Amanda's eyelids were lowered to half-mast, in mourning over the disaster.

"You too," Cynthia returned.

"Rain or shine her heart is mine."

"Don't mind my husband. This is one of his nights."

"Let prose expose but verse is worse."

"Would you like some cheese sauce on your potatoes."

"I wasn't always like this. I'm not like this now."

"All right everyone," Amanda burst in. "One more crack and I'm driving Miller home. I mean, are we civilized people or monkeys in the zoo?"

"That's it," Harold shrieked. He stood up. His face was white, his hands squeezed into trembling fists.

"Sit *down* love."

It was well after midnight before Miller prepared to go home. His burnt hand throbbed, he had grown even drunker during dinner but was becoming sober and exhausted as he gulped down one cup of coffee after another. With Cynthia and Harold he now felt entirely comfortable, as though they were strangers with whom he had witnessed one of those natural calamities that bring unlikely people together.

"Come back soon. *Promise*."

He kissed Cynthia. Her lips were surprisingly passive, almost asleep although her fingers hooked him between the ribs and crushed him against her. Harold offered his hand, then leaned towards Miller and whispered, "Be good to Amanda."

"Oh God," Amanda said, when they were finally sitting in her car. "I tried to warn you."

"You don't have to drive me home."

"I wanted to get out."

"You must be too drunk to drive."

"I've learned to survive them, Miller." She took his hand, kissed his palm where the match had fallen. "You see why I was so upset before we came? Forgive me?" Then she opened her coat and slid his hand up her sweater and under her brassière.

"Miller, I can't take you home now, let's drive all night."

Miller described later, on one of his television documentaries, how this drive had made him sensitive to the beauties of nature. Looking into the camera with the utmost sincerity—by then the plastic-framed glasses perched at their awkward angle had been replaced by Schweitzer-style spectacles with tinted lenses—Miller spoke in his most melodious voice. "Call me a romantic, but I believed then and still believe that our poor planet of earth and rock and water is in its own way the centre of the universe, an explosion of life that we mere men and women can only admire and respect." The truth is that while Amanda sent the car arrowing through the night, Miller, in the passenger seat of Amanda Nelson's MG, was in a daze of drunkenness and fatigue. He only woke up when the car hit a rough spot on the highway, tearing the muffler loose so that the car was filled with the roar and smell of exhaust.

"It happens all the time," Amanda said. "Open your window." And against Miller's protests, she kept driving. Miller fell back to sleep, and only woke up again, this time with a throbbing headache, when the car stopped.

"Here we are."

Miller stepped out of the car, tried to straighten himself, then his knees gave way and he pitched forward onto the wet grass.

"Miller, God, what's wrong with you?"

Miller rolled over onto his back. It was May, a light rain was falling, and he could feel his heart pounding its way free of the poisonous journey in the car. He held up his watch; science had provided it with numbers that glowed in the dark. Four A.M.

"Miller, get up, this is the place I told you about, my parents' cottage. We can stay here for days, forever, no one will ever find us. *Miller*."

Then suddenly she was on top of him and he was covered by the warm blanket of Amanda.

"Miller, please."

Exams were over, he had been staying in residence for an extra few days before going home, but now, lying in the rain, Miller felt the whole year peeling away from him, his skin throwing off its crust of failures, his father's sarcastic rages, his months of walking from one building to another with eyes scarcely open to receive the eternal grey light of the city. With absolutely no warning it was as if he was with Amanda for the first time. He wrapped his arms around her and the sweet smell of Amanda's skin, the earth's wetness, the falling grey sky broke him open. Rolling over and over on the grassy slope that led from the car to the cabin Miller and Amanda mixed themselves up in the falling rain until they didn't know who was who, which limb connected to whose body, what was water and what was sweat and love, what was the sound of their panting and giggling and what was the wind blowing little rivers of spring rain through the new spring leaves of the maple trees.

You will say that because I insisted, I deserved all the pain I got. Perhaps you will even accuse me of being interested in Miller not for himself but for his love for Amanda and the agony that it gave me. I admit it! More! More! After all, psychology is cheap—and, anyway, after the thousands of confessions I've heard from Miller, a few from myself are easily extracted.

In any case, we were talking of Miller in love. Miller discovering nature. Miller waking up for the first time in the morning with Amanda. They went to the picture window of the cottage and saw a picture of the sun splashing its light up from the lake in a golden sheet. They were naked, and when Miller turned to Amanda she was looking out at the water with her breasts cupped in her hands.

"Kiss kiss," Amanda said.

The next time they came to the window hours had elapsed, and the sun had shifted so that the light from the lake was a cool blue-green. Amanda was wearing clothes from her high-school days. Tight faded jeans, a sweatshirt so short that between the strained fastener of the jeans and the bottom of the cotton was a light brown stripe of Amanda's belly.

Amanda, young, was deliciously slender. Wasp-waisted, small high breasts, long legs with surprisingly dainty feet that turned slightly outwards. In certain lights the grooves between her ribs were shadowed channels. Then Miller had to run his tongue along them, especially the channel that led to a soft boneless place between her ribs on the left side where he could press in his tongue and feel her heart hammering back, a strong steady beat marred by unpredictable skips that made Miller's own heart race with the fear of losing her.

Of course Miller, too, had his charms. But Amanda never talked about sex with Miller, about Miller's body, Miller's heart. The obsession, the unstoppable love, the touch-by-touch recording—all that belonged to Miller.

"She was like a basket of peaches," Miller once sighed. A basket of peaches that Miller couldn't stop eating. By the end of the first day at the cabin he was totally intoxicated. Addicted. He was in the Realm of Happiness and he never wanted to leave.

Cynics will say that sex is bad for the brain and that Miller should have recognized the nature of his good fortune and been content with it. But Miller was no cynic. Miller thought that life had suddenly revealed its true nature to him—perfect happiness—and that, therefore, he had wasted his years up until this moment wandering in the desert of an Amanda-less existence.

When the moment came, Miller dove in. Whole-hearted, innocent, overdeveloped arms and underdeveloped mind. Nothing could have stopped Miller and nothing could have saved him. By the end of the first day Miller and Amanda had agreed never to leave the cottage except to buy food and cigarettes. By the end of the first week they had decided to get married, with or without the permission of the various parents. On their way home to request these blessings, they decided to save everyone the trouble by turning around and getting married right away. Amanda telephoned her father, at his office, to tell him the car needed to be fixed and that they would be staying at the cottage a few more days. Then Miller called *his* father to say that he was getting married to a friend and would communicate further details in due course. Finally they both crowded into the booth and telephoned me, asking me to join them at the cottage and be the witness to their nuptials. At that time, it is true that I hardly knew them. But every couple has their favourite unattached friend, the audience to their happiness, and for Miller and Amanda I was glad to be chosen, glad to say yes, only too happy to escape Toronto by taking the train to the small nearby town where they could pick me up. On the way I had plenty of time to compose my speech, which I never gave, and to remember all the thoughts I'd had while giving slide shows in the dark during Piakowski's classes. I was honoured to be the necessary third, to help to fill their happiness to overflowing, and when they picked me up in Amanda's MG it seemed only natural to be driving through the open air with Amanda on my knee and my arm around Miller's back.

The minister wore a vanilla ice-cream suit and a red shirt. He had moved to his country parish from the city, he said; now life was a permanent vacation. He had straight hair, combed straight back and plastered down with a moist combination of sweat and whatever kind of grease men learned to wear after the war; a red scarf was tucked into the collar of his red shirt and he had a strange habit of reaching into his jacket pocket every few minutes for a tube of nasal spray. His name was Albert Widdington; he claimed to be a friend of Amanda's father, and he didn't mind that Miller was Jewish.

"I've married worse," Widdington said, "Christians, that is, who were worse than heathens. So far as I'm concerned a Jew is just an old-fashioned sort of Christian, like you-know-who. Anyway," he added sadly, "you probably aren't a very enthusiastic sort of Jew, if you don't mind my saying so."

"I don't really," Miller assured him. In his pocket he had a freshly minted fifty-dollar bill, folded once. No, the bill was not the one his father had given him, saved for this fateful day: it was a gift, in imitation of his father's, from yours truly. Miller's plan was to give it to Reverend Widdington after the ceremony—as a combination tip and guarantee of good luck.

For his text Albert Widdington chose something he said was daring—a translation of a marriage sermon delivered by Teilhard de Chardin.

"I've become a sort of a mystic," Widdington confided. His wife nodded. She was a big placid woman whose head swung up and down in agreement every time Widdington spoke—as soon as he opened his mouth her assent began, like canned applause, so that listening to him and watching her I found myself nodding too. "People say that the Church is no place for mysticism," Widdington continued, "but I believe a man of faith deserves to experience God, directly, as a reward for believing." He held his hand over his heart. Mrs Widdington nodded vigorously. "Live your own lives," Widdington said, when the ceremony was over and Miller had passed him the fifty-dollar bill. "God will bless your union and keep you together, I know it in my soul. Amanda, your father will be proud to see you married to such a generous man. Give him my best regards, will you promise?"

I was the one to tell Piakowski. That was right after I got back to the city, and when I went to the hospital to deliver the news, Piakowski was in his armchair, drinking his afternoon glass of orange juice and reading the newspaper. The wild-man look of his earlier days in the hospital had disappeared altogether; now I could see that losing weight and resting in the hospital—away from his usual vices, myself included—had made him look a decade younger. Since I'd last seen him he'd gotten his hair cut properly, and instead of wearing pyjamas he was now dressed in proper clothes. Even his face had now accustomed itself to its new, less fleshy, incarnation: instead of looking haggard and loose it had taken on a square and aggressive look.

"You're looking wonderful."

"Life goes on," Piakowski said. He had lowered his newspaper and was staring at me. *You betrayed me, you went away*, was the message; a year ago, even six months ago, such a stare would have filled me with pain and remorse.

"I had to go out of the city. Miller and Amanda eloped."

Then I turned my eyes away from Piakowski and, looking out the window, told him the story of Miller's visit to Amanda's parents, the drive into the country, the minister with the agreeable wife.

"You're kidding," he said when I was finished. Slang never sounded right from him; this time the words dropped from his mouth with a strange leaden slowness. "I suppose this happened a few days ago, when you missed your visit."

"They asked me to be their witness."

"And so you saw it all." Piakowski's voice was thick with sarcasm—a tone from which I had always been exempt.

"I saw their marriage. It was very touching, if you want to know the truth."

"But I do, my dear, I do. The truth is what I want to know. The truth is *all* I want to know. Tell me the truth, please, nothing else."

A silence while Piakowski got a cigarette from his bedside table.

"And what do you think would make a suitable gift? Even a secret wedding, once it is no longer a secret, deserves to be celebrated. Would you mind if I asked you to do my shopping? They're still afraid that if they let me out of their sight I'll go back to my old ways."

Piakowski's features had taken on a familiar look, the hostile mask he wore when he had decided to exile one of his followers from the group that surrounded him. I remembered an attack he had made only a few weeks ago, an unexpected accusation against Leonard Spitzer. For two years Piakowski had been Spitzer's adviser and admirer. Then, one night in the restaurant, Piakowski accused Spitzer of stealing ideas from a journal and claiming them as his own. Denouncing Spitzer, Piakowski's face had grown rigid and totemic; and while the rest of us watched in uneasy silence Piakowski dispatched Spitzer from our sight like a five-star general sending a cowardly soldier to the firing squad.

"I would like to buy them something impressive," said Piakowski. "If you were getting married, what would you like to receive?" As he said this I remembered another Piakowski, the embarrassed and gentle man who, thinking I was a virgin, had so cautiously seduced me. "You are jealous," Piakowski said. "Never mind, my dear, I predict you will have a very happy marriage, when the time comes. All you lack is—patience."

"And you lack," I started, but looking at Piakowski I faltered and as I did Piakowski turned his eyes directly into mine, challenging me to complete the sentence. I didn't have the courage, instead I turned and walked out of the room. I was dizzy; unnameable feelings were swirling about in my stomach and throat. I knew that if I so much as opened my mouth everything would come streaming out, a Pandora's box filled with four years of Piakowski's humiliations.

I walked to a small park near the hospital, then sat down on a bench facing the traffic.

What had been my crime? Deserting Piakowski to assist at the wedding of Amanda? No doubt, even as I had walked down the hospital corridor Piakowski had begun to accuse me of being disloyal, the way he had accused Spitzer. Spitzer, whose real fault was not plagiarism, but his saying one day in the cafeteria—thinking he was outside Piakowski's hearing—that whenever Piakowski looked at Amanda his eyes always slipped away from her face and greedily glued themselves to her blouse. Spitzer had then screwed up his mouth and made obscene little sucking noises. Standing beside him at the coffee machine I had laughed—then looked over to see Piakowski advancing on us, his forehead wrinkled up the way it did when he was concentrating.

Sitting on the bench, I resolved never to see Piakowski again, to make the break immediately and without warning. My courses were over, my papers and exams finished. In a few weeks I would officially receive my Bachelor of Science degree, with first-class honours, and I already had two offers of graduate scholarships between which I could choose. I went home, took a bath and two sleeping pills, then sank into a deep and dreamless sleep.

The telephone woke me up. It was Miller. "I didn't know whether to disturb you, but Professor Piakowski has had another stroke." Miller's voice sounded hollow, a foghorn blasting through my skull.

"Nadine, are you all right?"

"Sorry. I just woke up. How is he?"

"Very weak. But he can whisper. They've put the tubes back in."

"Did he ask you to call me?"

"No."

"You're at the hospital?"

"I'm calling from the nursing station. Amanda's in the room with him now. He seems happy to see her."

"Good."

"I should go now," Miller said. "She's waving to me from the door." But he didn't hang up. Instead he hesitated, embarrassedly searching for the right thing to say. I was lying on my back, trying to force myself to breathe deeply, hanging on to the telephone so tightly that my whole arm was beginning to ache. Of course Miller had seen me leaving the restaurant every night with Piakowski. But now he was hesitating like a young boy confronted by some awful truth about his parents. "I'll see you later," he finally said. "Don't worry about here. We'll take care of everything." But again there was a questioning note in his voice and he paused, even, it seemed, holding his breath in order to make a space for me to speak. Then I had a sudden insight into Miller—that he would grow up into one of those people who are desperately eager to please, so much so that with each person in his life he would appear absolutely open, ready to absorb the least suggestion.

"We could have dinner later," Miller said. "We could come to pick you up when visiting hours are over."

"That would be nice."

"See you in a couple of hours," Miller said.

As I walked into the kitchen, Miller's last sentence kept repeating itself in my mind. I checked the clock: over twenty-four hours had passed since I'd come home and gone to bed. I went into the bathroom. The pill bottle was lying open and empty on the vanity: a few pills were scattered in the sink and on the floor beside it. I remembered coming home, looking at the full bottle, and having the absurd thought that it was squat and ugly, like a glass pig. Then I had taken two pills in my palm and screwed the bottle lid on tightly before swallowing the pills. For a moment I concentrated on what my palm had looked like: the skin, pale and creased in the flourescent light of the bathroom, the time-release capsules coloured missiles against my skin. Then, more dimly, came a second memory: waking up at dawn I had stumbled half-conscious to the bathroom and, opening the bottle, tried to pour the rest of the pills down my throat. My hand had been trembling, some of the pills had fallen from my mouth, and when I looked in the mirror I had seen not my own face but the foggy nightmare of myself coupling with Piakowski in the half-light of his bedroom.

Had I truly wanted to commit suicide? I think I had wanted to be rid of Piakowski, the nights in his apartment, the strange hold he had over me, his unwanted presence in my dreams. If I were braver, I would have given the pills to Piakowski, not myself. And if I had been braver yet, and more truthful, I would have recognized that the corruption I feared was not Piakowski's but my own.

By the time Miller and Amanda arrived, I had spent an hour in the bath and drunk several cups of coffee. There was still a slow insistent tidal wave resounding through my skull, but to make it more bearable I had convinced myself that the tide was ebbing, taking with it the double hangover from the sleeping pills and my bondage to Piakowski.

"He's all right," Miller said. Then he gave an exaggerated sigh of relief and ushered Amanda through the doorway. "I told him we were coming to pick you up for dinner."

"Good."

"I really think he's going to get better. I bet he'll be teaching again next fall. There's really nothing to worry about."

With the windows open and the last evening light streaming across them, Miller and Amanda looked beatifically happy.

"He asked you not to forget his plants and his fish," Miller said. "We could go on the way to dinner if you like."

Only a week of marriage had been enough to begin the transformation of Miller: it was as though he had been through one of those bizarre intensive therapies. The awkward and elusive student who moved furtively through doorways and didn't know where to put himself when he entered a room had given way to the newly espoused man of responsibilities. Not only had he ushered Amanda into the apartment like a shepherd managing a recalcitrant sheep, but he was now managing the entire situation, myself included. No doubt, after he had directed us through the caring for Piakowski's apartment, he would also order for us in the restaurant, bully the waitress if the service was slow, sue the management if the food made us sick or caused us mental anguish.

"I remember when I met him," Miller said. He crossed his legs, lit a cigarette, stared abstractedly at the window as though his mind was crossing a gap of decades instead of a year. "When he stood up behind the table he seemed overwhelming. Really. I don't mean just his size but his energy. Talk about magnetism. I couldn't believe my own father could know a man like that, let alone call him by his first name."

Amanda leaned over Miller, took a puff of the cigarette which, perhaps by telepathy, he had known to move from his lips towards hers. "We admire you, too, for being so close to him. We think it takes a lot of courage to be near someone who is so strong."

We went to Piakowski's apartment on the way to dinner. I didn't want to be there alone, so I asked them to come up. They followed me around while I watered the plants, Miller inspecting each one as though he was Charles Darwin on the Galapagos. Amanda waited in the living room, leafing through the classifieds of a month-old newspaper. Until they found an apartment they were, Amanda explained to me while I was siphoning off angel-fish droppings from the bottom of Piakowski's aquarium, living at her parents'. Which was fine except that Harold and Cynthia were suffocating them with kindness—sending them off to their bedroom every night with hot chocolate "to have their privacy" and then tiptoeing by every few minutes, slippers scraping their way to the door, to whisper through the keyhole that such and such a program was on television, if they wanted to watch, or that they were having a nightcap if the newlyweds cared to join them, or that they were going for a walk and would be back in an hour but were locking the door to avoid surprise visitors.

In the restaurant I continued to feel irritated by Miller's new personality. Perhaps, as Piakowski had suggested, I was only jealous. But the deeper truth was that somehow Miller, a junior student whom I had liked but felt superior to, whom I had helped out of pity and amusement, with whom I had become infatuated as a kind of crutch to help wean myself from Piakowski—Miller had somehow installed himself in the centre of my life at the same time as he had installed himself in the real world of maturity and marriage.

By the time I got home I had decided that Miller and Amanda were bores, that although I wished them the best with their married life, I was delighted to leave them to inherit the burden of Piakowski while I arranged to shift my own centre of operations to a different university—the further away the better.

The day Piakowski got out of the hospital he came to see me. It was mid-August, a blue summer day that sent its light exploding though the tunnel of my attic, bouncing back and forth from one treed window to the other. I was packing my trunk. Soon the entire weight and safety of an ocean would be placed between myself and the blurred purgatory I had gone through with Piakowski. I hadn't seen him since the night with the sleeping pills; I didn't recognize the sound of his footsteps on the stairs; and when he came through the door I was entirely taken by surprise.

For a moment he stood in the doorway, slowly surveying the room. More lost weight and months of drug-free living had transformed him into a younger ghost of himself, nervous and dangerous, as if he had just arrived in another foreign country. But then he stepped forward and whatever mask he was wearing dropped away as his eyes turned towards mine. I was so glad to see him, happiness slapped through me, unexpected. I wanted to leap forward, to embrace him and squeeze him in my arms. I was frozen.

"Mohammed has come to the mountain." Piakowski's voice was soft, his mouth sad.

"The mountain welcomes Mohammed. Excuse the mess."

Now I could move. I stepped forward, took his hands. Despite everything I was weeping.

"I hear congratulations are in order."

"Thank-you." Piakowski was referring to the extraordinary piece of luck that had come my way—I had a scholarship to go to England to study astrophysics at Cambridge University.

"I was very happy for you," said Piakowski. "You deserve it." He let go my hands, walked past me towards the armchair. "You'll excuse me if I sit down. I still get tired."

"You're looking wonderful." And it was true: I have never seen him better. His tailor must have visited him in the hospital because he was wearing a light blue summer suit cut to his new, more modest, dimensions; and under the jacket a white shirt was sportingly open at the collar. The only sign of his hospital stay was a red, coin-sized scar at the base of his throat where they had performed a tracheotomy to keep him from choking after the stroke.

"They've had me doing exercises." Piakowski folded his hands on his lap: where there had been only puffy flesh could now be seen the contours of heavy, knotted veins. "The doctor says that if I stay on my diet, and away from certain forbidden activities, I can expect to live to a ripe old age."

"I'm glad." And I was. The sight of Piakowski chastened and renewed had lifted such a weight from me that I could have flown. "You really do look wonderful. Am I allowed to offer you tea?"

"Very weak and without sugar." Piakowski reached into his pocket and withdrew a piece of paper. "Everything I am allowed to eat is written here. If you catch me trying to eat anything else, I give you permission to tear it from my mouth." He stretched the list towards me and gave me the same shrug that used to indicate it was time to lead him home. Despite myself, I felt the tears starting again.

"I'm sorry," Piakowski said. "Don't worry, I will find someone else to guard me from temptation."

"Good." I had turned away from him and was standing at the sink preparing the kettle for Piakowski's tea.

"You could still change your mind and stay here. I would supervise your thesis, protect you from the others in the department, make sure you got a good degree."

"I don't need your protection."

Now Piakowski suddenly laughed. "Listen to you. Because of the high marks you received from me, you have gotten offers of fellowships. Without me, where would you be? Teaching science to ten-year-olds."

"Goodbye, Stefann."

"Nadine, I'm sorry. Please don't be angry. An old man forgets—but I came here to make peace. At the hospital, as everyone says, I had time to put my thoughts in order. And you, what we have gone through together, were foremost in my mind. You see—" and here his voice broke—"you meant more to me than I might have shown. To you I am an old man who took advantage of a girl who was entrusted to me. A survivor of the Holocaust. A relative in blood. But to me, our relationship was something different. An island out of time. A little moment of eternity when I was happy because you made me so. And now, please stay where you are, don't look at me, let me leave you like this, before we do anything more to hurt each other. You have a wonderful future. I want you to depart with my best wishes. Take them, please, and go to your destiny with a clear conscience. Piakowski has loved you." I could hear his sigh as he got to his feet. "And Piakowski has forgiven you. He asks you only one more favour, and that is that you forgive him."

When Piakowski had begun his little speech I was holding a spoonful of tea ready to dump into the pot. Now the loose leaves were scattered over the counter and the spoon was twisted into a pretzel. Piakowski's arrogance filled the room. I could smell it. And my own anger, too. I squeezed the spoon between my fingers and clenched my teeth as Piakowski stepped towards me. But that was all he took: a step. Then he turned around and slowly went down the stairs. From the window I saw him make his way out the front sidewalk to a taxi which was waiting for him. As always, Piakowski had played it by the book. The tears started again, I called his name through the window, but the taxi drove away. When I turned back into the room I saw something white on the armchair. My first thought was that Piakowski, in a last dramatic appeal, had left me his diet list "by mistake" so that I would have to see him once more, returning it.

But what was on the chair was an envelope. The words on the outside read *with love*. Inside was a small piece of paper: a cheque for ten thousand dollars. It was only an hour later, when the first wave of my rage had subsided, that I noticed the date on the cheque: May 2nd, it was dated, the day I had walked out of the hospital and vowed never to see him again.

BOOK THREE
England 1964

Janis Farnham was an escapee from one of those British families who used to own castles but now take in lodgers. When she was young, she looked like a junior slightly overweight member of the Bloomsbury group: her blonde hair was long and tangled, she wore once-elegant clothes that were beginning to unravel. In photographs her large and intelligent blue eyes seemed to bulge forward, as if she was, even while the camera was on her, reading some impossibly righteous bluestocking tract. After graduation she worked in a London publishing house for a couple of years. Then a depressing affair with the managing editor convinced her that perhaps she should return to Cambridge and pursue a leisurely post-graduate degree. "I have stared love in the face and found it wanting," she wrote to her friend, Ellen Richardson.

When I met Janis and Ellen they were looking for a third woman to share their flat. During the day, in the week while I was waiting for classes to begin, I strolled about the town, soaking up the sunny weather and writing Miller and Amanda gay postcards about the wonders of life in Jolly Olde England. I had feared my return to Europe would be a homecoming to the dark shadows of the Second World War. But I had arrived in England at the exact moment when the war babies had grown old enough to want to forget. It was Carnaby Street time, England was ascending from the colonial to the psychedelic era on a magic carpet of smoke. Riding the carpet, front and centre, were my new flatmates; especially Janis. She was the original free spirit: untrappable, untameable, equally interested and uninterested in both sexes, she was a female Oscar Wilde who had joined the Optimist Club. Possessed of a beautiful face, a Reubenesque figure, and impeccably aristocratic vowels, Janis unleashed was a powerful magnet whose field of force daily attracted a new variety of marijuana or hashish to be tested, usually in the context of a ragtag dinner party well-lubricated with bottles of cheap Italian wine.

Into this easy and trivial life I plunged without hesitation. The sombre scenes with Piakowski had become a Wagnerian opera that had spent two years on the rinse cycle. I was delighted to have a chance to be superficial, to lose myself in brief unconsummated infatuations, to worry with my roommates about serious questions like the price of a bottle of wine, or whom to invite to the next raucous party.

After only a few weeks I felt like a new and carefree person. I even, for the first time in my life, got involved with a man of my own age. "Involved" is a safe word, but it suits the relationship, which started off as a bubbly sort of music hall dance, one which had its own little cycles of happiness and sorrow; but the happiness was never ecstasy and the sorrow never despair.

The object of my diluted desire was Ellen's brother, John. Their father was, they said vaguely, an American diplomat, their mother a blue blood whose ancestors had been related to those of Henry James. John and Ellen had been sent to Cambridge to get a suitable education in the Classics and to fix their accents—which had a vague floating quality due to the father having being moved across Europe like a hyperactive knight on a chess-board—into the Oxbridge mould.

John—a plain name but when I met him my first thought was that he was all dressed up for romance. He was tall and very slender. Wide cheekbones and strong jaw but eyes always slightly feverish as though he was recovering from a protracted illness. This invalid-poet theme was reinforced by the scarf that was perpetually wrapped about his neck and the raincoat that he always forgot, much to Ellen's dismay. Another first impression, and the one that endured everything, was of extraordinary politeness. He leapt to his feet when someone entered the room; he was the one who volunteered to go to the store, to pay for the drinks at the pub.

Handsome, well-mannered, vaguely effeminate, John Richardson was a suave and sophisticated—but also very minor because he was too nice—character in a European comedy. His father hoped he would end up in the diplomatic corps, but John preferred literature. At the slightest provocation he would pull a sheet of paper from his jacket pocket and read a poem he had just that day discovered and copied out. When he began inviting me to join him at the pub for lunch, or to go bicycling through the fields that surrounded the town, I assumed his attentions were part of the general stream of life at our flat. But one night when John had met me at the laboratory to walk me home, I realized what should have been obvious.

It was just after twilight, the evening was dark and misty. As our feet squished through the wet grass I found myself remembering a humiliating scene that hadn't come to mind for years; when I was eight years old and in my second year at the Borstein house, a girl approached me after music class and said she would like to walk home with me. The class had been rehearsing for the Christmas play in which I had been assigned the part of an angel—"our first Jewish angel," the teacher had explained, "to remind us that before Jesus there were no Christians, only Jews." Outside it was snowing big candy-like flakes that melted on our faces. Suddenly this girl, her name was Christine Mizener, grabbed my sleeve and said: "I like you. Let's be friends. Will you?" And then, embarrassed, quickly started walking again while I, silent, knew that nothing in the world could induce me to bring someone home to Earl and Emma Borstein and have them explain what a joy I was to their lives, what a miracle it was that I had survived.

"You want a drink?" John asked. But when I failed to answer immediately he didn't walk away as Christine had; he just stood in the rainy half-light outside the tavern, looking at me sadly.

Then we were inside, crowded together at a tiny round table. "You know, I don't know what I would have done if you had refused." He paused, as if unsure whether I understood what was really being discussed. "You won't refuse, will you?"

"No, if you don't ask too much."

"Well, cheers," John said.

That night we slept together but it didn't go well. After too many hours of tactful silences broken by cigarettes, John started to get dressed. "You'd think we had gotten married," he complained. I couldn't help laughing because this made me think of the amorous gambols of Miller and Amanda, their little megabombs of lust which made my own present armoured situation—covered with goose bumps, contraceptive jelly and tentative caresses—all the more ridiculous.

"It's not funny, Nadine. I really *wanted* you."

A week later John came to the apartment in the afternoon to retrieve some books. We went to bed right away, and this time everything proceeded according to the manual. We were both so relieved that we could actually do it that we went out and got gloriously drunk.

John was nice, I was relieved, but I didn't fall in love with him. At the time I thought there must be something wrong with me—that I was heartless, that I lacked what it took to be a real woman. In fact I was more like a turtle: the first layer of the shell had been formed in Paris, the second by my strange relationship with Piakowski. What I wanted, when I met John, was not less protection but more. But I could *like* John. Because he was so likeable, but also because he was weak and I could resist him.

Resistance, in fact, became the theme of our relationship. Every few days John would ask me to marry him and I would say no. He took these refusals like a true diplomat, giving off that perfect combination of disappointment and good cheer that made him so essential to me. The proposals were little rainy periods in an otherwise sunny season. How shallow!

How superficial! Just as every day with Piakowski had been a mountain to be climbed, England became one long and silly vacation.

Not that I forgot my work: Piakowski's parting gift was the fear that without him I would fail. So I declined the various druggy delights offered by Janis. With Piakowski I'd already experienced the numbing effects of that kind of oblivion— while the others smoked, I modestly drank wine and conserved my brain for another day. And then, every morning, while the others still slept in their self-induced fog, I was up with the sun, studying my texts and getting ready for my hours in the laboratory. And almost every evening, no matter how intoxicated, I would spend a few minutes before bed organizing the next day's work and writing my latest letter to Miller and Amanda. Letters, yes! Crossing the ocean had turned me into a compulsive correspondent. The Borsteins got postcards, along with Miller's father, Margaret and even Spitzer. But with Miller and Amanda I had graduated from postcards to lengthy epistles. In them, drinking a last glass of wine by the light of the candle, I would detail life in my flat, the various foibles of my professors and classmates, the advantages and disadvantages of my romance with John Richardson. Finally, pages later, I would end with a few perfunctory questions about their own affairs, the twins, the health of Piakowski.

Piakowski's name figured also in some other letters I was writing: these to Léonie. Now that I was in England, I felt only a thin elastic membrane separated the life I was living from the life I had escaped. And so, for the first time in years, Léonie and I began corresponding. At first the letters were hesitant, almost perfunctory—

Here in Léonie's apartment, I have those letters in front of me. It is strange to reread my own words, to watch myself—the scholarship graduate student—trying to impress my aunt, to build myself up for the inevitable meeting. Maybe I should have gone right away to confront Léonie and demand an explanation for what had happened. But—like loving John—it was too soon. And yet I thought that because I was young, I was free.

Piakowski had meanwhile come to represent everything that was undesirable in life. When his letters arrived, I dreaded opening them. For days the blue airmail envelope would lie sealed on the hallway table. Other mail would be piled on top of it. Cups of tea would stamp it with bronze rings and sometimes spilled liquid would seep through and dissolve the ink.

"My dearest," these letters always began. The words hammered home the whole sinister force of Piakowski's voice. "My dearest," I would read, and would instantly be back in the aqueous world of Piakowski's apartment, an innocent needy fish swimming in the shadow of Piakowski's sly net. Even at five thousand miles I was unable to bear the burden of his reproaches and the evening I finally opened one of his letters always ended in heavy drinking and me alone in my bed, crying myself to sleep.

One such night, when I was lying in bed, I heard a series of strange calls and shrieks from the living room. I rushed in to find Janis spread-eagled stark naked on the floor, her shining eyes fixed on the equally naked ceiling light bulb.

"Nadine, I have found God. He's in me, I know it, right inside me. Nadine, do I look different? God, I can't describe the feeling. Touch me, Nadine, I'm burning."

The room was heavy with the smell of marijuana smoke and incense. I bent down and laid my fingers against Janis's cheek. Her face was flushed and radiant, and from her skin heat was pulsing out.

"Nadine, please, lie on top of me. I'm freezing."

By the time I had gotten Janis a blanket she had returned to staring, open-mouthed and rapturous, at her light bulb. Her breathing had become so shallow that for a moment I was afraid she had lapsed into a coma. But seeing me she smiled ecstatically, then pointed to the ceiling as though she had seen through the peeling plaster to the vaulted arches of the Sistine Chapel. As it turned out, after several hours of semi-coherent babble interspersed by long ecstatic silences, marijuana had nothing to do with Janis's bizarre voyage: in fact she had blasted out of sanity with the aid of a much more powerful drug, LSD, the new superpill that was supposed to turn schizophrenics into poetic visionaries.

Writing Miller about Janis I explained my two theories: the first was that drugs had magnified her original problem, a screw irretrievably loosened. The second was that Janis, still unmarried in her mid-twenties, had opted to plunge back into the permanent idiocy of youth, before it was too late.

Was it too late? I should have emphasized even more how beautiful Janis was; but her beauty was the classical British one of fine creamy skin and delicate colouring mixed with a certain lushness of figure. Naked, Janis was an extraordinary flower in full bloom. Dressed, however, she lost in translation. This was a triumph of mind over matter. To be precise, as a result of one of her visits from God she decided to transform her wardrobe. Her first step was to throw away her underclothes. "My body has declared itself for freedom," she announced. "I won't have it imprisoned in the products of the multi-national corporate conspiracy." She made weekly trips to the second-hand shops where she found wide flouncy skirts and deep-cut blouses, all of which she dyed in earthy peasant tones. In her pantyless folkloric costume she wandered about Cambridge, a steady stream of avid males following in her wake. Janis handled them all with charm and love. She served them tea and read aloud, in her perfect nanny's voice, extracts from the *Bhagavad Gita*. "The uncontrolled mind does not guess that Atman is present," she would intone. "Without meditation where is peace? Without peace, where is happiness?" After each verse she would direct her shining porcelain-blue eyes straight into the eyes of the lovestruck supplicant. "Would you like some more tea? The leaves come from a small Buddhist village where the entire population is vegetarian."

Ellen soon found an excuse to move out, saying that her studies had reached a critical point and that she needed to be alone in order to concentrate. Shortly after this John made his own move: he invited me for a weekend in London. In the evenings John took me to plays which were followed by expensive suppers with vintage wines. During our afternoon walks John would drop lines like, "There comes a crossroads in every life," "Decisions are never pleasant," "I've realized I'm not getting any younger," "Now is the last time we can say our whole lives are ahead of us." Even without these I would have known that this was to be, as John said while dressing for the third play in three nights, "the crucial moment from which there is no turning back." After that ponderous gem, instead of lowering his eyes he looked at me directly to make sure that I caught the message.

At his worst, John was still the perfect gentleman. Even the leaden hints he dropped during our weekend in London were proof of his extraordinary sensitivity: they were his gallant effort to take onto his own shoulders the boring task of turning our carefree relationship into a marriage.

The night of "the crucial moment from which there is no turning back" John took me to dinner at an Italian restaurant. The decor was British rococo: brass and reds abounded in an explosion of plush velvet; sinuous naked statuaries clutched each other in self-protection from the candle-light that blasted them from every direction. It was late when we arrived, the restaurant was jammed by what seemed to be a gigantic wedding party, but the table John had reserved was nicely off to one side, between two gleaming replicas of Helen of Troy.

We had a glass of wine, then a second. It was a fancy Italian wine John had chosen after consultation with the waiter, a wine with a dry flowery taste that made me shiver.

"To us," said John.

I smiled.

"I know I've been pushing you," John said. "But I want to marry you. I think I'd be very good for you."

"You would," I said. "It's me I'm afraid of."

"I do feel stupid, proposing all the time. Yet it only seems right. Us, I mean. Together. When you turned me down at first it was a joke, I was only asking you to marry me because I love you so much. Now we've been together so long, it seems only natural to decide one way or the other."

It had never occurred to me that I was leading John on. But now, looking at his earnest face across the table, I realized that I had been completely wrong, that in his own perfectly polite and chivalrous way John had been looking to me not for a good time, not to forget old heartbreaks or to listen to the gems of Yugoslavian literature, but for a wife who would help him through the grim career ahead.

"I can't marry you."

"Why not? Tell me the truth, please."

I couldn't look at John any more so I looked down at my hands. As a girl I had desperately wanted them to be slender-fingered and long, but what I had were square and workman-like hands, hands that had caressed certain bodies, hands that would have looked ridiculous decorated by a ring. The truth? The truth was that I couldn't imagine myself married to John. The truth was that I was still waiting to be swept away in a tide of love and passion by a Prince Charming who could turn my leaden heart to gold.

"It's not you," I finally said. "It's just a promise that I made to myself, that I would never get married."

"And that," John said bitterly, "is what you always tell me. And I am supposed to believe that you are the little impover-ished Jewish orphan who has been rejected and scarred so often that in her poor orphan's heart of hearts she has vowed never to love, never to reproduce, never to—"

That was where he stopped. I had no defence. He had loved me, had been willing to risk a marriage that his family would certainly regard as disastrous; and I had returned neither his love nor his daring. Sitting in the restaurant I wished that some capricious god would snap his fingers and turn me into one of those brass statues that had been shoved into a corner or had its head lopped off to make a candle holder.

There was a long silence which John finally broke. "I'm sorry, but you'll have to forgive me if I haven't learned to hate you as well as you hate yourself."

I could feel my mouth shaping itself for a reply. But I could think of nothing to say. John was right: I had failed to respond to him. But what could I do? I still didn't want to marry him.

"Do me one favour," John whispered. "Let us leave this conversation behind and drink tonight until we pass out. Then we'll take the train home tomorrow and part the best of friends."

He raised his eyes to mine and then, when I didn't look away, took up the bottle from the table and emptied it into our glasses. Within a few minutes John had ordered a second bottle. Soon he was at his charming best—talking to the waiter in puppy-dog Italian, inventing the lives of the other patrons, telling me hysterically funny stories about the ways Ellen had tortured him during their school vacations.

When we went outside it was raining. I had tried to drink with John, but wasn't really in the mood. The rain sobered me up entirely and I began to dread the hours to be passed before the morning train.

I needn't have worried about John's intentions. A gentleman to the end, he staggered into the hotel room, pulled a flask of whisky from his briefcase, and drained half of it before falling asleep, fully clothed, in the armchair.

It was only midnight. John's laboured breathing swelled and filled the room the way Piakowski's once had. I took a sip of John's brandy, smoked a cigarette, then paced restlessly from the bed to the bathroom and back. Finally I put on my coat and went outside.

The rain had given way to a fine drizzle. There was a light mist, giving the streetlights a halo, and as I walked I could hear the eery echo of my shoes bouncing through the empty streets. Every now and then a cab would drive by, its tires swishing along the wet pavement.

This desolate sound drove me deeper into the gloomy thoughts I was having about myself. It was only a few months since I had arrived in England and those few months had been made bearable by John's unending attentions. It was true—he had almost accused me of it—that I had used him. Without John where would I be? An orphan again, but this time in a strange country, isolated with my unwanted memories of Piakowski and the knowledge that there was no future for me.

After an hour of walking, I became uncomfortably aware of the blisters that were forming on my heels and toes. I had no idea where I was. I felt like a character from one of the novels Janis liked to read, a Jean Rhys heroine who compulsively traded her body for the security of a man—but always ended up alone and unwanted, unable to do anything but drink until someone else came along.

When my feet became too sore to carry me, I stopped at a pub and went in. Thanks to John's unfailing generosity I had spent none of the money I'd brought to London. Now I splurged on a double Scotch whisky. I drank it quickly, then ordered a second. While I was searching in my purse for a package of matches, a man came and sat at my table. He had square rugged features, black hair, a smile that seemed very sure of itself. Before I had finished the second drink he had invited me back to his hotel. I refused that invitation but accepted another drink, then another. By the time we left the pub I was numb, barely able to stand. When my "host" followed me into a taxi I tried ineffectually to push him away. Then I passed out, coming to consciousness only when we were standing outside his room.

"I don't want you," I said.

Without speaking the man opened the door. Inside he began taking off his clothes. When he was naked he got into bed and lit a cigarette, waiting for me. As though nothing had happened I said good-night and walked out.

John was still asleep in the chair when I got back to our room. I drew myself a bath. For a long time I sat in the lukewarm water, smoking cigarettes. Then I decided to wake John up and beg him to forgive and to marry me.

I knelt in front of his chair, kissing his hands. They jerked spastically, then drew away from my lips. "John," I whispered. "John." No response. "John, please wake up."

His face was slack, a discouraging fish-belly colour. When his eyes opened they were cold and pale, the eyes of a dead man, the eyes of anyone but the warm and always-caring John Richardson. For a long time they rested on my face. Then slowly they travelled over my naked body, sometimes pausing as if to make notes.

"John, please forgive me."

He closed his eyes. Then his breathing deepened and he was asleep again.

On the train back to Cambridge John seemed to have a colossal hangover. Hunched in concentration, unshaven, he spent hour after hour staring at the same few pages of the *Manchester Guardian*. As for myself, I looked out the window. Gradually the city gave way to a still lush but dark autumn landscape, with heavy clouds rolling over the hills and filling the sky in sinister fashion, as if our little disaster had annoyed the ancient English weather gods. After a while rain began to streak long and angled canals across the soot-stained window, until finally the outside world was reduced to a blurred and pulsing green.

As the weather worsened, my mood followed. By the time the train reached Cambridge I had resolved to finish my degree as quickly as I could, then go back to Canada to teach.

Aside from soothing myself with promises of the future I also gave up my puritan resolve and turned to the crutch I had acquired from Piakowski; after my hours of study I would spend the evening with Janis and whatever drugs she had on hand. Of course there were already warnings in the newspapers that these new illegal substances were dangerous—but at this point I had nothing to lose. And, in any case, they had little effect on me—it seemed that opium had ruined me for anything else.

It was a cold winter. Months passed in a blur of rainy days and cold shivering nights. Then, in mid-January, a burst of warmth and sunny skies. I took the day off classes and went walking through the town. That evening, without thinking, I swallowed one of Janis's little magic pills. This time it took hold, and all the barriers inside of me seemed to explode. I spent the whole night lying on my bed alternately laughing with delight at the wonderful hallucinations and crying. When the sun came up Janis led me outside and we walked hand in hand to the bank of the river. I lay on my belly, licking drops of dew from the grass. I closed my eyes and nuzzled into the soft earth.

Suddenly I was back in the nightmare I used to have after the war: that the Germans had returned to Paris and I was being forced into a railway car by a shouting mob—faces contorted with rage.

I forced my eyes open. I stood up. But the movie wouldn't stop. Then I jumped. The water closed over me like a million frosty kisses. When I came to the surface I was laughing. Janis cannonballed through the surface of the water. Soon we were standing in the shallow river, embracing each other, roaring hysterically at the sensation of our four breasts bumping together like over-inflated balloons.

An hour later, bathed, dried, warmly dressed, I was dozing off into a kaleidoscope of half-seen dreams.

That was when the door opened and John appeared. Months had passed since that final disastrous night in London, and although we had occasionally found ourselves in the same room during parties or formal occasions at the university, we had not exchanged a word.

My heart skipped and stuttered. John's face, which I had always found weak and unresolved, now radiated goodness and warmth.

"It's good to see you," I managed to say.

"It's good to see you, too, Nadine." *Nadine*. He pronounced my name warmly, as though I were a very important person.

"Would you like some tea?"

"Tea would be wonderful," John said.

I turned to Janis. But instead of a single, slightly stoned woman collapsed sleepily in a worn armchair, I saw a thousand identical images of a rounded blonde angel floating against the background of a very unstable wall.

"Tea would be wonderful," Janis repeated.

John turned and walked towards the kitchen. I followed him.

"What's new?"

This was so unexpected that at first I misheard it, thinking that he had sneezed.

"Bless you," I said. John's head tilted towards that weird doggy slant it used to fall into when the going was rough. "Nothing much. Janis and I have been up all night."

"You look tired," John said. "You should go to bed."

I lay under the covers while John sat beside me and stroked my shoulders through the blanket. I closed my eyes. I was a little girl again, first night in the Borstein bed, curled up tightly with my knees against my chest and my eyes wet with tears that refused to be cried, ears wide open, listening for the sounds of footsteps coming up the stairs. I was speeding through the cosmos, travelling blind, searching for my lost planet. I was captain of the spaceship, eyes closed, zooming about the perimeter of the universe. I was curled into the egg that had borne me, whistling back from the moment of conception, destination oblivion.

I was waking up. John was lying on the bed beside me, on top of the covers. A strange, incredibly energetic sound was pounding through the apartment. I swung out of bed, aware as my bare feet hit the floor of John's warmth falling away from me. Undies, jeans, sweatshirt. Toes scrambling like mice, dragging me forward into the living room filled with voices. Music. Jolly boys' voices backed by an incredibly elastic rock-

and-roll band were powering out of the speakers of Janis's record player. Janis, half-naked, whirling through the apartment, singing along. Janis clapping her hands, looking at me, shouting—"Dance, little bunny, dance."

The night with LSD shattered me. But now I had a protector: John. Most nights he would sleep with me, and though we seldom made love I was absolutely dependent on the protective blanket of his body curved around mine.

John, meanwhile, had discovered his own immoveable object: politics. During our months apart he had virtually abandoned his studies to become a follower of a man called Langston Hughes—a sharp-faced foxy-looking physician turned guru with red hair and cheeks that became very pink when he drank. John had encountered Langston Hughes at a bizarre lecture where Hughes delivered his philosophy by way of a six-hour performance filled with aphorisms, bird-calls, ranting, chanting and piano playing. John was so impressed that he followed Hughes to London where he spent a week talking non-stop to the master.

Hughes lived in a communal house filled with converted disciples. In this strange place, not only middle-aged adults but entire families lived with common kitchen and bathroom, just like students. The house was called Hughes's House, everyone slurring the vowels together in a way they found comical.

In addition to their interest in Hughes and his own master, Carl Jung, the members of the house were also involved in the Peace Movement. Peace Movement? When I first heard these words, solemnly pronounced, I broke out laughing. "It's not funny," John said, "these people are devoting their lives to peace. War is the black shadow that curses mankind." After their sessions John and Langston Hughes would go to the peace demonstrations and marches that were sprouting up like flowers around the countryside.

From these weekends John would come back glowing. To make him happy, I began to accompany him to his demonstrations.

Because of his contacts with the London house he became something of an organizer, travelling by train from one group to another, carrying enthusiasm and information about the forthcoming Aldermaston marches. Soon the pseudotubercular Classics scholar with a predisposition for unrequited love became a minor political figure. While I took notes and made sure coffee and cookies were available, John gave increasingly eloquent speeches. At first these were delivered to small groups in the living rooms of Quakers and pastors. Then, one day in March, he spoke at an outdoor rally at Brixton. Two hundred spectators waved the by-then familiar Campaign for Nuclear Disarmament banners and applauded. There was even a member of the press.

It was a few days after this that a Labour party organizer came to see John and enlist his support in a local by-election. The interview took place at our apartment; the organizer was a large, florid man who was wearing a lime-green suit and smoking very strong cigarettes. He refused wine and tea, but then opened a very battered suitcase to bring out several bottles of stout. At the beginning I thought it impossible that this odd-looking man who had nothing in common with John could talk him into anything. But I was wrong. The next weekend John was speaking again, this time to a Labour-organized rally "Against War And For Socialism."

This speech made *The Times*. The headline read: "Soldier's Boy Proclaims NATO Should Be Scrapped." John's father, the "diplomat," turned out to be a high-ranking American general. Overnight John found himself in the midst of a political hurricane. But he decided to continue. Every weekend he gave a new speech. He was surprisingly persuasive. Long skinny arms waving with vehemence, his strong voice, nurtured on declaiming classical verse, carried easily to the growing crowds as he exhorted them to the convictions they already held.

By autumn it was clear that John's adventures were carrying him into a potentially explosive situation. Even the most trivial details of our life had changed. For example, during the summer months after our reconciliation, when John would come to stay the night at the flat, morning was a time when whatever sins of passion or its absence had been committed the night before were forgotten in the lazy ritual of breakfast and looking through the papers for comic scandals. Now, first thing in the morning, John would spring out of bed, and then rush to the store for the papers and two packs of the cigarettes he was now smoking compulsively. While Janis and I stumbled through the kitchen, John would be searching the papers for the various political items in which he felt personally involved. These he would inspect carefully for deviations from the truth according to himself, and then he would, in the same notebook he still used for copying out favourite poems, list the names of the various MPs and other public persons to whom he should be writing.

In the year since I had met him, John had turned himself inside out. Nonetheless, he was not exactly your standard drug-mutated wild-eyed visionary. Or, to be exact, he *was* wild-eyed and long-haired, *and* indulging in every vice that he could gather to his bosom, but the endearing thing about John was that despite his conversion to radical politics, he still wore his timelessly preppy oxford-cloth shirts and Harris tweed jackets. But instead of a scarf around his neck and poetry books in his pockets, John now had a gold astrological pendant hanging at his collarbone and the pockets of his jackets were filled with one-day-to-be-retrieved marijuana roaches and file cards listing the names of his various contacts.

The extent to which John's life had—and had not—changed became evident one Friday evening early in October. The moment I came into the apartment I knew that something was wrong. In front of Janis was a copy of a newspaper: "Is There A Communist Richardson?" was three inches high. Sitting opposite Janis was the Labour organizer. He was wearing the same lime-green pants but in honour of the occasion had topped them with a blue blazer. Beside him, smoking a pipe, was a short dapper man with hair slicked back and a dark suit. His face looked vaguely familiar but the aura he gave off was one of fame, not money.

"My name is Wyatt Browning," he intoned, and then I knew right away why his face had seemed familiar: I'd seen it a thousand times on posters and pamphlets. He was a very left-wing Labour MP, one of the backbenchers who was mixed in with the leadership of the Campaign for Nuclear Disarmament. He was said to have been a Communist after the war—not a Stalinist but a member of one of those tiny fanatical groups whose names are always changing. Now he was respectable; before entering electoral politics he had come into his father's inheritance, and speculation was that if he kept his hands clean until after the next election he would be offered a major cabinet post.

"You'll forgive us for breaking in like this on a Saturday. We were in the area and George said to me that we might have the chance to meet John Richardson. Can we invite you all to dinner? Students are always hungry, aren't they? I wish I could have given you more warning but George left his address book at home."

I took the article from Janis. This time a Conservative MP had made a speech in the House questioning whether the European NATO command should discipline American generals whose sons were involved with left-wing movements. "It is not," the MP had said, "a question of doubting the loyalty of General Richardson, who has served his country and her allies with exceptional courage. It is simply a question of common sense. Can the Department of Defence entrust important military secrets to a man who might at any moment be susceptible to blackmail?" The article went on to say that in an interview General Richardson himself, though deeply hurt by his son's activities, "was maintaining a tight-lipped silence." By the time John arrived, Wyatt Browning had taken off his jacket and, sipping tea, was telling us how much he admired the courage of the young people of England and the United

States who were putting their lives and careers at risk in order to ensure a peaceful world.

At dinner, Wyatt Browning waxed even more eloquent. We were, he said, a truly revolutionary group, an absolute mutation from the generations that had preceded us. I kept waiting for him to say something about the article in the newspaper and John's father. But he never did, until finally when he was shaking hands with us at Janis's door, he pronounced a wonderfully high-sounding sentence about a man who steps into the future having to pay the price of cutting himself off from the past.

As it turned out, Browning's words were prescient: a few days later there was another phone call—this time from John's mother saying she and the General had flown to London for the weekend, and that John was expected to appear for a family pow-wow. Ellen was already there, and the Richardsons were hoping that not only John, but also his "charming new companion," would arrive for dinner the next evening.

Harold Richardson was the kind of American impossible to ignore. A big man, almost oversize, with burly shoulders and long powerful arms. His hair was cut short, and that made his face seem larger; amazingly, despite the icy eyes and patrician nose, it was a very friendly face—seamed with lines and crinkles that leapt into action every time he smiled or laughed. I was alone in a room with him on only two occasions; like many big men he was always very careful to keep his distance in a polite way. I found him both charming and frightening. Of course Piakowski had been big also, but Piakowski's bulk was flesh and legend whereas General Richardson—the title seemed natural to him—was bone and muscle—a walking personification of the oversized American Empire that at any moment might somehow lose control of its enormous strength and accidentally reduce the rest of the world to a post-nuclear battlefield.

He had come from the mid-west; his thick blond hair, his confident drawling voice, his powerful arms and large expressive hands were incarnations of American-style intelligence and power. He had married his red blood to the aristocratic blue of Elizabeth Dawson—a dark and slender New Englander who had accepted the General the day she graduated from Bryn Mawr.

"John tells me you're an orphan," Betty Richardson said to me over pre-dinner sherry. "I think there is no greater tragedy than to be raised without a family. I hope that you w''' always consider our home yours, wherever we are."

"Thank-you very much," was all I could reply.

"The General lost his father very young. He was the eldest of six sons and I have always believed that he learned to be a leader while still a boy. Do you want to freshen up?" Before I could reply Betty Richardson had taken me by the arm and led me to the bedroom. "We wanted to have a large family, of course. Ellen came first, John two years later. He was a difficult child and General Richardson was always away. You can imagine it wasn't easy for me. Then, I got cancer. Do you mind me telling you this?"

Betty Richardson had drawn me down to sit beside her on one of the wide double beds, and still had her hand linked through my arm. Now she got up, took cigarettes from the dresser, offered me one before starting to smoke. "They said I had a year to live. I couldn't bear to tell Harold. Six months later there was another operation; of course I couldn't hide it from him that time—he was home. The, you know, what they call the prognosis was better. And then, the sickness was very hard on John. He was never *told* but it marked him. I told you he was difficult. We sent him to good schools, of course, but there were often incidents. We couldn't keep him at home, Harold was always on the move, we wanted John to find a stable environment. At least that's what we were advised. He had a very delicate mental constitution. He always reacted to everything, you understand. So Nadine, may I call you Nadine? We're hoping, I'm hoping, but I understand your position. I mean politically you must have your own opinions. God knows I wouldn't want to force my views of the world on someone like yourself. John tells me you are a very brilliant student. I've always thought that tragedy sharpens the mind. I understand that you have an aunt in Paris. I can see you are a sophisticated woman, the kind of friend my son has been fortunate to encounter."

"The good fortune has been mine," I broke in. I tried to stand up but Betty Richardson tightened her grip on my arm just as Ellen walked into the bedroom.

"There you are. I suppose Mama has been singing John's praises. Mother, don't you know that it's useless to preach to the converted? Anyway, dinner has arrived and Daddy has been sharpening his knife for hours."

Dinner was served in the living room, a bulky British repast featuring roast beef and root vegetables. We ate balancing our plates on our laps. "We're just camping out here," the General said. "Please forgive us, Nadine, but we're not such savages back home."

"I hope Nadine will come to see our house in Washington one day, then she can enjoy our true hospitality."

Before dinner John had primed himself for the occasion by smoking some hashish. "Don't worry," he had assured me, "I told them you were a co-worker. Nothing about romance. I promise." Now John had withdrawn deep into himself, only coming to consciousness every few minutes to wink broadly at me, a gesture that everyone else observed in silence.

"What's that around your neck, son?"

John looked down as if expecting to find some horrible surprise, then withdrew his pendant.

"It's a Leo," I said. "An astrological sign. John was born at the time of the lion which means he is a natural leader."

"He comes by that honestly," Mrs Richardson said. "If only he knew how to use it."

"He knows how to use it and I'm proud of what he's doing."

"Yes, of course you are, dear." Betty Richardson looked at her husband, who was staring directly at John.

"If you've got it, use it," Harold Richardson said.

"Don't get dirty, father."

Everyone laughed except John. "I can't believe this is happening," he muttered. "Can you believe it, Nadine?"

"John," Betty Richardson said in a high warning voice, "you promised not to talk politics tonight."

"Keep it in your pants," Harold Richardson said. "I believe in free speech, even among family and friends." Everyone had finished eating but him. While we watched in silence the General cut his roast beef into bite-sized pieces, each stroke of the knife so firmly carried out that it made a high shriek against the dinnerware, then slowly chewed his way through the remainder of his dinner.

When he was finished, John stood up. "Thanks for the meal."

"You're welcome," Harold Richardson said. He watched as John crossed the room and got our coats from the closet. "Where are you going?"

"We'd better get back."

"Sit down."

John brought me my coat.

"Sit down or I'll tie you down."

"John, please, sit down. We have to talk."

"There's nothing to say."

"John, he is your father."

"For Christ's sake, John." Ellen crossed the room and took his hand. "Do you want him to beg? Do you want us all to beg?" Then she looked at me. I had realized Ellen found Janis unacceptable, but now her eyes were filled with something other than social snobbery—hatred and rage. "Do you really have to be so selfish? Daddy is one of the most important men in the whole world. This isn't a movie, you idiot, this is true. Of course things are different here than at home. Everything is so very *very* polite here, the way you like it. People wipe their faces with napkins after they spill their food. They talk in fancy foreign languages and drive cars that don't work. But John, for Christ's sake, don't you see this place for what it really is? John, this place—" she gestured broadly, to take in everything from the Atlantic Ocean to the Urals—"this place is a backwater. It's nowhere. It's Appalachia. It's Florida. It's a one-room schoolhouse in Colorado with a fancy painting on the wall. *John*, if it weren't for the United States this place would be some crummy little country in the Russian Empire. And you know what, John? They know it. John, dear brother, why do you think everyone is so impressed with you? Do you think you're so smart that you've turned their heads with all your brilliant little droppings? John, dear brother, you know fucking well why your name is in the papers. It's because you're an American. They *love* Americans here. They *love* everything American. We came in and we won the war and now they'll listen to anything we say. You know why, John? Because we protect them, because we are the side their bread is buttered on. John, you're making a fool of yourself, and you're doing it at Daddy's expense. Don't you understand?"

"Ellen, dear. Of course John understands what he's doing but he doesn't mean Daddy any harm. Do you, John. Do you?"

"We really do have to go," John said.

"No one *has* to do anything, son. But let me tell you, before you put your coat on, let me tell you something. But first I want everyone to sit down and have a drink. One drink, because if Nadine will excuse us this little family pow-wow, I think it's important that we hash this out between us. Now Betty, I want you to go to the refrigerator and get that champagne. How often do we see each other, after all? Except for Christmas, this is the first time we've been together for years. Here, Betty, give me that bottle." With a twist the General had the wire undone, and sent the cork rocketing into one of the plaster angels that bordered the ceiling. "Let me propose a toast: to family, to friends, to truth."

We drank. Even John sipped cautiously.

"Now, son, you've had the floor for the past few months. You've made your speeches, you've given your interviews to the press, you've splashed your name—and mine—across the front page of every newspaper from Moscow to Washington. You've done that, John, and whether you're playing games or dead serious I've never stopped you, never tried to shut you up, never interfered with you in any way. The only thing I've wanted is to let this thing run its course. But it hasn't run its course. It's growing. So here we all are. Because, John, I think you've been pretty clever, but you haven't been too smart. The thing is, John, and it hurts me to tell you this, but there's a lot of truth in what Ellen said. No, I don't think these are tinpot countries. No, I don't think that the United States of America is perfect, but at this particular moment in history, John—"

"—Now, John listen to what your father has to say—"

"—At this particular moment in history, John, the United States of America has the most powerful army in the world. At this particular moment in history, right now, the United States of America owns the most powerful military force that any nation in the world has ever possessed. Now, John, you may feel that this is dangerous: I agree with you there. But it is still true that the United States of America could, at this very moment, obliterate any nation on the face of this earth. That, my boy, is military force."

"I can't believe you're boasting about this," John said. "Even you."

"Now dear—"

General Richardson had lit a cigar which he now waved benevolently.

"We're not boasting or deploring here. We're talking truth. We're talking reality. Anyone who doesn't understand this reality is as ignorant as an African savage."

"You're the ignorant savage," John shouted, "you're not talking about life, you're talking about death."

"That's right, son, I'm talking about death. I'm talking about the power to destroy. But son, don't forget, all life ends in death. Death is the umbrella that casts its shadow over all of us. And the power to destroy is the umbrella that keeps us all alive. That's deterrence son, in a nutshell. Or should I say bombshell?"

"You're crazy."

"I'm not crazy. I'm a realist. A pragmatist. You know what the difference is between you and me, son? We have no philosophical disagreement. We have no moral disagreement. We're both in favour of life, of children, of the lilies of the field. The only difference between us is that you're a child and I'm a man."

"Let's go," John said.

He stood up and began walking towards the door. As I started to follow, John's father leapt to his feet, and with one long arm swept John back into the chair.

"You'll hear me out." Harold Richardson was standing over his son. "You'll hear me out and then you can go back to your little crusade."

A few days later, another remnant from the past: this one arrived in a thick airmail envelope. I peered at it cautiously. *Nadine Santangel* was written in a familiar hand—Miller's. I picked up the letter and took it upstairs to read with my coffee. So I was sitting in the sunroom, as always in the morning, alone and peaceful with a cup of fresh coffee when I opened the envelope. Usually, though the envelopes were addressed by Miller, the letters from Miller and Amanda were typed by Amanda, Miller scribbling his comments in the margin; and in the year I'd been gone the letters had helped me to develop the image of how they must have become—a cheery young couple, happily raising their twin daughters while their various parents happily watched over their progress. Even the letters themselves, Amanda had made clear, originated from the very hearth of happiness, the kitchen, where she sat at the table typing after the twins were in bed and while Miller washed the dishes and had a nightcap. While reading her letters I could imagine Amanda reading the same words aloud to Miller, so that he might appreciate the wit with which she had described this or that Sunday outing, this or that little outburst of Piakowski's eccentricity at a faculty party. What a delightful story they made in my mind, Miller and Amanda, my childhood friend married to the class vamp, the sizzling college romance mellowed into a serene young woman's magazine family.

Now Miller was writing that life with Amanda had become "a nightmare," a "non-stop roundabout of deceit. Every day I hate myself more for staying with her. But what about the twins? I don't have the time, the money, the courage to go through a legal battle for their custody. Amanda, the bitch, she has me by the short hairs. And, what's worse, I still love her."

Alas, what had happened was a different woman's magazine story, the one about the dangers of marriages made too young. Miller, under pressure to finish his thesis and get the academic and financial security he needed, was working long hours at the university. But Amanda, with her income from her parents, was far from destitute—and, therefore, far from happy about Miller working so hard while she was left with the drudgery and boredom of feeding, changing, and caring twenty-four hours a day for two infant girls. Fortunately, being rich, such a fate was not necessarily hers. Amanda hired a babysitter to come for the afternoons. At first she used her free times to buy groceries and do other worthy errands. But when the pantries, the diaper shelves, the wardrobes had been stocked and re-stocked, there was nothing left to do but to go back to the scene of her youth, the Park Plaza, and have a drink or two in the bar to while away the afternoon.

And there, somehow, she had run into one of her old boyfriends, a fraternity rat who had seemed pallid beside Miller, but who, now that Miller was locked away with his numbers, had matured into a charming sort of person, the sort one could spend the afternoon with in Room 736. This arrangement went on for a while until the wife of the former frat rat grew suspicious and relations were terminated. Thereupon Amanda found another willing consort. But, as these things happen, the wounded wife didn't cease to be suspicious even after the causes for her suspicion were removed. She telephoned Miller. Miller, unbelieving, went to the bar of the Park Plaza to observe for himself. Where he saw Amanda and her current amour indulging in a little post-coital drink before rushing off to relieve the babysitter.

Poor Miller. Imagine the innocent, heart pounding, palms sweating, trying to stand in the shadows while searching through the darkened room for his lovely Amanda. Poor Miller—of all things, he was most unprepared for infidelity. Not for him a childhood where the father kept a second woman in a trailer park. Not for him a mother or a father sweating over pictures of the beloved with a stranger, over timetables and lists of meetings. Would Miller ever hire a private detective to bring him traces of the dirty deed? Such a thought, for Miller, belonged in the movies. Miller's parents—so far as Miller knew—had been perfectly faithful until death did them part. And Miller himself, tempted or not, had certainly never strayed from the sweet pastures of Amanda's blessings.

So. Betrayal. Amanda admitted it defiantly. Said she regretted nothing. Said she had no intention of spending the rest of her life as a cooped-up housewife. Said that her body belonged to her, to her alone, and that though she promised to love Miller uniquely, she demanded the right to spend her time with whom she chose—freedom of assembly.

"I don't know what I'm going to do," Miller concluded his letter, "but my fear is that I will do nothing at all." And so, of course, I wrote back to him right away, telling him that at least he should give himself a break in the action, a change of scenery, and that in England he had at least one friend who could try to divert him for a week or two.

A few days after Miller's letter, I found myself saying to John—as though I were Mother Amanda oppressed by child-care and household chores—that we never spent any time by ourselves. "All right," John threw back, "let's go cycling this very afternoon."

It was a perfect day, the sky clear and blue, though a stiff cold breeze whipped across the fields and roads. Eventually we stopped to wander through a woods filled with masses of wildflowers growing amongst the roots of gigantic oaks. In the shelter of the trees it was amazingly warm, and when John and I came to an inviting hummock covered with layers of leaves we sprawled on our backs and looked up through the branches to the sky.

"I'm happy," I said.

"It's good to be happy." John's voice gurgled through his chest direct to my ear. Lying against John's shoulder, I closed my eyes and gave myself up to the strange sensation of my heart slowing down, of each beat resonating strangely through my chest, of my heart leaking love as though it was an old boat finally ready to sink down into the warm bed of the ocean. For a few minutes we lay without speaking. The wind caressed us, the earth's dampness began to seep through my clothing. My breathing slowed down and the sentence *I am happy* revolved slowly through my mind. A handful of finches landed on a branch above us. For a few moments they chattered gaily. The light of the sun made their bright yellow feathers shimmer in the clear air. Then suddenly they looked down at us, saw us watching them, and in a shrill chorus of warnings flew away. A moment of silence followed by a deeper sound. A woodpecker had landed in the tree just abandoned by the finches and began to hammer at a limb where the bark had been torn away. Before each blow the woodpecker's bright eyes darted crazily around; then, finally focused, he plunged his head forward, tiny skull vibrating as his beak smashed into the hard wood. But the unyielding oak only made him more determined. The pace of blows accelerated, soon the thud-thud of his initial attempts became a loud staccato. Finally he stopped and stared at the oak, shook his head back and forth in bewilderment. His eyes were jumping like overheated ions and as he tried to straighten his neck I could see his chest feathers fluttering with the beating of his tiny heart. Then he flew away and instants later was hammering at another tree, machine-gunning his little brain towards oblivion.

Before returning to the flat we had supper at a pub. By the time we got back, one of Janis's famous impromptu parties was in full swing, and the apartment was overflowing with equal portions of loud music, smoke from diverse sources, and vegetarian snacks. That night I drank wine, I exchanged confidences with strangers, I danced with a shirtless boy until I was soaked in his sweat and mine. It was four in the morning before the guests finally left and John and I stumbled to my bedroom. I was completely satisfied, totally exhausted. But as I started to drift into sleep I became aware that John was still wide awake. I turned to look at him. He was sitting cross-legged, drinking a last beer and smoking a cigarette.

"What's wrong?"

"Nothing. Something. This afternoon, while we were cycling, I was thinking that we're so busy now, we hardly know each other any more."

"You talk as though we had been married for twenty years."

"Sometimes I wish I were married. As it is, I'm out on a limb, all alone. My sister is angry at me for betraying my parents. My parents are angry at me for betraying ten centuries of perfectly cultivated blood, to say nothing of the American war machine. Even Langston got annoyed at me the other day because I was too busy to do some little chore for him. And then there are all the scummy papers who want to find some gossip about the General's son. Sometimes I feel not a single person in the world would stand up for me."

"Don't be stupid. I would. Langston would. Janis would. Even Wyatt Browning would."

"I mean stand up to my heart. Stand by me no matter what, even if things change."

I thought of John's father, the General, cutting so precisely into his slices of roast beef. The sound of his voice booming through the telephone when he called John from the airport. "I would."

"You didn't used to like it when I asked you to marry me."

"Ask me now."

"Don't play games."

"Don't you play games."

"Will you marry me?"

"Yes."

The first time I saw Miller on a television screen I was absolutely astonished. What relationship could there be between the smooth and confidently famous man of science, the discoverer of Miller's comet and the author of *Shooting Stars*, and the Miller I had once known? During the entire program, an afternoon talk show of the type I never ordinarily watched, and on which Miller would have never—later—appeared, I was practically glued to my chair, waiting for the inevitable—that is, for this new televisionized Miller to break his pose and collapse back into himself.

When Miller accepted my invitation and came to England, I thought of him as being in a bad period, a time when the demands of work and marriage were too much for him to bear; but in fact Miller was going through something much more profound: under the pressure of necessity—or, who knows, perhaps because some genetic time bomb had unexpectedly exploded—Miller had become a man absolutely determined on success—the man, in fact, whom I would eventually see on the television screen.

On the surface, Miller in England was the married man on vacation. Even now I have the photographs. Here is Miller in pigeon bespattered Trafalgar Square; Miller and myself arm-in-arm in front of the British Museum; Miller, John and Langston sitting in a triangle at the site of the hunger strike; Miller with his arm around Janis in front of our flat in Cambridge.

But despite his holiday air, the Miller-to-be was hard at work. For example, we were both studying spectroscopy. I was finding the mathematics almost impossible. One afternoon I showed Miller what I was doing. The next morning Miller came and woke me up: he had stayed up all night rearranging the entire tangle into a few simple lines. How had he done this? Concentration, you'll say. Miller was working while I was putting my energy into my relationship with John. True, but the question remains. After all, just a few years previously, Miller had come to me for help. Why could his mind now wrap itself around concepts that had previously eluded him? Of course there is no answer to these questions. No one knows why a child one day can't speak a word, and the next day is talking. Intelligence, despite those who seek to explain it, is absolutely mysterious: it proceeds in discreet little jumps, quantum jumps you might say, and some people make more jumps than other people.

There was another way in which Miller had changed. Whereas he had previously seemed in a fog either because of Amanda or his family, he was now—despite his problems— much more outward-looking than he had been. Everything interested him—tourist sights, our political activities, British theatre, Janis's religious monomania.

One night I told Miller about Piakowski's statement that whereas my own mind was second class, Miller had a "great mind."

"Well," Miller replied, "at least someone believed in me then."

There was something in his tone, a flat achieved confidence that I had never heard before. I waited.

"Actually," Miller said, "I've discovered a comet. It happened one night when I was at the observatory, photographing stars. It was in all the papers back home, just a couple of weeks ago. I thought you might have heard about it."

"No, I hadn't." I was absolutely astonished. All I could think to do was to ask him if it had a name.

"AS2998674 Miller. There's a formula for naming them. They say it's going to be quite bright."

If there was ever a cat who could swallow the canary and keep it hidden, it was Miller. "How bright?"

"Second magnitude," Miller answered. "Possibly first. In fact, they say it will be the brightest comet of the decade. Possibly the century."

"AS29 whatever is going to be the brightest comet of the century?"

"It was straight luck. Every other observatory in the world must have been covered by cloud."

"Miller, for Christ's sake, why didn't you write?"

"I wanted to surprise you. Actually, I'm supposed to go to Greenwich next week to firm up the details. Then there's going to be a press conference in London to announce the event to the world."

"And it was pure luck."

"Luck, that's it." He grinned at me and looked away. "Actually, I had been studying the light from some adjacent stars and there was a strange disturbance, as if a veil had been inserted between me and the stars. I took a wild guess that there might be the tail of a comet involved and then arranged to spend a few nights taking photographs of that section of the sky. I lucked in. The comet showed up on the third night. I telephoned Spitzer; he's gone to Stanford, and he double-checked from their observatory in the desert. That was that."

That was that. While others had gone on to more exotic locations, Miller had stayed home. Now, in one leap he had passed us all: myself, Spitzer, Piakowski.

The hunger strike was Langston Hughes's idea. It took place outside the American Embassy in London, a glass and concrete structure crowned by a large golden eagle.

Langston began his strike on a Monday at noon. The press had been invited, and while Hughes positioned himself on the steps of the embassy under a gigantic Campaign for Nuclear Disarmament sign, a group of twenty supporters distributed leaflets to the crowd. The leaflets explained that Langston Hughes, well-known psychologist and anti-war activist, had decided his conscience could not allow him to eat so long as Britain and America were allied in the cause of nuclear suicide. It invited onlookers to join him for a few hours, and since there were a hundred or so sympathizers who had already agreed, by two o'clock the steps of the American Embassy were very crowded. That afternoon Wyatt Browning introduced a private member's bill in the House advocating nuclear disarmament, and the evening papers gave the whole event extensive coverage. When closing time at the embassy came, most of the demonstrators left the steps. That, too, had been arranged. Langston Hughes refused to move. He made a speech, already printed in a press release, saying that he refused to walk or eat until the Prime Minister of England

and the President of the United States came personally to have dinner with him and discuss their situation.

The next day the scene was repeated. Unfortunately for Langston, a sex-magazine scandal diverted both the House and the newspapers. Nonetheless, he persisted. John's role was to co-ordinate activities behind the scenes, telephoning lists of sympathizers, recruiting new members of the organization.

The plan had been that the action would last for a week, and that on the final day a huge crowd would march from the American Embassy to the Prime Minister's residence on Downing Street.

The strike had begun the day Miller arrived. The second afternoon we joined Hughes on the steps of the embassy for a few hours. Then, that evening, Miller and I drove up to Cambridge. I had classes to attend and research to continue; the idea was that on Sunday we would all—Miller, Janis and I—come down to London to rejoin John and Langston for the final day. This schedule continued with Miller proceeding to Greenwich before we all, once more, gathered in London for a new triumph—Miller's press conference. Our plan had everything to recommend it except, as it turned out, reality.

Our flat in Cambridge was on the second floor of a red brick house that gave onto a large common. The landlady must have gone through a very individualist phase, because although the woodwork of all the adjoining houses was painted a subtle off-white, the front door and windows of our house were a strange lively yellow, a colour that in the rain looked like atomic egg yolk.

When we had the car, however, we entered from the back lane, which was where the parking was. For me, city girl *extraordinaire*, the lane back of our row house was nature run amok. Between the tire tracks rose thick clumps of violently green grass, and on either side of the dirt tracks, cowslips and bluebells grew in profusion. We had a glassed-in sunroom that extended shakily off our kitchen; in the morning I loved to sit there, windows wide open, looking out at my tiny wild garden and drinking my coffee.

Since Ellen had deserted us we'd had a spare bedroom, which was where Miller slept the night we arrived from London. I was in the sunroom going through the coffee routine when I heard Janis get up. She had a red kimono with very fancy brocade—the gift of an admirer—and when she was feeling well she looked, with her blonde hair and bright blue eyes, like a healthy Wagnerian doll.

But on this particular morning Janis was pale and washed out, her hair hanging in strings and her skin dry and sallow.

"You look sick."

"I'm pregnant," Janis said.

As she said these words, her face became, there's no other word for it, naked; and then upon her naked face was laid another, new expression, and that of course was fear. I felt as though she was appealing to me, that her appeal was one even more abject and total than the one I'd made the night I'd knelt before John's chair. But then, pregnant women have always been able to make a convincing case. Whether I had these reactions at the time or in retrospect is impossible to say; after all, the psychologists tell us that, like Stalin, we are continually reconstructing the past.

But whatever psychologists say, I have now, and have had for many years, what is like a photograph in my mind. My eyes are the camera. In the foreground are my own hands and the thick white porcelain mug in which I always drank my coffee; these are not in sharp focus, but they make the bridge over which I am staring—and in the place of the troubled waters is Janis. She is standing framed by the open window, and in the warm glow of memory even the grey morning light is enough to suffuse the room, to surround her shoulders, her face, her golden hair with a pulsating brilliant edge.

"Are you going to keep it?"

"I guess so."

That is when the image breaks, because that is the moment when Janis steps towards me. What I can't remember is what happened next: did she rush forward, arms extended for a forgiving embrace? Or was the movement of her arms only a stray notion to maintain her balance as she walked past me, out of the room and my life?

I returned the embrace, whether or not it was intended, not knowing what there was to be forgiven.

"I'm four months gone," Janis said. "I should have told you earlier. I don't know. I thought I might have an abortion. But I didn't have the heart. So." These words spoken while clinging to me. Then she stepped away and opened her bathrobe. Janis's belly, always a bit pillowy with its gentle burden of rice and vegetables, had now begun to rise. I had always found the sight of Janis naked slightly arousing, but now that I knew she was pregnant, the reddish-gold muff beneath her belly seemed more of an afterthought than an attraction. "I really wish it weren't happening."

"Four months," I said. I was trying to remember, but couldn't recall Janis having any particular boyfriends at the time. For some reason I then thought of Miller, and that it was too bad he was asleep since he was an expert in these scenes. "Who's the father?"

"John," Janis said. The word was coughed out, as if she hadn't been able to decide whether to whisper or to shout it.

I sat down in the wicker chair where I sometimes read the paper on weekends. I stood up. Closed the window against the suddenly irritating breeze. Opened it. I felt a familiar confused resentment, the way I used to feel at the end of a school day when I realized it was time for me to go back to my attic at the Borsteins'.

"I'm sorry," Janis said. "I didn't want to hurt you." These words spoken in Janis's perfect Oxbridge way, each one dropping like a little cultured pearl into my burning ears.

I walked from the porch, through the kitchen and into the living room. Still feeling numb, still buzzing, I began picking up loose objects from the tables—cups, saucers, lamps—and throwing them at the wall. They made sharp brittle sounds as they broke, and after a few moments the buzzing was replaced by the pleasant song of porcelain exploding. Then I saw Janis standing in the doorway, watching.

"It was an accident," Janis said. "It only happened once, before you and John started going out again."

"The pause that refreshes."

In my hand was a King's College beer mug that Janis had given me for Christmas. I threw it at her. She stood, without flinching, while it arced across the room. When it struck her on the head she fell heavily to the floor. The mug clunked down after her, not breaking. Janis struggled to her feet. Her forehead was cut, a trickle of blood had begun to make its way down her cheek. She extended her arms to me.

"Don't desert me. Please?"

"Does John know?"

"No. And he doesn't have to."

"Yes he does."

"I'm sorry. It wasn't on purpose. I was going to have an abortion but—I couldn't bear to kill—".

She was in my arms, crying.

I moved away. "You're going to have the baby then?"

"Yes."

"John has a lot of money."

"I don't want John or his money. I just want the baby. And—" Again the pleading pregnant look.

"And?"

"And you, Nadine, if you want to, I wish you would."

"You wish I would what?"

"Marry John," Janis whispered. "He loves you. But until the baby is born, do you think you could stay here?"

What was I thinking? Nothing. Everything. My mother handing the infant me to the waiting Léonie. Léonie's cold lips kissing me goodbye as I headed off for a new life in the New World. John asking me to marry him and me saying yes, wanting to be worthy of him, even willing to risk a whole lifetime pretending to love.

"We'll see," I said. "I have to think about John. No big promises."

By the time we had finished cleaning up the mess in the living room, it was almost noon. We were sitting on the back porch, Janis still in her bathrobe, when Miller staggered into view. Lucky Miller, still catching up on his jet lag he had slept through everything.

"Suppose the universe has a code. Suppose the maps we make of the sky are the maps of our own psyches, and the constellations in fact the ancient countries of the heart"

These words begin Miller's first and most famous book, *Shooting Stars*. It is amazing to think that while Janis, John and I were going through our convoluted little tunnel of love, Miller was having such lofty thoughts. And yet, he's since told me, it was during his visit to England that he began writing his book: I have even seen the small black notebooks which he used; and having been shown them remember noticing them in his luggage. I had thought they were record books for tracking the future progress of his comet.

Now, as Janis joked over the telephone the other night, the pen is in the other hand. And I am sitting at Léonie's table again, trying to use words to make sense of lives that don't. Of course on the surface we have all—the survivors—our own little successes. Miller achieved his books and his television image, I my full professorship and my medal of honour from the Royal Astronomical Society, Janis her literary friends and a glamorous life. But even our successes make it easy to judge us harshly: we who thought ourselves in the vanguard of a new generation, a new history, are now propping up and being propped up by the amenities of middle-class existence. We have, you might say, traded our youth for middle age, our radical ideas for the comforts of money. But who can defend themselves against the charge of having grown old? In retrospect, we may have made the wrong choices; at the time, we didn't know we were choosing.

The three of us returned to London the next morning. Janis was at the wheel, driving, as always, a little too fast on the winding roads she preferred to the freeway. Despite the fact she had been up most of the night, a quick bath had restored her to her usual ravishing self; the sunglasses she wore to hide her swollen eyes only added to her dramatic appeal. I sat beside her in the passenger seat. From time to time Janis removed her sunglasses in order to give me sad looks begging for forgiveness. Her eyes were full of sorrow, complicity, guilt and—I couldn't help thinking—delight at being the centre of attention. Now that I knew she was pregnant, an unexpected sentimentality—along with my other reactions—had let itself loose in me. Overnight, it seemed, her face was fuller, more feminine. The delicate tones of her skin were heightened, and within her seemed to burn the mysterious vitality of the unknown life she was carrying.

Miller sat in the back, turned sideways so that his legs could stretch out along the seat. Though Janis and I scarcely exchanged a single word, Miller talked to both of us equally, dividing cigarettes, comments on the English countryside, questions about the hunger strike, with scrupulous fairness.

Each jolt of the car bounced through my bones. The frayed leather of the seat was uncomfortably harsh against the backs of my thighs, and the constant turning of the car as it swayed through endless tight curves made me feel slightly nauseated.

I didn't want to arrive in London. The prospect of seeing John, of sharing his bed again, repelled me. And, of course, I was dreading the confrontation. We had talked on the telephone but I'd said nothing about Janis. John was his usual sweet self. He reported that Langston Hughes was taking mineral water now, on the advice of his doctor, but that he had eaten nothing else for a week and was beginning to weaken. John, also, had started to fast; after two days he felt pleasantly dizzy, and was sometimes very thirsty. He said that

there had been several interviews with newspapers and that a
BBC television crew had been filming them. A few minutes of
this bland chit-chat was enough to set my stomach churning.
Then John asked how Miller was enjoying his visit to Cambridge; and after I assured him that Miller was having an
excellent time, John asked me to give his regards to Janis.

"You'll say hello to Janis, won't you?" were his exact words.
Janis. He pronounced her name no differently than ever, no
differently than any other word. It was so casual, so studied,
he must have said the sentence to himself a thousand times in
order to get it right. Or perhaps it had meant nothing to him.
Another night, another *trou de mémoire*. But why be unfair
to John? He might have been feeling lonely. If Janis had
seduced him, she had meant it only as an absent-minded gesture of friendship, one that no doubt had been a welcome
surprise for John. But not so welcome that he had pursued
Janis. Not so surprising that he had behaved any differently
with her since.

The sun is setting, the sky over Paris has turned a deep,
pulsing red. It is odd work, remembering Janis, her voice
made husky by two extra decades of cigarettes and cocktails;
odd to place my good friend Janis back into that other time,
twenty years ago, when Janis and I and the soon-to-be-famous
cosmologist D.B. Miller drove together in a tiny car on our
way to London to join John Richardson and Langston Hughes
in a hunger strike against the atomic bomb.

Janis endlessly repeated that we were the mutant generation, and that with us, history was over. If history stopped
then, where has it gone since?

What could we have thought was going to happen as a
result of our protest?

Were the bombs going to rise up in their silos and eject
themselves from the foolish grasp of mankind?

Were John's father and all the other field marshalls and
admirals and generals and commanders going to choke on
their double whiskies?

Were the nameless and numberless masses we tried to avoid sitting next to at lunch going to leap to their feet and join us in a great angry roar?

I know what Janis believed: she believed that when the atomic bombs were dropped on Japan all of humanity had mutated, that we—the generation of the future—were destined to sweep the world clean of war, injustice, hunger, sexual restrictions and boring music. In their place a green glowing planet where people exploded out of their destinies like flowers springing from the bud.

But that day in the car Janis was less than ecstatic: she had been caught, you might say, taking her own secret ride with the comet between her legs. By the time we got to London her softness had turned to nerves and she was fiddling with her sunglasses and chain-smoking cigarettes in anticipation of the meeting to come, when we would tell John, jointly, that he had gotten Janis pregnant. That was the agreement we had come to, Janis and I.

The plans for the demonstration had certainly included people: why else would John have distributed leaflets, telephoned supporters who in turn telephoned their own contacts who in turn urged as many sympathizers as possible to witness the hunger strike at the American Embassy. And yet, in all the planning of the hunger strike, although Langston had talked about how wonderful it would be to get wide press coverage so that all of England could see what their government was doing, no one had ever thought about the actual number of people who might be attracted, the possibility that the hunger strike might not only fill up the steps, or the street, but that thousands or even tens of thousands might be drawn to the centre of the storm.

But that was what happened. When we arrived, or came as close as we could get—the steps themselves, the street in front of them, the square, was a seething mass of spectators waving signs. Surrounding the throng, not quite threatening and not quite passive, was a cordon of police. Still polite, still per-

fectly polite and happy to let us through. Also at the edge of
the crowd, more ominously, were ambulances and police cars.

Eventually, at the trials, witnesses said ten thousand people
were present, although the police claimed only five. Such
figures and estimates are beyond me: even five thousand is
the population of a fair-sized town. Let's say there were a lot
of people—more than I had ever seen in one place, more
than I could count, more than I was comfortable pushing
through. At first, also like a town, everyone seemed to know
their place. There were signs being waved, there was chanting and songs from different parts of the crowd, but there was
also a certain looseness to the whole occasion, clumps of spectators standing and talking to one another, as if at a gigantic
picnic, waiting to see who was going to win the three-legged
race.

But by the time I reached the sidewalk in front of the steps,
the human mass had tightened, almost frozen. Pushed from
behind, unable to move forward, people were pressed together, trying not to break the human barrier a chain of
policemen had formed between them and the embassy, where
John, Langston, and about twenty others were sitting on the
steps, holding their own signs, waiting for the next item on
their own agenda. In the front row of the crowd, looking on,
were about a dozen journalists taking pictures, and even two
men with television cameras adorned by the BBC logo.

As soon as I got to the front row, John saw me, waved and
grinned. I felt a stab of pain. Jealousy? Yes, I suppose I was
jealous. But more than that I was depressed. Ever since Janis
and I had agreed to confront John with the knowledge of the
baby, I had been wondering what his reaction would be. Of
course he would apologize; in his perfectly diplomatic manner he might even find a way to say that Janis, not exactly
monogamous herself, could hardly be certain who *was* the
father of the child-to-be. Then, no doubt, he would plead
with me to marry him. After all, he had had and neglected
his opportunity to pursue Janis. It was me he wanted. The
trouble was, I didn't really want him. I suppose I *had* wanted

him—good old steady reliable John. But now he wasn't so
steady and reliable. Instead of being my protector, he was the
one I needed to be protected from. If I had been in love with
him I might have wanted to forgive and forget. As it was, I
wanted to forgive and—in return—be granted my freedom.

On the way to London the weather had been perfect: one of
those soft English days when the sun sparkles out of the baby
blue sky. But now the sky had completely clouded over and
a light drizzle began to fall. Umbrellas sprouted quickly
through the crowd—pushed together it was easy to share.
And—obviously having predicted even the weather—Langston
and his cohorts on the steps pulled out CND-decorated plastic rainhats to keep their faces dry.

I waved to John as he motioned me to come forward,
through the police, to join him on the steps.

I put my hand on the policeman's arm, asked him to excuse
me. He looked down at me and grinned. I noticed how tall he
was, how thick was his uniformed arm. When he smiled the
strap holding his bobby's helmet in place divided the flesh
under his chin, making his face enormous. He shook his head.

"They want me there," I said.

"They want all of you there," the bobby said. He grinned
again and I noticed that one of his eyeteeth was missing. That
was how I recognized him in the photographs displayed at
the trial. The same grin, the same missing tooth.

Tentatively, I pushed at his arm. The arm pushed back. No
particular force. No violence. Just an automatic readjustment
of the situation.

"Are you going to let me through?"

"No, I am not."

He wasn't smiling any more. I could see where he had
nicked his throat shaving that morning. His cheeks and the
sides of his chin were pocked with the souvenirs of teenage
acne. His hair was sparse and lanky, his face puffy. On his
wedding finger was a ring: somehow that was oddly reassuring. I thought that a married man probably had children,
regular sex, was less likely to be sadistic than a lumpish single

man who had only a policeman's future. Or maybe I didn't think these things then, but afterwards, trying to remember. That is the problem with memory: it has no respect for the difference between now and then.

It was drizzling and John was still waving at me. I began to feel impatient, that I should do something definitive in order to join him on the steps. Even if I wasn't going to marry him. Especially if I wasn't going to marry him, I should at least have the courage to join him in this.

I pushed the arm again. "Please, I *must* pass through."

This time the arm pushed back harder. But before I could react there was the screech of whistles. I looked to their source. A column of policemen had made a path through the crowd, made a space through which a van was driving up to the steps. Out of the van leapt a dozen men who climbed the steps immediately, without pausing, while one of them read loudly from a piece of paper declaring that those persons sitting on the steps of the embassy were breaking the law by trespassing.

But the words were drowned in shouts and jeers from the crowd. And, in any case, it seemed that Langston and the others knew what was coming because they now all lay down on their backs, Gandhi-like, their placards like faithful companions beside them.

Cautiously the police advanced.

There was no further movement on the steps.

The first to be approached was Langston Hughes.

"All right, get moving mate," the policeman barked.

"I refuse," Hughes said.

The policeman pushed him with his foot. "I said get moving."

"No," Langston shouted. "In the name of world peace I refuse to move."

Now the crowd was silent. We all knew what was supposed to happen: as in the Gandhi movies the police were supposed to pick up the protesters and transfer them to the van. The television cameras and the newspaper photographers would record the event, it would go out on the evening news, and the whole world would applaud another brave day in the non-violent achievement of peace.

There was only one problem: the policeman in charge had obviously not read the script.

He nudged Langston again, this time a kick in the ribs. Langston groaned.

"Carry him, you idiot," someone shouted from the crowd.

"It's non-violence," I said to the policeman in front of me.

He shook his head and shrugged his shoulders.

Finally two of the bobbies picked Langston up—one grasping his shoulders, the other his feet. Langston hung hammock-like between them. Then they dropped him. Langston fell heavily on the stone steps. For a moment I thought his back must have broken. Then he curled into the foetal position.

"Sorry mate, the rain is making you slippery. Better stand up and get going."

But it was John who was the first to move. He was bending over Langston, wiping blood from his face, when the two policemen tried to pull him away.

"Just a minute," John said.

They yanked him to his feet. John looked me in the eyes, smiled as if to say that despite everything the movie would go on as planned, peaceful and triumphant. Then tried to lean down to Langston again.

"Hey," said one of the bobbies. The other sank his fist into John's stomach. John doubled over, then jerked back up, his own fist like a wounded bird in flight, hobbling and bobbing towards the policeman's face where it landed on his nose with a little burst of red. There was a surprised little bracket of silence—then a bobby's nightstick made its own little trajectory—high in the air, then down on the back of John's neck, crumpling him onto the steps. The last thing I saw clearly was Langston trying to struggle to his feet, because with the blow to John the crowd went crazy, thousands of throats screaming "Peace" and pushing forward. I was knocked to the ground. I remember the funny "clonk" sound my forehead made on the pavement, but before I could be trampled I was being dragged up. It was Miller to the rescue. The awkward angular Miller with his high-school biceps had been following me all the way; now he hugged me close and dragged me backwards, against the grain, me blinded by the blood that kept pouring over my eyes, my ears filled with shouts and screams of the crowd battling the police.

At the hospital they gave me three bristly stitches and a fat white aspirin: despite all the blood, the cut was just a little opening on the upper edge of my left eyebrow. Then Miller and Janis and I drove back to Hughes's House. As we pulled up I saw a long black limousine parked in front of the house. And walking in the door it was immediately clear that something was terribly wrong. Wyatt Browning was in the living room. He stood up as we came in, shook hands with Janis and Miller and then, as I extended my hand, surprised me by stepping forward and putting his arms around me. Then he stood back and looked at me. At first I thought he was concerned about my injury—my forehead was swollen and I could feel dried blood against my cheek. Then I recognized the expression on his face: it was one I had seen before—on the faces of Piakowski's doctors after the stroke. Sitting in the living room, morose and silent, were some of the other members of Hughes's House. There were signs propped in one corner, and on the coffee-table was the usual collection of empty bottles of wine, ashtrays overflowing with the cigarette butts.

"Langston Hughes had a heart attack," Wyatt Browning finally said. "He's in hospital."

"Where's John?"

"He was arrested."

The white defeated faces surrounding me were frozen. I wanted to sit down but there was nowhere. Then the floor was rushing towards me.

"You fainted," Janis said. "I've never seen anything like it. You went down like a stone." I was being propped up in a kitchen chair and Wyatt Browning was squeezing cold water onto my face. It collected under my bandage, ran down my cheeks and neck, pooled in my collarbone, trickled down the inside of my shirt.

"Is Langston all right?"

"He's resting. The heart attack was a mild one, brought on by the excitement. He was lucky it wasn't worse: if the crowd hadn't reacted the way it did, I think the police might have killed him."

For a moment there was something almost vulnerable about the face of Wyatt Browning. The danger his friend had been placed in? The shock of the British police departing from the script and resorting to violence? But then the smooth politician's mask was back in place. A bland smile, a pat on the shoulder, a lightly murmured excuse as he went on his politician's errands—this time to get John released from jail. The charge: assaulting a police officer.

Janis, Miller and I were left alone in the kitchen. Until today I could never have believed John would actually hit someone. But then I wouldn't have been able to picture John sleeping with Janis. As Piakowski used to say, the most dangerous failures are the failures of imagination.

By the time John arrived, there were a dozen of us sitting in the kitchen. Some, like me, had various cuts and bruises that required bandages. Others had suffered only torn clothes or a certain loss of political innocence. As John walked in, apparently unharmed, I looked at my watch: seven o'clock. It had been after noon when we had arrived at the demonstration.

John came right to me, put his arm around me. We kissed, the perfunctory peck we always gave each other in public, then admired each other's wounds. John said they had made Wyatt Browning put up bail of five hundred pounds.

"A public menace," someone called out. Laughter. John wedged a chair in next to mine. A bottle of beer was passed to him. He tipped it back, drank half of it in a swallow.

"God, I'm starved." More laughter. The hunger strike was over. It had been a victory after all. Names of restaurants were shouted out, soon an expedition was being organized to a nearby Italian eatery.

I tried to picture myself going to the restaurant, drinking gallons of wine, stumbling back to Hughes's House with John, smoking marijuana, collapsing into our cosy bed in Langston's study. Now was the time to forgive and forget. Now was the time for me to be swept back into John's orbit, to make love in the afterglow of our triumph, then to tell him about the baby and say that I was going to be a good wife, an understanding wife, a wife who could forgive a little slip made when we weren't even going out together.

I tried to picture all of this but the picture wasn't there. The only picture I had was of me by myself, alone in a bed, asleep.

I looked over to Janis. "Are you ready to drive back?"

Janis nodded.

"Let's go then."

We were in the front hall before John caught up. "What are you doing?"

"Going home."

"Home? This is our home. Aren't you hungry?"

His face was puzzled, hurt, uncomprehending.

"I want to leave, John. I'm exhausted."

"If you leave, I'm leaving with you."

Janis and Miller were already in the car. John and I were still standing the doorway.

"I'm sorry, John."

"Don't be sorry." He brought his hand up, tenderly touched my bandage. Gentle, reliable John. He had been a hero today, risked his life for a friend. But I didn't love him, couldn't bear his touch.

Finally I was the one who walked out of the house. Miller was in the back seat. I joined him. John, the long-legged one, climbed into the passenger seat beside Janis and Janis, without speaking, started the motor and began driving.

I closed my eyes, hardly able to stay awake. As we jerked our way through the city traffic I tried to reason with myself.

I knew I was being terrible, irrational. I was no longer even able to rouse myself to jealousy: instead, over and over in my mind, played the scene of my inviting John to marry me, of my saying I would stand by him, no matter what. Finally I fell asleep. When I woke up I had a headache from the roar of the car's engine.

I leaned over so my mouth was next to Janis's ear. "Stop the car."

"I can't. We're in the middle of the freeway."

"Stop right now or I'm jumping out." I opened the door. Janis slanted the car through the traffic and then pulled up on the shoulder.

"John, Janis and I have something to tell you."

John looked at us, his face bland, quizzical, showing nothing but polite curiosity.

"John," I said, "Janis is pregnant."

Now John's face twitched, at first puzzled, then went a deep red.

"It's true," Janis said. "You're the father."

Trucks passed, buffeting us. It began to seem that our only hope was that one of them would smash into the car, sending us all to oblivion. Janis began to hit her head against the steering wheel. "Jesus Christ," John said, "everything happens at once."

I got out of the car and stood by the side of the road. Miller followed me. Leaning against the car we could hear Janis weeping, then interrupting herself to tell John that the three of us would live together and raise the child in a happy family.

"This is crazy. We're going to get killed." Miller took my arm and led me to the grassy ditch. We sat down. The ditch was filled with an unmoving stream of cigarette packages, pop bottles, crumpled potato-chip bags. "This is a crazy vacation. I wish I had someone to write home to." He lit a cigarette. "I thought you came to England to get away from messy scenes like this."

"So did I."

"Do you love him?"

Miller's question was such a surprise that at first I thought he meant Piakowski. Then I tried to imagine myself with John again. "No."

"Love is what matters," Miller said. He looked at me, the awkward and sincere Miller of old. "I don't like him either." Then he laughed nervously, the way he had when detailing the means he had used to discover Amanda and her hotel-room games.

There was a hand on my shoulder. Janis lowered herself beside me. "He still wants to marry you." She was leaning against me. She felt tremendously heavy, inert. "I feel terrible. Please take me home."

"John can take you home."

"Nadine, please."

"John can drive."

"Nadine, I need you. You promised."

The traffic had intensified and it seemed the highway was nothing more than a long conveyor belt of trucks, belching their diesel exhausts as they roared by.

"I wish I'd had the abortion."

"It's too late now."

Janis's head slipped down onto my lap. Automatically I began stroking her hair, making soothing sounds. I was aware of John sitting alone in the car but the thought of John miserable and repenting his sins was not unpleasant. Finally we got back into the car. This time it was I who drove, with Miller beside me. John and Janis were in the back, and when I looked at them in the mirror I could see how stiffly they sat.

When we got home we were able to agree on at least two things: thirst and hunger. I began cooking dinner. It was almost as it might have been a week ago. Tasks were divided up, bottles of wine were emptied: Janis even tried to smoke marijuana but I took it away from her, saying that if I was going to help with this baby I would prefer its brains intact. She agreed meekly and returned to chopping vegetables. Meanwhile I drank: an idea had begun to form in my mind—a plan to ensure Janis's security, John's happiness, my freedom.

With dinner steaming on the table I set out candles, the way Janis and I used to on festive occasions, then opened a new bottle of wine.

"To the baby." I raised the glass. Janis smiled and looked relieved. John blushed. Then I proposed a second toast. "To the bride and groom, Janis and John. A quick and happy marriage."

This time Miller was the only one who smiled.

"I want to marry *you*." John protested.

"You'll marry Janis. She needs your name and your money. And you both need me." I raised my glass. "Cheers."

"Cheers," Miller said.

Janis and John didn't move.

I emptied my glass and poured another. I hadn't realized how drunk I was. Being drunk wasn't part of the plan. There was no plan.

"Nadine," John said. His voice had that deep syrup-like sincerity that had won me back once before.

"John," I returned. "John, I have to tell you. I forgive you for Janis. I even forgive you for not telling me. But I can't marry you. I won't." I put down my glass, then went to the bedroom and locked the door.

Two weeks after the demonstration I went down to London to visit Langston Hughes. He was out of the hospital, in the care of one of the women in his house who had been a nurse. Before she sent me up to his room she asked Langston if he wanted to see me. I found him in bed, cheerfully reading the papers. He had started to grow a beard so his cheeks and chin were covered with stubble alternately red and grey, like an old man.

"I hoped you would come."

"Thank-you."

"You see, it worked just the same." He showed me the papers piled up on his bed. They all had articles about the hunger strike, the burgeoning British peace movement. "Amazing, isn't it, that a bit of violence could make peace so famous." There was a slight tell-tale slur to his words; he was on sedatives, the way Piakowski had been.

He was sitting up in bed, propped against a series of pillows. Now he angled his head to one side, and gave me a cautious smile. "John's been here all week," he said. "He's taking things very hard."

"I know." John had always been the diplomat, but my refusal to keep on with him seemed to have unhinged something. There were frequent—almost daily—phone calls—filled with recriminations and nasty remarks. It had been my suggestion that he go to London and see Langston.

"I suppose you've been feeling guilty."

"Angry, now."

Hughes nodded. The room was oddly silent. Langston's attentiveness had filled up all the space. I wondered if this was his professional manner, with his patients. I felt soothed—doubly so because I tried to imagine that John, too, must be calmed by all of this attention.

"Do you think what John did is a terrible thing?"

"No," I said.

"I wish I knew you better," Langston Hughes said. Then he laughed, an unexpectedly inviting laugh that made me feel suddenly important, as though there really was something in me to be known.

This was followed by a new silence, a less comfortable one. I tried to imagine the next few minutes: was I supposed to explain my feelings for John, justify my decision not to marry him?

Langston smiled at me, then surprised me again: "It's for the best," he said. "John needs all his energy for himself right now."

After about half an hour I stood up to leave. Hughes made me promise to come back. In retrospect I think Hughes is the only saint-like person I have ever met. In the whole time I knew him Hughes never contradicted himself, never lost sight of the vision that propelled him.

Busy though John may have been, he was still part of our lives. After my visit to Hughes's House there was another phone call from him. This time his voice had the hard edge of his political speeches. "I think we should meet for a drink. Talk things over. I promise not to ask you anything difficult. But we have to reach an accommodation, you and I, for Janis's sake."

"Perhaps you should talk to Janis."

"Nadine, don't be thick."

So we met in a pub. John kept his promise, and I must admit I found his company enjoyable. After an hour he stood up to leave. When we were outside he shook hands with me, solemnly, then asked if he might drop into the apartment from time to time.

"Of course, of course." And then: "You know, John, if you and Janis *do* decide to be together, I would be genuinely happy for both of you. Really. I know that wasn't the idea when you started. But now—"

"I offered already," John said. "Thank God, she turned me down."

"You'd be good together, you and Janis."

John laughed. "I don't think so." I felt an unexpected jolt—jealousy again. I suddenly remembered that when we started out together John had always refused to admit to any previous girlfriends; of course I knew he was lying, but it was a lie I had enjoyed. The moment of jealousy passed as quickly as it had begun; now I was standing outside the pub with a friend, a semi-stranger, an ex-lover whose ex-ness had quickly become a comfortable wall never to be breached.

"Well," John said, "I have a meeting." Once again we shook hands. Then he leaned over to kiss me. I felt a little butterfly of fear leap from my chest to my throat. Then he was walking down the road, briefcase swinging jauntily, long scarf wound round his neck and trailing down the back of his jacket.

The weeks passed quickly. I had my own routines; they were boring but boredom and escape were what I wanted. Before I knew it, Janis's due date was about to arrive.

By this time Janis was enormous. Despite her doctor's warnings she had, in the last two months of her pregnancy, ballooned into a gigantic caricature of a pregnant woman.

Meanwhile John had gone to London for his trial. He, Langston and six others were accused of assaulting police officers. Langston, completely recovered, used the witness stand as a podium for his pacifist beliefs. John, too, had his picture in the paper. His eyes stared intensely at the camera but he looked puffy-faced and tired—twenty years older than the carefree boy I had gone cycling with only a few months before. Finally the trial ended, the judge reserving his decision for several weeks.

That night I phoned Langston to congratulate him on his good showing. He thanked me graciously, a thespian taking his bow. Then I asked after John. He was well, Langston said, all things considered. I didn't ask what those things were—I supposed they must be myself. Then Langston said that John had left London right after the trial and was probably in Cambridge by now.

Another week went by. Janis's due date arrived. And it passed. Janis, bedridden, began to swell. Meanwhile John had not yet appeared.

In the morning I went to get the doctor. He came to examine Janis, then informed her that the baby might be born in the next few hours—or the next few weeks. He advised her against eating too much and asked her to contact him again when labour pains started.

It was mid-summer and Cambridge was gripped by its own humid version of a heat-wave. Immobilized in her bed, Janis heaved and perspired. Her normally perfectly pale skin had broken out in a blotchy rash; she had taken on so much weight that her fine features were blurred with new flesh; in an attempt to cool down she lay naked under a thin cotton sheet with a damp washcloth plastered to her forehead.

When the doctor left I went to the kitchen and put on the kettle for tea. Waiting for the water to boil I swung open the windows of the sunroom, to look out on the back lane. It was barely nine in the morning, but the air was already hot and a wilting breeze blew across the roof-tops. Playing in the lane were almost a dozen children, rushing back and forth in some complex game of tag, their raucous voices rising and falling like the calls of overgrown birds. On other back porches, on the tiny rags of lawn, could be seen other women like myself, women of my age and Janis's. Soon Janis would join them and would be changing the diapers already neatly stacked in the nursery, rocking the cradle that had long dominated the centre of the living room, hanging out on the clothesline the dozens of tiny little jerseys and shorts she had already washed and carefully placed in the baby's dresser.

"Where are you?" Janis's voice was weak and pathetic.

I found her lying almost comatose on her pillows, trying to smoke a forbidden cigarette while sobbing fountains of tears. She cried for an hour without stopping, tears streaming forth until her whole face was wet and swollen. Finally she began to cough and choke—I forced her to drink her tea, however cold, and allowed her a second cigarette—but though she stopped crying nothing would console Janis that day until finally, late in the afternoon, she fell asleep.

While she slept, I anxiously watched over her. Then, when she woke up, I made her get dressed and we went and walked across the commons to the river. Only a few seasons had passed since that hilarious day when we had pushed each other over the bank and into the water. Then it was I who had been sad, I who had needed to be rescued—and when I needed it, Janis had rescued me.

Janis took my hand. She was breathing heavily, she always breathed heavily now, but I had gotten used to her laboured breathing, the almost ceaseless movements of her hands over her tummy, the sudden depressions and the bouts of dependency. For me, Janis's pregnancy had become the normal state of affairs, something that could go on forever.

"I don't know why I fucked him," Janis said.

Nietszche wrote that in life everything happens twice—first as tragedy, then as farce. This leaves no room for joy, which is perhaps the difference between women and men. This may seem cruel, but the days I waited with Janis while she sweated out the hours before Leandra's birth, I was feeling cruel about men, about the whole race of men who seemed to view women as earthbound carrion to be fed off then deserted, but also, of course, towards John in particular.

Every few hours I telephoned the house of Langston Hughes, but I was unable to reach John. Finally, when Janis insisted, I rang Ellen Richardson to ask if she'd seen him: she replied very formally, as though I were a bill collector, that they had lunched together two days ago and that she wasn't in the habit of asking her brother to leave his address.

So we waited. When another week had passed the doctor came and examined Janis once more. "Two fingers," he announced, meaning the opening of the cervix. "Don't worry. It doesn't mean a thing."

Janis looked at him, pained at his diffidence; and then, just as her face was settling into the frosty neutrality that was one of her best expressions, she gasped and her mouth twisted.

"That's better." He pressed his hand on Janis's belly and held it there while her face sank slowly back to normal. Then, once more, he probed his way up the tunnel of love. "Why don't I stay for a cup of tea?"

At midnight the doctor was still there, still drinking tea. At slightly diminishing intervals Janis was seized by ever-longer contractions. Each one brought new waves of moans and whimpers. But she refused to take painkillers; instead she made me read to her from the manuals she had laid out for the occasion—snatches from the *Tibetan Book of the Dead*, her favourite bits of *Winnie the Pooh*, the La Leche League breast-feeding manual. By ten o'clock there wasn't enough time between contractions to get through more than a paragraph. At midnight, the doctor made me scrub my hands thoroughly, then slipped a rubber glove on my hand so I could reach up and feel the baby's head for myself.

Incredible: after hours of hearing the doctor describe its progress—"it's descending, it's turning, it's caught on the bone"—the baby was suddenly real.

"Is it there?"

"It's there."

Through the gloves I could feel a warm soft skull, tiny bumps that must be matted hair.

A few minutes later the head emerged into the light. The hair, it turned out, was sticky with blood.

Now with every contraction I held Janis's shoulders. "Push," I chanted as Janis groaned. "Push."

One squeeze and the forehead was visible, another and the tiny closed eyes followed by a nose flattened like a baby broadbean. Janis's moans had become loud screams. The baby's mouth opened. It was filled with blood. "Now," said the doctor. He had the head in his hands, his face was black with concentration.

Suddenly Janis's belly vibrated and Leandra floated out, sliding on her own bloody back like Moses floating down the Nile. There was a tiny apologetic baby cough, then she was in my arms, her eyes still wide open, and I brought her up to Janis's waiting hands while the doctor began to pull out the cord.

When I finally picked up a towel to wipe my hands, I realized that the telephone had been ringing for ages, a loud insistent buzz that grew louder with every repetition.

It was Langston Hughes.

"How are things going?"

"It's a girl."

A silence. "Congratulations," Langston said.

"Did you find John?"

"I think so. We're not sure. Could you come down to London tomorrow?"

It was two days before I got to London. By that time the body was beyond seeing. According to the coroner's report, John

died of a sharp blow on the head. They had found him, already
dead, in a hotel room. His blood was half alcohol and there
was an empty bottle of sleeping pills on his bedside table, the
place where he might have hit his head, if that was what killed
him. The autopsy report said he had taken enough pills to
kill himself twice. His wallet was empty, too, so it appeared
he had been robbed—dead or alive. Also, according to the
autopsy, he had had sexual relations shortly before his death.
On our way to pick up John's parents at the airport, Langston
told me there were two kinds of suicides, the ones who are
calling for help and the ones who are determined to succeed.
John wasn't calling for help, Langston said. After the funeral
I fled to Paris, to Léonie, the only place left for me to go.

Léonie is thin. The embarrassingly lush buttocks and thighs
have been whittled down to mortal size, and as she walks back
to the living room to make excuses into her telephone, her
slacks seem to hang from her hip-bones. Watching her bend
to hang up the telephone, then return to me, I am delighted
to see how completely the embarrassing aunt has survived to
become the elegant Parisian professor, white-haired but in
fact more youthful and mercurial than the unmarriageable
spinster with her hopeless gentleman callers. Only her face
has aged: a dark and leathery glove drawn tightly over her
knife-blade nose, the too-prominent cheekbones.

When I came to see Léonie after John's death she embraced
me. And then: "Look at you," her voice that amazed and
wounded croon I'd grown used to twenty years before, Léonie
welcoming me home after a rare excursion into the street.
"Look at you, Stefann telephoned me last night about your
friend. You must be terribly upset. I was hoping you would
come."

Of course I had brought John to meet Léonie—even after
the letters, I had needed him with me to give me the courage.
Like a diplomatic summit, our first meeting in so long had
been preceded by a series of invitations, prospective dates,
exchanges of photographs, then finally telephone calls to seal

the agreement. But even after all these precautions we had still been shocked to see each other. Unable to do anything but stand in the open doorway, our mouths open and quivering like the mouths of baby birds until John rescued us. That week in Paris had been one of our very best times, a week when under Léonie's benevolent mothering I really believed John and I could love each other and make a life together. It was the week I most wanted to marry John—to exchange the manless existence I seemed to have inherited from Léonie for family love and togetherness. That week John and I had even let ourselves talk about children—first in a joking way in front of Léonie and then finally lying on the fold-out couch in what had once been my old bedroom and now was Léonie's guest-room. Whispering in the dark, the windows open to the summer heat, those nights I imagined my body suddenly freed from its prison of birth control pills, my square mannish body blossoming with pregnancy, babies, nursing. John coming home from work with his scarf around his neck and shirt undone, leaning over our nest of little ones. Léonie the maiden aunt and guardian angel, watching over us and keeping us safe.

Except that she hadn't watched over us. Hadn't been our guardian angel. Hadn't kept us safe. A month after our stay in Paris, on a day when I had looked at my pastel plastic circle of birth control pills and wondered what would happen if I missed just one day, Janis had dropped her little bombshell.

Less than a year later John was dead: and I was back in Paris, seeking solace from Léonie. She hugged me, she kissed my cheeks. Then she smiled, an old familiar smile and said: "Nadine, someone is here." She gestured towards the kitchen and before I had time to react she had opened the door and was on her way down the stairs.

"Nadine." When I am describing Yaakov I have to say first of all that his voice had turned into a saxophone, a tenor saxophone with mellow notes but sudden birdy flights to harsh gutteral sounds that would then smooth out into song again.

Yaakov as a boy had been an undernourished little twig with a beak nose and large vulnerable eyes. The man in front of me was wearing a short-sleeved shirt that emphasized his sinewy arms and showed the black hair that matted his chest. In the open collar of his shirt he was wearing a small star of David. His eyes were still large and glowing, but were overhung by thick black eyebrows. He had black hair, also thick and straight. His dark skin was so deeply tanned that I hardly needed to ask if he had been living in Israel. His corded neck, the thick muscles of his arms, the ruddy glow of his cheeks all exuded extraordinary health and vitality, as though he had become an athlete or a health-food guru. A soldier, as it turned out.

We shook hands. "Isn't that just like us," Yaakov said, and then he opened his arms and held me against him. I was aware of the sweet-sour salty smell of Yaakov's sweat. I stepped away. John's sweat had been purer and rarer. Occasionally, after bicycling, there would be a line of fine drops from the space between his eyebrows down to the tip of his nose—each drop, as it descended, growing slightly larger. John's nose had been straight and thin. Looking at his sealed coffin, it had been one of the parts of him that I'd imagined.

"Léonie told me about your friend. I'm sorry."

"It's all right. He wasn't really my friend anymore." I was crying, or at least there were tears coming out of my eyes— the way they had at the funeral—tears that flowed on their own, unaccompanied by sobs or any of the other apparatus of crying—just little streams of tears that needed to escape.

It was evening, but even so I could see that in the short time since my visit with John, Léonie's place had been modernized into a bright, North American style apartment. Everywhere there were new light fixtures; the shabby wooden floor had been covered with tile and carpet; the walls were painted in light-reflecting colours or papered with cheery floral patterns. Most revamped of all was that most revampable of rooms—the bathroom. Lights, mirrors, gleaming fixtures, a tiled shower stall. "Look at this," I said.

"Try it," Yaakov said. "After a funeral, a shower is just the thing to wash away the tears."

While I was drying myself Yaakov walked in. He had stripped off his shirt and the mist from the hot shower settled onto his muscular shoulders and back. His torso was as tanned as his face, and as he bent over the sink to splash water on himself I was aware of the play of his muscles beneath his skin.

"Definitely not my type," I said. "I go for skinny intellectuals."

Yaakov turned around. Scattered across his shoulders, chest and belly were small scars. They were the size of coins, but they weren't quite round; then they suggested flower petals but when I made him let me examine them more closely, I saw they weren't like petals at all, they were like splashes made by drops of paint when they fall accidentally to the floor, the splashes of a boiling liquid melting into the skin. From his waist to his neck there were forty-three of these marks—each the same delicate lavender, each a small smooth crater that had burned away the first layers of skin. On his buttocks there were four more—two on each side—but these craters were for some reason white rather than lavender; and then, down the back of his left leg, the colouring returned for each of the twelve final tear-drops—one for each month, that began at the crease of his left buttock: January was followed in a burst by February, March and April—then there was a gap before May, June and July—which was the largest of all and was located behind his left knee. Then the rest of the year followed at even intervals down his calf with December placed squarely on his heel.

Forty-three plus four plus twelve: fifty-nine splashes to be counted and kissed. Fifty-nine craters left by shooting stars. Fifty-nine tiny acid cannon-balls burning into soft skin.

And so, beneath the sheets. My skin covered with the grainy summer sweat of Paris. Lying side by side in the night.

Too hot to be in each other's arms. Only our hands touching. My eyes closed. Yaakov's slow breathing carrying me while Janis, Leandra and John swirl about in my mind. Bittersweet, bittersweet. I am crying, soundless, the tears are leaking from the corners of my eyes and making warm paths down my cheeks. Eventually, just as I have forgotten I am in Paris, in bed with Yaakov, I feel his breath like a warm wind on my face, his beard scratching against my skin as he licks my tears away.

I put my arm around him and draw him over me. I feel his soldier's muscles moving against me: I feel soft, defenceless, a spring field waiting for the plough to descend, a city waiting to be invaded. He is suspended above me. The matted fur of his chest brushes against my breasts. I pull him down. I want to feel his whole weight. I want to know what it is like. I want to make stupid jokes about him sticking it inside me and popping off his gun. I want to be his target practice. I want to be obliterated.

The next day Yaakov was out doing business. By the time he came home from his fund-raising meetings it was almost eight o'clock—a neatly exact twenty-four hours since my arrival in Paris. I was making a chicken cassoulet in the old black iron cooker we'd had years ago.

"Look at you," said Yaakov. "What a good wife you are being." He took off his suit jacket and hung it on a chair. Between his broad shoulders, the back of his white shirt was bunched and damp with sweat. He reached into his jacket pocket and withdrew a thick yellow envelope. In an instant pictures were spilling out on the table—for a few terrible moments I thought they were going to be his old concentration camp photographs. But of course they weren't: a letter had arrived that day from Israel and he was showing us new pictures of his wife and children.

They had all been taken outside and in the bright sun the people, the buildings of the kibbutz, even the trees were bright and clean.

I bent over to look at them. The children were already almost elementary school age, almost as old as Yaakov and I had been in our imaginary kingdom. Now, finally, Yaakov came to stand beside me. I was looking at a picture of his wife. She was squinting into the sun, her face was very tanned and she was smiling broadly, showing large, slightly uneven teeth.

"That's Ruth," Yaakov said. The hand on my shoulder squeezed reassuringly. I said something inane about how beautiful she was, about how her beauty was so human.

"She was a dancer," Yaakov said. "She has a great body. Big tits."

I straightened up. Yaakov was standing very close to me, his hand still on my shoulder, grinning. Léonie had gone to her bedroom to change.

"Is that how you like them?"

"Nadine, I'm trying to tell you I'm married."

"You told me that last night."

Yaakov shrugged and poured himself a glass of wine. The child Yaakov had done that, too; made his nasty jokes then shrugged his shoulders to telegraph the audience that the act was over and intermission was now resuming. But when we were younger I'd had the advantage of age and strength on Yaakov.

Léonie came into the kitchen. She was wearing a new blouse I'd bought her that afternoon—a dark blue silk blouse with long sleeves that gathered at the wrists.

"Do you like it? I think it makes me look very important. Yaakov, haven't you set the table yet? I insist, Nadine, that I will make the salad."

So, Léonie was in her element again and Yaakov and I were two children once more, harmony restored.

After dinner, Léonie said she was going to retreat to her bath and then to bed. As she stood up, so did Yaakov. "Let's walk down to the river." We had drunk a lot of wine, and I was swimming in a warm and sentimental sea of carefully selected

memories. Even Yaakov, beside me, had changed from the
malevolent tormentor of a few hours back to the unsure boy
who had been my loyal and charmingly devious subject in
the kingdom of our childhood. On the street, in the dark,
Paris was mine again—its shadows slipping over my shoulders like an old forgotten coat.

We were walking down the Boulevard St Michel. It was
close to midnight but there were waves of people on the sidewalk. Students, tourists, lovers with their arms around each
other's waist—the way John and I had walked six months ago.
"I can't believe you really lived here," John had said. "You
must have hated to leave."

Beyond the last rows of traffic and street lights we could see
the dark gap of the river and smell the half-rank summer
water and the oily fumes from the barges. Then we were
winding our way down the stone steps: it was so familiar I was
spiralling through the centre of my own mind. For a while we
walked along the water without talking. There was a light
breeze, making a ripple of leaves in the riverside trees that
masked the traffic and the murmured conversations. Overhead was the compulsory moon, brilliantly white in the pillowy sky, sending its sculpted light through the pollarded
chestnut trees, scattering an army of bright reflections on the
water, shining down on Yaakov's white shirt and transforming
it into a brilliant sail ready to whisk us across the ocean to—but
where? That was the question. It was Paris in the summer but
I had my bittersweet memories of John and Yaakov had his
wife—with her uneven teeth, big tits, and dancer's legs that
had spread apart to give him two children.

"I love Israel," Yaakov said.

"I know."

"Why don't you come there with me?"

"You keep telling me you're married."

"My wife and I are not slaves to each other. She will welcome you because you are my friend." Yaakov's hand was on
my shoulder and the back of my neck, rubbing in little cir-
cles, predictable soothing patterns, the way one strokes a child,

a pet, an accident victim. "How can you decide about what you don't know? Let me tell you something. Last year I went to New York to raise money for Israel. They sent me to congregations which were worried about Israel's military policies, and they said, 'Here is someone who can set you straight. Here is a nice soldier who regrets what he has to do but can speak eloquently about the terrible conditions in which his people must survive. Here is a soldier you can understand, a man with big strong muscles and scars who almost weeps every time he kills another human being.' And so I went to New York and made my eloquent speeches and nice girls like you offered themselves to me. For the most part, I declined, but one evening I went to a Manhattan apartment building with a very beautiful young Jewish woman who is a lawyer and a civil rights activist and has even visited Israel on several occasions. We got out of her car and a security officer escorted us into the building through doors of bullet-proof glass. Then we went upstairs and into her apartment after unlocking many locks, which we locked up again before looking out her window at the glittering lights and the night sky and the cars driving brightly up and down the street.

"The next morning, I went past the armed guard and was out on the street again.

"Let me tell you something. That apartment building is like the entire Western world. There are people inside and people outside. The inside people try to avoid the outside except on the television news. Sometimes they traverse the outside when they are in an airport or a foreign country for a vacation. But even in a foreign country they protect themselves by going to good hotels, putting pills in the water, or taking guided tours through carefully selected wilderness areas where nothing unpredictable can be encountered. They think they are being safe but really they are pacing the walls of their own prison. Your own prison, Nadine. I know you have commitments, but the life to which you have committed yourself is dead. Leave it behind, Nadine. Come to Israel and build something worth having. Don't be afraid to live."

"You sound like a bad propaganda movie," I said.

"And what do you think you sound like? Every second of your life, Nadine, you have played it safe. Even your Communist boyfriend was the son of a general. And when he knocked up your girlfriend you had a great excuse to leave him. Are lovers always faithful? Are you being faithful now? Am I? I have killed men but at least I admit to it and am sorry about it. You killed John Richardson and you pretend not to know it."

"He was always a devil," Léonie said. This was hours later, after she had announced that she was going to bed, after we had stood up and then—as though we were at an airport—embraced and shook hands before going to our separate destinations. For a long time I sat on the window ledge. I smoked a cigarette, then another. But I was just about to go to sleep when I heard the footsteps in the hall, Léonie's hesitant knock on the door.

"He was always a devil."

"I don't mind."

"The two of you," Léonie said. "I never knew whether to make sure you stayed together or apart."

"How did you decide?"

"The camp pictures. Then I knew you couldn't stand up to him. It was like your mother and father all over again. Yaakov would have had you shooting a rifle by the time you were ten. You would have been killed."

"Now I can do whatever I want."

"That's right. You're a woman now."

"Yaakov says I'm a coward."

"I don't think so."

Since Yaakov and I had returned from our walk a light rain had begun. Now the sound of tires on wet pavement echoed through the street, mixed in with the patter of rain on metal awnings. The sounds, the odours, the sweet buzz of excitement that is always in the air. I would, I realized, give a lot to make it my home again; people had, I realized, already given a lot—sacrificed much, compromised much, to keep living in Paris. Léonie, for example, had compromised me. On the bed she now drew a cigarette from her housecoat; in the blue flame of the lighter her lips were carved and stony—then the flame snapped out and the pale sheet of her face reappeared, instantly shrouded by a violent cough of smoke.

This was it, finally, the gap in the conversation—the opening. The enemy's defence was exposed—now was my invitation to blitzkrieg. It was Léonie, in fact, who had explained to me exactly how the German army had attacked the French from behind their own fortifications. How the French had been defeated in six days. Or how, according to those who had not been sent to concentration camps or suffered other unfortunate fates, the French had lulled the Germans into believing they were defeated, lulled them into an Occupation which didn't cost them an entire generation reduced to trenches and blood.

So: Léonie had showed me an opening in her Maginot Line of nervously lit cigarettes, meaningless chatter about the changing architecture of Paris. Now was my chance to wheel in the heavy artillery: what had happened to Henry Brimmer? What had she done with my letters to Yaakov? Why had she never followed me to Canada?

I walked from the open window to the bed, took one of Léonie's cigarettes and lit it.

Then I found myself thinking of a book I'd read during a period when I had decided to recapture my French heritage by reading French novels. The book was *La Condition humaine*, by André Malraux—another war romance. The best scene was the opening one, in which a revolutionary assassin is in the bedroom of his intended victim, watching him sleep. Being a good intellectual French novel the knife was long suspended in the air while the hero contemplated the political, the historical, the *philosophical in the broadest sense* implications of his choice. Because it was a choice. In a British novel the scene would have been excised straight from the imagination, not even giving an editor a chance to label it excessively sentimental; in an

American novel the hero would have been on a quest to prove himself a man by committing murders; but in this French novel the only thing that mattered was the sweet taste of digression.

And so it was as Léonie sat in front of me, more or less inviting the outbreak of war. Should I assassinate her with the past? Or, better yet, forget the whole enterprise, breathe the Paris air, ask for the wine list, listen to the prosperous sound of birds enjoying the rain and conversations moving at the comfortable pace of a midnight walk.

The silence extended itself. Finally Léonie spoke. "You came back. How long are you going to stay?"

"A few days."

"You could live here if you want, Nadine. I would like that."

My heart thumped in my chest, a noise so loud I thought Léonie would surely hear it. *I would have liked that too, twenty years ago*, was what I thought. But I didn't say it. Didn't say, either, that I knew I was responsible in some way for John's death, and that therefore, from now on, my life would be bound to Janis and Leandra. All I could do was shake my head, no.

"Stefann says you are going to be a professor."

"Yes."

"You were always very good about your schoolwork."

I was? How would she know? But though she had shown me the openings I wasn't ready to attack. Instead I stubbed out my cigarette and said that I was tired. We kissed again before she left the room—a fierce kiss like the one we'd given to each other when I arrived.

I am lying in bed, feeling the breeze. The windows are ajar, white toile curtains swaying. In the morning I will take my last shower in Léonie's revamped bathroom and then I will go to the airport.

According to the glowing numerals on my clock it is two hours after midnight. I have been in Paris now one night, two nights, four nights, ten nights. In bed, in the night, I think of the darkness surrounding John. But John is dead and so quickly my mind switches from him to my own oblivion.

Officially I am mourning John but in reality, I am ashamed to realize, I am waiting for Yaakov.

I want him to open the door, to come to my bed. Some nights I fall asleep waiting and wake up to discover I have spent the night alone. Other nights he arrives and we make love—without speeches, without feeling. It is a mechanical, physical love that jerks me along—even in the throes of passion my body is sullenly playing out its role. My geometry teacher, Piakowski, John Richardson, Yaakov: these four men have been my lovers. But I am still the Sleeping Beauty waiting for her Prince Charming, the little orphan girl imprisoned in the Borstein attic, praying that one day I will discover how to escape.

BOOK FOUR
Toronto 1968

Piakowski stands up when I come into his office. In life he is not so large as memory made him. We move warily. When I reach out to shake his hand his palm is warm and friendly, but it insists on nothing. Then we both sit down. It is unclear whether we are to be friends or adversaries. Piakowski's desk is between us and in the midst of a pile of papers I see a bound copy of my thesis.

"You're looking well."

"And you," I return. An opening gambit, but also the truth. Piakowski *is* looking well. His black hair has grown silver wings, and his eyes are protected by gold-rimmed glasses that give his eyes a gentle, *genteel*, European professor air. His suit is a richer blue than it used to be, his shirt and tie more carefully chosen.

It is twenty-seven years since our first meeting, eight since we became lovers, four since last I saw him. It is still unknown what these lengths of time are supposed to signify: but when Piakowski smiles I find myself smiling back, needing his warmth, forgiving the past that seems more than a lifetime away.

At first the conversation is slow. Fits and starts interrupted by well-intentioned smiles, awkward silences. Piakowski tells me that he has read my thesis and that it is a brilliant piece of work. I remember his comment about second-rate minds but don't repeat it. A student comes to the door and I stand to go, but Piakowski waves her away. An attractive blonde girl in a tweed suit carrying her books pressed against her breasts. Piakowski's most recent conquest?

Piakowski takes me to lunch at the faculty club. On the way Piakowski walks slowly, but more easily than he used to. I offer him my arm. He takes it. Once his step falters and his body lurches into my own. My heart jumps but Piakowski regains his step, moves away from me.

We have sandwiches and glasses of beer. Piakowski tells me that as Head of the Department he has stopped doing research. No time. He still teaches the introductory course in astronomy. "I like to get them first," he says. His eyes are grey and hooded. I feel a few sparks of the power he used to have over me, but they recede, like stray bits of a comet tail zooming away from the sun and towards the limits of the solar system. I remember a night with Piakowski when we talked about that, comets: comets have two homes, Piakowski said then. One is the sun, the other a mathematically determined point somewhere in outer space. Comets are like hearts, Piakowski continued, alternately attracted to heat and nothingness.

I don't repeat this, either, but can't help wondering if Piakowski remembers such things, and if Piakowski, too, has moved away from heat to nothingness.

After lunch we walk slowly to the meeting we are both to attend, the faculty meeting where Piakowski will be in the chair and I will be introduced as the newest member of the Department.

The event takes place in a room with windows protected by yellowing venetian blinds. Piakowski speaks graciously. He cites my publications and when he describes my thesis he makes it sound better than it is. Miller is sitting across from me. After an hour of small business Piakowski excuses himself to go to another meeting. He stands up. A chunky man of average height. The woman who had been to one side, taking notes throughout the meeting, rises to go with him. At the doorway she takes his arm and I see Piakowski lean possessively into her body as they start down the corridor. The jealousy that I didn't feel with the student stabs into me now, a little explosion of pain that makes me gasp. To cover up I cough and light a cigarette. Then I look around the table at my new fellow workers. Some are former professors, others new faces. When the meeting is over Miller offers to buy me a drink but I have another engagement: it is time for me to pick up Leandra from her play-school.

When I arrive she runs to me and while I am talking to her teacher, Leandra clings to my leg. Then we walk home, across the campus again.

There is a small grocery store near our house where I buy what we need for supper. By the time Janis gets home, Leandra has eaten and I am exhausted.

"How was it?" I ask.

"You have a strange country," Janis says. She is smiling with her happiness and I am happy too—for Janis, for Leandra, for myself. It is September and Toronto is serene and beautiful. Warm days, cool nights, leaves beginning to change on the tree-lined street. I feel ridiculously proud of myself, as if I have invented this safe, secure place where broken lives can be made new. After Leandra goes to sleep it is still possible for Janis and me to sit in the backyard. On the weekend I will take her and Leandra on a promenade through my old neighbourhoods—the houses where I used to live, the schools I used to attend. When night falls we go back inside—I to work on my lectures, Janis to read manuscripts. She is the most junior of all editors at a publishing house on the verge of bankruptcy. I am the lowest of lecturers in a department known mainly for the fluke discovery of a comet by one of its graduate students. We are happy.

I was the neophyte; Miller was the prodigal hero, the great white hope of astronomy. His comet was now known throughout the scientific world not by its numbers but simply as Miller's Comet; and in addition to his scientific status, Miller had twice actually been interviewed on the radio for a program which specialized in telling laymen about scientific discoveries.

The second of these broadcasts was played just after we had arrived from England. I was in the kitchen, putting a coat of wax on tiles that had been unknown years without it, the radio turned on to help me pass the time, when suddenly I was aware of Miller's voice filling the room. Not his usual voice—the agitated voice in which he told me of his problems with Amanda—but Miller's voice transformed into calm and sanity. As he talked about the late nights he had spent looking for his comet, the sleep he had foregone, the quizzical looks on the faces of his twins when he came home from a night at the observatory, I was caught up in the story—as though it were being told by a stranger.

The next day I congratulated Miller. Miller blushed, gave me one of those sincere looks he always had in store, then said that the only good thing about the broadcast was that it had impressed the director of the university press which was publishing his doctoral thesis as a book. "He told me they might use colour for the cover," Miller said. "I don't know what that's supposed to mean."

Then Miller, who had only one thing on his mind, returned to the topic of Amanda. Amanda—unleashed, unrepentant, uncaring—was still being unfaithful to Miller. Poor Miller. Neither his moral indignation nor his obvious distress seemed to make an impression. "You'll get used to it," she kept telling him. But he didn't. The worse she made him feel, the more addicted to her Miller became. And the more Miller talked about Amanda, the more she changed from the actual person whom I remembered into a fictional Medusa-bitch. Until one morning, Amanda herself appeared at my office.

It was November, a freak cold snap had brought snow and Arctic temperatures to Toronto, and when I got up to answer the door I glanced out the window to the street which the wind had turned into a tunnel of ice.

Amanda was wearing a fur coat, her long hair glistened with a fine layer of melting snow, the cold had reddened her cheeks and lips. Standing breathless in my doorway she looked as though she had arrived to audition for *War And Peace*.

"How are you? You look wonderful. Miller said you hadn't changed so of course I knew you must have blossomed. How are you adjusting to life back in the frozen North? Or is this just a quick stop on your way to God knows where?"

She shrugged off her coat, took a package of cigarettes from her snow-covered purse, and then she settled into the chair opposite my desk. Time and hydrogen peroxide had turned her hair a spectacular white-gold, and the sensuous teenager had become a full-figured woman. But despite her new voluptuous self, Amanda's main message had become raw nerves. Of course, Miller's descriptions of her hotel manoeuvres were impossible to forget, but nothing he had said had prepared me for Amanda five years later: her edginess, her uneasy sexuality, the sudden bursts of conversation followed by uncomfortable silence.

"You *have* blossomed," Amanda said. "I've always expected Miller to fall in love with you." Then she laughed. "Don't I sound like the jealous bitch? Of course, Miller has been in love with you forever. Loving you is one of his biggest virtues. I don't know why I'm talking about Miller's virtues— between us, Miller has *all* the virtues."

"I'm glad you came," I said.

"My plan was to invite you to lunch."

"And now?"

"It still is."

As she used to, Amanda was driving a sports car. This one seemed newer and longer. It was also double-parked at the entrance to the Physics Building. As we climbed in I remembered Miller that first night he came for help with his mathematics problems, emerging so tousled and ground-up from his session in the front seat that he could hardly make his way up the stairs.

By the time we got to the restaurant we were both freezing. Amanda ordered drinks right away, lit a cigarette, then began talking about her children like any other mother.

Amanda's arms were resting on the table. She was wearing a dark angora sweater, sleeves pulled so that the cuffs of her

white blouse were made to surround her wrists like large
linen petals. Her hands were both elegant and confident: narrow palms; longish fingers with short, transparent nails; on
the knuckles a slight fuzz of blonde hair. I was aware of these
details because a few days previously those fine blonde hairs
had emerged as major characters in one of Miller's most
amazing adventures—a scene which I found to be the most
poignant of all his confessions ...

One evening, after dinner, when the twins are already asleep,
Miller and Amanda are sitting in the library of their house.
This library, a long narrow room elaborately surrounded by
walnut-faced bookcases, is Amanda's creation. On the floor is
a thick oriental carpet. Real art adorns the one wall free of
books. Between the two armchairs in which she and Miller
respectively pursue their respectively solitary evenings, a glass
table supports an imported marble chess-board furnished with
imported marble chess-men. It is Amanda's hope, Miller be-
lieves, that this chess set symbolizes the friendly harmony and
competition that are the virtues of their marriage.

Alas, the unfortunate, absolutely inescapable reality was that
the marriage was hardly the same proposition for Miller and
Amanda. Amanda did not have occasion to sit in the library
festering with paranoia and outrage while Miller added to his
sexual scorecard. Amanda, even at the restaurant with me,
was not worried about each move of Miller's as though her
skin would be the wire through which every little change in
Miller must be registered.

Miller, on the other hand, was hooked on Amanda. Ob-
sessed, addicted and afflicted with a terrible illness of which
she was both cause and cure. That night in the library, Miller
decided that the only tactic left to him was to beg.

Dropping to all fours, doggy-style, he crawled across
the oriental rug. At the chess set he paused, then sank
to the ground so that his stomach would actually drag
along the carpet. Inching along, his tongue lolled out and he
began to pant and whine—the servile dog pleading for
forgiveness.

Amanda, reading, seemed hardly aware of him. Miller woofed gently to get her attention. Then he slunk forward. Beneath his palm he could feel the strands of silk that had been fastened into place by starving children in Afghanistan, apprentices to the great rug makers about whom Amanda had collected a shelf-full of brochures.

"Woof," he said again.

"For Christ's sake, Miller, what are you doing?"

At this point, a lesser man might have shrunk from the task: "Sorry, dear, I thought I dropped my diamond stick-pin." Or even: "Would you mind calling the doctor, my knee—." But Miller, as always, had bigger ideas. In fact, at this very moment, he told me, he meant to blurt out to Amanda what years of nervousness and fear had repressed; he had intended, once and for all, to make clear to her that with each of her frivolous flirtations she was violating the happiness of a fellow human being who loved her in a way he had once believed she had loved him. Imagine the scene: Miller, belly-flopped on the carpet, awkward and sincere as ever, but with a certain new confidence due to his worldly success, finally makes the long-awaited pitch. Horizontal, he levels with Amanda—play ball or you're out!!! Easy to imagine, also, is the result Miller hoped to achieve: shocked and impressed by the unexpected strength and forgiveness of her too-often-cuckolded husband, Amanda—imagine her a planet experiencing a little unexpected intercontinental polka— begins to feel her plates move, a veritable series of fissures open up in the encrusted surface, earthquakes shake down millions of years of civilization, until finally, suddenly, totally—repentance.

Miller and Amanda—O unhappy couple—leap into each other's arms and make love like crazy until the morning when, as the sun pours through the windows, the blonde-haired twins descend the quasi-spiral staircase of their model home to find their parents entwined like naked Gods on the library carpet.

Let's say the above almost happened. (According to Miller only a warning cough from Amanda discouraged him). But

almost isn't good enough, as Emma Borstein used to say about
the kitchen floor when it wasn't quite clean. The reality is
that Miller grabbed Amanda's hands, brought them to his
mouth, and then—for reasons he himself couldn't say—bit the
ring finger of her right hand with such force that the severed
vein began to gush dark red blood and (as hospital X-rays
later established) the bone that leads from the knuckle to the
first joint was cracked along its entire length.

Sitting in the restaurant with Amanda my eye was drawn to
the finger Miller had described so minutely—even down to
the blonde fuzz, even down to the taste of the blood (which,
he said, was surprisingly sweet at first but then syrupy and
nauseating so that he spent the whole night getting up to
brush his teeth.) Beneath the golden fuzz the expected scar
could be seen. It was a crooked white hieroglyph that re-
cords the violation of a finger—but I wondered what, when
Amanda looked at it, she thought about Miller, whether she
imagined the scars she had left across his heart, whether she
realized his oriental crawl had been intended for a more noble
destination.

"I was glad Miller went to see you in England." Amanda
said.

"So was I."

"You're the only person that he really talks to. At least, the
only woman. I've often thought things would have worked
out better if you two had gotten married. You've known each
other forever."

"Perhaps that's the reason we wouldn't want to."

"Miller told me what happened in England, with you and
John. I was sorry about that. I meant to write you after he
died—but after Miller came back we had such a row that I
stopped writing you."

"That's all right."

"It's not. Now you're back and we're not friends anymore.
We used to be—you and Miller and I—remember? And you
were the only guest at our wedding."

"I remember."

Amanda laughed. "Isn't this crazy? We're not even thirty years old and already we're drinking too much at lunch and bemoaning our lost youth. I mean, are our lives over? I'm still waiting for mine to begin. God, that sounds stupid. Tell me about your students or something."

She turned away from me, embarrassed, but I reached across the table, put my hand on her face, and turned it back to mine.

Then her cheeks flushed, and I dropped my hand. Amanda said, "Thank you, I was afraid you were only Miller's friend.

Miller's friend. Yes, that was the role everyone had cut out for me. Even Miller and I. That is why, I suppose, one drunken night when he had come round to see me, he was entirely undeterred by the fact that the houselights were off. Lights off? Nadine in bed? Well, better wake her up! So Miller simply tried the front door of our house and, finding it unlocked, walked through the halls and into my bedroom. He did make one concession: seeing I was asleep, he lay down on the bed beside me.

"Nadine."

I had been dreaming about Léonie in Paris, imagining her with a whole new set of suitors.

"Nadine, God, were you asleep?"

Miller drunk, smelling of cocktails and cigarettes. I switched on the light. He was lying beside me fully dressed: he was still wearing his overcoat and even his tie was properly knotted.

"Oh God, turn that off, it's killing my eyes."

"How did you get in here?"

"The door was open. I needed to see you."

"Here I am."

"I know. Do you mind if I take off my coat?"

"Miller, make yourself at home."

"Sorry." Miller rolled to the floor, which he hit with a sodden thump. Then he extracted himself not only from his coat but from all of his clothes.

"Do you mind if I get into bed with you?"

"Miller, you're drunk."

But Miller paid no attention, only lifted up the covers and slid between the sheets. We were lying side by side, Miller's cold body unmoving next to mine.

"Miller, you're freezing."

"I know."

Then Miller twisted in the bed and kissed me. Soon I was surrounded by Miller's universe, lying beneath Miller, being pumped full of Miller, exploding with Miller.

Once, and then again, slowly, without speaking, kissing, licking, savouring until I felt like a long-banked fire brought to a full blaze. Did I think about what I was doing? Did I ask myself what was going to happen in the morning? Yes, the question would appear, in tiny letters in my mind, and then I would feel Miller growing in my hand, or need to have him suck my breasts one more time, or need to impale myself on him to see if I was going to shake and shudder and moan the same way I had a few minutes ago.

How many times had I laughed at Miller for selling his soul to Amanda for a few overvalued orgasms? And now I was in a happy semi-coma beside Miller, feeling that for the first time in my life I knew what love was, *real* love, love that pours out of you the way light pours out of the sun, love that is not yours to give or hold back but love that exists, sweeps you away, blasts you out of the person you thought you were into—

"I've got to get home," Miller said when he woke up. "The twins will be wondering where I am." Miller took a shower. Dressed. "That was great," he said, drinking coffee at the kitchen table. "God, we should have done that years ago."

It was a Saturday morning. After Miller left I drew myself a bath, complete with some never-used bubbles Janis had given me the previous Christmas, and sitting in the scented water, drank coffee spiked with brandy and inspected my toes. They looked, I thought at that moment, like the toes of the Queen of Sheba after a night spent with her favourite lover. Watching my toes, sipping at my coffee, letting the unfamiliar feelings of fatigue and sexual exhaustion spread through me, I periodically closed my eyes and allowed myself to imagine that the hot water pressing on this or that part of me was Miller tonguing and kissing me once more. And then I began to think about Miller, Miller driving home, Miller equally exhausted but trapped in yesterday's clothes saturated with yesterday's sweat and yesterday's booze. It was, according to the clock over the sink, now an hour since Miller had left me. By now he would be at his house, walking in the door, seeing Amanda.

The image of Miller confronting Amanda made my heart bump. I had been able to imagine Miller all the way from here to his house, but now I couldn't cope anymore. What would happen when Miller saw Amanda? Would he smile, pat his unshaven cheeks, say that he had been working at the office all night? Would he give her a kiss, and then go upstairs to lie on his bed and think about me?

Miller had once told me that after her infidelities Amanda always took care to make love with him as soon as possible, so that she would be filled, as it were, with domestic semen. Would he honour the tradition? For a moment I almost smiled, at the thought of Miller searching in vain for something with which to fill Amanda. Then I saw Amanda at my office. Amanda so coolly beautiful, Amanda so coolly in control, Amanda so used to winning with Miller.

I got out of my bath and poured the brandied coffee down the sink. When I tried to breathe, my lungs pushed back as though dark jagged mountains had suddenly erupted inside my chest. And then the telephone rang.

"Nadine?"

"Yes."

"Nadine, it's me. I couldn't go home without knowing when I would see you again."

"How about right now?"

The sound of Miller laughing.

"We could cancel some classes next week," Miller said. "Get away for a couple of days. Would you like to do that?"

"Of course."

"We could go on Tuesday. Is that okay?"

"Tuesday. Yes." I tried to think about Tuesday. It was now Saturday. Did this mean I wouldn't see Miller for three whole days? When he had left I had felt full enough of Miller to last a lifetime.

"I'll pick you up Tuesday morning," Miller said. And then he hung up. Was he at home after all, hanging up the telephone lest he be discovered by Amanda? I started to dial his number, then stopped. But I didn't feel destroyed anymore. Only dazed, in shock, suspended between two unfamiliar places. I was pouring myself another cup of coffee when Janis came into the kitchen.

"What are you doing up so early?" she asked me. Stopped, looked at me, her face suddenly full of concern. "What's wrong?"

The telephone rang again. I barged in front of Janis, picked it up. "I just wanted to tell you," Miller said, "I miss you already." I was left, the receiver in my hand, looking foolishly at Janis.

"Did something terrible happen?"

Of course, as it turned out, I heard from Miller before Tuesday. And saw him, also, every day. But we didn't have a chance to make love until he had driven us out of town to an "Inn" he had seen advertised in the newspaper. It was supposed to be a place for rich city couples to spend country weekends, but they serviced our type, too.

We got to our room after lunch. Through the window came a hard grey light, not very promising, and putting my suitcase beside the bed I had the terrible feeling that it wasn't going to work this time, that what we'd experienced that one night was a drunken interlude in a sober and chaste relationship. Miller, too, seemed to be having second thoughts. He produced a bottle of whisky from his suitcase and poured us stiff drinks. Only after the bottle was almost half empty did Miller come from the armchair where he had been sitting, towards the bed where I was dutifully perched. Then he lay down on his back and stared at the ceiling.

"This is crazy," he said. "I want to be with you, but now that I'm here I feel paralysed. What are we going to do?"

I lay down and inspected my own section of the ceiling. Unlike my comfortable bed in the city, this had a lumpy mattress set on springs that poked into my back.

"I told Amanda I was going to Montreal. Why didn't we go to Montreal?"

My section of the ceiling was growing boring so I closed my eyes. Miller was right, we should have gone to Montreal. Or stayed home.

"Sometimes I think that I love you," Miller said.

I began to try to imagine what I was going to do. Right now I was drunk from Miller's whisky. Not happy drunk, not numb drunk, but on-the-verge-of-crying-jag drunk. Eventually I would open my eyes and look at my section of the ceiling again. After that I would get up, roll off the bed, put on my coat, take my suitcase, go downstairs. "Could you call me a taxi, please," I would say. The key was to sound as though it was perfectly normal to be calling a taxi a half hour after arriving.

"How are you feeling?" Miller asked.

I didn't answer. I decided I would count backwards from ten down to zero. At four, Miller rolled on top of me. I started to push him away but he was kissing me. Miller kissed me and held me, and murmured in my ear that he loved me. Then he got up from the bed and closed the curtains and shut off the lights. Soon we were under the covers, back in the Garden of Eden, warm rivers of our joined sweat twining through our perfect little countryside.

"Over there," Piakowski murmured. "Don't let him know you're watching him."

The man Piakowski indicated was bent over a menu. He was perfectly suited to Piakowski's fantasy: ferret-faced and needing a shave, he had sallow skin, was balding, and wore a shabby blue blazer and grey flannels that had seen better days. When he spoke to the waiter it was with an accent.

No doubt he was one of the Hungarians who had come to Toronto after the 1956 uprising; but according to Piakowski he was an agent who periodically followed him and once had even questioned the tailor in the shop below his apartment.

His *former* apartment I should say, because Piakowski had moved from his loft above the tailor's to a fashionable high-rise following the fire which had destroyed the shop below and would have killed him had he not been in a semi-wakeful opium doze instead of an ordinary sleep.

"Do you still eat dinner with your students?"

"Nadine, he's listening to us." Piakowski took out a cigarette, sheltered it in his hands while he lit it. Then suddenly his face relaxed and he smiled—strong white teeth the embodiment of sanity, the scarred eyebrow shooting up as always. "What are we talking about? Isn't this crazy? Let's order a real meal. You know I'm still always hungry, no matter what the doctors say."

Later we walked back across the campus. Piakowski, in his new slimmed-down version, put on running shoes every evening and went on these forced marches no matter what the weather. Diet and exercise: that's what the doctors had prescribed to keep him alive. But in order to diet Piakowski needed to take pills, and the pills seemed to be pushing him towards the edge. On the other hand, for Piakowski, paranoia had always seemed a suitable companion.

"Nadine, you know I really am delighted that you're back."

"It was kind of you to offer me a job."

"There was no kindness, Nadine. I was hoping you would accept—in spite of everything."

He stopped and looked at me. He put his hands on my shoulders. I twisted away.

"Nadine, you're a woman now. I understand that."

"Thank you, Stefann." What had I been before? I wondered. And then we were walking again. It was early December. A week of rain had melted most of the snow. In the afternoon the city had seemed grey and listless, but now from

the ground rose a mist heavy with the colours of streetlamps
and store-front signs.

The streets were still crowded with students returning from
late classes and the library; I remembered how uncomfortable
I used to feel, seeing young couples together and thinking of
my own strange alliance with Piakowski.

"Do you want to come up for a drink?" Piakowski offered,
when we were standing in front of his apartment building.

"Another time."

"Nadine, it took a lot of courage for me to ask you out to
dinner."

"I appreciate that."

"Some day, there are things I want to tell you."

That was the promise Piakowski always used to make when
I would ask him to tell me everything he remembered about
my parents. "Some day, Nadine, I'll tell you everything about
those years. But you don't want to spend your life living in
their shadow." "But I already *am* living in their shadow."
"Nadine, believe me, I know you better than you know
yourself."

"Some day," I said.

"Good-night, Nadine."

He turned and walked slowly to the apartment door. I
waited. Was he going to turn around and beg me to come up?
Hiss some insult that would shatter my composure? Threaten
to have me dismissed? The truth was that I had accepted the
job because I needed to establish myself professionally and I
needed a familiar place to go. When the time came, I had rea-
soned to myself, I would face down Piakowski. But now that
the moment had finally arrived, I couldn't believe he would
leave me unharmed.

That, however, was what happened. Piakowski crossed the
lobby to the elevator, turned and waved a benign farewell. As
I was walking home I looked across the street and saw the
man who had been in the restaurant with us. I couldn't help
wondering if he had been lurking in the shadows behind us
the whole time. But a street before my house he turned away

and I was left, as after all my encounters with Piakowski, to draw my own conclusions.

I did not understand what was happening to me with Miller. Twice before I had thought I might be "in love." First with Piakowski, and then with John Richardson. Now looking back, both of those affairs seemed to belong to an inferior being.

Yet, I *had* loved Piakowski in a certain sick way. I had needed him, been dependent on him. In memory I see the girl who slept with her uncle as desperately young, desperately unhappy. Her hair is badly cut, her body is white and featureless, she hides her nakedness in shadows or under blankets even when she has been smoking Piakowski's opium. What did she know about Piakowski then? Nothing. Only that near him, the walls of independence and self-possession she had carefully maintained during her ten years in Canada collapsed. With Piakowski, at least, she could be herself: a remnant; a lump spewed out by history; a war orphan still in the shadow of an overwhelming past.

And then, later, with John Richardson? A good try. At least I had had the courage to escape Piakowski by then. And in John Richardson I knew exactly what I was getting. Mature love, I had called it at the time. Mature love—yes, perhaps the love suitable for someone in their dotage needing comfort and security. But had it been passion? Had I ever cried and begged him to come to my bed? Had I ever thought the world would explode if I could not wrap my legs around him and feel his body slamming into mine? No, that was not how it had been with John, although he might have wanted it. With John I was the fearful little girl, the good daughter looking for a safe daddy to protect her from the rest of the world, yes, but most of all to protect her from her own violent feelings.

Or, so I thought. Because with Miller it seemed my life had started anew. One night with Miller had been enough to make me realize my past and future had to be rewritten. I was happy with him and, at first, even happy when I was alone.

Life was mine, in my body, ready to break out at a touch, a whisper, the ringing of the telephone, the sound of Miller's step in the hall.

Then Amanda showed up at my office again. It was a week after my dinner with Piakowski; the temperature had plunged and now the city was frozen solid. Amanda came in wearing her fur coat, a cigarette gripped in the leather fingers of her gloves, her cheeks pinched red by the cold. I hadn't seen her since the day of our lunch. She looked nervously about the office, then pushed the door closed.

"Nadine, congratulations. Miller told me everything."

"Everything?"

"Yes. All about you. The two of you. Sorry. I should have telephoned. But you know I can't talk over the phone. Yes, he told me everything. I want to tell you that I am truly happy. Really. You see, I always said the two of you should have been together." This delivered in a breathy, intimate tone.

Of course I had known that Miller must eventually tell Amanda. But somehow I hadn't thought it would be so soon. Now, with her in the office, our stolen weeks together seemed suddenly smaller, insignificant, a little house of cards that had already been swept away.

"You know, Nadine, I haven't always been perfectly faithful to Miller. So I am glad he has been getting some compensation. Of course I would have preferred him to search somewhere outside of the family circle. But when it comes to sexual matters, Miller's imagination has never functioned very well."

"Is that so?"

"Excuse me. Of course I shouldn't say such things to you. Anyway, I just wanted to let you know that everything is okay. Really. Just enjoy yourselves and have a good time with my blessing."

"Thanks, Amanda."

"About Christmas. I know you'll want to spend some time with him then. But it's important for the twins, too, to see the family together. Do you think you could leave Christmas to us? Instead, you and Miller could have New Year's together. Perhaps you could even go south. I have a travel agent. I'll get him to arrange something for you. I'm sure he knows just the kind of thing you'd like. I use him all the time."

And then she was gone, slamming the door behind her. I waited a minute, then ran down the hall to Miller's office. But Amanda had arrived first, and the two of them were standing on opposite sides of Miller's desk, staring at each other as though ready to kill.

"You'd better leave," Amanda said when she saw me.

I looked at Miller.

"I'll call you later," he said.

I was dismissed. It was twenty minutes to two. I had a two o'clock lecture. When two o'clock arrived I telephoned the secretary and asked her to tell the class that I was sick. At fifteen minutes after two I heard footsteps again, this time leading away from Miller's office. After a few moments I telephoned Miller's number. No answer. I went down the hall to his office. The door was locked.

I didn't hear from Miller that night or the next. The first night I drank a bottle of wine: all that happened was that I got drunk, fell asleep dressed, then woke up in the middle of the night feeling horrible. The second night I went out walking until the cold numbed my cheeks into leather. But when I got home there were no messages—only Janis looking very concerned but pretending that everything was normal.

The next afternoon I went to his office again; it was locked. The department secretary informed me that Professor Miller would be back in two days. Then she handed me an envelope which he had left for me. It was a request that I substitute for him in his graduate astrophysics seminar.

So: dejection, rejection. Every joint in my body ached, and every time I heard a telephone ring or a door open my stomach frothed into action. This was pain—real pain, physical pain. This was torture. "I feel so terrible," I said to Janis, "I must be in love." And Janis didn't even laugh, only looked at me sadly, the way she looked at Leandra when she was sick, and offered me a hot toddy.

The weekend came, no word from Miller. I got out buckets and sponges and spent Saturday morning scrubbing floors. I was bent under the kitchen table, my knees raw and aching, when I remembered how Emma Borstein used to wash the floors whenever she discovered that Earl had spent another night at the trailer park. On the other hand—I had to admit— the floors were filthy. I had washed them often enough, in ordinary states of mind, but now I learned that only misery can get floors *really* clean.

When I was finished with the floors, I decided to go to the supermarket and buy all of those basic supplies, at a reasonable price, that we always ran out of and had to spend a fortune for at the corner store. There, lined up at the cash register, I ran into Walter Miller. I wouldn't have recognized him at first: the always elegant doctor was dressed in baggy jeans and a cable-knit sweater under his stained sheepskin coat. Age had blown away the rest of his thinning hair, steel-rimmed spectacles had been replaced by rose-tinted glasses, thick grey-curled sideburns had sprung up on his cheeks.

"Nadine. My God, what a surprise. Dennis told me you were back in Toronto. You remember Bernadette?"

Whom I had never met, except through Miller's descriptions, but now hove into view, arms loaded with groceries; as she dumped them out I could see that she was pregnant. Miller had told me that Bernadette had converted and become an orthodox Jewess—a real fanatic, according to Miller, who actually followed the dietary laws and forbade his father to eat bacon sandwiches for lunch. But the woman in front of me seemed only another exhausted housewife.

"Congratulations."

"Our third," Walter Miller said, and then, turning to Bernadette: "Nadine used to live across the street."

Bernadette gave me a slightly nasty smile, then began to push their groceries towards the cashier.

But when I got outside, and was loading my things into the car, Walter Miller came up to me and said again how delighted he was that my life had turned out so well. "You'll come to visit us, won't you?" I nodded, and couldn't help wondering what exactly Miller had told his father about me. "You want a surprise?" he asked as we were saying goodbye.

I nodded.

"Watch the news tonight."

And so, at eleven o'clock, I switched on the television. As usual, the news began with the horrors: fresh movies of troop actions in Vietnam, faces of the victims of war frozen in agony, President Nixon looking deeply into the eyes of the free world and assuring us that we were "winning"; a story about our own government, the possibility that taxes might force the middle class to dig deeper into our pockets; various plane crashes, train derailments; coverage of a student demonstration that did not require tear gas or rubber bullets; and then, suddenly, we were up to the "light" piece that always concludes the Canadian news on the government station, a happy little item guaranteed to make us go away smiling. And there, suddenly, was Miller—Miller *fils*—wearing a white lab coat and with a picture, bizarrely, of the Mount Palomar observatory in the background. I called to Janis—together we watched Miller as he explained how tiny was the danger of a satellite being knocked out of commission by a piece of flying space rock.

The next Monday, Amanda appeared once more. "Knock knock." She was wearing her white fur coat as always, and in one hand held out a bouquet of flowers stiff from the cold. In the week since our last meeting I had not seen Miller, except to pass him in the hall, and had spoken to him on the telephone only once—after his stint on the news. After saying hello he had—as if reading from a prepared statement with Amanda watching over his shoulder—informed me that "although I do love you and want to keep seeing you, I feel I should straighten things out at home with my children. They, after all, are my first responsibility."

"They are?"

"They are only children," Miller had pronounced.

"I had no intentions of eating them, alive or otherwise."

But Miller had only continued on to explain that they were currently very sensitive to disruptions in their parents' lives, so that he wouldn't be calling me for a few days after which he would get in touch with me.

"A peace offering," Amanda said.

"Peace?"

"Nadine, I want to make it up. Miller has been terribly unhappy."

"I see."

"Please, Nadine, let's start again. I promise not to interfere with your relationship with Miller. Even if he wants to leave me and live with you, I won't stand in the way. Only please, don't fight with me? You know you're stronger than I am. Anyway, I want you to be with Miller, you're good for him. The thing is, I've been so jealous this week I've made him think that he must choose between you and the twins. I promise, Nadine, he doesn't have to choose. Can't we be friends? I know this is bizarre, the wife coming to bless the triangle, but Nadine, we're such crazy people, we have to do things crazy ways. Won't you forgive me?" She was standing right in front of me, the bouquet of flowers lying on the desk, and now her hands reached out to grip mine.

That's how we were when Miller came into the room. He started to leave again but Amanda called him back. "Miller, you're going to spend this evening with Nadine and explain to her how everything is all right, after all. Won't it be perfect?"

That night Miller and I went out to dinner. The week apart had made me afraid, but Miller seemed so relaxed, that with the help of a bottle of wine we were soon planning trips we would take together. But later, in bed with Miller, I looked at his face when he was in the middle of his own private ecstasy and I saw the little boy who had closed his eyes when I had kissed him in the snow. "You'll never be mine," I whispered, but of course Miller didn't hear me.

In bed without Miller. My clock glowing in the dark. Twisting in the sheets. The memories of Miller's touch like insects crawling on my skin. Wanting Miller. Needing Miller. Aching for Miller. Wrapping my legs around nothing and squeezing while I pray for Miller.

Hours stretch into nights. Nights into weeks. For a time there was a pattern. At least twice, even three times a week Miller would come into the house late at night. By then he had a key so he could surprise me, the way he had the first time. During those months I went to sleep easily enough, even if Miller hadn't telephoned to warn me he might be coming by.

Then came January. The promised vacation took place at the end of the month. Only we didn't go south the way Amanda had suggested. Instead it was up to our little lodge again. This time there was snow enough for skiing. Feet and feet of snow. We were there for a week. Miller's work made a real vacation impossible. For most of the daylight hours he was buried in his notebooks, so it was I alone who put on skis and went skimming over the hard-packed trails. I liked that. Cold air pinching my nostrils together, biting into my lungs, making my hands and feet tingle for the first half hour. Until finally, warmed up, skiing between the pines in the bright sun, I would feel as though I could spend a lifetime gliding along the crisp snow.

Sun. Snow coated with tiny crystals of ice. Air colder than a stone wall. Then inside again to take a bath and have lunch with Miller. We were working on a project together at that time, but Miller had other projects, too. Listening to him talk about them I would sometimes hear something other than his words, a note of desperation in his voice. The truth was that Miller, like so many scientists, like Piakowski, had made his big find at a precocious age. It had happened so fast that—in retrospect—Miller couldn't know if he had been touched by genius or merely luck. The only way to prove that he had deserved what he had gotten was to make another strike. And although he had written worthy papers that had been read to eminent conferences, he had never quite come up with something to equal that first splash.

Sometimes, as he talked about this, every time Miller said comet I would substitute Amanda. Because, in love, Amanda had been his great discovery. And just as he couldn't shake off the early success of his comet, he was having trouble shaking off Amanda. The nights he came to surprise me, he often arrived with a few drinks under his belt and I had taken it for granted that Miller had simply used the bottle to keep himself company during his long hours spent poring over his numbers. But now, at the lodge—just as when we went out to dinner—I noticed that Miller was by any standard a heavy drinker. There were always cocktails before dinner, wine during, liqueurs after. And then, sometimes, if he was too drunk to leave the restaurant, Miller would order a beer or two just to wash out his throat.

In our room he had a couple of bottles of Scotch which he worked away on once we had come upstairs. And when those two bottles were used up we drove into town and bought more. Always in pairs, I noticed, so that killing the first bottle wouldn't leave him dry.

In the restaurants he didn't get drunk, only loving and sentimental, so that I liked to see him drink. Alcohol relaxed him, I thought, loosened the grip of his everyday cares and—most of all—the grip of Amanda. But at the lodge, it seemed that no amount of drinking could erase Amanda from his heart. In fact, the more he drank, the more he sank into the spell of their relationship. And then, suddenly, as if his gears had slipped without his being aware of it, I would find myself holding my own glass while Miller slipped into his old mode of making confessions of his jealousy of Amanda, his continued spying on her, the terrible tortures she inflicted on him and the terrible feeling he had in his gut now that he was torturing her just as she had tortured him.

"You feel guilty!" I exploded one night. "I can't believe it. For fifteen years you've been complaining that the bitch Amanda made you suffer in every way, you practically describe her pulling out your fingernails and toenails one by one, and now you feel guilty about the prospect of hurting her? Miller— you're crazy. Crazy once because she deserves everything you might do; crazy twice because she couldn't care less. Where do you think Amanda is right now? And who do you think she's with?"

Miller, stunned, got up from the armchair in our room— where he had been carrying on his soliloquy about Amanda— and refilled his glass.

"Look at you. Every time you or I say Amanda's name you need to have a drink. What are you? Amanda's faithful little robot?"

The night ended in more drinks, more accusations, and though we finally made love I was unable to go to sleep. Instead, lying in bed and looking out the window to what should have been the romantic view of a half-moon perfectly poised over a jagged row of pines, I felt not romance but the death of romance. Ever since Amanda's strange plea I had feared that she would somehow manage to hypnotize Miller into staying. But now I was beginning to realize that Miller didn't need to be coerced by Amanda. He wanted to stay with her, needed to stay with her, was going to stay with her. The week we had planned in the Bahamas at New Year's had become a week in the frozen North not because of Amanda, but because of Miller. And just as our holiday had cooled, so had our relationship. During the first weeks I hadn't even thought about such things as whether Miller would leave Amanda for me. And then, as I became more involved with Miller, I had taken it for granted that we would talk about such things when the vacation finally came and we had time to breathe and make our world of love again. The way it had been at first. The way it had been when it didn't need a week away to spring into existence.

There was only one flaw in my plan. Miller didn't love me. Not the way I loved him. The way I loved him was the way Miller loved Amanda. The way I knew I would always be loyal to Miller was the way Miller was always going to be loyal to Amanda. Whether he wanted to or not, and no matter what he said.

On the way back to Toronto in the morning I said to Miller that I had been thinking about our relationship and that I wanted to be sure it wouldn't upset our lives. Not mine with Janis and Leandra, nor his with Amanda and the twins.

"You know," Miller said, "I've been thinking the same thing. If only we can go on as we are, everyone loving each other. Can't we just love each other, make love to each other, enjoy each other's company?"

"Is that how you feel about Amanda?"

"Are you asking me if I make love to Amanda?"

"Do you make love to Amanda?"

"She's my wife, Nadine, can't a man make love to his own wife?"

"Of course, Miller. I was only trying to follow your logic."

"I don't know where it goes."

"It goes to bed, Miller. Just like us. Why don't we give it a big kiss and put it to sleep."

"You know, Nadine, sometimes you are so cynical I can't believe what you say. You want to hear something crazy? When you used to live across the street I thought you were like that because of the war. I knew your parents had been killed in concentration camps and I used to try to imagine what I would be like if my father was put in an oven."

"Your mother was killed."

"That was different. You know. An accident. In fact I used to be jealous, too, that my mother had been killed in a stupid accident while yours had been wiped out in the big lesson of history that everyone always talked about. It seemed that in comparison I had lost mine for nothing. Isn't that crazy?"

"No. It isn't crazy at all."

"Well, here *is* something crazy, Nadine. In some weird way I was in love with you then, when you lived across the street. And do you know why? It was because you had been touched by death, like me, but the death you had been touched by was public death. There I was, shell-shocked because I had lost my mommy in an accident I couldn't understand—and there you were, the young-old witch woman with Death painted all over your face. I used to look across the street to your room and wonder what you were doing in there, what you were thinking. Then I would imagine your mind and it was like a big dark cave all jammed full of skeletons."

It had started to snow. Soon the car was moving in a grey and luminous cocoon down the highway. "I always wanted to tell you these things," Miller said. "Do you mind?"

I was breathing. One breath in, one breath out. The car was full of electricity. One wrong word and everything might explode. I reached into my purse for a cigarette. *A big dark cave jammed full of skeletons.* Not exactly romantic but difficult to forget.

"I think you're good for her," Miller said a few days later. "I've been thinking about our conversation in the car, and you know what? I think this affair is actually good for my marriage. Today Amanda brought me breakfast in bed. We used to do that for each other, when we were first married." We were at the faculty club. Miller had ordered a carafe of wine, always a dangerous sign at lunchtime, and was looking at me anxiously as he launched himself into the new episode of the Miller-Amanda soap opera. Anxious? More than anxious. But I, the well-behaved girl at the Borstein house, I just gave my perfect mistress smile so that my lover could tell me his latest adventures with his wife. But Miller still hesitated.

"I have told you about the breakfasts, haven't I?"

"Yes, yes."

Of course I knew all about them: by this time Miller's confessions had mapped out the architectural details of his disastrous marriage and all that was left to be filled in were the menus and the descriptions of furniture. From the moment I had arrived back in Canada, Miller had been on a roller-coaster binge of compulsive self-exposure. Before our affair had begun, the confessions would take place anywhere—a few words slipped in while we were walking down the hall to a meeting, a whole episode quickly related during a coffee break, whereas lunch gave room for an almost operatic treatment. But now, most frequently, Miller preferred to pursue his muse in the deeper hours of the evening. Sometimes these bursts of inspiration took place at my house, in bed; others, when Amanda was exercising her own freedom, Miller would invite me to come and pass the time with him in his library. There we would sit—lights out, smoke making dragon's tails against the window panes, drinks in our hands—while the twins enjoyed the trusting sleep of the innocent.

Miller's admiration for Amanda was endless. "She has the courage to live," was one of the stupidest things he came out with. It was amazing to see Miller so in awe of Amanda just because she had so defeated him; nonetheless, he would often be singing her praises when she walked in the door (another of her virtues was trying not to stay out all night, for the sake of the children). Then—though these postludes deserve a story of their own—the three of us would cosily drink hot chocolate.

Also after dark were the times when Miller, instead of waiting at home to hear the exciting details of Amanda's adventures, hired a babysitter and came to visit us for dinner. Miller was always the perfect guest, charming and discreet. And yet, except for the very first weeks of our affair, after a bottle of wine you could see that the whole disaster of his relationship with Amanda had him in its grip: there would be breaks in the conversation when Miller would be gazing at the clock, unaware of the silence he had created, or at times he would just lower his eyes and look down at his half-eaten food like a dog remembering some vivid shame. When these gaps became too painful Janis would excuse herself and go upstairs. Then the floodgates would open again.

So now, at lunch, while I ate my slimming Greek salad and drank coffee without sugar, Miller triumphantly related how Amanda had brought his breakfast to him while he was still lying in bed. Poor Miller—so eager, so unable to escape. Our lunch-hour passed. Miller looked at me guiltily, broke off in the middle of describing how Amanda liked the butter to pool and soak into the pores of her toast.

"I knew she was up to something," Miller concluded hastily. He reached for his wine glass. It was empty, his sandwich half-eaten. "This isn't easy to say, Nadine."

"Then don't."

"I have to. You see, Nadine, in all this time—since our first night—I haven't actually touched Amanda. Not—do you understand?"

"Of course. Of course I understand."

Miller stood up. "I've got to get back. And I wanted to give you the material for the project."

I am sitting in my kitchen, it is night-time, working on the charts that Miller has given to me. This is the work we share— and so, missing Miller, I instead roll out the maps and stare at a certain portion of the sky—to be exact, the western section of the zodiac.

Zodiac. Zo-di-ac. A strange word. And if zodiac sounds as foreign to you as it once did to me, imagine that broad highway across the southern sky shared by the sun, the moon, the planets.

Or imagine for a moment that you are suspended above it all. That a flying rocket ship, a magic pill, a grenade in your belly has sent you shooting into space, whooshing past the moon and looping like an atomic yo-yo towards the Milky Way. For a moment you pause for one last look.

In front of you is the solar system. In the centre the sun glows like the eye of a nuclear frog: around it move the planets in their orbits, ever receding children circling the mother at their own stolid pace. Soon your miraculous journey will carry you beyond them, but for this moment, please, stay to admire the perfection of the planetary dance.

Third from the sun—that's the earth, that's where you come from. Even from your privileged position in space you don't need a guidebook to tell you that earth is the one with the broken hearts, the unanswered telephone messages, the late-night, nothing-is-right, alimentary love song.

Your life is over, you're whizzing towards that great black hole in the centre of the sky, you're looking back one last time at the crazy kids who set off firecrackers to celebrate the dawn—except this time the little exploding chains are stretched across the skin of the planet. And then, just as you can't bear it you're free, outside the invisible bubble, beyond the ken of planetary laws.

But Miller and myself, the years we worked together, stuck closer to home. From our part of the planet the zodiac is a section of the sky best seen in summer, just after the sun is set. Then Venus is the brightest object in the sky: low by the horizon, a white pulsing jewel in the twilight. And if you wait until the twilight is almost over, then just above you will see a fainter, redder object. That dark stained light is Jupiter. And now—don't move—if it is a certain year and the night is clear your eyes may pick up an even more delicious reflection. This is red too—not the brilliant red of a jewel but the dark and patient colour of running blood. This is Mars, the God of War. This is where, in ancient times, astronomers at their maps would sketch the vengeful hero with his chariot of fire. In those days star maps were wonderfully romantic. When I was a child I saw those maps—with their angry gods, their animal constellations, their annotated borders—and I felt I was being invited to join a mythic heaven of victories and defeats. But when future children see the maze of numbers to which the sky has been reduced, what will they think of the gods of science, of the conquests science has made? Will they feel invited to join in a universe where men and women are

shadows of gigantic gods with a destiny large enough to fill a
whole sky? Or will they see, in the numbered stars, the numbered blobs of matter, a clue to their own reduced destinies?

For Miller and me the area of interest is between the two
reds—Jupiter and Mars. And so, on Miller's charts, on top of,
around, and between the numbers, Miller and I have made
our own additions: notes about the varying radio frequencies
emitted by certain flying bits of the solar system. These notes,
of course, are also in the form of numbers.

In my kitchen I inspect Miller's findings. Our project is
something we had discussed as students—the kind of ridiculous enterprise that might come into the minds of children.

Because, you see, if you were to look at the solar system
from just the right vantage point, you would see that when
the planets are lined up there is—between Jupiter and Mars—
an inexplicable space. A missing tooth in the planetary smile.
According to the ancients there was once an extra planet in
that gap. And then, one day millions or billions of years
ago—cosmic catastrophe! War of the worlds! Collision with
destiny! Or who knows, perhaps the cosmic catastrophe was
actually a nuclear war or some other unthinkable breach of
planetary laws. In any case, the result is known: the unknown
planet was destroyed. In its wake—millions of asteroids whizzing about the sun in sloppy variations of the original planet's
orbit, comets that shoot in and out of the solar system to
brighten up our skies and make the reputation of astronomers like Miller, renegade chunks of rock that sizzle through
the earth's atmosphere and make showers of shooting stars.

First as a distraction, then as a serious project, Miller and I
have spent a certain amount of time trying to put together the
evidence of the exact nature of this lost planet. For Miller this
is science, the discovery of the real; for me it is an exercise in
nostalgia, a continuation of the childhood fantasy of a perfect
kingdom—a world without war, without violence, without
trains headed into oblivion.

From the bedroom I bring out my own briefcase, filled with
my own calculations and charts. Soon I am lost in the work

we have made together. Hours pass. Janis and Leandra appear, but I say I don't want dinner, which is true. At this moment what I want is nothing at all.

"Nadine, did I wake you up?" Piakowski's voice was full of harsh and rasping notes.

"No." But in fact that was only part of the truth because although I had been working away at the kitchen table all evening, when the telephone rang I had been lying with my head on the charts.

"Nadine, are you there?"

"I'm here."

"Nadine, I telephoned you so we could talk. Do you want to talk to me?"

"Stefann, it's the middle of the night."

"Are you awake?"

"Yes."

"Are you expecting someone?"

"No." In fact, Miller had already telephoned earlier, as though nothing had happened at lunch, and informed me he would be spending his evening with Amanda, making a duty visit with the twins to her parents. On such evenings Miller would make his excuses to me as though I were an extra wife to be placated.

"This fascination you have for Miller. I've watched it for a long time. Do you know that? Nadine, are we really going to talk tonight? I want to talk to you tonight. Now. That's why I telephoned you. You and I, Nadine, we share things. Can we really talk tonight?"

The possibility of sleep was totally gone. I rubbed my eyes, stood up and walked, carrying the telephone, from the kitchen table to the stove where I switched on the kettle. This was a new routine, one I had developed a couple of months ago when Miller, unable to come in the middle of the night, would sometimes make clandestine phone calls from the library and we would spend hours on the telephone, Miller drinking whisky while I drank coffee to keep awake.

"Say yes, Nadine."

"Yes."

"Good girl." I could hear Piakowski lighting a cigarette, the sharp inhalation, the slow breath out. "I should have been a father to you. A real father. Someone you could rely on. I always wanted to do something for you, do you know that?"

"You did a lot."

"No, Nadine, I'm serious. To be protective, the way a father should be. That's why I want to talk to you tonight about Miller. I want to help you with him."

"I can't be helped."

"Nadine, are you in love with Miller?" Piakowski's voice over the line: a whole new incarnation, a rough-edged freight train rushing through my mind.

"Yes I am." Piakowski had never alluded to my feelings for Miller before, never shown any awareness of the torture I was going through.

"I thought so." Piakowski said gloomily. Then suddenly he laughed. I felt a flash of anger.

"Did you telephone me in the middle of the night to ask if I was in love with Miller?"

"Nadine, what's wrong with that? Who else do you talk to about Miller?"

"I haven't been talking about it."

"Not at all?"

"Amanda knows. And Janis. But what is there to say? Girl falls in love with boy. Boy loves someone else. Girl wishes things would change. They don't."

"You're not a girl, Nadine. You're a woman."

"Thank-you Stefann."

"Those were the days, Nadine. The best days for me. I want you to know that. I want to tell you that."

"Thank-you."

"Now it is all shit. *Shit*," Piakowski hissed and the sudden burst of static made me push the telephone away. "You love him, Nadine, but the love you have for him is a bad love. It's eating you away. You know why I want to talk to you about it?

I'm afraid it will destroy you, that one day I am going to discover that my lovely Nadine has taken an overdose of pills or stuck her head in the oven, all over a certain worthless Miller."

"He's not worthless. Remember the night you told me he had a great mind?"

"I remember. And I was wrong. I was right and I was wrong. I sensed there was greatness in him, near him, possessing him. In those days Miller was like a child in the lee of a demon. That girl, Amanda, he fell into her like an ant into a honeypot. Then there was the comet. Those were the moments I sensed for him. When they passed Miller became like the rest of us again."

"You said his *mind* was great."

"I didn't know Miller then the way I know Miller now. Perhaps Miller did have a great mind. But he has sold it—mind, body and soul—sold it all as quickly as he could."

"What are you talking about?"

"Over the telephone? You have to be crazy. This is a private matter. Miller's sell-out, Miller's collaboration, Miller's degeneration into a plastic scientist trying to invent secrets. You expect me to talk about these things over the telephone. I thought we were going to talk about real things, Nadine, about our hearts."

The kettle was boiling. I turned it off. Then looked at the clock: one A.M. I was entirely awake now. If my agony for Miller had not already existed to ensure my sleeplessness, Piakowski's crazed rantings would have guaranteed it. I made myself a cup of instant coffee, lit a cigarette.

"Nadine, are you there?"

"I'm here. It's now one o'clock in the morning and you were going to tell me about our hearts."

"Your heart, Nadine. The heart that Miller is breaking. Nadine, the truth is that Miller is in trouble. Very serious trouble." Piakowski was breathing heavily, a reminder of the beached-whale sound he used to have when he smoked opium. I wondered if he was on drugs again. "Nadine, do you hear me?"

"Yes."

"Nadine, your friend is in very serious trouble. I want to tell you about it."

"I'm listening."

"I can't tell you over the telephone. Could you come to my apartment?"

"I have classes all day tomorrow."

"Tonight, Nadine. After tonight it could be too late."

"Stefann, I'm exhausted."

"So am I, Nadine. But what I want to discuss with you is so serious, so *confidential*, that if you are unable to come here I will take a taxi to your house." Here he stopped again, again trying to catch his breath. I imagined the ranting, half-conscious Piakowski arriving on my doorstep, talking in my kitchen until he slumped into sleep hours later.

"Don't come here, Stefann."

"I need to tell you things."

"I know. I'll be there soon. But only for a few minutes. Is that agreed?"

"Of course, Nadine. A few minutes."

The streets were almost empty but most houses—like ours—had at least a few lit windows. The air was so cold that the snow squeaked as I walked along the sidewalk; and when I exhaled, my breath threw a new foggy cloud into the air. It was March, but a sudden cold snap had brought clear skies, and as I rounded the corner to the street where Piakowski's apartment was located, I looked up and through the bare branches of a gigantic maple I saw the Milky Way shining like a silver studded scarf carelessly abandoned.

I found Piakowski ensconced in his usual chair. The glass coffee-table which had once been my pharmaceutical ware-house was now obscured by a copy of the chart that had been putting me to sleep earlier in the evening. Holding it down were two glasses and a bent-necked bottle of Armagnac—one of the affectations Piakowski liked to attribute to his years in France, as though he had been there on assignment to search out good restaurants and refine his palate. While I dug through my purse for cigarettes, Piakowski crossed the living room and checked that the door was locked. I have already reported that after his heart attack Piakowski had gone on a regime of careful eating and exercise. In retrospect, with the clarity hindsight gives to what was blurred or even unperceived, it is difficult to say at what point such and such a detail fell into place. But I do remember that on this particular night I noticed the actual spring in Piakowski's step, the unexpected *physical* vitality, the way his shirt hung from broad shoulders to his belt with only a slight swelling where it had once ballooned with abandon; and I noticed, too, that with his sleeves rolled up I could see the actual shape and play of his arm muscles as he reached up to deadbolt the various locks he had installed on his door. At that point, also, it occurred to me to wonder if Piakowski's meltdown had been entirely a result of medical necessity. Or, had Piakowski, feeling hunted, felt compelled to become the soldier once again, the night traveller—let us not say coward or informer—preparing to take to the road once more. As though reading my mind, Piakowski smiled shyly at me, then he opened his hand to reveal a small pocket-knife, which he used to unscrew the face-plate of the intercom so that the wires could be disconnected.

He crossed the room and sat down again, opened his mouth to speak, then interrupted himself to pour our drinks. "Put it this way: I have locked the door so that no one can burst through it too suddenly, and I have disconnected the intercom so that no one can use it to listen to us. On the other hand, if there were a truly interested party, surely he could have planted a microphone, interfered with the wiring, rented the apartment next door and be listening with a glass to the wall. After all, who is to say who might interest themselves in the little collaboration in which you and I and Miller are indulging."

I sipped at my Armagnac. It was sharp against the tongue, but a welcome flash of heat as I swallowed.

"Now, my dear Nadine, let us admit collaboration can be an ugly word. Suppose we lived in a certain time in a certain country, for example, and that country were invaded. Suppose the invaders of that country used certain cowards, certain weak-minded liberals, certain sympathizers to form a puppet government to ensure that the conquered country remained conquered—but in a restful manner. In, let us say, the sweet repose of sleep, give or take a few interrupted dreams.

"Then what would you call these cowards, these weak-minded, these sympathizers? *Collaborators.* Of course. A rose by any other name. But, not jumping to conclusions, what we have here, back at the obvious, is a piece of paper, a map of the sky, a future for humanity mixed with—let's face it—a few military secrets. Naturally on this low level of importance there are so many secrets that no one—no army—could ever be bothered to learn them all. Let us be more accurate, then, and say that what we have on this piece of paper is information which is confidential because we esteem "confidential" more than "non-confidential." A flattering thought, to us poor scientists, that others esteem our work. In this case works in which the interest is purely scientific because it will eventually allow us to learn certain tiny routines for tracking objects in the solar system. On the other hand, let us admit, we live in an era when governments have also developed an interest in tracking objects through space.

"So my dear, here we are: you, me, D.B. Miller—not unaware of why we have received funds for our innocent little enquiries into the ways of the sky. . . . "

I have tried to remember Piakowski as he was at the different stages when I knew him. The night he accused Miller of selling our secrets Piakowski seemed to have the greatest of his transformations—from the bloated body of a drug-addicted refugee had emerged a powerful man in his early sixties. Over the decades I had known him Piakowski's black hair had become grizzled, his smooth baby face carved with lines, but most amazingly of all—the force which in the fat man had seemed purely mental had in his successor flowed down into his body.

"I have proof," Piakowski finally said. "You and him together." Then he gave an odd, uncontrolled giggle. "I don't know what I think. *You* must think I'm crazy."

"Just drunk."

"No—just—don't make me say it—lonely. I love you, Nadine. What do you say to that?" He was swaying back and forth in his chair, drunk, in his hands the pocket-knife with which he had tried to lock away the outside world. "Nadine, do you suppose—Nadine, do you want to—Nadine, you bitch, do you want to go to bed with me?"

"Stefann. It's time for me to leave."

"Please, Nadine—I've found out that I'm dying. That's why I asked you to come tonight."

"Stefann, for God's sake, you really should see a psychiatrist."

"A doctor, Nadine, that's who I see. I have brain tumours. They're making me crazy." His voice had changed once more—transformed itself from the voice of the paranoid slimmed-down Piakowski to that of the enormous and legendary professor who was surrounded by awe-struck students.

"I don't believe you."

"It's true, Nadine. Don't argue with a man about his death."

"I'm sorry, Stefann."

"Nadine, I didn't want to tell you over the telephone."

"I understand," I said. But I hadn't decided whether or not to believe him. How could I?

"Nadine, you know I was in Paris during the war."

"Of course."

"I was looking at these tonight. Have you ever seen them?" Piakowski reached beside his chair and handed me an old brown envelope, paper so worn it felt like thin cloth. I opened it: out came dozens of photographs. One by one Piakowski picked them up and explained them to me: until, arranged in front of me, I had the life and times of Stefann Piakowski—

Piakowski young, Piakowski in Warsaw with his wife and daughters, Piakowski in Paris the first time as a student, Piakowski with his mentor Marie Curie, Piakowski with my father, Piakowski with both of my parents, Piakowski holding the infant me and cooing handsomely into the blanket.

"You know, Nadine, your father was a remarkable man. He came to Paris before I did, to study. And he would have had a brilliant career as a doctor but he stopped studying in order to work and make enough money so that I could join him."

"No one ever told me that."

"I was the only one who knew."

"I always wanted you to tell me about my parents."

"I know. But I didn't want you to spend your whole life looking back." Piakowski leaned over the coffee-table and picked out a picture of Léonie and Lemieux. Léonie had shown me the same picture once, saying only that Lemieux was a journalist she had known during the war. "There's your aunt," Piakowski said. "Do you recognize her? She's with the man she was in love with. I always thought they should have gotten married."

"I thought she was supposed to marry Henry Brimmer."

"That was pity. He had tried to help your parents escape. Then he got caught and put in a concentration camp. After the war he was sick for years. Then he came to Paris and began seeing Léonie again."

"What about Lemieux?"

"He had a wife, in Lyon. After the Liberation he went back to her."

So that was it: no wonder Léonie had made herself unattractive, had wasted hours on unlikely suitors, had rejected Henry Brimmer even after she had promised to marry him.

"I was married too, Nadine. You knew that. I had a wife and children in Poland."

"I know."

"She was a very proper wife, but I didn't like her very much. When I got to Paris I used to wish that when the war was over I would discover she had fallen in love with someone else. On the other hand, you understand, it was my duty to go back to Poland. Anyway, where else could I go? I couldn't remain in Paris—that was too dangerous. Lemieux offered to try to get me to England or Spain, but I couldn't allow myself to escape the war while my family was being killed. So I said I would go back to Poland and fight the Nazis."

"I know," I said. That was part of Piakowski's legend—he had risked everything to get to North Africa where he was going to join the Free French Army and cross back into Europe. Instead, he had been pressed into other activities, where he had distinguished himself heroically—winning medals that he himself had shown me decades ago.

"Nadine, I never went to Poland."

"I know."

"I never went anywhere, Nadine. It was too dangerous. On the day I was supposed to leave I went to the house of one of my old professors. I begged him to hide me in his cellar and he did, until the war was over."

"Then what?"

"I had the identity papers of a Frenchman and some money. I used the papers to get to England and then to Canada. In those days everything was so confused—I was accepted as a refugee. Then I came to the university, where they knew my work, and I was given a job. After that—well, you would be surprised how easy it is to buy old medals."

Again Piakowski reached down beside his chair, then pulled up the velvet bag I had often seen, the one filled with various medals commemorating his heroism under fire.

"So," he said. He laughed and poured himself some Armagnac. "Even an old man has to confess."

"Do you feel better?"

"Yes, Nadine, thank you."

He was leaning forward, he was smiling, he was the old smooth and confident Piakowski. The con Piakowski. The uncle who had slept with his half-brother's daughter.

"You know Stefann, I have to tell you, I really think you're lying. Yes, I do think you're hiding something." I stood up. I

was angry in a way I had never been, angry with an anger
that was literally making my blood boil, my skin burn, my
hair stand on end. I was in a white heat, a red rage, a wrath of
God. I was so angry I couldn't do anything but stand in front
of Piakowski and quiver as it gripped me.

"Nadine," he said. He stood up.

"NO!" I screamed, and pushed him back into his chair.

"Nadine."

"NO!" I picked up one of the photographs. This was Piakowski in the Polish army reserve: handsome, in a square-
jawed sort of way, impressively military with his steel-rimmed
spectacles and his broad shoulders. I tore the photograph in
half.

"Nadine. Sit down. Give me time. I'm going to tell you
everything. I *want* to tell you everything." His hands were
shaking. He leaned forward. He leaned back. He lit a cigarette. He stubbed it out. He took a sip of Armagnac. He lit
another cigarette. He looked at me helplessly. Like jumbled
frames from a movie, like a chain of firecrackers, like a death
train crawling from Drancy to Auschwitz, Piakowski's body
stumbled through its changes.

"I told you about Lemieux."

"Yes."

"Lemieux was married to a woman from Lyon."

"You said that."

"Yes. Well, this woman had a father. And the father was
unhappy seeing his daughter left alone. So he had certain
friends in Paris investigate Lemieux and they discovered that
Lemieux was working for the Resistance. Except in those days,
before the war ended, it was nothing so fancy. Just a few
people taking chances because they were too foolish or too
brave. The particular specialty of Lemieux and his friends
was the procurement and delivery of false papers. I was the
mailman. One afternoon I got caught. That day I was carrying the papers for myself and your parents—as well as documents for a dozen others. They took me to a police station.
The man in the cell with me had been beaten and was

moaning all the time. Let me tell you, I was very frightened. Then they sent for me. The man who interrogated me was the father of Lemieux's wife. He knew all about me and what I was doing. He told me that if I delivered my "mail," then I, my friends, my family would be spared. No one would know what I had done, he said, because the people for whom the papers were intended would all be picked up on the same day they were supposed to escape.

"I was sent back to my cell. That night some guards came in and worked me over. I thought they were going to kill me. Then one of them kicked me in the head and I passed out. The next morning someone came to clean me up, then I was led upstairs again, this time to a friend of Lemieux's who arranged for my release.

"After that, I did as had been arranged. I thought of telling Jakob and Gabrielle about what had happened—but in the end, I had to trust Lemieux's father-in-law."

"But he was a collaborator."

Piakowski sighed. "Either we were all dead or he would allow some of us to escape. And to escape, Jakob and Gabrielle had to play their roles convincingly. I thought I was helping them."

"The way you help everyone. By playing God."

"I had no choice, Nadine. And—you survived. You and Léonie and Lemieux."

"What about those who died?"

"They would have died anyway. They were all marked."

Piakowski stood up. "I'm tired," he said. "I want to go to bed." He began walking very slowly out of the room. This was a walk I recognized because it was not the strangely rejuvenated step of the new slimmed-down version of Stefann Piakowski; it was the cautious, stiff-legged, drugged fat man's walk. Habit pulled me to my feet and holding Piakowski's arm I helped him to the bedroom.

Piakowski lay down on his back. His eyes were open but he was breathing slowly, each breath dragged rasping from his lungs, each new cargo of air hoarsely taken in. I lifted the cigarette from his fingers and stubbed it out in the ashtray on his night-table.

"I'm cold," Piakowski said. From the cupboard I took a quilt—not the first time I'd seen that quilt—and laid it gently over Piakowski. His eyes were still open, on mine, waiting for forgiveness. Then I took off his glasses, folded them carefully, and sat them on the table beside his cigarettes. That was the way Piakowski always slept—even in Paris he had probably carefully composed his glasses and cigarettes before closing his eyes and whisking himself off to dreamland.

Piakowski was shivering. I should have lain down beside him. I should have lifted the quilt and slid beneath it so that like King David his body was warmed by a young woman. That was what I had done before, when he needed me, when I needed him. But it was too late. I bent over and kissed his forehead, the way Léonie had done. But when Piakowski's arms reached up for me I slipped through them and walked away. I suppose I expected him to call after me. Then I put on my coat and rearranged the deadbolts so I could leave the apartment, all the time waiting to be drawn back by the sound of his voice. When I got outside it was still dark and in this darkness the temperature had fallen far enough so that my cheekbones began to ache. When a small wind whipped down the empty snow-covered street I felt as though my clothes and flesh had been stripped away and my bones were beginning to chatter. Even as I was getting into bed and falling asleep to the new nightmares Piakowski had given me to dream, I was waiting for the telephone to ring. But it didn't, and the next day at the Department Piakowski merely looked at me and nodded as always.

In bed without Miller. Twisting in the sheets. A few months before I had been twisting with desire, with the need for Miller's hands on my skin, Miller's kisses to stop my mouth from forming words I didn't want to say, Miller's weight to crush out of me all my thoughts and fears. But now I was being kept away by other feelings—my need for Miller, my loneliness without him, my anger at the way he was ignoring me. Some nights Miller still telephoned me. "Nadine," he would gasp out, as soon as I answered, his voice heaving with relief as though he were stumbling onto an oasis after weeks in the desert. "Nadine, thank God you're there. I was afraid I might miss you."

"I'm marking papers tonight," I would say.

"You looked beautiful today when I passed you in the hall. Why don't you come to talk to me in my office anymore?"

"Why don't you come to me?"

"Nadine, you know I'm swamped with work. I'm supposed to be preparing papers for three different conferences. And you know Piakowski has made me the undergraduate supervisor. Every time I turn around there are six students sitting outside my door."

"I know. I'm sorry."

And so the conversation would go. Within a few seconds the excuses had been made, the barricades erected. Sometimes, miraculously, a breach would open in the walls. And then Miller, perhaps feeling safe, perhaps even for a moment feeling for me what I did for him, would propose: "Nadine, can I see you tonight?" Then he would come over and we would end up where we had started, entwined in my bed. Except that somehow it was different now. In the beginning when my body had exploded for Miller I had thought this was it—cosmic, unalterable, perfect love. My body still exploded on command. But the love I felt for Miller, though unalterable and overwhelming, was no longer perfect. It was torture. Miller, by a phone call, a sudden whim, could decide to appear at my door or absent himself for two weeks. But if I asked him to come, he would back off, citing some long-standing obligation to Amanda or the twins.

One night when Miller called I told him I was too tired to see him.

"What's wrong, Nadine. Are you sick?"

"No, just tired. I want to go to bed early."

"Don't you like going to bed with me?"

"I love going to bed with you. But tonight I want to sleep."

"You can sleep any night."

"Miller, what do you think I am for Christ's sake, your sex slave?" Then I banged down the telephone. After waiting for a few minutes for it to ring again I got dressed—I really *had* been intending to go to bed, and then I went up to the attic where Janis was buried in her manuscripts. With a little convincing she agreed to get the teenage girl next door to babysit and then went out drinking with me. By the time we came back it was the middle of the night. I wrapped my telephone in two thick towels, swallowed a few sleeping pills, and passed out until noon.

When I got to the university there was a vase of red roses on my desk, with a note from Miller asking me to dinner. I telephoned Janis and told her what had happened.

"Now you've got him. Tell him that he has to choose between you and Amanda."

But trying to make Miller choose—that was what I had never done. Of course I wanted Miller for my own. At least at the beginning I had wanted him, craved him, needed to be with him every second. But as time had slipped by and I'd had to watch our glorious love shrink itself down first to a glorious affair, and then to a not-so-glorious one, I had begun to make excuses not only to Miller but to myself. And besides, what about the twins? I wanted Miller, but did I want to play mother to the twins with Amanda coming onstage every fifteen minutes?

And suppose it went the other way: that I had Miller but the children remained with Amanda. Miller's whole rationale for ten years of his marriage had been the children. If he lost them, he would be totally miserable. And then *I* would be the bitch, *I* would be the one who had separated him from his own flesh and blood.

No, there was no solution. The affair had been wonderful, yes, but now I had to seize my freedom, or at least the shreds of my dignity, and tell Miller it was over.

But that night at supper, after the drinks I encouraged Miller to have so he would take the news more easily, Miller had plans of his own. "Nadine, you look incredible these days. Absolutely ravishing. You know what Nadine? I think I'm falling in love with you all over again. Do you think that's a record? To fall in love with the same person twice in six months?"

"Miller—"

"Nadine, let's go away together for the whole summer. You and I alone. Get a cottage on a lake somewhere, big rocks that stick out into the water. We'll hide all our clothes under the cottage and run around on all fours like monkeys for two months. Would you like that?"

"Miller, what about the children?"

"I've thought of that. Amanda can take the twins for one month, then we'll take them for the other. It will be great for them. And that way they can start getting used to you."

Start getting used to you. What was Miller saying?

"You know, Nadine, this has been a terrible winter. I really want to make it up to you. Will you?"

"Miller, I have to think."

"Of course you do. But we'll do it, won't we? You and I. Like monkeys."

That night, back at my house, everything was perfect again. Recently, without even knowing it, I had been closing myself off from Miller. Fear, the decision that I must leave him, self-defence, all had shut me into myself. Now I felt uncaged, almost wild. We made love all night, the way we had the first night, but when the morning came I clung to him and started to weep, unable to stop.

"Nadine. Nadine, what's wrong?"

But I couldn't, didn't want to say that somehow I knew it was over, no matter what promises we made or what lies we told each other. Finally I took a bath and calmed down. Then we ate breakfast together, munching toast, drinking coffee and reading the newspaper like a happily married couple celebrating our fiftieth anniversary.

"We will do the cottage, this summer, won't we?"

"Of course we will," I said.

But when the weekend came that we were supposed to go
and look, one of the twins came down with appendicitis. The
next week Miller was giving a speech in New York. The weekend after that Amanda broke her leg skiing in Vermont and
Miller had to stay home to take care of the twins.

A few months after Miller's first television appearance, *Shooting Stars* made its appearance on the paperback racks and
Miller's face stared out at us from every newsstand, every
bookstore window, the review pages of every magazine and
newspaper. But suddenly Miller was no longer simply Miller.
In fact, the D.B. Miller who occasionally dropped by the
university to pick up his mail, or even the D.B. Miller who
still made his late-night visits to my apartment, was only the
representative, the earthly agent, of the cosmic Miller, the
media Miller, the television personality and magazine-article
mogul, the man whose voice you heard while you ate breakfast, the face you saw on the cover of the magazine you read
while you went to the bathroom.

Meanwhile Janis and I had moved from our first place to
what would become our permanent home in Toronto—a house
divided into two apartments, one on top of the other, with
identical layouts. It was the perfect combination of compan-
ionship and privacy—but I felt that my privacy was turning
into loneliness. At first, when Janis had proposed buying the
new house, I had even resisted on the grounds—which under
the circumstances were too ridiculous to voice—that Miller
and I might still somehow come together in a permanent way.
But then I looked in my datebook, the one in which I marked
not only my official engagements but, with an *M* discreetly
tucked beside the number, every time Miller and I had made
love. During November and December there had been weeks
when almost every single number was accompanied by that
desirable little *M*. Even in January and February, despite
week-long dry spells, there were little clusters of nights when
Miller and I would begin to re-explore whatever it was we

had. But by the time April arrived and Janis started looking through the real-estate advertisements, my nights with Miller had become occasional at the most. Every week, or two, a single *M*. One weekend there were three consecutive nights: that was the weekend, during Easter break, that we finally drove about the countryside to talk about our plan of spending the summer together. Unfortunately, predictably, by then it was too late to find anything. Miller had not yet told Amanda, Miller's work was pressing, Miller's armies of the night were withdrawing from my camp whole legions at a time and even the ever-evasive Miller was beginning to admit to me that Amanda was what he wanted and needed.

"The thing is," he said, the last night of our weekend, "she's become like a disease I've learned to live with. I can't shake her. I can't even live without her."

"I know."

"Without you, I don't know how I would have survived this year. I owe you a lot."

"Don't be stupid."

"I feel stupid. First I spend years complaining about Amanda. Then I fall in love with you, only to discover that I can't live without her."

"That's the way it goes."

"I still love you, Nadine. We'll keep seeing each other, won't we?"

"Of course."

"And can I still stumble over to your house in the middle of the night?"

"Of course," I said. "Stumble away."

But when I got home, I decided again—as I did every time after seeing Miller—that the hangover was no longer worth the drunk. I stayed up half the night with Janis, looking at real-estate advertisements, and when we moved to our new house I vowed to myself that what happened in my bedroom was going to be my own life, not just an extension of Miller and Amanda. And so it was that the first guest in my new bedroom was not Miller, but a chemistry professor

who had been taking me to dinner every week for a few
months. I had resisted him because I was afraid that after
Miller he would be boring, because I wanted to be faithful to
Miller to prove to myself he was important to me, because the
professor was married and the last thing I needed was another married man. In bed, however, I discovered that some
of the magic I had thought belonged to Miller must have
rubbed off on me. Thereafter, every fortnight or so, there was
a furtive evening yielding another initial to tuck beside the
date.

It was two months before the obvious happened: one night
Miller telephoned while the competition was visiting. I told
him not to come, but an hour later Miller was knocking at the
door, unable to understand, apparently, that I might actually
be busy. After a farcelike interval during which my terrified
professor hobbled out the back, one hand grasping his shoes
while with the other he tried to hold his pants up, Miller and
I had the conversation I'd put off for too long.

"But why would you want to stop sleeping with me?" Miller
asked, like a bewildered child. "Don't you like it?"

"Of course I like it."

"I like it, too," Miller said, "better than anything."

"Not better than Amanda."

"So that's it," Miller said suddenly, as if he had just seen his
comet for the first time. "You want me to choose between you
and Amanda. But why? Isn't it perfect this way? We see each
other. We love each other. We work together. Yet you have
your own life. You don't have to worry about my habits, about
the twins, about the way I work all night but never do the
dishes." Miller was in his best, most charming mood—smoking
cigarettes, glasses perched crazily on his nose in the old style,
beer in one hand while the other waved to the Rational God
of the Cosmos. "Why would you want to live with me? I'm a
disaster, you know that."

Silence.

"Don't you love me anymore?"

"I don't know."

"Christ, Nadine, don't go all *dead* on me. You love me. I *know* you love me. Let's quit talking and go to bed." He stood up and drained his beer. "Come on."

"No."

"Why not?"

"Miller, I've already made love with someone tonight. When you called, I wasn't alone. That's why I told you not to come over."

"Jesus Christ, Nadine, I don't believe it. Where is he?"

"He left the back way when he heard you knocking at the door."

"Nadine. *Nadine*. I can't believe this is happening to us." Miller turned away from me. For a moment I thought he was going to leave, but then he opened the refrigerator and helped himself to another beer. "I've really done the wrong thing with you, haven't I, Nadine? Have I given you a terrible time?"

"Not so terrible."

"Let me think things over, Nadine. Maybe we can work something out."

"No."

"Nadine, tell me what you're really thinking."

"Do me a favour, Miller? Just leave, right now, no more talking. Walk out the door without saying another word, without looking at me, without anything at all."

"Nadine?"

"Miller, I asked you not to come tonight. Now I'm asking you to leave." As I spoke I could hear how abrasive my voice had become. Of course I knew I was hurting Miller, but I didn't care. For one hour he could feel what I had been going through for the past six months. Or maybe I wanted him to beg me the way he had so often begged Amanda. But Miller just poured the rest of his beer into the sink and walked out the door. I stood in my living room and through the curtains could see the lights of his car switch on, hear the motor start, watch him drive away. The next day in the mail-room of the Department, Miller smiled and said hello to me: friendly, composed, distant, the approachable face of the famous scientist who stepped out of the television set once a week to share a few mysterious marvels of the cosmos.

Another absence in my life: Piakowski. Since our bizarre night meeting he had refused to speak to me, other than to nod coldly in passing and inquire after my health—as though I were the one who had announced my own death. As the winter months passed, Piakowski aged rapidly. The weight loss which had flattered him at first continued. His suit jackets hung sadly from his broad shoulders, the lines on his face multiplied and deepened, his hair became greyer. *Was* he suffering from brain tumours? I made an appointment with his doctor to find out the truth. It turned out that there was nothing at all wrong with him. "Of course," the doctor said, "survivors of terrible situations often break down decades later. A delayed reaction because the original defences were so powerful they can take a lifetime to crumble. Perhaps we are seeing this in Professor Piakowski. Sympathy. Caution. Patience. These are what we counsel in such cases. Unfortunately the professor lives alone. The support of wife and children sometimes makes a difference."

I resolved to try once more; by coincidence that very night Piakowski telephoned me, his voice all business, to say he was reviewing course assignments for the next semester, and did I know what Miller's plans were.

"No."

"He has been offered a very good job, you know, at Stanford."

"I didn't know." But remembered now that Miller had gone there twice in the past few months—once to deliver a paper, once to discuss various research problems with Spitzer and to inspect their radio telescope.

"And Nadine, how have you been? Are you well?"

"Yes."

"I always wish you well, Nadine."

"I wish you well."

"Do you? I wonder sometimes. Perhaps you are angry at me."

"No, Stefann, I'm not angry with you."

"Nadine, I am only an old man. Peace be with you." And then Piakowski hung up and there was the sharp buzz of the dial tone.

I waited a moment, then called him back. Piakowski didn't answer. Ten minutes later I called again. This time he picked up the receiver, but he didn't speak.

"I love you," I said.

"That's something, Nadine."

"I can't forgive you," I said. "But it doesn't matter, I want to see you again. Can I come to see you now?"

"Please," Piakowski said.

When I arrived Piakowski was sitting in his usual chair. I locked the door behind me then hurried to kiss him. I wanted to kiss him quickly, to get it over with, to kiss him before there was time to reflect. His lips were slack and cold, but he smiled at me. In front of him was a book—Proust, his favourite—Proust, the half-Jew who had taken French society and turned it into an exotic butterfly, pinned it forever in the intricate web of his prose.

As he used to, Piakowski read to me. Only a few pages, but it made us both feel peaceful. And then, as I used to, I read to him. It was the book in which Swann falls in love with a lady whose charms are greater than her innocence.

"This is a great love story," Piakowski said. "No one understands better how love must always become decadence."

His voice was so weak I thought he must have something stuck in his throat. But then his eyes closed, opened again, closed.

"Stefann—"

"Nadine, I'm not feeling so well." I was already on my feet, leaning over him. His face was turning grey. I loosened his tie, opened the collar of his shirt. Piakowski shuddered, then his mouth opened and his tongue protruded, swollen and purple. There was a brief convulsion, then his head fell back on his chair and he was breathing regularly. By the time the ambulance arrived there had been two more convulsions. After

each one his breathing smoothed out again, but each time it
grew more shallow.

At the hospital he was put on machines. I stayed with him
all night but it wasn't until morning that he regained consciousness. Then he opened his eyes, stared at me briefly,
died.

Afterwards, sorting through the papers, I found a letter written by my father, addressed to me. It was in a folder containing other letters—also from my father: some to Piakowski,
others to Lemieux. The letters described my father's life in
Drancy, the prison camp outside Paris from which, altogether,
about one hundred thousand Jews caught the weekly train to
Auschwitz. One letter described the camp itself, a large concrete barracks surrounded by barbed wire. Others were about
life in the camp, tailored to pass the censor: for example,
early on he wrote to Piakowski describing the excellence of
the weather, saying that he was on a very healthy diet, and
asking only that toilet paper be sent as it was in short supply.

Beside this letter Piakowski had folded an old report from
the Red Cross, a medical analysis of starvation in Drancy,
where the average prisoner lost fifteen kilograms in the first
two weeks of confinement. According to this report the nutri-
tional bounty consisted of the following: breakfast—coffee;
lunch—"vegetable" soup; supper—more soup; bread allow-
ance 220 grams per day; total calories—500.

Ideally, the camp was to provide one thousand persons per
week for deportations. The night before, those whose names
were read were put into special rooms. Then, in the central
courtyard where all could see, their heads were shaved. The
barbers worked at this task non-stop, growing more harrassed
as the hours wore on. Meanwhile, a multi-coloured blanket of
hair—white, red, blond, black—piled up on the courtyard
and the wind blew the stray bits and curls around the whole
camp like so many fallen leaves. "The night before," wrote
my father, "is an interminable chorus of weeping, screaming,
cries for mercy. Each remembers his life, anticipates the

dreaded future, burns with love for those they are about to leave. When dawn finally comes they are emptied. The protests that greeted the calling of their names only twenty hours before are replaced by exhausted docility as they are shuffled into the railway cars. Spiritually they are already dead."

My father, perhaps somehow protected by Lemieux's friends, survived two years at Drancy. Then, when his turn came, he wrote last letters: a brief one to Lemieux saying he had still not heard what might have happened to Gabrielle since their separation, one to Piakowski begging him to take care of me should we both survive the war, and finally one to me.

My dear Nadine,

If you receive this letter, you will have become a child who can hardly remember her father. But although I am unknown to you, every moment I spent with you is engraved in my heart. Nadine, believe me, I love you, you are in my thoughts every second, my hope for you and your life is what keeps me alive. Tomorrow I die: the first day of Hanukkah. Believe no one who tells you anything unfavourable about your mother and myself: God alone is our judge.

Piakowski's death was a blankness that swallowed everything. A hole in the centre of my life and I fell through it. The night before the funeral I dreamed and dreamed again the last moments I had spent with him, that tiny irreducible moment no fraction is small enough to describe when life suddenly ended and nothingness began. As it had rescued the old ladies of his beloved Proust, Death plucked his face from old age and made it beautiful. Even his eyes, open when he died, turned a mysterious violet colour, as though Death had sent him off with wonderful visions. Through their perfect blankness the sun's light reflected a spectacular prism of nothingness. For a moment I had a wonderfully comforting thought—Piakowski an ethereal foetus whizzing through space and time. Then I looked at the face again, saw the young boy who had been forced from country to country, whose mouth

had wrapped itself around strange languages, around his own
cries of pain, around anything that could be swallowed. Even
until the last moment of his life my feelings for Piakowski
were anger and resentment for the day he had patronized and
manipulated me. But then he was gone and the love I had
held back flooded through me: first love, then pain and sorrow.

Working into the night. Sometimes, from outside, an unexpected shout or the roar of a passing car will break the silence
which blankets me and I will start from my chair, certain that
my privacy has been invaded.

Then the noise fades, silence recommences; at least what
begins again is what used to be silence but is now only the
temporary absence of disturbing sounds, an emptiness in which
I can think of the deaths of those close to me. In the months
following Piakowski's passing there is no real silence in me
anymore, no true untouched oasis of calm. There are only times
when I am completely absorbed: staring at a chart, reworking
figures, trying to construct the lost planet. But the locus of
the lost planet has shifted for me now. I no longer look to the
sky but the history books. I learn about Drancy. I imagine my
father picking his way through the concrete barracks that become as familiar to me as my own house. The recorded voices
and memoirs of survivors have become the voices of his last
friends. I hear the crying of children, see the line-ups of the
naked and starving, watch the death train pull away, offering
another week of life for those who are left behind.

The nights go by, one at a time. Each night I try to make
my peace with darkness.

Janis paces above me. She has her own life, her own loneliness, her own regretted passings of which she tells me nothing.
Periodically her steps slow by the place I know her telephone
is located. In a few seconds I'll hear the nervous sprint of the
dial. I will lift up the receiver, make a face that has become as
familiar to me as it is invisible to her, and say "hello" with the
appropriate anonymous enthusiasm of an orphan answering
the door for a blind date. Completely willing to pretend that

we haven't parted only a few hours before, I'll settle into my armchair for a stiff dose of gossip and banal conversation. As the end approaches, signalled by a certain tell-tale running-together of the consonants on Janis's part, I'll feel free to initiate the long goodbye. Then finally, at least half an hour or perhaps even a whole hour after Janis's initial impulse, I'll be back with my own thoughts. Disturbed, to say the least. Angry at Janis for wasting the tail-end of my evening. Too tired to work. Underneath, though, contented that another day has floated away without my being plunged into any one of a number of terrors. In sum, the call from Janis establishes that I am not only a digger into the grisly details of the past but a normal human being; I feel wanted and I can go to sleep knowing I am just another regular person, not too much worse than most, still judged suitable for the social comforts.

So, give Janis her due, I have much to be grateful for. And just as she thinks of me, I am often thinking of her. Because, despite her beauty, despite the endless supply of men wishing to take her out to dinner or more, Janis is lonely. And Janis sees that I am lonely. Sometimes, instead of telephoning, Janis comes down to my apartment, leaving the door open in case Leandra has her own nightmare problems, and helps herself to my bed. Her body, still warm from the bath, radiates heat. I hold her to me. I touch her the way she likes me to and sometimes I let her touch me, too, so for a few minutes we are lost in our own little race to serenity.

"You're haunted," she says. "You'll get over it."

Months pass. I write to Léonie telling her that on this first anniversary of Piakowski's death my life has returned to normal. I begin to see my chemistry professor again. His wife finds out and he breaks it off. But I don't mind. As the snow melts Janis and I rent a car and drive Leandra north of the city for a couple of days. We rent a cabin and make fires while Leandra discovers spring.

When summer finally came that year, Miller announced to me that he was leaving Toronto to accept a job in California.

"Amanda and I have decided that this is our last chance. We're going to give it two years. Really try to be a family." The plan was for Miller to go ahead and find a house, then Amanda and the twins would follow in time for the school year. I was the one chosen to drive Miller to the airport because on the morning of his departure Amanda had an appointment with a real-estate agent.

"I'm going to invite you down to give a lecture," Miller said as I parked the car. "We have to keep working on our project." On the way into the airport I saw our reflection in one of the glass doors: a young, professional couple. Miller was wearing a suit, summer loafers, sunglasses in his breast pocket. Getting onto the plane and watching Toronto recede, Miller would be leaving his youth behind, moving into the prime of his life. As for me, I was not yet thirty. I had a good job, a family of sorts, from now on it was going to be smooth sailing.

"Thank-you for driving me, Nadine. Are we going to kiss each other goodbye?"

"Let's shake hands. That way it won't be goodbye."

BOOK FIVE
1982

"**N**adine." Then a silence, the transcontinental hiss filled with electronic buzzings and the murmurings of other urgent conversations.

"Miller, for God's sake, it's the middle of the night."

"Not here," Miller said. "It's a wonderful evening here. I'm sitting on my balcony looking out at the ocean. The moon is shining across the water. Can you hear the moon on the water?" Another silence, so that I could imagine Miller, rich and successful, sitting in his San Francisco condominium with a bottle of California wine by his chair.

"I miss you," Miller said. "Where have you been?"

"I was out of town for a week."

"Did I wake you up?"

"Yes."

"How sexy." Then Miller laughed and I joined him.

"Christ," Miller said, "I really did miss you. I telephoned every night for at least a month. You must be up to something. Why don't you ever come to visit me? We haven't seen each other for years."

This time I was the first to laugh. It *was* ten years since I'd seen Miller—except on television or in magazines where he was photographed escorting various starlets to glittering occasions—but Miller always refused to return to Toronto, preferring instead to telephone once a month and play the tune of the rejected suitor.

"*Hey*," Miller said, "let's go somewhere together. Let's *see* each other."

"Come for the weekend."

"Neutral territory."

"We can go to Mexico."

"The food makes me sick." Now Miller's voice dropped into that sad tone he sometimes had, the sad doggy tone of his worst confessions. I could hear him breathing, the sound of swallowing: Miller was the original telephone alcoholic—every Christmas he used to send me a case of California wine so I could have something to drink with him when he called.

"Have you gotten married?"

"No," I said. "Have you?"

"Almost. She was great in bed but, you know, stupid."

"Poor boy."

"Come to Israel with me. Have you ever been there?"

"It's too far. I can't afford it."

"Jerusalem. Wouldn't that be crazy? I've always wanted to go there. I'll pay for everything."

"She must have been *very* stupid."

"We'll meet in New York," Miller said.

"New York terrifies me."

"I'll come to the airport and get you. I promise." Then Miller hung up. I listened to the dial tone for a moment, then went back to bed. A few minutes later the phone rang again. It was Miller, announcing he had reserved the tickets. "Can you get away?" Then a word I hadn't heard from him for a long time: "Please?"

"Was this to be your honeymoon trip?"

"For Christ's sake, Nadine." Another transcontinental pause, the sound of wine pouring. At least he was still drinking from the glass. "Actually," he said, "it's a religious odyssey. You know how Jews have to go to the homeland once before they die."

"Are you sick?"

"No, nothing like that. I just want to see you because you didn't answer your telephone for a month. Or was it a week? And why not go to Israel? Aren't you sick of your house? I'm sick of mine. I'm serious. Let's go."

Do I have to say that at various times in my life I would have given twenty years for such a proposal from Miller? Do I have to say there were whole years when I lived for his monthly phone call? And anyway, Miller had caught me at exactly the right moment. Yet another affair with a married man had recently ended in disaster; I *was* sick of my house and my circular life; worst of all it was the beginning of March and Toronto was still endowed with a layer of dirty snow which wouldn't be gone for at least a month.

"All right."

"All *right*," Miller whooped, and across four thousand miles I could hear the happy sound of his glass shattering. "All *right*, let's *go*."

La Guardia Airport, New York, March 1982: smoke, jet fumes, anxiety are mixed together in equal proportions. I am wearing a coat because otherwise the strap from my carry-on bag chafes my shoulder. But the coat is too warm and now I am sweating. I stop my aimless search, finally, put down my suitcase and rummage in my purse for a cigarette. Light up and inhale deeply: after twelve years I've started again. Janis said this trip to the Holy Land would teach me about paradise — but now I'm on my way and so far the only change is that I've been dreaming every night about terrorists and bombs. At least, smoking, I've got my own little weapons in my hand, cancer sticks and a propane lighter guaranteed to burst into flame on the first try.

"Would the party meeting Dr Miller please come to the American Airlines ticket counter. Would the party meeting Dr Miller please come to the American Airlines ticket counter."

I catch the message on the second round, then start walking before I even know in what direction to go. I drag my suitcase up a set of stairs, down a long curving corridor. Finally I see him. He's standing, cool and collected, in front of the counter. His own huge suitcase is sitting on a trolley, behind which a porter stands at the ready. Miller, too, is wearing a coat, but it is cashmere, the kind you never sweat in. The glasses are gone, the hair is silvering, on his upper lip is an elegant narrow moustache.

"There you are."

He leaps forward, plucks the suitcase from my hand, folds me into his coat.

"Excuse me for paging you. My flight was late and I got held up signing autographs." He looks at me sheepishly and for a moment I almost believe him. Then he bursts into the crazy old Miller laugh and I laugh with him.

"You bastard," I say.

"Let's go before they arrest us." I link my arm through Miller's and we proceed towards the El Al desk, porter in tow, an absolutely middle-aged and unarrestable couple on their way to Israel to see a few sights and catch up on an old friendship.

We come down through the clouds into the sun. By then I am in the circle of his charm again, leaning against the armrest so that my shoulder is joined to his, laughing without hesitation at his jokes. I am happy to be with him because he is my oldest friend and I have known him almost my whole life, a younger-older brother so knitted into the fabric of my past I can't remember being a child without in my mind walking down the street where we both lived, without seeing the houses which faced each other, without smiling over our first snowy kiss.

As the wheel carriage is lowering we hit a small air pocket; our descent is then stopped by a rising cylinder of hot air that throws us up into the clouds again. Miller's hand clenches mine; I look at his face and the fear is already beating a hasty retreat as his grip loosens and he smiles at me almost shyly, finally transformed into the Miller I used to know. I keep his hand in mine, caress it as we make our smooth final landing and taxi along the tarmac. Miller's arm slides around my back, he pulls my head to his shoulder. I sit without resisting—inside me the young woman once in love with Miller has come alive; but between that young woman and Miller's arm is a shell I've never felt before, a husk of experiences unshared, nights wasted, skin toughened by too many romances.

I open my eyes to see that the No Smoking signs have been switched on and the other passengers are starting to get to their feet.

"Hey," I say to Miller, "when they fly like that it makes me nervous."

"Me too," Miller says.

"I will be your guide." I looked down to see a young boy: black curly hair, sparkling blue eyes, skin the colour of toasted almond. His head nodded back and forth expectantly, like a puppy desperately hoping to be taken for a walk. With one hand he had already grabbed my sleeve. The other arm ended in a stump, neatly wrapped in a brightly coloured swatch of cloth.

"I will show you everything. I promise you. Usually I am very busy but today I am entirely free. At your service. Please call me Yitzhak."

I was standing alone, outside the hotel, but before I could speak Miller had joined me.

"Mister, good morning. Today you are in luck. I am going to show you and your wife Jerusalem. Everyone comes to the Holy City but only I can show you its true face. Ten dollars, American. For example, right at this very moment you are standing on stones made from the original Holy Temple of David. When David was King of Israel these stones made the walls of his palace. Your very feet are resting on the remains of the bedroom wall of the king. When he prayed to God he would look at these stones you are standing on and call out to God to make him young again, to make him worthy of the trust of Solomon, to make him once more the young and powerful king of the Israelites, ready to slaughter the enemies of the Jews and make their land safe for the Hebrew God."

"Let's go," Miller said to me.

"Please." The boy's hand shifted from my arm to Miller's. "Let me come with you. Is ten dollars too much? I will make it five dollars. Nothing at all. How is that for a bargain? What could be cheaper than nothing? For absolutely free I will show you the city and it will be a favour from me, a grateful citizen of this fine country, to two of the Americans who have been so wonderful to us. Let me give you this gift from Israel, it will be my pleasure."

"What happened to your hand?" Miller asked. I could have killed him, but the boy was unfazed.

"It was an accident. I was on a bus that exploded. If you like I can take you to the spot. It happened in a square opposite the old palace of Nebuchadnezzar, the famous Babylonian King. I was very fortunate because there is a hospital nearby. It specializes in wounded like myself. The most famous surgeon in Jerusalem tried to save my hand. And now he is making me a new one; next year, when you come back and we have our reunion, you will see that I am just like you again. Please believe me, there is nothing to be frightened of. I can take you to the hospital where you will see many miraculous things. Believe me, in America you have space ships, but here there are miracles too, every day."

"You are a miracle," Miller said. He smiled uncomfortably at the boy, who gave back a radiant milk-toothed grin.

"Please call me Yitzhak." His hand still grasping Miller's sleeve he hooked his other arm through mine and began to lead us forward. "First I will show you the Wailing Wall. Everything is in walking distance because you are young. At the end of the day your feet will be sore, just like the pilgrims. Then in the evening you will eat and drink wine. Take it from me. This is the way to see the Holy City. Are you Jews or Christians? It doesn't matter. Tomorrow I will take you to Bethlehem. My father has a car. Don't worry, everything is free, a gift from the heart, because love is what makes us brothers."

"I am a Jew," Miller said softly.

"I knew it. Be proud of it. Not *I am a Jew* like a little whisper because you are afraid someone might overhear and stick you in an oven. Look—" Yitzhak pointed to a wall which had a niche dug into it—"this is where Christ, staggering under the weight of the Cross, paused to catch his breath. His hand right here—put your hand there. By the time you have seen the Holy City you won't be whispering *I am a Jew* in a frightened little voice. For the first time in your life you will stand up straight and say, *Listen world, here walks a Jew. For five thousand years God has protected my race and now I have come out from my dark little corner to see His land, my land. I am a Jew!!*" The boy looked at us in triumph. "Be proud. Walk on the ground that was given to your ancestors. Sink your feet into the dirt that they died for."

By the time we reached the Wailing Wall hours had passed and I was dizzy from the heat. On the way through the Arab market Yitzhak, who seemed to know every merchant in every stall and doorway, had made us buy tidbits to sample and fruit drinks to wash away the heat, but now the food, which had looked so appetizing in the open air, growled danger-ously in my stomach.

The Wailing Wall was made of the light sun-coloured sand-stone from which all of Jerusalem seemed to be built. In the niches between the stones were thrust thousands of tiny bits of paper. Some had become almost transparent from the rain and their blurred messages could be seen through the paper. Beside the wall were the tourists, hundreds of them. The women wore hats and summer dresses, the men dressed in slacks and sport shirts. Almost everyone, like Miller and myself, wore sunglasses against the glare, cameras slung around the necks to record the Holy City for posterity.

"This is where you pray," Yitzhak informed us. "People spend their whole lives deciding what they will say when they get here."

To Yitzhak we were just another tourist couple—appropriately exhausted after our first day in Jerusalem. After assuring us that we had made excellent progress, were in fact the most sensitive and perceptive Americans he had ever encountered, he escorted us back to the hotel.

There we were furnished with adjoining rooms with a door that opened between. Miller had arranged that, of course, he was always an expert at arranging just the perfect combination of comfort and tact. Emerging from the shower I stood in a private corner of my room to dress. My face and figure are not destined for Hollywood, but at this ridiculous moment I noticed in the mirror that my body was almost unchanged since its last encounter with Miller: small-waisted, thighs and hips a little over-padded, breasts still resisting the blandishments of gravity and nursing infants. In fact, I must admit when I stopped smoking I decided that I should start taking care of my body. At the women's health club I belong to we all stare at each other—covertly of course. The feature I am most self-conscious about is my nipples: adolescent pink buttons that are my badge of spinsterhood beside the dark splotchy nipples of the women who have borne children.

Just as I had finished pulling on my dress, Miller knocked at the open door, then came into my room carrying the bottle of duty-free Scotch he had purchased on the plane.

"Kills the germs," he said, pouring us each a healthy dollop and filling the glasses from the hotel room tap. Then we sat down, and for the first time since meeting Miller in New York almost fifteen hours before, there was a moment of calm between us, a space in which we could try to find our way back to our old friendship.

The first drink was poured into the silence. Then there was a second. While I was still sipping on that, Miller started a third. Let's say I can't help noticing these things: irreducible little details. And so I found myself noting, too, that although the bottle had been full when Miller came into the room, it was now half-empty; and that although Miller had stepped into the washroom and run the tap vigorously to top his Scotch with water, the contents of his glass were a dark, unwatery amber.

By the time dinner was over Miller had consumed an enormous amount of alcohol. I don't want to say that he was absolutely drunk, because he wasn't, but whatever he had been so desperate to escape must surely have been put to sleep. I myself was exhausted. Not only from the drinking and the strain of being with this new, middle-aged Miller, but also I had been up for almost thirty hours and I couldn't keep my eyes open. When Miller positioned himself in my arm-chair and tried to find something to watch on the television, I kicked off my shoes, then lay down on my bed and drew the blanket over me.

While I dozed, Miller rambled on about his life in San Francisco, the various romances he amused himself with, the constant demands from Amanda for more money, the trials of being a part-time father. Poor Miller, his obsessive love for Amanda finally exhausted, he was beset with the same boring problems as the rest of his generation. I was almost asleep when I realized he had changed tack entirely and was talking like a teenage philosopher about the books he read at night, and his need to find the single act that would redeem his flaccid life.

"But what's wrong with your life?" I protested. "You have your books to write, classes to teach, beautiful women dying for your embrace. You're important, you're busy, you have the twins. What more is there?"

This only launched Miller into a new tirade. "Can't you see we're living in a bubble? Look at that boy who took us through the market today. If one of the twins had her arm blown off I would go crazy. Yet here's a child in the middle of the mael-strom: impoverished, maimed, no future to look forward to except the next explosion—and here we are, his bread and butter, voyeurs come to gawk and then flee to safety. Do you know I was going to come here to join the army? I thought to myself that instead of wasting my life as I am, I could let it be my blood instead of someone else's that helps build some-thing worth having."

"I didn't know you were so involved with Israel."

"I'm not. But I'm a Jew, by birth if nothing else. Even if Israel is totally wrong, they are being wrong on my behalf.

Why shouldn't I die for them? Better to die for a cause than
for nothing."

"If you're going to die for a cause," I mumbled, "isn't it
better to die for a cause you believe in? If you're so interested
in Israel, why have you never been here before? Why haven't
you read books about it? Learned Hebrew? Miller, you're the
same as ever. A total romantic in search of a windmill." And
then, unable to help myself, I fell asleep. The next time I
looked up it was morning. I went to the bathroom and stood
for a long time in the shower: the soap had the exotic smell of
tropical woods, its wrapper sported Hebrew letters I couldn't
understand. They looked ancient and primitive, characters
suitable for carving into stone. When I came out of the shower
I saw that Miller was lying naked on his bed, dead asleep. I
rolled him under his covers: his skin was cold to the touch
and he was so skinny that his ribs dug into my palms. As I
was pulling the sheet over him, Miller opened his eyes. They
were glazed, half-conscious. "I love you, Nadine."

"I love you too," I said automatically. "Have a good sleep."

Then Miller reached up for me. I could have backed away—
half of me wanted to. Instead, I bent down to kiss Miller. A
kiss, a moment of hesitation, then I lay down beside Miller on
the cool linen sheets. When we made love it was the way it
used to be.

Compared to the air-conditioned hotel, the streets of Jerusalem were like a furnace. I retraced the walk we had taken
the first day until I got to the Arab market. There, my stomach cramping in warning, I detoured through a few side-
streets until after a while I found myself at a temple surrounded by tourist buses. Others were lined up; I lined up
too. When I finally got into the temple I was asked to take off
my shoes and I discovered that it wasn't a Jewish temple at
all. Men with guns at their hips herded us towards the centre
and explained in Arabic and English that this was one of the
most holy places of the world of Islam. Beneath its golden
dome hundreds of Arabs knelt in prayer. In its centre was an

enormous white rock—the place, the guides said, where Abraham had been told to sacrifice his first-born son to God. Then we were led below the rock to the dark chambers where the blood from hundreds of years of ritual sacrifices had flowed. Beside me was a British couple, and I heard the husband whisper to wife: "Look at this. They're *all* savages, what did I tell you? Worse than the Irish."

Outside my eyes were still adjusting to the sun when Yitzhak took me by the arm. "I would have showed you this," he said disapprovingly. "I waited for you the whole morning at the hotel but they said you were sleeping. Tomorrow I will come with my father."

The next morning Nathan Haidasz picked us up in his taxi. Yitzhak looked the perfect Mediterranean child, but Haidasz was an East European. He was a tall slope-shouldered man with black hair combed straight back except for a channel of tanned skin down the centre of his scalp. He wore a beard, black laced with silver, and sweat had plastered his white shirt against his broad belly and back. On the way out of Jerusalem he told us his life story: he had been born during the First World War to Jewish parents who hid in a tiny village until the war was over. Later he studied engineering in Cracow; when the proscriptions against the Jews started in the thirties, he and his parents escaped to America. "Just as the door was closing." After the Second World War was over he followed his parents once more, this time to Israel. They settled on one of the first socialist kibbutzim—just in time for the War of Independence which killed his parents and his brother. But not him. He had been in the army. After the war, he moved from the kibbutz to Jerusalem where he went into the construction business with army friends. Following the Six Day War, when the old section of Jerusalem was captured by Israel, his company worked on the excavation and restoration of the great wall. "It goes," he said, "hundreds of feet below the ground." Somehow he met and married an Arab woman, had four children of whom Yitzhak was the youngest. But his marriage caused his business partnership to break up, so he began driving a taxi and running a tourist-bus business. Yitzhak had been on his best bus when it was blown up. There was no insurance.

By the time we were out of the city and on the road to the Dead Sea, Haidasz had finished his story.

"This is what I call hot," Haidasz said. "Open your windows or close them, it doesn't help." His window was closed. Yitzhak, sitting directly behind him, had his own window wide open. The desert air whipped through the car, hot and stale, every breath burned the lungs. Miller had taken off his jacket and sitting behind him I could see the lake of perspiration spreading on his back. I, too, was hot, but bothering me equally was the machine gun Haidasz kept on the floor in front of me: my ankles were shoved up against the barrel and with every jolt of the car they were forced against the uneven edges of the metal.

When we got to the Sea itself, Nathan and Yitzhak led us to the shore. We stood among the salt-encrusted branches, looking out at the water. It was a strange light green. And even the sky above, which had seemed so brilliantly blue during our drive, was now the colour of hot milk. According to the guidebook, the Dead Sea was also known as the Sea of Sodom, the Sea of Lot, and the Sea of Death. In fact, as Haidasz offered, we could go to Sodom for lunch if we wanted. "God destroyed Sodom and Gomorrah in ancient times. But the Israelis use everything: now there is a potash plant where Sodom used to be. That way we can say that none of the Lord's work is wasted, even his vengefulness." He laughed, showing gold-rimmed teeth. From the Sea a very slow breeze was sweeping over us. The Wailing Wall had given me a deep haunted feeling, as if it had the power to touch my soul. But here I felt nothing. Only hot and tired and slightly nauseated. Miller, on the other hand, was transfixed, staring out at the water as though he were having visions of the ancient Israelites fleeing the wrath of God.

"You must be very moved," Haidasz said.

"This is incredible," Miller whispered. He waved with one hand at the tent a few hundred yards away from us, a bedouin tent with camels enclosed in a rough corral. We had parked near the tent, beneath which Pepsis, hamburgers and oranges were sold, and walked across the sand to the water's edge. "It's so *hot* here. How could anyone have lived in such a place?" The day before Miller had bought a straw hat. Only a few hours in the sun had blackened the California tan on his face and arms. "What a place for an observatory. Can you imagine the stars at night?"

"The university has some of the best telescopes in the world," Haidasz said. He was always interjecting these observations about the modern state of Israel, as if it were a prize pupil.

I looked at Miller and smiled. But Miller shook his head and his mouth turned down in a worried look.

"I could arrange for you to see it," Haidasz offered.

But Miller had taken my arm now because two jeeps filled with soldiers were roaring along the sand towards us. When they reached Haidasz a man leapt out and began talking excitedly in Hebrew. To me, who barely knew a single word, the sound was harsh and gutteral.

"There has been an incident," Yitzhak translated. "A bomb in a supermarket in Jerusalem. Twenty-two killed, a hundred wounded. The Prime Minister has placed the country in a state of alert. Tonight there will be a curfew."

Only after the jeeps had driven off did Yitzhak add that the soldier talking to his father was his elder brother. "When he is in the service he never comes home," Yitzhak concluded. "That is because of my mother, you understand." Yitzhak looked at me, the woman, for confirmation, and I nodded. I have not had children but of course I oppose war. Of course. Every decent person opposes war.

As we were driving back to Jerusalem Yitzhak pointed out their household, one of a row of tenement flats with laundry strung outside the window. On top of each flat was a weird contraption, a solar-powered water heater, Yitzhak explained, that his father had helped to invent.

As we drove through the streets towards our hotel I saw more jeeps filled with soldiers. They wore their machine guns slung casually over their shoulders, or rested them in their laps like favourite dolls. We were standing in front of the hotel, thanking Nathan Haidasz, when gunfire broke out. Suddenly the street began to clear. I was paralysed. The sound of the guns was like hearts popping open. A car came roaring down the street, a dusty old American car that should have been scrapped twenty years before. Two of its tires were flat. At the wheel was a young woman who was shouting in a language I couldn't understand. The windshield was smashed and she had blood flowing from her face. The car veered towards us, I saw a man in the back, shooting randomly into the crowd. Then the car was gone and all I could hear was a strange clattering sound, the sound of a grenade as it skipped across the pavement towards us.

The grenade is made to fit in the palm of a hand. It is the size of a heart, the colour of baked mud. With each bounce my own heart slows, threatens to freeze. With one arm Nathan Haidasz scoops up his son and throws him behind the taxi. I admire this quick action, a father saving his son. Then with his other arm, Haidasz is reaching for me. His mouth is open, shouting a warning that has no time to turn into words. But for once in my life action comes easily. I am already in motion, twisting around Haidasz's hand, watching it clutch at air as I dash forward. I am running towards the grenade, unsure what to do—only *something*—and then I am arriving. I hear Miller behind me. He is shouting my name but I am aware only of the grenade. It is grey with flecks of rust. It has metal scales. I am almost on top of it when my feet give way. Even at this moment I don't know if I've acted by accident or design. But as I fall, I reach out gratefully, happy to know that—when my moment finally arrived—I was not a coward. My hands close around the grenade. Between my palms it is amazingly hot, as though it had already gone off. When the explosion comes I shut my eyes and my mind takes off like a V-2 rocket, a shooting star buzzing straight for the sun.

UPI—In Jerusalem today a Canadian tourist, Dr Nadine Santangel, was wounded in an incident outside the Four Seasons Hotel in downtown Jerusalem. No one claims responsibility for the attack but the Embassy has said that investigations are being made. Dr Santangel is Chairman of the Department of Astronomy at the University of Toronto. She has received many honours for her scientific research and is a past president of the Royal Canadian Astronomical Society.

The situation is complicated. The situation is dark. The situation is that when I open my eyes I am in a hospital of which I do not know the name. Perhaps I will never know its name. Perhaps I am dying. Perhaps the situation is that I am already dead. These and other thoughts parade through my mind as I take in the surroundings: metal tree holding two bottles of intravenous, oxygen machine (currently unused), pale green plaster ceiling, large rectangular window with an excellent view of the hills surrounding Jerusalem.

To focus on my body, or what is left of it, is not easy. The situation is that I am feeling, as they say, no pain. In order to arrange this they have also had to arrange that I am feeling nothing at all. I try to flex various limbs—there are no sensations. Then I get more specific: "Fingers right hand, fingers left hand. Toes right foot, toes left foot." These commands are more successful: I feel or think I feel a low-level buzzing. I am lying on my back and now I can see that I have all of my arms and legs. A blanket is covering me up to my neck. My left arm is strapped to the bed, to receive the liquid gifts of the intravenous, and there are straps lightly laid across my hips, too, in case I have an ambulatory dream.

The following idea arrives: I could, with my free right hand, lift the blanket and look under it. Then I would know my situation exactly. But I feel like an insect who has suddenly grown a thorax and without even looking I know that things are bad, very bad. To lift the blanket would take much strength, more courage. Even thinking about what might have happened to me gives me my first physical sensation, a flutter of fear around my heart.

"It can't be that bad," I say to myself, and I reach for the blanket to pull it down and inspect the damage. At least I decide that is what I am going to do and I expect to see my hand obeying this command. Instead nothing happens—nothing but a wave of pain that sends me back into darkness.

The next time I awake my eyes are already open and I am watching the face of a person from the army. I even know that he is a corporal. I don't know how long he has been talking to me, how long my eyes have been open, how much I remember or forget. Apparently, the entire situation is due to the grenade.

The grenade in question was American manufactured, designed for use in Vietnam. Most likely, the corporal in charge of such details tells me, the grenade was captured by the Viet Cong during the mid-1960s. He smiles when he tells me this, like an archaeologist sharing his moment of triumph at reconstructing an unlikely artifact. After the grenade's capture it might have been stored for almost a decade, always intended for us. Then, after the war, along with other now ageing or obsolete weapons, it was sold to some other guerilla group. After any number of further resales it ended up as part of the arms hoard of some sub-group of the Palestinian Liberation Organization.

Because of its age, its many journeys, the various and perhaps unideal conditions under which it had been stored, the firing mechanism of the grenade had become imperfect. Perhaps my heroic gesture had been unnecessary. Perhaps only my heroic gesture had caused it to explode.

"Actually," the corporal apologizes, "weapons are almost a personal possession here. When a man switches his loyalty from one group to another he takes his rifle with him like a dowry."

At that point a doctor takes over and becomes the expert. He shows me a film that recorded how various shards of metal have travelled through my clothes and skin and lodged themselves variously in my ribs, my backbone and my lungs. One stopped beside my heart, but hadn't had the pep to penetrate. Of course I have lost buckets of blood, blood that is being replaced by the donated blood of some of the Israelis I had wished to save.

The situation, in brief, is not good. But it is not hopeless. In a total of eight operations the situation could be entirely repaired. Two to remove the fragments (one front, one back). Four to do the skin grafts that would leave my shining self desirable to the eye and hand. Two more for reparations of the spine. The process would take several months but of course even during those months I would be making progress.

The doctor excuses himself and the corporal resumes. He explains to me that whether the PLO itself can be blamed for this attack is unknown and probably unknowable. The state faces so many enemies, there are so many arms caches, so many groups and sub-groups, so many free-lance terrorists with no affiliation at all, that it might never be discovered who planned and executed the aborted mission of which I am the only casualty. "Unfortunately, those who spent their childhoods as orphans in the refugee camps can easily be convinced to spend their lives overthrowing the Jewish State."

That is where our interview ends. I am in a more-or-less lucid moment. Which is to say that I am mentally clear despite being taped from neck to knees in bandages and plaster. Most of all, though, my situation is one of continued floating. Floating through the air as the grenade explodes, floating on the bed where I have been lying for an unknown number of days, floating on a sea of the drugs and painkillers they have given me.

Yaakov comes to see me. "I read about you in the newspaper," he says. "You didn't have to do anything so drastic to get my attention. Why didn't you just telephone?" He bends to kiss me. His lips, against my drug-dried lips, feel large and moist. I am aware, too, of his beard scratching my face.

My heart is in the sky and it is dying. I am dying. I am finally on the train, but there is no train for me, no windows, no anything at all except my soul shooting free of gravity, shooting into orbit, shooting beyond this planet, beyond the Lost Planet, beyond everything but the hiss of oxygen being pressed in and out of my lungs, the taste of plastic on my lips, the dull pain of intravenous needles being eased into my arm.

In this dream I am with Piakowski. We are hovering above the cemetery where his funeral took place. He has been explaining to me that this cemetery—a large tree-filled place called The Mount Pleasant Cemetery (no puns intended, we are to assume)—had always attracted him and so he bought himself a space there, decades ago, so that in his afterhours he could rest among the wealthy of Toronto.

When he says all this it makes sense to me: after all, Piakowski has lived most of his adult life imagining the bodies of his wife and children in a variety of unattractive circumstances. So, in the end, that is what he fears.

In the dream Piakowski is young. He is wearing an expensive grey suit, a little number made up for him by his favourite Warsaw tailor, a high-collared white shirt, a snap-brim fedora. His olive skin is smooth and shining, but shining even brighter are his eyes, little circular stages back-lit by opium.

"So you went to Jerusalem," Piakowski says. "I never thought you had it in you."

"What is that supposed to mean?"

"My dear Nadine, it can mean anything you want it to."

"I wasn't trying to be a hero, it just happened."

"Nadine, you know better than that. Nothing just happens."

"I don't mind being dead," I said. "I think I've wanted to die for a long time."

Another dream: It is raining hard but a taxi is waiting at the curb. When the driver sees me he opens the door. Someone is inside.

I am sitting in the taxi and Léonie is talking. Rain sheeting down the windows. Smoke from our cigarettes whorling in the grey light. Léonie's voice a husky song telling me her love for Lemieux. I am hardly hearing the words. I am seeing Léonie's face turning sacred colours as her voice freights out the pain of Lemieux, the sorrows and the trials of loving Lemieux, the betrayal of Lemieux. I am watching her face. Now she is talking about Piakowski. Somehow he and Lemieux have become confused, merged into one. Everything she is saying is so totally unexpected that my mind has been blown clean, each word is exploding like its own little firecracker in the empty pond of my mind; I can't hear them, only the noise of the explosions.

"*You* loved him," Léonie is saying, "I know that you loved him. That was his final revenge—on me, on his brother, on you—on all of us who witnessed what he did."

We are in the taxi. Smoke surrounds us. Somehow Léonie knows that I have died, but she keeps talking anyway, her voice carrying the pain and sorrow of everyone she has watched die, all the shooting stars that have burned themselves out trying to reach the heart of the sky. Rain is sheeting down the windows. Then the motor stops. I wake up. I am not in some anonymous taxi, after all, but in the car of Nathan Haidasz. The door opens. Miller is gallantly lifting me over the wet pavement. Everyone is waving goodbye as my wheelchair crosses the tarmac to the waiting airplane. Soon I am ensconced in a plush seat, Miller beside me. I lean on his shoulder and drift back to sleep as the jet engines roar and carry us into the sky.

Here in Paris, I have become a heroine of sorts. An amazing Jewish Joan of Arc who has had her week in the magazines—the exiled French orphan of the Holocaust come back to the homeland. That is what happens when you are blown up by a grenade in Jerusalem and flown first-class to Paris.

"You brought good weather," one of Léonie's neighbours remarks every day. The whole building knows me, is friendly to me. Of course everyone saw me arrive: a van drove me direct from Charles de Gaulle airport and then I emerged, blanketed like a sausage from neck to feet, pale face bathing in the popping of flashbulbs. Miller was carrying the suitcase, but it was Yaakov who was pushing the wheelchair. As you might expect he was the one to attract the cameras: a burly black-bearded soldier, nice white teeth that look good in the photographs; but he could use a haircut, it's been twenty years since he was the *wunderkind* of the Israeli infantry.

After a few days, Yaakov went back to Israel. Then Miller returned to his classes in California. But there is still Léonie to take care of me. She watches over me. She holds my hand when I have nightmares. Bit by bit we exhume the past.

Lemieux is waiting for me, everything has been arranged. He is sitting in a dark café, elbows riding the raw wood of a small rectangular table. In one hand a glass, half empty. In front of him an open package of Gitanes, cigarettes extended like so many white-tipped fingers. Léonie's pictures showed a man with dark lank hair. But now the hair is short and grey, combed neatly to one side, and the thin face has become gaunt and furrowed.

He watches me as I come in the door, offers his hand to me without rising.

"Please excuse me, but my back has been sprained this week." Then he takes out a cigarette and puts it in his mouth. Nicotine and smoke have stained his fingers.

"It was very kind of you to agree to meet me again."

"It was my pleasure. Our lunch with your aunt was only a beginning, I hope." His English is fluent, spoken with a sardonic Parisian accent. "Now, make yourself at home. This place is my living room. Or should I say parlour, said the spider to the fly," Lemieux suddenly adds, and then he laughs. He must be in his mid-sixties, and until that moment he looked even older—but the sudden flash of teeth makes him seem youthful, and I laugh with him.

I sit down opposite him. Without my asking, a glass and a carafe of red wine are brought to the table.

I am looking at Lemieux. Somewhere between the dashing youth of the pictures and the greying man in this café is located a resistance fighter, a man who took chances. There were decorations, though he is too proud to wear them; there was an article in the press describing some of his exploits against the Nazis and including testimonies by many Jews that he saved their lives; there was his own autobiography detailing his life in Paris during the war. On the back of his autobiography was, of course, a photograph: the compulsory romance, it showed a shadowed face, dark burning eyes, a cheekbone scarred by the Nazi bullet that had grazed him during one of his many miraculous escapes.

"You deserve the truth," he says. He begins to talk. He recreates the hotel room where he and Piakowski would drink the night away. He pulls out yellowed newspaper clippings. He drinks more wine and his voice becomes incoherent as he tells of the times Piakowski vowed he would return to Poland. "To me they were all heroes—your uncle, your parents, Léonie. I admired them more than I have ever admired anyone else. From me, believe me, that is a big compliment. When your parents left for Spain, I truly believed that they would return at the end of the war. In my mind, let me say it exactly, your mother and father were giants. Human beings of infinite courage. It was a privilege to assist them. When I found out what happened to them—" Pause for another cigarette, another glass of wine, then Lemieux is telling how he arranged for Piakowski to leave Paris.

Lemieux leans back in his chair. He sighs. Consideration is given to the thought of Piakowski discovering he is afraid. Piakowski's betrayal of my parents, Piakowski going to the house of his old professor and begging for shelter.

More wine is drunk. A second carafe. "Once you called me papa," Lemieux says.

And after the war? Why didn't he keep in touch? Why didn't he become one of the men who climbed the stairs of our apartment to see Léonie. A silence. Another white-tipped Gitane. "We weren't for each other," Lemieux finally says. "I had my duty to my wife." He is finished. He turns his glass upside down on the table and he closes his eyes. After a few moments he says goodbye. I remember he promised me the truth. Perhaps it never existed. Perhaps he has forgotten. Perhaps I am the only one who cares and it is waiting for me to invent it.

This morning I went to the doctor's. "Madame will remove her blouse, please." At one time I would have been embarrassed to stand naked in front of a doctor, even a woman doctor, but now I am a patient, an object. "Excuse me Madame," says the doctor, touching the newly grafted flesh. "Does Madame have sensation?"

The tip of her finger is cold and sandpapery, like her voice. "Yes."

We pass on to other, less sensational injuries. It is amazing to think what a mess an explosion can make.

At lunch-time I go to meet Léonie in the park. In the bright sun her skin is beautifully pale, almost translucent. She would be hard for a man to resist, I think, and, as if she is almost reading my mind, Léonie starts talking about Lemieux.

"Ten years after the war I had almost forgotten him. That is to say, I no longer thought about him every day. Then his book came out. But I didn't rush to buy it. In fact, I was a bit nervous about what role he might have given me. After all, at the time of the famous episode where he was discovered and tortured by the Pétainistes, he was living in the apartment he had procured for us.

"I suppose I never would have read it, save for a coincidence. One night, a few months after its publication, I went into his café. I wasn't really thinking about him, I only went in because it was a familiar place and I had been out walking on a hot summer's night that made me thirsty. Lemieux sat down with me and we had a drink.

"It was the time of year when no sane person is in Paris. Lemieux offered to take me for a drive. Soon we were in his car, whizzing through the streets at first and then—although nothing had been agreed—we were outside the city.

"It was dark, through the open windows blew a cool breeze, we weren't talking but there was a wonderful feeling of escape. When Lemieux pulled up at a hotel and suggested we go inside, I didn't object. We had whiskys and a sandwich at the bar, then we went upstairs to bed. "Just like old times," Lemieux said, before falling asleep. He had brought a briefcase with him, for appearances, then taken out a copy of the book to show me. While Robert slept his satisfied sleep, I found myself lying on my back in the dark, reliving every night we had spent together, remembering each of his letters, and then finally remembering when the nights and the letters had stopped and only memory and desire remained. I had often told myself that Robert and I had had not an affair but a movie without an ending. Now, after all these years, the last scene had finally been scripted. I was to be lying in bed, smoking cigarette after cigarette, inhaling the unchanged odour of the hero's sleeping flesh. Getting out of bed I took his book and my cigarettes into the bathroom. Of course Robert had been too—let's say discreet on Marguerite's behalf—to put my name or yours into print. He didn't even mention the epilogue to his night of torture, which was my discovering his bloody, half-dead body and then nursing him back to health until he was well enough for one of his friends to drive him back to Lyon and the arms of his wife.

"You wouldn't remember that, Nadine. Why should you? I never wanted you to have the war hanging over you."

We are at the Luxembourg Gardens, sitting on a little bench near the pond where children are taken by their nannies to lose their sailboats and throw breadcrumbs on the water. The sun bobs up and down on the tiny waves. I close my eyes. Points of light ricochet through my brain; I am lying on the street again, the noise of the explosion has blocked out my whole life, my soul has torn free and is flying through the universe like a runaway star.

When I get back to the apartment I make myself a cup of tea. It is time for me to begin my afternoon's work—looking at photographs and writing. Soon—today or tomorrow or next week—I will be finished. It will be time to allow the past to seal over, my life to resume. I try to imagine how it must have been for Léonie and Lemieux. First in Paris, during the war, and finally now, seeing each other when their lives—lived and unlived—are almost over. Which were their real lives? The ones in which Léonie lived out her spinster years while Lemieux put himself through the paces of his marriage? Or their phantom lives, the forbidden underground ghosts that spent useless decades yearning for each other?

Restless, I stand up. There is still a knife of pain across my abdomen every time I get to my feet. But even in that wound I was lucky: a little deeper and my womb would have been torn; as it is I have only a long and jagged scar, needle marks crossing it like railway ties, running from my left hip to a point just to the right of my belly button. I go to the windows and pull them open. Below me the thick traffic has paused momentarily as a woman pushes a baby carriage across the street. From the handles hang plastic bags of groceries—and as I look down, the infant's eyes suddenly stare at me. Explosions go off in different parts of my body: every time I feel something all of my wounds have the sensation of splitting open.

The telephone rings and this time it's for me. The man's voice at the other end is full of tenderness. Miller is telling me that he loves me, that he is coming to see me, that when he arrives he is never going to leave me.

"Idiot," I say. "What makes you think I would wait for you?"

Miller laughs. "I forgot to tell you, I am already in Paris."

His taxi arrives while I am still looking out the window, wondering whether I want to believe him.

Matt Cohen

The Disinherited

This is the first of Matt Cohen's highly acclaimed series set in the fictional town of Salem, Ontario. Witty and ironic, immense in the scope of its conception, brilliant in its execution, *The Disinherited* can be seen in many lights.

"A finely-told story of the decay of a generations-long way of life and of the fierce family infighting over who is to inherit or escape."

Margaret Atwood

"A beautiful book about people discovering each other too little and too late."

Peter C. Newman

"The sense of warring past and present is splendidly created, the characters swell to giants as they recede into memory, and the whole novel... has a largeness of texture that leaves a massive shadow on the mind."

Maclean's

"One reads and lives Matt Cohen's *The Disinherited*... he has expressed his vision of man and the land in this corner of the continent in terms you won't ever shake off again."

The Ottawa Journal

Matt Cohen

The Colours of War

The second of Matt Cohen's Salem novels, *The Colours of War* is set some time in the near future, when both Canada and the United States are in a state of civil disorder, with food and fuel shortages, corrupt government and armed forces patrolling the streets.

In the centre of this world of unpredictable violence is Theodore Beam, journeying by train from Vancouver to the small Ontario town of Salem. His mind flooded with childhood memories and experiences, Theodore wavers between past and present, fantasy and reality, innocence and corruption.

The Colours of War is at once science fiction, political fantasy and an unforgettable story of alienation, loyalty and love.

"...a technical *tour de force* for Cohen, a real virtuoso performance."

The Globe and Mail

Matt Cohen

The Sweet Second Summer
of Kitty Malone

This is the story of two lives inextricably intertwined. After twenty years of loving each other, hating each other and ignoring each other's existence, Kitty Malone and Pat Frank have reached the point of no return.

"The people in this book are all striving to come of age the second time around and the story of their struggles is both intriguing and marvellously told."

Timothy Findley

"A violent and tender story of love... human and triumphant in spirit... splendid writing."

George Woodcock

"Funny, potent, bittersweet... a work of joy and mastery."

Dennis Lee

Matt Cohen

Flowers of Darkness

Looking for an escape from their life in Ottawa, Annabelle and Allen Jamieson move to an old stone house in the sleepy town of Salem. There, Annabelle begins to adjust to the muted rhythms of a town dominated at one end by the brooding Presbyterian church and at the other by a smoky tavern.

Annabelle, an artist, starts work on a mosaic depicting the people of Salem. As autumn gives way to winter, and then to spring, they step one by one out of the mosaic and into her life.

Flowers of Darkness tears away the serene façade of a small town to reveal undercurrents of passion and hatred. Alive with the spirit of a man and two women and their haunting and unforgettable story, it is a stunning achievement by one of Canada's finest novelists.

"*Flowers of Darkness* is a strong, deeply felt, adult work of fiction... Cohen writes lyrical, wide-open, yet masterfully sure and skilful prose."

Maclean's

Printed in Canada